Hawaiian Dreams

by

Sheri Lynne

DORRANCE
PUBLISHING CO
EST. 1920
PITTSBURGH, PENNSYLVANIA 15238

Dorrance Publishing Co
585 Alpha Drive
Pittsburgh, PA 15238
Visit our website at *www.dorrancebookstore.com*

ISBN: 978-1-6376-4039-5
eISBN: 978-1-6376-4886-5

Hawaiian
Dreams

Acknowledgments

Hawaiian Dreams was written in memory of my dear husband who passed away in 2013. The love that Gordon and I shared as a married couple for 41 years was unsurpassed by anything either one of us could ever imagine. Even after a heated argument, he could always make me laugh. Although this book is fictional, the events in the military in the first chapter actually did happen to him and his identical twin brother, Gilbert Ross. Gil, thank you for sharing your time in the military with me and your support to make this book happen.

A special thanks to retired Detective Sargent C. Goch, and Detective Sargent T. Baker, and all the troopers at the Michigan State Police department, you know who you are, for helping me put the crime scenes together. I love you all!

And last but not least, my beautiful daughter Wendy Janca who kept prodding me to write and finish the book. She was an endless help to me with research, editing, and the story line. I love you!

This is my first book in the trilogy, staring the TreVaine brothers. My hope for all of you who read this book, enjoy Mike and Jenna's story, and how they found true love in the midst of chaos, and the love and never-ending bond between identical twins. May you escape to an island paradise, and from the world that is uncertain, and find a love that is stronger than life itself.

— Sheri Lynne, author of *Hawaiian Dreams*

Be on the lookout for the next book in the trilogy, *Hawaiian Flames*, coming soon.

Chapter 1
July 2010

Michael James TreVaine, serving in the United States Air Force, stationed at Joint Base Pearl Harbor-Hickam, on the island of Oahu, Hawaii, was called to train a new Airman on a C-17 Globemaster III sitting outside a hanger off the flight line. Seems there was a clogged latrine that needed to be cleaned out located behind the cockpit. Airman trainee Doug Baker and Mike walked down the tarmac to the aircraft. The breeze from the Pacific Ocean felt good against Mike's skin as the temperature on the island climbed up into the 70s.

What a way to begin training, Mike chuckled to himself as he thought about the new Airman's first assignment. As they neared the aircraft, Mike turned to Airman Baker. "Let's head up into the aircraft and see what we'll need to clean out the clog."

"Yes sir," replied Airman Baker.

Meanwhile, up in the aircraft, two technicians were working on the instrument panel in the cockpit. As Mike and Airman Baker approached the cockpit, Mike nodded and explained that he and Airman Baker were there to clean out a clog in the latrine. The technicians nodded back, one of which jokingly commented, "Good luck with that!"

Mike and Airman Baker continued towards the latrine to determine what equipment they would need. Exiting the aircraft, Mike sent Airman Baker to get an air compressor over at the far side of the hanger while he went to get a bunch of rags.

Back at the aircraft, Airman Baker lined the air compressor underneath the front of the aircraft. Mike and Airman Baker worked to attach the hose of the air compressor to the drain pipe with a supple.

"Airman Baker, go make sure the air compressor is attached to the extension cord," said Mike. Mike waited by the compressor until he got back.

Airman Baker replied, "All set sir!"

"Okay, I'm going back up into the aircraft, and when I yell down to you, set the air compressor at 50psi. You got that Baker?"

"Yes sir!" he replied.

Mike headed back up into the aircraft, nodded to the technicians, and went into the latrine to cover the hole in the toilet with the rags he brought with him. When he got them all in place, he yelled down to Airman Baker.

"Airman Baker! Can you hear me?"

Airman Baker confirmed, "Yes sir!"

"Okay, start the compressor!" Holding the rags in place, Mike heard the compressor start up. Suddenly, the toilet in the latrine started shaking. As the shaking became more violent, it was getting harder and harder for Mike to hold the rags in place. When the shaking wouldn't stop, Mike yelled down, "Airman Baker! Shut it off! Shut it off! Can you hear me, Baker? Shut it the hell off!"

It was no use; it was far too loud for Airman Baker to hear Mike. Meanwhile, underneath the aircraft, Airman Baker heard a loud BOOM and saw the two technicians running towards him yelling, "SHUT IT DOWN!"

Up in the aircraft, Mike stood there in the middle of a blue/green slime shower. Kinda like Ole Faithful, only worse! When it finally stopped, Mike looked around the latrine. There was blue/green slime, bits of toilet paper, and who knows what all dripping down the walls, ceiling, and all over him! As he turned to leave the plane, he saw the cockpit. It was all over the instrument panel!

"Shit! What a damn mess!" he groaned. As he came down out of the aircraft you could hear every swear word known to man come out of his mouth and then some! He walked up to Airman Baker with a fierce look in his eyes and angrily said, "Why the hell didn't you shut the compressor down when I yelled down to you?"

Airman Baker with eyes as big as saucers backed away a little, as the horrific smell radiating from Mike hit him like a ton of bricks!

"Sorry, sir, I couldn't hear you with the compressor going!" exclaimed Airman Baker.

"Well, what in the hell did you have it set on?"

"Five-hundred psi, just like you said sir!" replied Baker.

"I said 50psi, you knucklehead! Now go call clean up," Mike yelled. "I'm heading back to the barracks to get cleaned up!"

Mike turned and walked away when Airman Baker called, "Uh, sir?"

Mike turned back and glared, "Yes?"

"Uh, nothing sir, nothing," Airman Baker responded. As he watched Mike leave, he thought to himself, *Damn, he really looks bad and the smell! Whew!*

Then, without warning, Sargent O'Rourke approached yelling, "Airman Baker! What the hell happened here?"

Baker jumped and turned towards the Sargent softly mumbling to himself, "I'm in so much trouble here!"

Mike was walking back to the barracks when he heard a military jeep pull up beside him. He turned to see that it was his twin brother Mark along with two other Airmen. Mark took one look at his brother, and with a shit-ass grin asked, "What the hell happened to you bro?"

Mike glared at his brother firing back, "I had a major incident with a latrine in a C-17 Globemaster III!"

Mark chuckled, "Well hell bro, you're a damn sight, and you smell like shit!"

"This isn't funny, Mark!" Mike responded angrily and walked off! Mike could hear his brother and his crew laughing hysterically as they drove off. "Real funny, ha-ha!" he angrily said to himself.

Back at the barracks, Mike stripped down outside, walked into the building and headed straight into the shower. He scrubbed himself down several times, toweled off, looked in the mirror and groaned, "Oh this is not good!" He still had blue/green colors all over his body. He then sniffed himself, "Oh damn! I still smell like shit, too! No woman in her right mind will want to get near me! This is really going to play hell with my sex life!"

Meanwhile, back at the flight line, Mark and his crew arrived at the aircraft they were scheduled to work on, an aerial refueling plane, KC-10 Extender. The oil relief valve needed to be repaired. They all got out of the jeep still laughing.

"Damn, Mark, your brother looks like someone out of a horror movie! And the smell! Whew! No one is going to want to get close to him for weeks!" laughed Airman Shaw.

"I know, I know!"

With a grin and a glimmer in his eyes, Mark laughed, "This is really going to play hell on his sex life! And you know how well Mike likes the women!"

"I know right!" laughed Shaw.

Still chuckling Mark said, "Okay, men, let's take a look at this relief valve and see what we will need." Mark sent Shaw to get a ladder, McConnell to grab the tool box, and Mark went up into the cockpit to turn the oil pressure gauge off. Shaw placed the ladder underneath the aircraft, and Mark went up to see what part he would need to fix the relief valve. Once that was taken care of, Mark gave instructions to Shaw to go up into the cockpit of the aircraft.

"When McConnell gives you the go ahead, you can turn the oil pressure gauge back on. McConnell, you stand here by the entrance to the plane and watch for my signal. Are we clear on what we are all supposed to do?"

"Yes sir!" Shaw and McConnell said in union.

"What's the signal sir?" asked McConnell.

"I will give you a thumbs-up and yell okay," Mark said.

"Got it," said McConnell.

Mark turned, climbed the ladder, and went to work on the relief valve. He was having a little trouble with the part that needed replacing. He threw his arm down and started swearing words that no one should hear! This alerted McConnell.

"Did you say it was okay, sir?" he yelled.

"This damn relief valve," Mark swore, not paying attention to what McConnell was saying.

"Hey Shaw!" McConnell yelled up to Shaw, "I think TreVaine said to turn on the oil pressure gauge."

"Are you sure?"

"Well, he threw his arm down and was yelling something. It's hard to hear with all the noise of the other aircraft. I say go for it!"

Mark was just starting to come down off the ladder when oil gushed out from the plane and covered him from head to toe! He stood there for a minute in shock as black oil slid down his body. He walked up to McConnell, with only the whites of his eyes showing.

"Did I give you the signal to turn the oil pressure gauge back on?" he yelled.

McConnell looking at Mark with unbelieving eyes said, "Well sir, I saw your arm come down, and you were yelling something, but with the noise of the aircraft taking off on the flight line, it was hard to tell for sure. I just assumed it was the signal."

"Well you assumed wrong!" Mark snapped. "Get Shaw and get started on cleaning this damn mess up!"

Mark turned and walked back to the hanger, grabbed some rags and cleaned himself up the best he could. He was headed back to the mess when he ran into Sargent Mason.

"What the damn hell happened here, TreVaine?" he yelled. "Can't you TreVaine brothers do anything right! I heard about your brother's escapade this morning! Which one are you anyway? I can never keep you two straight!"

"Mark sir!" he said.

"Go get this damn mess cleaned up!" Sargent Mason yelled.

Mark sighed, "Just headed that way, sir!"

After Mark and his crew finished cleaning up the oil spill on the tarmac, Mark headed back to the barracks and was itching all over. He went into the shower and scrubbed himself clean. When he toweled himself off and looked in the mirror, he saw red splotches all over his face and body. *And I thought my brother looked bad!*

Mark put calamine lotion on his splotches to keep from itching and got dressed. He decided to go over to Mike's barracks and see how he was doing. When he arrived he saw Mike sitting outside on a bench.

Mike looked up at his brother in surprise and said, "What in the hell happened to you? You look like a pink lobster with red bumps all over you!"

As Mark explained what happened, Mike started laughing.

"You know bro, we're quite the pair! We both look like we stepped out of a horror movie, but at least you don't stink!"

"Sorry if I don't sit next to you, bro, but you really do stink!"

Laughing, they both turned and looked at each other and said in union, "This is DEFINITLY going to play hell with our sex lives!"

PRESENT DAY

Looking back on his Air Force days, although it wasn't funny at the time, Mike had to laugh. He and his brother did more disrupting than fixing! *Thank God after a year in maintenance we were able to get into administration working in the message center!* After a short time, Mike was asked to become General Daniel McCall's aid. Daniel McCall was a 1 Star Brigadier General who gave all of himself to his country and to his family. It was an honor to serve under him for the rest of his tour.

Mike looked out over the blue waters of Hanauma Bay. The waves were almost high enough to do some serious body surfing. With the wind blowing across his broad tan chest, Mike breathed in the fresh clean air and thought, *It just can't get any better than this!*

Last night was stupid busy at the restaurant, and with the upcoming meeting with Mark this afternoon, this was just what he needed!

Mark and he were now co-owners of the Hawaiian Lanai, located on Waikiki Boulevard. It took years of sweat and hard work, but it paid off. Their restaurant was the most successful restaurant on the island of Oahu, where locals and tourist come from all over the world for an American-Hawaiian experience.

Mark handled the financial aspect of the business while he oversaw the whole operation and made sure everything runs smoothly. Mark approached him last night and mentioned he was concerned about some shortages in the liquor inventory, and asked if they could meet at 1:00 today to go over his findings. He also informed Mike that he had taken on an intern from the University who was studying to get her degree in Certified Public Accounting. She would also be attending the meeting.

As he headed out into the ocean, he was curious about this intern. What did Mark say her name was? Jenifer, Jenny? Well, he'd find out soon enough. Time to catch some waves and lose himself in the thrill of riding those waves back to shore!

Chapter 2

*J*enna Hathaway was a senior at the University of Hawaii-Manoa, and she was in her final semester for her BA degree in Certified Public Accounting with a minor in Marketing. As she changed her clothes for the third time, her cat Cuddles, a beautiful black and white tuxedo cat with huge green eyes, laid on her bed and stared at her.

"Don't judge me, Cuddles! I want to look my best! I am so nervous to meet my bosses and start my first day as an intern!"

Her cat meowed.

When she finished dressing, she bent and placed her hand on her cat's head and scratched behind her ears, "Okay, Cuddles, do I look good?"

She stood before her mirror, twisting and turning to look at herself in the outfit she finally decided on. She chose black dress pants, a short sleeve turquoise V-neck silk blouse, and black pumps. To accent, she chose a silver necklace with a heart, turquoise stud earrings, and a silver watch. Although Jenna didn't see herself as beautiful, her choice of clothes complimented her soft features and rich Hawaiian tan.

Jenna left her bedroom with Cuddles at her heels to go into the kitchen to fix herself a quick sandwich and grab a Coke from the fridge before she had to leave for her 1:00 meeting and orientation at the Hawaiian Lanai. As she started to fix her sandwich, Cuddles let her know she was hungry, too! Jenna stopped what she was doing and went to get Cuddles favorite cat food. She put it in her bowl and set it down by her water dish.

While Cuddles dove in, Jenna finished fixing her sandwich and popped open her Coke. Sitting down at the counter to enjoy her sandwich, Jenna looked around her apartment. The open living space included a living room and small dining area off the kitchen. The walls were painted a soft eggshell color. Colorful prints of Hawaiian landscapes adorned the walls. The teal sofa and matching loveseat brought warmth to the room along with an off-white area rug to cover the hardwood floors. Off the living room was a lanai, which Sasha and her used for studying and relaxing. In the kitchen, the beach wood cabinetry, white counter top, and stainless-steel appliances made it a gem to cook in. Coming from a large family in southern Michigan, Jenna loved to cook and create dishes of her own.

Jenna shared the apartment with her best friend Sasha. Jenna met Sasha in their sophomore year at the University, and they became best friends almost immediately. Since this was their final year, they decided to get an apartment together and share the expenses. It was a great feeling to be free of dorm life! One of the things she liked about where the apartment was located, was that she could walk anywhere she wanted to go: to the University; the International Market Place; there were trails leading to Diamond Head, and to the Bistro where she works part time. When she wasn't working or studying, you could find her jogging along Waikiki beach.

Jenna looked at her watch and realized it was almost time for her meeting! She put her dishes in the sink and ran back to the bathroom to check her hair and makeup. With a quick application of her favorite lipstick, she grabbed her purse, notebook, laptop, said goodbye to Cuddles, and headed out the door. Good thing her apartment wasn't far from the restaurant. She would just make it on time.

Chapter 3

Sitting at the conference table in the office, Mike and Mark are having coffee and discussing Mark's upcoming divorce, currently in a custody battle over their 7-year-old son Cameron.

"I don't know, Mike," said Mark. "Sherry won't give! She only wants to give me Sundays, and I want every other week. That way we would have two weekends a month to explore other relationships."

"Any chance you two could get back together?" asked Mike.

"Oh, hell no! After her affair with my best friend, she crushed me, Mike! I couldn't sleep or think straight for weeks!"

"Sorry bro, I know you've been through hell these past months, and you've come a long way since the initial shock. Maybe you both should sit down with your lawyers and discuss what's best for Cameron, and not for you or Sherry," said Mike.

"You're right bro, I just wish it were over, and we'd quit dragging Cameron through the middle of this mess! I love him so much, and he needs consistency in his life!"

"Just hang in there bro, it will happen." Mike looked at his watch. "Its five minutes after one. The intern is late! I have a 1:45 meeting with the staff!" Mike said irritability. What did you say her name was again?"

"Jenna, Jenna Hathaway. She's in her final semester at the University and will be receiving her BA Degree in Certified Public Accounting in June. I'm hoping she can give us some insight to the problems we are having with the liquor inventory. It could be the software. Maybe with new eyes, she'll find something I'm missing. I would hate to think it was one of our employee's stealing."

"I agree, Mark. I've always prided myself in hiring good people, but there's always a chance that I missed something in their back ground check."

As they continued discussing other issues involving the restaurant, outside, Jenna rushed through the restaurant door and was met by a beautiful Polynesian woman. Out of breath, Jenna extended her hand.

"Hi, I'm Jenna Hathaway. I have a meeting with Mark and Mike TreVaine."

The woman looked at Jenna with disproval in her eyes as she shook Jenna's hand.

"You're late!" the woman said curtly.

"I am so sorry! I misjudged the distance from my apartment!" She literally had to run the last two blocks! She must look a sight. She wished she had time to go into the restroom to run a comb through her hair at least!

"Come this way." The woman said curtly. Jenna followed the woman to the back of the restaurant and got a quick look at the décor and found it very inviting. No wonder it received such great reviews!

At the office, the woman opened the door. Mike and Mark both rose from the conference table.

"Gentlemen, Jenna Hathaway. Can I get you anything before I leave?"

"Yes Kalea (pronounced: kah-lee-ah)," Mark said. "Please bring in a carafe of coffee with an extra cup for Jenna and also some of those little cakes."

"Yes sir," said Kalea. As she left, Jenna stood shell shocked! Mike and Mark were identical twins! She didn't know which one was which! When the school told her she would be working under the TreVaine brothers, she had no idea!

"Hi, I apologize for being late, I misjudged the distance from my apartment. I hope I haven't held either of you up. It's very nice to meet you both, but can you tell me which one of you is Mark?"

Both Mike and Mark chuckled. Mark came up to Jenna and extended his hand. They shook hands, "I'm Mark, and this is my brother Mike." As Jenna turned to shake Mike's hand, Mark chuckled, "He's the serious one."

When Mike took Jenna's hand, she felt an electric jolt that penetrated up her arm and all the way down to her mid-section!

He smiled, "Don't believe everything my brother says. He likes to give me a hard time."

Jenna and Mike's eyes locked. She couldn't help but get lost into the sea of deep blue. His smile when he looked into her eyes was so captivating, showing off perfect white teeth. Jenna smiled back and thought if she didn't sit down soon, she would melt into a puddle right there on the floor! He let go of her hand, and she felt an immediate disconnect.

A knock at the door made Jenna jump, and the spell was broken. Kalea came in with the tray of coffee and an array of little cakes. Circles and squares, all in different colors of icing with tiny little flowers on top. They looked simply delicious! She set the tray on the conference table and asked, "Will there be anything else?"

"No, Kalea, that will be all for now. And thank you for bringing this in for us."

"You're welcome."

When she left the office, she noticed that Mike was staring at Jenna the whole time she was in the office with them. *This girl is going to be trouble, I know it!* she thought angrily. *I'm going to need to keep an eye on her. Nobody is going to keep me from Mike no matter what the rule around here is!"*

She stomped back to the hostess station to get ready for tonight's reservations.

In the office, they all sat down at the conference table, and Mark began to pour the coffee.

"Do you take cream or sugar, Jenna?"

"Two creams and one sugar, please."

Mark handed her the mug of coffee.

"Jenna, help yourself to some cakes. They're one of the house favorites, and we sell them out at the front counter."

Jenna took one of the cakes and took a bite.

"Mmm, this is so good!"

Mike sat staring at Jenna and was enthralled with watching her eat the cake and wished he could lick the frosting off those beautiful pink lips of hers! Her long chestnut hair was a little windblown but fell softly around her face and cascaded in waves down her back. It was sexy as hell! Looking into those big brown eyes of hers, a man could get lost in them! Jenna turned and looked at him and a surge of energy went right through him!

Jenna felt Mike's eyes on her and was a little embarrassed at the thought that she might have frosting all over her face! She took a napkin from the tray and wiped her mouth as Mark started the meeting.

Mark started explaining how the business was set up. Jenna tried to focus on what Mark was saying, but could feel Mike's eyes still on her. It gave her goose bumps just thinking about him.

Mike couldn't stop looking at her! He has never felt this way about any woman! This electrifying surge going through him was new to him.

"Mike. Mike! Are you with us?" Mike jumped and looked at Mark.

"Sorry bro, what were you saying?"

"I was saying," Mark said a little irritably, "or should I say, explaining to Jenna that we have some problems with the liquor inventory, and we're not sure if it's our software or possible theft. Stay with us man!"

"Yes sir!" Mike replied just as irritably.

Jenna looked at Mike and then at Mark.

"I've taken some software classes, and they can have glitches in them. After the meeting, would you mind if I take a look at what software you are using?"

"Well, we use several different software applications, but no, I don't mind. But first, I would like to go over your schedule and what role you will be playing here," said Mark. "Mike has a 1:45 meeting with the staff, so we will need to take a look at what days and hours your internship allows."

Jenna took a sheet of paper out of her notebook and gave it to Mark with her schedule on it and went over it with him. "Monday, Wednesday, Friday, I have a morning class. Tuesday, Thursday, and Saturdays I work part time at the Bistro from 4:00-10:00. So, I thought I could be here on Monday and Wednesday from 12-5," said Jenna.

"That's a pretty full schedule," Mike said. "When do you have time to relax and have fun?"

"It is a little hectic, but on occasion I go out with some friends on Friday nights."

As they looked at each other, Jenna felt like he could see right through her. She felt that tingling sensation again. She looks away and tries to concentrate on what Mark was saying.

"I think we can work with that. How about you, bro? Mike!" Mike brought himself out of his trance and shook his head.

"That's fine with me." Mike looked at his watch, "I need to get to my meeting. I'll leave you two to get started. Jenna," she turned to look at Mike, "before you go and before we get busy, I would like to show you the outlay of the restaurant and how things are done."

Looking into those blue eyes of his, Jenna shivers.

"Thank you, I would like that." Mike stood and looked at his brother, nods, "Mark".

"Mike," Mark said as he left the office.

Mike stood outside the office, turned, looked at the door and thought, *What the hell just happened in there! I've never let a woman get to me like that! Well, not since I was in high school. When I went into the service and the Dear John letter came, my heart was shattered! I swore I would never lose my head over another woman again!*

And so far, he hadn't. He'd dated a lot of women, and none made him feel what he felt in there! Not even his first love! He could still feel that surge of energy when he shook her hand. Mike shakes his head and starts walking.

Get your head back into the game, Mike!

As he entered the bar, he took a deep breath, went in, and started the meeting.

Jenna, sitting at the conference table, was still reeling from the effects Mike had on her. She never felt this butterfly, tingling all over with any man! Not that she dated much. She never had time! She wasn't even experienced in those types of relationships! But when she remembered the feel of his hand and those eyes that looked like they wanted to devour her, she got all tingling again.

Mark was busy bringing up all the reports and printing them off the computer. As she studied him, it was amazing how much they looked alike. Same broad shoulders, same blue eyes, same chiseled face. But she did notice some subtle differences. Mark was not as tan as Mike. Mark had a slight slant to his left eye, Mike didn't. Mike's hair was a lot lighter than Mark's due to the Hawaiian sun. Mark appeared to be more laid back, but she sensed an undercurrent that she couldn't put her finger on. Mike, on the other hand, was all business and full of electrifying energy that got her all worked up again!

Mark sat back down at the conference table and began to go over the reports with her. As she tried to focus on what Mark is saying, she was thinking about Mike, his meeting, and what role the Polynesian beauty Kalea played here. She wasn't very pleasant to her when she arrived at the restaurant.

At the meeting, Mike went over the specials for tonight, including the specialty drinks.

"We have a party of 25 coming in tonight, and they requested the lanai. The reservation is for a 50th wedding anniversary for General Daniel McCall and his wife. General McCall is a personal friend of mine, and I want everything perfect for them. Carol and Tammy, you will be the servers for the party, and Jeff you will tend the bar. Set the tables up at the far side of the lanai with a few smaller tables around the pond."

Looking at the rest of the reservations for the evening, he divided the work between the staff.

"As always we aim to give our customers an experience they will never forget. Good food and excellent service. I am proud to say through your efforts and hard work, we have become one of the top restaurants on the island."

Mike closed the meeting, turned, and was headed toward the kitchen when Kalea grabbed his arm.

"Mike, can I speak to you for a moment?"

"Sure, what's up?"

"I was curious about this Jenna Hathaway. She's very attractive. Will she be working full time?"

Mike looked at Kalea and wondered what this was really about.

"No, she's an intern from the University and will be working with Mark a couple of days a week. She is here for three months to earn her BA degree. I would appreciate it if and when she has questions pertaining to the restaurant, you will answer her truthfully and with courtesy."

"Well, of course, Mike, I will be glad to help all I can," she smiled demurely.

Mike turned and left to go talk to his head chef. Kalea, with her arms folded, glared at Mike's back. She got very jealous when it came to Mike. She had wanted him to notice her for a long time. He was such a handsome man. They would make a great couple. This rule of "no dating the employees" was bullshit!

…*Yeah, Mike, I'll give her all the help she needs,* Kalea thought sarcastically.

Mike entered the kitchen.

"Hey Palani (pronounced: pah-law-nee), how are things going today?"

"Hi Mike! Going great," said Palani.

"How's the family?" asked Mike.

"All is well except our son is still having a little trouble at school."

"Let me know if you would like me to talk with him again. I remember what it was like when I attended middle school."

"Thanks, I appreciate the offer," said Palani.

"Let's take a look at the specials for tonight and see if we need to make any changes," said Mike.

"Of course!" said Palani. Mike went over the specials, made one change in the desert for tonight, asked if there were any questions, and headed back to the office.

When he went to open the door, he couldn't believe how his heart started to beat a little faster at the thought of seeing Jenna again. He opened the door and saw Mark and Jenna with their heads together looking over the reports and had an instant surge of jealousy hit him. He entered the office and closed the door with a bang.

"How are things going? Are you making any headway with the reports?" Mike asked curtly. As Mike sat down at the conference table, both Mark and Jenna looked up at the same time.

"Well Mike, looking over the liquor inventory and comparing it to the sales receipts. There is definitely a problem. Last night, two bottles of Jack Daniels were used and then the computer automatically ordered another case as if we were out. Six come in a case. According to the inventory report it was a new case that was opened. Four bottles are missing. Jenna thinks it could be a possible glitch in the software, but we would need to do inventory by hand and count each bottle every day for a week and compare it to the sales receipts to be sure," said Mark.

"According to these reports, do you think that theft is a possibility?" asked Mike.

"I think we may have to consider it," said Mark

"May I say something?" asked Jenna.

"Yes, Jenna, go ahead," said Mark. "I noticed that you use several different software applications to run your business. And there is a possibility that when you run your reports that inventory and sales don't match up correctly. I mentioned earlier that I work for a Bistro near the University, and their current software is an all-in-one POS and restaurant management system. Knowing that I was studying to become a CPA, the manager let me view the software. It's pretty slick."

"How does it work?" asked Mike.

"Basically, it can do everything from fulfilling orders, update online and in-house menus, ordering inventory, employee time sheets and sales receipts all in one program. It can be set up for touch screen or regular screen. It has dramatically cut their costs and increased profits."

Mike, watching her, asked, "Are you sure you are an accounting student because that was good!"

Jenna laughed, "I suppose it did sound like a sales pitch!"

Mark chuckled, "What is your input Mike?"

"Well, I think we should definitely do the inventory check and cross checking the sales reports. Let's do it for a week, possibly two to get an idea of what we're dealing with. Let's also go ahead and check out this new software, the cost, and the timeline to set it up and have it running. Then we'll meet back here in two weeks and go over our findings and go from there."

Jenna made notes in her notebook while Mike was speaking.

"Let's keep this confidential between the three of us and not to be discussed in front of any of the employees." Mark said. "Are we all in agreement?"

"Agreed," Mike and Jenna said.

"Jenna, I will have you reading the reports and checking on the new software. I will start counting the inventory Thursday morning, and every morning before the staff comes in at 2:00. And since tomorrow is Wednesday, I will see you, Jenna, at noon," said Mark.

"I will definitely be here," said Jenna

As they all got up from the conference table, Jenna looked at her watch. It was 3:00 already! She turned to Mike, "I'm so sorry, Mike. I have to be at the Bistro at 4 today. May I take the tour of your restaurant tomorrow?"

As their eyes met, he smiled, and there went those butterflies again!

"We'll see you tomorrow."

"Again, it was very nice meeting you both, and I look forward to working with you." Then she was gone. Mike watched her go and instantly felt a sense of loss. *This is crazy!*

Mark took one look at his brother and said, "I see that there's some chemistry going on between you and Jenna. You know our rules about dating employees."

Mike turned to his brother and smiled, "She's not an employee, Mark. She's an intern. Last I knew, interns didn't receive a paycheck. I'll see you out on the floor."

Mike went out into the restaurant and left Mark staring after him.

Chapter 4

That evening, Mark was sitting at the bar having a Jack Daniels on the rocks, watching their wait staff and bartenders busy serving their customers. Listening to the upbeat music coming from their state-of-the-art sound system, Mark always enjoyed watching their customers, young and old, having a good time.

Mike came up behind his brother and sat down next to him.

"Hey bro, you look pretty intense. Aren't you supposed to be home tonight?"

"Sherry called and said she would keep Cameron tonight, so I thought I would hang out here for a while and do some observing."

"I thought it was my job to do the observing."

"It is, but you do a lot of PR work to make sure our customers are satisfied. Why don't we go over to that back corner table, I'd like to talk to you about some concerns I have about the restaurant."

Mike slid off the bar stool and headed that way. Mark grabbed his drink and followed after him. As they sat down at the table, Megan, a pretty green-eyed, blonde with her long hair done up in a ponytail, came up to them and asked if she could get them anything.

"I'm all set, Megan, how about you, Mike?"

"Just bring me a Johnnie Walker on the rocks, Megan."

"You got it!" She winked and smiled at Mike.

As she left to go get his drink, both Mike and Mark watched

her. The outfits Mike chose for the staff fit her nicely and showed off her long beautiful legs. She was well put together, Mark thought.

"You do a good job hiring the staff, bro!" said Mark.

"Remember our rule, which you reminded me this afternoon, no dating the employees!"

Mark took a sip of his drink.

"Maybe we should take a second look at that rule," he said grinning. Megan came back with Mike's drink, set it down on the table, and gave Mike a brilliant smile.

"Can I get you gentlemen anything else?"

Mike smiled back, "No thank you, Megan."

As she turned to serve other customers, Mike took a sip of his drink and turned to his brother, "Okay Mark, what's this all about?"

"I just thought it might be a good idea to sit and watch the comings and goings of our staff to see if anything suspicious is going on," said Mark.

"So you do think someone from our staff may be stealing from us."

"I didn't want to concern you until I had proof, but the shortages on the reports have been happening off and on for a couple of months now. There is still a possibility it could be the software, but my gut instincts are telling me that someone is taking liquor out of here. And not just the cheap stuff; our high-end liquor."

Mike leaned forward.

"Mark, you should have informed me of your suspicions long before this," Mike said sternly.

"I know, I'm sorry, at first it was a bottle here and there. I actually thought it could be a glitch before Jenna mentioned it in the meeting today, but it started happening more and more. What do you think about bringing in Zack and have a consult with him?" ask Mark.

Sgt. Zackary Williams was a detective for the Police Department and a regular customer of the Hawaiian Lanai. Both Mark and Mike built a solid friendship with Zack as well as several other officers at the police department.

"No, let's see if you and Jenna can come up with anything substantial in the next couple of weeks before we call him in," said Mike.

"Alright bro, we'll wait and see if my gut instincts are correct... Jenna seems like a nice young woman. Very attractive," Mark commented.

Mike tensed and glared at his brother.

"Whoa, bro, I misspoke earlier. I know she's not an employee and fair game. But I wouldn't want her to get hurt, or you for that matter. I saw how you two looked at each other at the meeting. The chemistry was unmistakable."

Mike relaxed.

"I do not intend to hurt her. But I'll be honest. I have never felt anything like I felt with Jenna today. Not even Selena, who I thought I was madly in love with. As you know, I've dated a lot of women since the breakup, and none of them made me feel. Right now, bro, I'll try and keep my distance until we see how she handles herself in her role at the restaurant. After that, I give you fair warning, I'm going after her," said Mike, smiling.

"Before you do, maybe you should find out if she has a significant other." Mike glared at his brother. "Just saying," said Mark.

Tammy, one of the waitresses serving the party in the lanai came up to their table. They both looked up and smiled.

"I'm sorry to interrupt, but General McCall would like to have a word with you Mike."

"Tell him I will be with him in a moment. And Tammy?"

"Yes?" she asked.

"Thank you for letting me know," said Mike still smiling.

Tammy looked at them both and then back at Mike and smiled, "You're welcome." She turned to head back into the lanai with her face all flushed.

Damn, those two are just too handsome, she said to herself.

Mike turned back to his brother.

"So, are we good, bro?"

"We're good," said Mark.

Mike downed his drink and got up from the table.

"See you tomorrow."

Mark lifted his drink and said, "Tomorrow."

Mark watched his brother head into the lanai.

I hope you know what you are doing bro concerning Jenna. I have a feeling that she will keep you in line, he said to himself. Smiling, he finished his drink, threw some bills on the table, and decided to go home.

As he was leaving the restaurant, a woman and one of the bartenders were huddled at the far end of the bar watching the two brothers conversing and then leaving.

"Do you think they are on to us?" asked the bartender.

"We need to keep an eye out, we don't need them suspecting what we are doing," said the woman.

"Will do, but just so you know, if I go down so will you!" said the bartender.

"Then you better make damn sure you don't get caught!" said the woman angrily.

"I'm doing the best I can!" he replied just as angrily.

She looked at him exasperated.

"I just don't want to end up in jail with everything else that's going on!" she said as she stomped off!

Mike was coming back into the bar after speaking with General McCall. It was good to know they were happy with the food and service his restaurant had to offer. As he came through the door, he scanned the bar and saw his brother had left for the night. He looked over to the far end of the bar and saw one of his hostesses and bartender in a heated argument. He was just headed that way when they broke apart and the hostess stomped off. He made a mental note to keep an eye on the two of them. He didn't need his customers upset because they had an attitude!

Chapter 5

_T_he next morning, Jenna felt a little paw gently touch her face. Then a minute later, her alarm went off. She rolled over to turn it off. As she rolled back, Cuddles was above her head, staring down at her. She closed her eyes. She did not want to get out of bed this morning. A paw came down and touched her forehead. She looked up and lifted her cat and laid her down beside her. Jenna scratched her ears and petted her back and heard the familiar purring.

Last night, they were slammed at the Bistro. When she finally got home, she was exhausted. She managed to study for an hour and then fell into bed.

Jenna reflected back to the meeting yesterday at the Hawaiian Lanai and remembered the explosive chemistry she felt for Mike and wondered if he felt it too. Both Mike and Mark were extremely handsome men, but there was something about Mike that drew her to him.

Cuddles flipped on her back and grabbed her hand with her paws. When she started biting her fingers in a playful gesture, she knew it was time to get up.

"Okay, Cuddles, let's get up and get you something to eat.

Her cat jumped down to the floor as Jenna climbed out of bed and headed to the kitchen. Sasha was already seated at the counter eating a bowl of cereal with a text book beside her.

"Good morning Sasha! How's it going?" asked Jenna.

"Just trying to read up on my chemistry class," she said. Sasha was studying to become a doctor and would be going on to medical school after she gets her undergraduate degree. "What about you? You came in awfully late last night."

Jenna was busy getting her cat some food. She turned to her friend.

"We were swamped at the Bistro right up until 10:00. By the time we got the place cleaned up and everything put away, it was close to 11:30. I'm still feeling it this morning."

"Wow, it's not usually that busy on a Tuesday night."

"No it's not. We were all surprised," said Jenna.

"How did it go on your first day as an intern at the restaurant yesterday afternoon?"

Jenna started the coffee pot and put two slices of bread in the toaster.

"You ask a lot of questions so early in the morning!"

"Can't help it, I'm a curious person by nature. I need to know the details!"

Jenna buttered her toast and filled her mug with coffee and sat down next to Sasha. Once she fixed up her coffee with cream and sugar, she took a sip.

"Ah, that is so good!"

"Come on, Jenna! Give!"

"Okay, okay. It was interesting."

"Interesting?" Sasha stared at her, "How so?"

"Well, first of all, when I walked into the meeting I was shocked to find that the TreVaine brothers are identical twins! And when I tell you their identical, I mean it's hard to tell them apart! I had to ask which one was Mark!" As she took a bite of her toast, "They're really hot, Sasha," she said dreamily. "I mean really HOT! Other than that it went good."

Sasha just stared at her.

"Are you going to keep me hanging here?"

"What do you mean?"

"What else happened?"

Jenna finished her toast and most of her coffee. She took another sip.

"Well, we had a short meeting. Kalea, this beautiful Polynesian woman, I might add, brought in coffee and these cute little cakes that were so good! Then Mark and I went over some of the financial reports."

"And?" asked Sasha a little frustrated.

"And, what?" asked Jenna. "What about Mike?"

Mike, Jenna wasn't ready to talk about, nor was she ready to talk about the explosive chemistry she felt for him.

"He's all business."

"That's it?" ask Sasha with a surprised look on her face.

"For now, will see what happens today." Jenna looked up at the clock. "And speaking of which, I've got to get going." She got up, walked around to the sink, rinsed her dishes, and put them in the dishwasher.

As she left to go get ready, she heard Sasha yell, "This conversation isn't over! I know you're not telling me everything!"

Jenna smiled as she went to shower, dress, and put her makeup on. As she left the apartment for her class, her only thought was seeing Mike again. The anticipation was nerve-wracking!

After her class, Jenna decided to stay and study in the common area until she had to leave for the restaurant. Kenny, a classmate of hers, came up to her and asked if he could join her.

"Sure, have a seat. Are you all done with classes today?" asked Jenna.

"I have one more in just a little bit. Just wanted to see how your first day at your internship went yesterday."

"Well, there's not much to tell. Mark, my boss, started to show me some of the financial reports, but we didn't really have time to dive into them. I'm looking forward to getting back into them today. Speaking of which," Jenna looked at her watch, "I have to get going. I'm supposed to be there at noon." Jenna closed her book and got up from the table. "You have a great rest of your day Kenny!"

"You too Jenna, and good luck!" said Kenny.

"Thank you!" said Jenna.

Kenny watched her leave and wondered if she would go out with him. She had such a warm personality, and she was so beautiful. He sighed. Maybe someday he would get brave enough to ask her out. He got up from the table and went on to his class.

Arriving at the restaurant 10 minutes early, she found the doors locked.

"Great now what?" she mumbled. Just as she was about to call the number for the restaurant, Mark came up behind her. At least, she thought it was Mark. She was not feeling any electrifying energy, so it must be Mark!

"Hi, Jenna, sorry, the doors are locked until 4:00 unless we have a meeting and Kalea is here to unlock and relock the door. I will give you my cell phone number when we get inside."

Jenna followed Mark to the back of the restaurant and into the office. He flicked on the lights, turned towards her, and gave Jenna his cell number. Jenna put it in her contact list. While in the meeting yesterday, Jenna didn't pay much attention to the layout of the office. As she looked around, there were two large offices, one on each end with a smaller office in between them. The conference table was centered in the open area as you came through the main door. Mark led her to the smaller office and flicked on the light. There was a large desk with two computer screens centered in the middle with a large copier and file cabinets set on the far wall.

"This will be your office while you're here. I have the office to your right as you come in the main door, and Mike's is on the left. I'm going to have you begin by getting familiar with our software and how the reports are run on a daily basis. Then next week you can check into the new software. Have a seat, and I'll show you how to get into the program and pull up the reports. You will need to set a password, so no one but you can get into them."

Jenna sat down at the desk. Mark leaned over her, showed her how to set her password, and pull up the reports. While they were discussing and comparing the reports on the screens, they heard a door slam! They both jumped!

"Hmm, must be Mike's in. He usually doesn't come in at this time of day." Jenna's stomach fluttered just knowing he was in his office. "Do you have any questions for me?"

"Not at this time, but I'm sure I will once I get into this."

"Okay, I'll just be in my office if you need me."

"Thank you!"

Jenna worked for the next two hours going over the inventory and sales receipts. She was so engrossed in her work, she didn't hear the knock at the door. She sensed an energy in the room that gave her goosebumps! She looked up and saw Mike staring down at her.

"Mike! I didn't hear you knock!" she said nervously.

Mike stood with his hands in his pockets, catching her eyes.

"So I noticed. I see my brother has you knee-deep in reports."

"Yes, I am looking over the inventory and cost analysis."

"It's time to take a break. Come with me."

"But I need to finish this and check in with Mark before 5:00." It was already 3:15!

"This won't take long and I'm sure my brother can wait!" said Mike curtly.

"Oh, okay. Just let me sign out and I'll be right with you." Jenna was nervous as she logged out and hoped Mike didn't notice her hands shaking as he stared down at her.

Mike watched her as she signed out and was irritated that this woman had him all tied up in knots ever since he laid eyes on her at the meeting yesterday. He tossed and turned all night, just thinking about her. When she came over to him, he took her arm and felt that zing go up his arm and into his heart. He wondered if she felt it, too. He led her out of the office and into a large room with a pond in the center and bridges crisscrossing over it. Each bridge led to a pagoda, which looked like a hut with lush tropical shrubbery and colorful flowers in and around each one.

"This is our Hawaiian room. Each pagoda can seat up to 12 people. Tourists from all parts of the world and locals come to enjoy the Hawaiian experience. Of course, we offer American dishes as well as our famous Hawaiian cuisine." They walked along one of the bridges, and Jenna gazed down at all the different colored gold fish swimming aimlessly in the water.

"Who takes care of all the fish?"

"We have a company who is skilled in maintaining the ponds and feeding the fish."

As Jenna looked around the room, she looked up at Mike.

"This whole atmosphere is so relaxing. I can see why people would come here time and again. It's beautiful."

Mike looked deep in her eyes and wondered how it would feel to kiss her right here right now. As he lowered his head, he heard a noise off to the right of the room. Jenna's heart was racing in anticipation of Mike's lips on hers.

"Sorry Mr. TreVaine, don't mean to interrupt, just setting up for tonight."

Mike lifted his head and placed it on her forehead. He took a deep breath and smiled still looking deep into her eyes.

"It's okay Markus. We were just leaving." He took her arm and led her out and into the bar area.

The bar was set for the younger crowd, with the dark wood paneling, the upbeat music, and a wraparound bar that gleamed in the indirect lighting. There was a large mirror set in the middle behind the bar, with the words "The Hawaiian Lanai" etched in it. Two bartenders were working behind the bar, and Mike introduced them to Jenna.

"Outside there is a lanai with another pond in the middle that is used for overflow and parties. It has a beautiful view of the Pacific Ocean with colorful tropical plants placed all around and palm trees standing tall as you head down to the ocean, as you can see looking out of the windows here in the bar area," said Mike.

"Yes, it's enchanting. You have a wonderful establishment here," said Jenna.

As they entered the kitchen, Jenna's only thought was, *Wow! To work in a kitchen like this would be amazing!* Behind the counter was a tall Polynesian man with a broad chest and large muscles. His long black hair was tied behind his neck. He appeared to be doing some prep work for tonight's specials. He looked up as they came in.

"Jenna, I would like you to meet our head chef Palani." Palani washed his hands in the sink and toweled off. He came up to them and extended his hand. "Palani, this is Jenna Hathaway. She will be working with Mark over the next three months to earn her BA degree in accounting."

Jenna shook his hand.

"It's nice to meet you, Palani"

"Same here."

"Palani is an expert in Hawaiian cuisine," said Mike.

Jenna smiled.

"Sometime, I would like try one of your dishes while I am here. I've heard they are extraordinary."

"I'll be sure to make something special for you."

"Thank you! I would love that!" Jenna checked her watch and looked over at Mike. "I really need to get back to the office. Thank you for the tour. And again, it was nice to meet you, Palani."

"Same here," he said grinning. When she left, Palani looked at Mike. "Nice girl! She just might be a keeper!"

As Mike watched her go, he thought to himself, *Yes, she just might.* He turned to Palani. "How is your son Makaha doing in school now?"

"He's doing much better since I had you talk with him about the fights he was getting into. It's going to take time, but he has agreed to try harder to get his grades up."

"That's good to hear, Palani. Let's go over tonight's specials, and then I'll let you get back to work." Mike went over the menu and specials that were scheduled for tonight, asked if he had any questions, and headed back to the office.

Back at the office, Jenna went directly to work on the reports. She wanted to recheck the liquor inventory. She thought she saw something before Mike came to take her on the tour. She reflected on Mike and the almost kiss that she had wanted so badly. She wondered what it would feel like, his lips pressing next to hers. Those hands, when he touched her, sent chills throughout her body. She sighed.

Focus Jenna, you need to get this done!

Mike came in and went directly into Mark's office and shut the door. Mark looked up as Mike sat down.

"How was the tour?" asked Mark.

"Good."

"What was with the door slam earlier? Are you jealous much?"

"Sorry bro, I shouldn't have done that. It seems I do have a jealous streak concerning her." Even a possessiveness he feels whenever he is around her, he thought.

"Look Mike, Jenna and I have to work together. I have no romantic intentions for her. Did we not have this conversation last night?"

"Yes, I apologize, I will try to keep better control over my emotions," said Mike.

"I would appreciate it. Did you happen to see anything last night that might be suspicious?" Mark asked. "Nothing out of the ordinary, although when I came in from the lanai after speaking with General McCall, I did see one of our hostesses and bartender arguing. When I went to see what the problem was, the hostess stomped off. It could be personalities clashing, but it might be worth keeping an eye on. I don't want our customers to become upset if our staff can't get along."

"I agree," said Mark. There was a knock on the door. "Come in." Jenna opened the door and saw both Mike and Mark in the office.

"I'm sorry, I'll come back."

"No, Jenna, come in," said Mark. Jenna came in through the door. Mike was sitting in front of Mark's desk.

"I don't mean to interrupt, but I found what you had mentioned in the meeting yesterday where a new case of Jack Daniels was ordered just five days ago and then re-ordered yesterday. The sales report shows that it couldn't have been out to warrant a re-order. Plus, the same thing happened to other cases of your higher cost liquor off and on throughout this past month."

Jenna slightly leaned over the desk to show Mark her findings. Mike was just about to lean forward to have a look when he noticed her cute little ass and instantly started to feel himself getting aroused. He started thinking thoughts he shouldn't be thinking. Mike suddenly got up and was about to leave the office when Mark looked up, "Don't you want to take a look at this, Mike?"

"Show it to me later, I just remembered some paperwork that I need to finish."

Mike couldn't get out of the office fast enough. As he walked into his office, all he could think about was getting his hands on her and feeling every soft curve of her body!

Mike! he said to himself. *You need to get a grip!* He sat down at his desk and ran his hands through his hair. That was going to be easier said than done.

After Mike left, Jenna turned to Mark, "I did interrupt your meeting with Mike!"

"No, you did not. I have my own suspicions as to why he left, but we won't get into that. Let's take a look at what you found."

Over the next half-hour, they reviewed the report.

"I'm pretty sure there is theft involved but feel like we still need to do the manual inventory check to make sure," said Mark. Mark looked at his watch, and it was after 5:00. "It's getting late, and I have to meet my soon-to-be ex-wife to pick up my son Cameron at 6:30. Why don't you go ahead and log out? I want to go over this report and some others with Mike before I go, and I'll see you on Monday."

"Okay, see you on Monday then. Goodnight."

"Goodnight Jenna."

Jena left the office, and as she was coming out, she saw a young woman with long red hair coming out of her office.

"Can I help you?"

"I was looking for Mike," the woman said nervously.

"He wasn't in his office?"

"No, so I thought I would take a peek in here."

"Maybe he is out on the floor of the restaurant somewhere. You can check there," said Jenna.

"Yes, I will." She couldn't get out of the office fast enough. Jenna went into her office and checked her computer screens. She didn't see anything out of place, but it bothered her that she was in her office. She would be sure to mention it to Mark and be more cautious about logging off whenever she left her office. Jenna shut down her computer and locked her office. She was ready for a relaxing evening and a nice glass of wine.

Mark put all the reports in the file folder and locked them in his desk drawer. He went out into the restaurant to see if he could find Mike since he wasn't in his office. He went up to Kalea and asked, "Have you seen Mike?"

"He just went out the front door to catch your intern," she said curtly. "I thought we had a rule around here. No dating employees!"

"She is not an employee. She is here to get her BA degree, and the rule still stands!" he said with a glare in his eyes. "When you see him, tell him I need to see him in my office." Mark turned and walked off.

Mike came into Mark's office a short time later and as he sat down.

"You wanted to see me?"

"Yes, I haven't much time, but I wanted you to see these reports and get your take on it."

Mike looked over the reports, he looked up at Mark.

"We definitely have a problem here."

"I think we better call in Zack and not wait. He could give us some insight as to how to proceed and catch who is doing the stealing."

"I agree, but let's meet at the police station or at another location. We don't want whoever is doing this to know that we're on to them," said Mike.

"Okay, what is your schedule look like on Friday morning?"

Mike checked his calendar in his cell phone. "Looks good, I'm free all morning."

"I'll give Zack a call and shoot you a text when I confirm the time and location," said Mark. Mike got up and headed toward the door.

"Sounds good, I need to get back out on the floor. I'll keep my eye out for anything unusual."

"I'll walk out with you," said Mark. "I was supposed to meet Sherry at 6:30, and I'm already late." Mark put the file back in his drawer, locked it, and headed out the door with Mike. He locked his office and checked Jenna's. "We need to keep our offices locked from now on," said Mark. Mike went and locked his, and they headed out into the restaurant. As Mark left, he turned to his brother and smiled, "You have a good day off tomorrow, bro."

"I will, and give Cameron a big hug from his Uncle Mike!"

"Will do," then he left. One of his waitresses came up to him to let him know a customer wanted to see him, and the rest of the night went by in a blur. Meanwhile, out behind the restaurant three people were talking.

"Look man, I don't know how long we can keep this up without the owners getting on to us."

"Well, the boss is going to want his money, and he's not going to like me coming back with nothing to give him."

The man glowered at them both, a rough looking character with long, dirty, brown hair, and teeth that looked like they could use a good brushing. His smell wasn't too good either.

"I'll give you two weeks to cough up the money, or you'll regret ever being born!"

"We'll have the money, and then were done!" said the woman.

"The boss will let you two know when you're done! Don't give me any shit!" The man grabbed her arm and threw her against the wall.

"Hey! Don't be roughing her up!" As he stepped in between the two, he got a fist to the gut! He groaned.

"You can count on more of this if you don't have the money in two weeks!"

"We'll have it," said the woman.

"See that you do!" and he left.

"How are we going to come up with$2,000? Even if we can find a way and pay him, he always ups the ante!"

"We'll find a way and then we will make it clear we are done with this," replied the woman.

"Well, I happen to value my life, and if we can't come up with the money, I am going to the police and turn myself in. Maybe we can turn this loan shark in, so he can't keep doing this to people!" he said angrily and walked back into the restaurant, leaving her to wonder just what have they gotten themselves into.

Chapter 6

The next morning, sitting out in the lanai, Jenna was enjoying her favorite smoothie made with vanilla protein mix, coconut milk, fresh strawberries, blueberries, and bananas. Cuddles sat on her lap and purred loudly as Jenna scratched behind her ears, her favorite spot. It was a beautiful sunny morning, perfect for a jog on the beach. She finished her smoothie and put Cuddles on the floor, which she wasn't happy about.

"Going to go jogging this morning, Cuddles. You be a good cat while I'm gone."

Cuddles meowed at her and jumped back up on the chair to curl up and take a nap.

Jenna put on her tennis shoes, grabbed her iPhone and earbuds, said goodbye to her cat, and headed out the door. Listening to her favorite iTunes, she decided to take the trail to Hanauma Bay. It was gorgeous out, and the temperature was perfect. The light breeze caressing her skin felt good as she started down the trail. As she jogged the trail, she admired the beautiful tropical plants and shrubbery that landscaped the homes in the area. There were couples and singles already out for a walk or bike ride, enjoying the weather that was so common on the island of Oahu. Sometimes, there'd be a shower during the day, then it cleared up and was beautiful again.

It wasn't long before she was approaching Hanauma Bay. She looked out over the ocean and saw the surfers sitting on their boards, waiting for the biggest wave to ride back in. The beach was pretty crowded already with tourist and locals sunning themselves and watching their children build sand castles in the sand.

She stopped to watch for a moment as the surfers started to go out on their boards to catch the wave. It always amazed her how once they turned the board and the wave caught them, they could jump up on their feet and steer the board how they wanted and ride into the beach. It took a lot of skill and balance, and yet some still toppled over into the ocean, then got back up on their boards and did it again. She walked down the beach to see if anyone was body surfing. She saw several surfers riding the waves, using their arms and hands to steer them where they wanted to go. As they came closer to the shore, the waves slammed them down. She had a friend that liked to body surf, and when they come down, he said you had to let the ocean take you where it wanted and not fight it. She saw some of the surfers come up and start walking out of the water. One in particular looked familiar to her.

He had a broad tan chest, narrow hips, strong muscular legs, and his whole body was glistening in the sun as he came up on shore. His suit was skin tight, and as she looked at him, she recognized who it was. Her heart went ballistic, and she was about to turn tail and run when he called out to her!

"Jenna! Jenna, wait!" he yelled.

She stopped and watched him put his sandals on, grab his towel and dry himself as he came toward her. She couldn't stop looking at him. The butterflies in her stomach made it hard for her to breathe. She had never in her life seen such a magnificent and virile man.

"Mike!" she said breathlessly. "That was some body surfing out there!"

"Thanks. I love to body surf. I'm out here every chance I get. Looks like you've been out jogging. What brings you out this way?"

As he gazed at her, he had to keep himself in check. He didn't need to become aroused in this form fitting suit! But he couldn't help but notice her perfect body in those tightfitting shorts and form fitting tank top she was wearing. It showed off those perky breasts that he'd like to get his mouth and hands on. Her hair was up in a ponytail with strays clinging to her pretty face. He had all he could do to control himself and not take her in his arms and kiss her senseless. His heart was beating so loud, he was sure she could hear it.

Jenna felt a little self-conscious as he gazed at her intently. She must look really bad with her hair all over the place, and she was sweaty to boot!

"Uh, yes, I usually jog on Waikiki Beach but decided to take the trail here. I always enjoy watching the surfers."

He smiled down at her, knowing she was self-conscious about her appearance.

"I'm glad you did. Have you ever body surfed?"

"Oh no!" she said, shaking her head. "I'm not a strong swimmer. I wouldn't be comfortable in such turbulent waters. I'm sure I would drown! But I do find it amazing how people can ride the waves with a board or their bodies."

"It's a thrill of a lifetime! I try to get out here as much as I can. It helps me to release some of the stress in my life!" he said with a grin.

"Well, I don't know how that works, but okay!"

Mike just laughed.

"Do you have time for coffee? I live just up the way, and I need to get into the shower to get this salt off my skin."

"Uh," Jenna didn't know what to think. Going to his home, should she? Mike noticed her hesitancy.

He smiled down at her, "It's only coffee Jenna." Although he would like to do more with her than just have coffee, he thought. *Whoa Mike, slow down!* "I might even have a pastry or two to go with it!"

Well, how could she refuse that smile of his and the pastry! She smiled back at him, her heart beating fast and said breathlessly, "Okay."

They started walking towards his home, and while they were walking, Mike asked her, "What made you want to become a CPA?"

"Well, when I was in school, math was my favorite subject. I loved to work with numbers. Actually, before I graduated high school, I always did my parents income tax returns."

"Wow! I never really cared for math. I learned the basics but didn't want to handle the accounting part of the business. That's why Mark handles that end, and I oversee the restaurant-aspect of the business. It was a lot of work in the beginning, not much time to socialize, but it was worth it."

Jenna smiled, "As I saw yesterday, you and your brother have a beautiful establishment. I've read some of your reviews on line, pretty impressive!"

"Thanks, that means a lot. Here we are!"

They stopped. Jenna looked up a small flight of stairs and saw a beautiful, sprawling ranch painted a light olive color with white trim. The main entrance door had a beautiful stained-glass window in it, and the door was also painted white. There was patio furniture on either side of the entry door and a big crystal light fixture hung down above the door.

"Is this your home?" Jenna asked in awe.

"It is," said Mike, smiling. They started up the stairs, and from what Jenna could see the home was on a large lot, and the landscape was immaculate. Palm trees in both the front and back yards with shrubbery lining the perimeter of the home and beautiful hibiscus in an array of color were placed perfectly around the property. It was pure paradise. Mike unlocked the door, turned towards Jenna. "After you," he said with a smile. Jenna smiled up at him and went inside.

It was amazing! For a brief moment, she wondered what it would be like to live in a home like this. As she looked around, she saw an open floor plan with the living room, dining room combination, with sliding glass doors leading out to a screened-in lanai. The gray granite counter separated the kitchen from the living area. Bar stools were set in front of the counter. All the walls were painted white, but were bare of pictures. Mike closed the door and watched Jenna take it all in.

"It's a little cold isn't it?"

"I wouldn't exactly say it is cold, but the rooms could use some color and pictures on the walls to bring warmth to the rooms."

"I just purchased the home six months ago and haven't had time to do any decorating or figure out what colors I would like for the walls."

"I love the skylights, as they soften the rooms," she said.

"I agree. That's one of the reasons I bought this home. I looked at a lot of them, but this one drew me. Well, make yourself at home. I'm going to take a quick shower and be right back."

As he started down the hall to the right, Jenna called after him, "Would you like me to start the coffee?"

He turned back with a surprised look on his face and said, "Sure! The coffee and coffee pot are on the counter."

She went into the kitchen when Mike left to go shower. She found the coffee pot and coffee and started putting the coffee grounds and water into the coffeemaker. She pushed the start button and looked around. It was a state-of-the-art kitchen with everything nicely laid out and everything at your fingertips. She wondered what it would be like to cook in a kitchen like this. She went to find a bathroom to freshen up a bit and found one down the hall to the right. She could hear Mike in the shower in the master bathroom and thought she might take a peek and see where he slept. The master bedroom was huge with a king-size bed centered in the room. The headboard and two end tables were made of dark oak, and a round table made of the same wood sat in front of the window with two comfortable chairs on either side of it.

She heard the shower stop and hurried back down the hall and slipped into the bathroom. She took one look at herself and groaned. She was a mess! She did the best she could by rinsing her face and putting the strays of hair back in place. She had no makeup on and felt like a wilted flower. She was sure she didn't smell good either! She needed to stay far away from Mike.

When she came out of the bathroom, she ran right into him—literally! He caught her by her arms, and her hands landed directly on his chest. She could feel his muscles beneath her palms, and his musky scent after his shower just about did her in. Her heart started racing as she looked up into those blue eyes of his.

"Oh! I'm so sorry! I didn't see you!"

Mike, caught off guard, wanted to hold onto her, as he liked the feel of her hands on him, but she broke away from him and started towards the kitchen. The electric current going through him was staggering. She took a seat at the counter while he went into the kitchen and took two mugs out of the cupboard. She was shaking a little from that brief contact with him. She wished she looked a little better, especially when he was heart-stopping gorgeous!

As she watched him pour the coffee, he looked up and grinned, "Cream and sugar right?"

Jenna was surprised he remembered!

"Yes!" When he handed her the mug of coffee, she took a sip. "Perfect!" She grinned.

As she looked at him over her mug of coffee, he had put on navy twill shorts and a matching t-shirt that stretched across his broad chest. She read the yellow lettering written on his shirt.

"Oh no," she exclaimed.

He looked up surprised!

"What?"

"Don't tell me you are a U of M fan?"

"Yep, and what do you think you're going to do about it?"

"Well, I'll think of something, but know this! The MSU Spartans will beat the socks off of those Wolverines come this fall!" she laughed.

Mike burst out laughing.

"We'll see little one, we'll see."

It felt good to laugh with him.

Mike took some pastries out of the refrigerator and warmed them up in the microwave. He sat in the bar stool beside Jenna and offered her one.

"Thank you!" She bit into her pastry and groaned, "Oh, this is so good."

"Definitely hits the spot!" said Mike.

While they were enjoying their pastry and coffee, Mike was thinking, *Wouldn't it be nice to wake up and have this time with her every morning...? Whoa Mike, where did that thought come from. Never getting married, remember?* He quickly dismissed his thoughts when he realized Jenna had asked him a question.

"I'm sorry, Jenna, what did you ask me?"

"I was curious about how you came into the restaurant business."

Mike smiled.

"When I was growing up, my parents owned a small family

restaurant in a rural town in the southern part of Michigan. After school, all of us kids would go and help in the kitchen and do our homework. Mom and Dad would always work the dinner crowd, and it was just easier to have us all there. As we got older, our schedules got a little crazy with sports and after-school activities. So, Dad hired someone to take Mom's place, so she could keep track of all of us. After I graduated high school, my brother and I signed up for the Air Force, and after basic training, we were stationed here on the island at Joint Base Pearl Harbor-Hickam. We both fell in love with the island and all the culture here, so we started to look into buying a restaurant. My dream was to one day own a restaurant, and here I am today."

"Wow, do you have any other siblings besides your twin?"

"One older sister who lives in the Detroit Metro area with her husband and two boys, and an older brother, Peyton, who is still serving in the Armed Forces as a special op for the Army Rangers. He's currently on a special mission, and we have no idea where he is or if he's okay."

"OMG! And there's no way you can get in touch with him?"

"Nope!" he said. "Every mission is top secret, and they are not allowed to disclose any information to anyone, including family."

"That must be really hard on all of you, not knowing."

"It is, but we are hoping this will be his last tour. What about you, Jenna? What's your family like?"

"Well it's not as exciting as yours," Jenna chuckled. "I grew up on a small dairy farm, also in a small town in southern Michigan. Small world—we are both from Michigan!" They both smiled at each other, and her eyes lit up. "My parents had six children, me being the last one born. I have three older brothers, all married, and two sisters, one married, and lots of nieces and nephews."

"What made you want to study in Hawaii?"

"I've always wanted to travel. I was studying at MSU at the time, and this opportunity came up where I could study any where I wanted on a full scholarship in the CPA program, so I applied, got accepted, and chose the University of Hawaii. I love it here. There is so much diversity here. I miss my family, but I try to fly home at Christmas. Hopefully, some of my family will be able to come over for my graduation."

Mike gazed into her big brown eyes and could imagine her growing up on a farm and running around in her bare feet. She had to have been the cutest little girl on Earth! Jenna finished her coffee and looked at her watch.

"Oh, my, gosh!" she exclaimed. "I've been gone over three hours! Sasha will wonder what happened to me."

"Who's Sasha?"

"My roommate, I left a note on the counter that I would be back in an hour."

"Would it help if I drove you back to your apartment?" ask Mike.

"Oh, that's very kind of you, but the traffic is heavy this time of day, and it would be faster to jog it back." She got up from her chair and headed for the door. Mike followed her and opened the door for her. She turned back and looked up at his handsome face, "Thank you so much for the pastry and coffee. I enjoyed being here with you and getting to know you."

"Me too," said Mike. He didn't want her to go. "Jenna."

"Yes?" she whispered.

"Are you doing anything tonight?"

"I'm working at the bistro from 4:00-10:00."

"Oh, that's right, the Bistro."

"Well, I'll see you," she said.

"See you," said Mike.

Then she turned and hurried down the steps. Mike closed the

door and went back to the kitchen to clean up the plates and coffee cups. As he picked up the cups, he noticed she left her I phone and ear buds on the counter. Mike smiled and thought, *Looks like I'll be having dinner at the Bistro!*

Chapter 7

When Jenna came back into her apartment, she was met at the door by her roommate, Sasha.

"Where have you been? I've been worried! I thought maybe you were mugged or even worse, kidnapped!"

"I'm so sorry, Sasha. I decided to jog over to Hanauma Bay and ran into Mike. He asked me if I wanted to have coffee, and the time just flew by."

"Well, you could have called! Wait a minute. You ran into Mike? Your boss! OMG! I need all the deets!"

"Sasha, it was all very innocent, and—oh my gosh!" Jenna felt around in her pockets. "I left my cell phone on his counter!"

"On his counter!" exclaimed Sasha. "You had coffee at his home?" she asked with a stunned look on her face. Jenna nodded her head yes. Sasha grabbed her hand and sat her down on the sofa. "Okay, spill it!"

"Sasha!" Jenna exclaimed.

"Jenna, you are not leaving this couch until you tell me everything!"

"Okay, okay! When I got over to Hanauma Bay, I decided to stop and watch the surfers go out and catch the first wave. It always amazes me how they stay on the board!" Jenna shifted a little on the couch to look directly at Sasha. "Then I went a little further down the shore to see if anyone was body surfing. There were several out riding the waves and a few coming out of the water, and one of them was Mike!"

"Go on," said Sasha.

"When I saw him coming out of the water, his body glistening in the sun, looking sizzling hot and me all hot and sweaty, all I wanted to do was run! He saw me and called out for me to wait and invited me for coffee." Jenna sighed, "Sasha, he's so good looking. I get all hot and bothered when I'm around him, and my stomach feels like it's all tied up in knots."

"Wow, so you went to his home. What was it like?" Jenna had a dreamy-eyed look on her face.

"It was beautiful, a big, sprawling ranch on a large lot with palm trees and colorful tropical flowers all around the property. Inside was just as beautiful. It has an open floor plan and a state-of-the-art kitchen. His bedroom was huge with dark wood furniture and a king size bed."

"Jenna!" Sasha's eyes were about ready to pop out! "You were in his bedroom?"

"NO! I was just exploring and peeked in until I heard the shower stop."

Sasha was looking at Jenna flabbergasted! "OMG! Did you see him naked?"

"NO! I hightailed it out of there before he came back in his bedroom! Then we got to know each other better over coffee and pastries." Jenna sighed, "He is just so hot! Now, I've got to figure out how I'm going to get my phone back. I don't have his phone number."

"Hey!" exclaimed Sasha. "Maybe you can get it from his twin! What's his name?"

"Mark!" exclaimed Jenna. "That's a great idea! I'll just text him and see if he can get a message to Mike! Can I borrow your phone?" asked Jenna.

"Of course," she said. Sasha got up from the couch and went to get her phone. Cuddles came from her bedroom and jumped up on Jenna's lap for some cat time attention. Jenna scratched behind her ears and petted her back. Her soft purring relaxed Jenna as she waited for Sasha to come back with her phone. When she came back in, she handed Jenna her phone and Jenna put Cuddles down on the floor. She was not happy about her time being cut short.

"Sorry, Cuddles. We'll spend more time after work."

Jenna got up from the couch and went over to the desk. In the top drawer, Sasha and her kept all their information and phone numbers where they worked in case there was an emergency and couldn't get a hold of each other on their cell phones. She found Mark's cell number and punched it into Sasha's phone for a text.

> Hey Mark! I ran into Mike at Hanauma Bay. We had coffee at his home and I left my I phone on his counter. Could you please contact him and let him know?
>
> I will be working at the Bistro tonight so you can have him call this number, my roommate Sasha Winslow, will get the message to me.
>
> I would really appreciate it. Thank you!
>
> −Jenna.

She pushed send and handed the phone back to Sasha.

"If he calls, call me at the Bistro and give me the deets! I'm going to take a shower and get ready for work."

"Will do, Jenna," she returned.

When Jenna went to shower, Sasha went into the kitchen to fix her some dinner to prepare herself for a night of intense studying for an exam tomorrow. As she was getting everything out to prepare her dinner, she smiled and thought, *I knew she wasn't telling me everything, and I'm pretty sure she is starting to have feelings for Mike. It's about time she found someone! She's always been way too serious and stubborn about dating before she gets her degree.* Sasha stopped what she was doing. *Come to think of it, I can't remember a time she ever went out on a serious date since I've known her.* Sasha shrugged and went back to preparing her dinner. *I sure can't wait to see how this all unfolds, should be interesting!*

Mark was working in his office when he heard his phone ding to let him know a message came in. He picked up his phone but didn't recognize the number, but saw Jenna's name at the bottom of the message. He quickly read the message and got a grin on his face. *Brother, how do you do it?' Women just fall into your hands.* He sent a text back to Jenna to let her know he received her message and would get ahold of Mike. Then he sent a text to his brother.

> Hey Bro, Jenna sent me a text via her roommate's phone. You have her I phone which I'm sure you already know. I will text you the number if you need it, but I am sure you have something else up your sleeve. And just FYI, we have a meeting over at the police station with Zack at 10:00 am tomorrow.

Mark hit send and put his phone back on his desk.

Mike was working in his yard and thinking about Jenna. He can't seem to get her out of his mind. He was looking forward to seeing her again at the Bistro where she works and returning her phone. He heard his phone ding. He took it out of his pocket and checked the message. It was from his brother. As he read it, he chuckled. He sent a text back:

> You know me so well brother! (smile emoji) See you in the morning at the police station.

He pushed send. His brother returned his text, with a thumbs-up sign. He put his phone back in his pocket and finished up his yard work. He had a feeling it was going to be an eventful night!

Jenna was getting ready to go out the door for work when Sasha called from the kitchen.

"Hey Jenna!" she yelled.

"Yes?"

"I got a text back from your boss and said he sent a message to Mike about your phone."

"Did he say anything about when Mike was going to return it?"

"No. Just said he sent him a message."

"Okay, if you hear anything else, give me a call at the Bistro."

"Will do, Jenna," she said. With that Jenna headed out the door and on to the Bistro.

The Bistro was busy tonight, and Jenna hardly had time to sit down. Her section was full the whole night. She was glad she only had a few more hours to go, and she could go home and crash! One of her booths opened up, and a tall man with his back toward her went to sit down. He had on faded blue jeans and a black tee that showed off every muscle in his arms and back. She noticed he also had a very nice butt!

She went to grab a menu and a glass of water and took it to his booth. She sat the water and the menu down in front of him. He was looking at his phone when she said, "Welcome to the Bistro. Can I get you anything to drink?" He looked up and grinned.

Jenna's heart stopped. "Mike!" If her face wasn't 10 shades of red, it sure felt like it! She smiled back at him.

"Hi Jenna, I'll have coffee with cream."

"I'll be right back!" Jenna hurried over to the counter. Her belly was in knots and her nerves were shot! Why does this man have such an effect on her?

Lilly, one of her co-workers came up to her.

"Are you alright? You look a little frazzled." Lilly looked over at the customer who just sat down in Jenna's section. "Who is the hottie in your booth?"

"Lilly, he's my boss at the Hawaiian Lanai where I am doing my internship. He makes me so nervous! I need to get him his coffee, and he has my phone!" Jenna went to get a mug, filled it with coffee, took some cream out of the cooler, and headed towards Mike's table, leaving Lilly starring after her with her mouth opened thinking, *He has her phone?*

Jenna walked up to Mike's table, praying he didn't notice her hands shaking as she set his coffee and cream down on the table. Mike looked up and caught her eyes. With a gleam in his eyes and that sexy smile of his that gets to her every time he said, "Thank you Jenna. I have never eaten here before. What do you recommend?"

"Well, if you like fish, we have a Fisherman's Pot Pie that is really good." *Calm down, Jenna,* she says to herself.

"Okay, I'll try it. Have you had your break yet tonight?"

"No, we've been so busy tonight."

"Is there any way you could take a few minutes and sit down with me?"

"Oh, I don't know," she said nervously. "Let me put your order in and finish taking care of my customers. I'll see if anyone can cover for me for a few minutes."

"Good! I'll be waiting right here!" he said with a wink and a smile.

As he watched Jenna go about taking care of her customers, he couldn't help but notice the bubbly personality she projected. She was wearing khaki capris and a burgundy tee with "The Bistro" embroidered just above her left breast. He was starting to get aroused as he watched and admired every inch of her. *I can't believe how this woman affects me!* he thought to himself.

Another waitress brought him his dinner. She smiled and said, "Enjoy!"

He started eating and thought, *This is really good!*

A few minutes later, Jenna came and refilled his coffee, smiled, and took the coffee pot back behind the counter to put it on the burner. Mike watched Jenna say something to her co-worker. A few minutes later, she came and sat down in the booth across from him.

"How did you like the pot pie?"

"It was very good. Thank you for recommending it," he said.

"You're welcome. Um, do you by chance have something for me?" Jenna asked.

Mike gazed intently at her and their eyes locked. With a smile he said, "And what might that be, little one?"

"Mike! I left my cell phone on your counter! didn't you get Mark's text?"

Mike laughed. She was so cute when she gets all riled up!

"Number one, yes, I did find your phone on my counter. And number two, yes, Mark texted me, but I had already decided to bring your phone to you tonight."

"Oh, well, thank you. I'm so lost without it." She looked around the table. "Where is it?"

"In due time, little one. What time do you get off tonight?"

"It's my turn to go early, so I should be finished by 9:30."

Mike looked at his watch. It was quarter to 9:00.

"I'll wait for you and drive you home."

Well, that's a little presumptuous of him, Jenna thought. "Look Mike, I don't live very far from here, and I always walk home. Could you please just give me my phone?" she pleaded.

Mike did not like the idea of her walking home every night she worked! Anything could happen to her!

"No, Jenna!" he argued. "I will drive you home, and then I will give you your cell phone!"

"It's really not necessary." The look in his eyes stopped her short. "Okay. I'll finish up what I have to do, and you can drive me home. Would you care for any desert, or more coffee?" she asked. The gleam in his eyes told her that he won this round.

"Just some more coffee," he said.

Jenna got up and out of the booth a little peeved at the situation and asked Lilly to take coffee around for her. She finished giving guest checks to her customers and did some clean up. By the time she was done, the restaurant was emptying out. She picked up her tips and said goodnight to everyone. Her heart started racing when she walked up to Mike's booth and said she was ready to go. Mike got out of the booth and handed her $20.

"That's yours," he said with a smile. She went to hand it back to him when their hands touched and that same jolt that she felt when she first met him went up her arm!

"This is way too much!" she whispered. He took the bill, folded it, put it in her hand and closed it.

"It's just right. Let's go."

He led her out into the parking lot, and when he opened the door to a classic yellow Corvette T-Top, she was in awe!

"What year is this?"

"It's a 69."

"It's beautiful!"

As he held the door for her, she slid inside. The saddle leather interior was immaculate. Mike went around to the driver's side and got in. His long muscular legs and body fit perfectly behind the wheel. She noticed that it was a four-speed on the floor. As he pulled out of the parking lot and into the traffic, she couldn't help but notice his strong hand on the gear shift. It made her wonder what it would feel like to have his hands on her body. It gave her goosebumps and took her to a whole new level!

"Where do I go?" asked Mike.

Jenna came out of her thoughts and gave him directions. It didn't take long before he was pulling up in front of her apartment.

"This was nice, Mike. It felt like I was riding on air."

He shut the engine off. He turned towards her and gave her a smile that made her heart start racing.

"Anytime," he reached over and opened the glove box. His arm brushed her leg and she just about lost it. "Your iPhone, my little one."

She took the phone from him and smiled.

"Thank you." When she looked at him, she couldn't move. Mike wanted to kiss her so badly but didn't feel it was the right time yet.

"Do you hike, Jenna?"

"I love to hike."

"Would you like to go with me up to Diamond Head on Sunday morning?"

"I would love to go, but I go to church on Sunday mornings."

"Church, I haven't been to church since I went into the Air Force."

"Well, you are welcome to join me anytime. Pastor Kingsley is very warm and welcoming."

He thought a moment.

"I don't think that's for me. Sorry, Jenna."

"It's perfectly okay. I will keep the invitation open if you change your mind. If you don't mind hiking in the afternoon, I would love to go with you."

"It's a date!" he said grinning and gave her a wink. Mike got out of the car and came around to open the door for her. He extended his hand to help her out of the car. He pulled her up and against his chest. Jenna thought for sure he was going to kiss her, but he pulled away and led her up to her door.

"Mark and I have a meeting in the morning with Zack. He's a detective over at the Police station."

"What time?"

"Ten o'clock. We are hopeful he will have some suggestions on how we can catch who's stealing from the restaurant."

Jenna was thoughtful for a moment. She looked up at Mike and gazed into those blue eyes of his.

"I'm sure he will. Well, goodnight Mike," she whispered.

Mike put his hands up along her face, and with his fingers, he gently swept some stray hair away and placed them behind her ears. He bent his head and placed a sweet kiss on her cheek. His blue eyes gazed into hers.

"Goodnight Jenna," he whispered back.

She watched him get back in his car, and with a quick wave, he drove off. Jenna stood there and watched till he was out of sight. She touched her cheek where he had kissed her and smiled. As she went into her apartment, she knew she would have sweet dreams tonight.

As Mike drove home, he thought about the kiss he had given her and knew the perfect place where he was going to finally kiss those perfect lips of hers. Sunday couldn't come soon enough!

Chapter 8

*F*riday morning at the Police Department, Mike and Mark were met in the lobby by Detective Sargent Zackary Williams. After they shook hands, Zack led them back to his office.

"Have a seat, guys."

Mark and Mike took the two seats in front of his desk, and Zack sat down in his chair. He leaned forward with his arms on his desk pencil in hand ready to take notes.

"Let's look at what's been happening at your restaurant. You mentioned in your phone call Mark that theft may be involved."

"Yes, and for starters," Mark leaned forward with his arms on his knees and his hands folded, "For the last two to three months I've been noticing that our sales reports are not matching up with our liquor inventory reports. At first, it was just a few bottles that seemed to be missing, but then lately, it's been getting quite a bit more."

"Can you tell me why you haven't come to me sooner?"

Mike leaned forward.

"Zack, we didn't want to involve the police unless we had something solid to give you. "Jenna—"

Zack looked back at Mark.

"Jenna! Who's Jenna?"

"Oh sorry," said Mark.

"I brought on an intern from the University, and I had her go

65

over the reports for the last three months. We both thought, at first, it might possibly be a glitch in the software, but when she reviewed the reports, she pointed out that within a week, a case of Jack Daniels was ordered and then re-ordered five days later, as if it were out. When we checked and compared the sales to inventory reports, two bottles were used and four are missing. This has happened to some of our other high-end liquors as well over the past three months. We've always relied on the computer software to keep track of the inventory and re-order when necessary."

Zack was taking notes as Mark was speaking. He looked up at Mark.

"Have you thought about taking inventory manually, just to be sure?"

"Actually," said Mike. "Mark started yesterday morning. We thought we would take inventory for the next week or so, to get a better idea of what has been taken."

"That's good," said Zack. "And how about security?" he asked.

Mark and Mike looked at each other and shrugged.

"We've never felt the need for security," said Mike. "I do a complete background check on every employee we hire. And honestly, Zack, we have never had a problem in the eight years we have been in business until now!"

"Well background checks aren't always reliable. They can be clean and then something happens in that person's life to make them turn to a life of crime."

"What are you thinking?" asked Mark.

Zack thought for a moment and leaned back in his chair.

"What would you think about putting some hidden cameras at different points in your storeroom and also at the front and back entrances of your restaurant? That way, you'll be able to see if anyone slips out with a case of your high-end liquor."

Mike looked at his brother.

"I don't have a problem with that. What do you think, bro?"

"Sounds good to me," said Mark. They both looked at Zack. "How long do you think it would take to set all this up?"

As Zack looked from Mike to Mark, "If you can get the surveillance equipment and the cameras, we should have it up and running quite quickly depending on when you want to get it set up."

"We are closed on Sundays, but I think we should plan on installing the equipment at a time when there is no tourist or locals walking by the restaurant, and we don't want any of our employees to know what we are doing," said Mike.

"I agree," said Zack. "Looks like a third shift job."

"Since we have no idea what equipment or cameras to get, could you help us out with that Zack?" asked Mark.

"Sure, I can do that for you. I'll get started today after my shift ends. And since I have the day off tomorrow, I should be able to get everything we need. Which one of you would like a follow up call?"

"Give me a call, Zack, and then I'll inform Mike. Sound good, bro?" asked Mark.

Mike looked at his brother and shrugged, "It's fine with me."

"Do you have any more questions for me?" asked Zack.

Mark and Mike looked at each other and shook their head.

"Not at this time, but I'm sure we will have plenty once we start to install the equipment," Mike chuckled.

They all got up from their chairs, and Zack led them back out into the lobby. They ran into Lieutenant Fillmore on their way out. They shook hands, and Mike asked how the family was.

"The wife and girls are great! The girls seem to be growing in leaps and bounds."

Ray and his wife Maggie had a set of twin girls that kept them running when they weren't working.

"Hey! Zack mentioned you were having some trouble over at your restaurant. Is there anything I can help you with?" asked the lieutenant.

"We'll let Zack fill you in, and if you want to help with some surveillance equipment, we could use it," said Mike.

"You bet! I'd be glad to help. I'll be bringing in the family tomorrow night for dinner. Any chance you could reserve a table for us? Say around 6:30?"

"Consider it done! We'll see you tomorrow night," said Mark.

Zack led them to the entrance door of the police station, turned and shook hands with both of them.

"Any chance you could save a table for two for tonight? I may be bringing a date!"

"You bet! We'll save the best seat in the house. What time?"

"Seven o'clock?" asked Zack.

"See you tonight," said Mike.

When they left the police station, Mike turned to Mark.

"Do you think we can pull this off without any of our employees finding out?"

"I sure hope so. If not, we may never know who's been behind this." Mark looked at his watch. It was 11:30. "I'm going to head over to the restaurant and get started on the liquor inventory before we open."

"Okay Mark. I have a few errands to run for the restaurant, so I will see you a little later. We're pretty booked tonight with reservations. It's going to be busy!"

Mark smiled, "Just the way we like it! See you later, bro!"

"See you, Mark!"

Mark arrived at the restaurant around noon. He went to unlock the door but saw it was already unlocked. *Hmm, that's strange. Nobody is supposed to be here at this time of day,* he thought. *Maybe*

Kalea is doing some set up early with all the reservations tonight. But still, even if she came in early, the door should have been locked.

He went inside and walked around. Silence, there were no lights turned on, and he didn't see anyone. He moved toward the kitchen and called out, "Is anyone here?" Nothing. He turned and went to the office.

When he reached to unlock the door, he heard a loud bang. It sounded like it came from the store room off the kitchen. Mark took his phone from his pocket and punched in Zack's number.

"Detective Sargent Williams," answered Zack.

"Zack, Mark here, someone is in the restaurant. I'm going to check it out. It might be a good idea to get over here."

"Mark! Do not go looking around! I'll be right there!"

"I'll have the front door open for you," said Mark and hung up.

"Mark!" Zack looked at his phone. "Damn it!" He put his phone back in his pocket and flew out the door. Mark immediately went to unlock the door. *I am not going to wait for Zack to get here,* he said to himself. Besides, he kept himself in prime shape since the military. He could handle it. He may be able to catch the culprits red handed and end this! He went into the kitchen and looked around. He didn't see anything out of place, but noticed the store-room door was propped open. He slowly went inside and looked around. In the middle of the floor was a broken case of Jack Daniels. He looked behind shelves and nothing. Whoever it was must have left out the back entrance already.

Detective Williams came in with his gun pulled.

"Mark! You okay?"

"Yeah, I'm okay." Zack took a look around the storeroom. It looked like it was safe, and he put his 9mm Glock back in its holster. He went over to Mark.

"Looks like someone tried to make off with a case of whiskey."

Mark was down on one knee, looking at the contents in the case. He looked up at Zack.

"Yeah, there are a couple of bottles that didn't break, but the rest is a loss." Mark got up and put his hands on his hips. "You know what really makes me mad Zack? It's one of our employees doing this! It's not like we don't pay them enough for what they do!"

"Mark, we are going to catch who is doing this. I promise you."

"I hope it's soon. I'll get a hold of Mike and then clean up this mess."

"Okay, I'm going outside to have a look around, and I'll be back to let you know if I see anything or anyone suspicious."

Mark went up to Zack and extended his hand.

"Thanks, Zack, for coming so quickly."

"Hey it's my job! I would do anything for you and Mike. You know that. You're good friends." They shook hands, and Zack left to go check outside. Mark sent a text to Mike:

When you get this message give me a call. Urgent!

With that sent, he went to get a broom and a mop.

Outside in the back of the parking lot sat two people in a black Camaro, watching a police officer canvas the outside of the building.

"That was close!" said the woman.

"Too close! What is Mark doing here so early? He doesn't usually come in until 2:00 on Fridays."

"I don't know, but we are going to have to be more careful. Especially now that a police officer is involved," said the woman.

"I don't like this, Tonya, I don't like this at all!"

Mike was at the International Market Place picking up some salmon and a few other items for the restaurant when he ran into an old flame of his. The relationship didn't last very long. She was too clingy. Mike tried to dodge her but she was too quick.

"Hi Mike!"

"Oh, hi Heather!" he said.

She got up close and personal.

"How have you been, Mike? I've missed you!"

Well, he hadn't missed her! She put a hand on his shoulder. He backed away.

"I've been fine, Heather, just very busy!"

Heather gave him a seductive smile.

"I was hoping we could get together again, if you know what I mean." She tried to touch him again, but he stopped her. He looked at her. She was a beauty. Long, straight, blonde hair, blue eyes, and a body that was a knockout! They had had a sexual relationship, but it didn't last very long. She wanted more out of the relationship than he could give her. He wasn't the happily-ever-after type. Suddenly thoughts of Jenna popped into his head.

"I'm sorry, Heather, but I'm seeing someone else."

"Is it serious?"

"Possibly, maybe, time will tell." Just at the right time, his phone dinged. He took his phone out of his pocket and looked at the message. "Sorry, Heather, I have to make a phone call." He looked at her and said, "It was good seeing you again," and walked off.

"You too, Mike!"

As she watched him go with a pout on her face, she wondered about this new person in his life. He didn't sound like it was too serious. Maybe she would stop in at the restaurant some night and try again. She really did miss him!

Mike pulled up his brother's number. When he answered, he said, "What's up bro?"

"Mike! We had an incident at the restaurant, when will you be coming in?"

"I just finished picking up a few things for tonight's specials, I'm on my way in."

"Good! I'll see you when you get here. Zack and I will be in my office."

Mike ended the phone call. Zack was there! He headed to the restaurant. When he arrived, Palani was in the kitchen with his crew prepping for tonight's reservations. He handed the items to Palani and headed to Mark's office.

Mike entered the office and saw both Mark and Zack sitting at the desk. He closed the door behind him and took a seat next to Zack. With a concerned look he asked, "What's going on?"

"Someone tried to take a case of Jack Daniels out of the storeroom. And they didn't break in. They had a key. When I arrived here at noon, the door was unlocked," said Mark.

"But the only two people that have a key to the place besides us are Kalea, and Palani. And I know that neither one of them would steal from us."

"I agree, but we are going to have to come up with a game plan to catch whoever is doing this and find out how this person got a key," said Mark. "Zack and I were just discussing changing the locks right away, but I think that would let the perpetrator know that we are on to them. Plus, the employees would want to know what's going on." Mark turned to Zack, "Zack, once you have the cameras and the rest of the equipment, can you come and install it on Saturday after we close, say around midnight?"

"This is my weekend off, so yes, I'll be here. I keyed the lieutenant in on what's happening here, and I'll check to see if he can lend us a hand. Between the four of us, we should be able to get it done."

"How about you Mike?" asked Mark. "Do you have plans for Saturday night?"

Mike's thoughts turned to Jenna, "I was going to go pick up Jenna after she got out of work and take her home, but it shouldn't take very long, and I can be back here by midnight."

"So, are we seeing Jenna now? What happened to waiting a while?" asked Mark.

"This Jenna must be pretty special," said Zack.

Mike smiled and looked from Mark to Zack.

"I don't know what it is about her, but I can't get the woman off of my mind! I was attracted to her the first moment I laid eyes on her."

Mark and Zack looked at each other and grinned.

"Sounds like you have the hots for her," said Zack.

Mike grinned, "Maybe I do. In any event, I will be here to help."

"Good! The quicker we get this done the better!" said Mark.

"Well, men, I need to get back to the station to file my report. I will see you both tonight."

"Thanks again, Zack, and we'll have your table waiting for you," said Mike.

"Thanks."

After Zack left, Mike looked at his brother.

"Did they make off with any of the other liquor?"

"I don't know. I found one case in the middle of the floor. There were only two bottles that didn't break. I haven't been able to get back to the store room to check." Mark looked at his watch. He got up from his desk and started to walk out of his office. He turned to Mike. "The restaurant opens in two hours, so we better get ready for tonight. I'll come in tomorrow morning to check inventory and see if anything else was taken."

Mike followed Mark out of his office.

"Okay, let's keep our eyes open for anyone of our employees acting strange or nervous. I'm going to go and check my emails. I will be right out to help get ready for tonight," said Mike.

"Sound's good! I'll see you out on the floor."

Jenna was in the kitchen at her apartment trying to decide what to make for dinner. She was looking forward to a quiet and relaxing evening after the crazy busy week she had. She also wanted to try and make this dessert she had been thinking about. She was getting the ingredients out of the cupboard when Sasha came in through the front door.

"Hey Jenna, what are your plans for this evening?"

"I was just about to make dinner, and I want to try to make this dessert I have had stuck in my head. Why?"

"Some of our college friends and me are going out to a club tonight. It's been a hellish week with tests and work. We want to go hang loose and have fun. You want to go?"

"Oh, I don't know, Sasha. I was looking forward to a quiet night and maybe a movie."

"Oh, come on, Jenna! How long has it been since you let loose! You're always working or studying, and now you have an internship!" Sasha swung her hips around and started dancing. "It's time to have some fun!" she said with a grin.

Jenna thought about it. It had been a hellish week.

"You know Sasha, you're right! It has been a while. Let's do this!" She came around the counter and started dancing with her friend. They both giggled. "Is this place casual, or do I need to dress up?" asked Jenna.

"They want to go to a new club at one of the hotels not far from the restaurant where you work, and I hear it has great music and a lighted dance floor. So, let's dress to kill!"

"Okay! I know just what to wear!" They both rushed off to their bedrooms to get ready.

When they came out, Sasha had chosen a black, snug-fitting dress with thin shoulder straps. The dress hung down above her knees and showed off her perfect figure. She wore her long, black hair down, and to compliment her outfit, she wore black, three-inch sandals and a gold necklace with a single black onyx stone. She looked gorgeous!

Jenna had on a pale blue sundress with a halter top, bare back and a flared skirt that came down above her knees. She also wore her hair down, but curled it around her face and down her back. She wore two-inch, navy blue wedge sandals and her makeup was flawless.

"Ready?" asked Sasha. "Ready."

Sasha decided she would drive, and when she pulled in to the back parking lot of the Hawaiian Lanai, Jenna turned to her friend and asked, "What are we doing here? I thought we were going to the Club."

"We are. We decided to eat dinner here before we went to the club. Kenny already made reservations for the Lanai. It's such a beautiful evening. Besides, I want to meet your hot bosses!" she said with a grin.

Jenna didn't know what to think. She didn't know which one of them were working tonight. What if it was Mike? Just the thought made the butterflies in her tummy go ballistic!

"Jenna, are you okay? You went quiet on me." Sasha parked the car and looked at Jenna.

Jenna returned the look and said, "I wish you had told me we were coming here. Maybe neither one of them is working tonight."

"Well, I'm sure one of them has to be working. Look at the parking lot it's packed!"

When they went into the restaurant, they were greeted by Kalea.

"Good evening, ladies. Do you have a reservation?"

"Yes," said Sasha.

"It's under Kenny Stevens."

While Kalea was checking the reservation book, Jenna looked around the restaurant. She didn't see either Mark or Mike anywhere. Of course, they could be with customers in the Hawaiian Room or in the kitchen. It was such a big place.

Kalea glanced up and said, "Oh yes! They are already here and seated in the Lanai. I will take you to their table."

"Thank you," said Jenna.

Kalea looked at Jenna. "Oh, hello Jenna, I almost didn't recognize you," she said curtly. You look nice tonight."

"Thank you," said Jenna.

Kalea picked up some menus and walked toward the Lanai.

"This way ladies," she directed.

As they followed Kalea into the Lanai, Sasha whispered to Jenna, "What's with her?"

"I don't know; she's been rude to me ever since my first day here."

As they walked to their table, Jenna kept looking for Mike but still didn't see him. When they arrived at their table, Kalea sat the menus on the table and said, "Enjoy your dinner."

When she left, everyone greeted each other, and it looked like they had a good start on drinks. Jenna sat next to Kenny, and Sasha sat next to Barb and Bruce seated across the table.

"What is everyone drinking?" asked Jenna.

"I'm having a piña colada," said Barb.

"Just a beer," said Bruce.

"I went all out and ordered a Tropical Itch!" said Kenny with a big grin on his face.

"Kenny," said Jenna, "do you know how much liquor is in one of those?"

"Yep! But it will last me the rest of the night."

"Okay! But just so you know, I'm not carrying you out of here if you get too drunk!"

"Ha! Never!" said Kenny. They both laughed.

Their waitress came up to their table with a big smile, "Hi! I'm Tammy, and I'll be your waitress tonight. Can I get you ladies anything to drink?"

"I will have a Mai Tai," said Sasha.

"Do you have a white Moscato?"

"We sure do!" said Tammy.

"I'll have a glass of that," said Jenna.

While their waitress went to get their drinks, Jenna looked around the Lanai. They were seated next to the pond with a full view of the ocean. The tropical plants and vibrant flowers were placed around the lanai, making the area seem like a tropical paradise. The waterfall along the wall set the atmosphere. The tiki torches were placed around the perimeter of the lanai and would be lit closer to dusk. She looked down at the pond, and the some of the goldfish were swimming up to the edge to see if they could get a handout.

"Sorry, fish, but the sign says 'Do Not Feed the Fish'!"

Their waitress came back with their drinks and asked if they were ready to order.

"You guys go ahead. I haven't looked at the menu yet," said Jenna. They each gave Tammy their order, and when she got to Jenna, "I'll have the Hawaiian steak, cooked medium, with red potatoes and a salad with your Hawaiian dressing."

"Thank you," said Tammy. "I'll put this right in for you."

When she left, they all started talking about college, what they were going to do after graduation, if they were going to spend time with their families before they get a job or just jump right in. Their food came, and all was quiet as they dove in. Everything was delicious! Out of the blue, Barb turned to Jenna, "When are we going to meet this hot man of yours?"

Jenna blushed. She turned to Sasha with a look that said, "What have you been saying!"

Sasha just looked away and knew she was going to be in trouble when they got home.

"Well, for one thing, he is not my hot man, he's my boss. I'm not even sure he is here tonight, as I haven't seen him."

Everybody roared "OH!"

"So you've been looking for him," said Sasha.

Jenna blushed again.

"It's not what you think."

They were interrupted again by Tammy to see if anyone wanted dessert, thank the Lord! Everyone said they were full and asked for their checks.

While they were waiting, Jenna got up from the table and said she was going to find a restroom.

"We'll come with you," said Barb.

They got up and followed Jenna into the bar area. Jenna stopped short. There, leaning against the bar was Mike, with a long blond-haired beauty with her arms draped around him. She was smiling up at him, and he was looking at her. The shocked look on Jenna's face said it all. Mark seemed to come out of nowhere.

"Jenna!" You look beautiful tonight!" She looked at Mark and said a brief thank you. "And who are these lovely ladies that are with you?"

Jenna introduced her friends to Mark. She then excused herself and ran to find the restroom. As she ran past Mike, he stood and took both Heather's arms off him and told her again he was not in-terested in starting a relationship with her again.

She gave him an angry look.

"Fine! But don't think I will come crawling back to you if you decide later that you want me!"

As she stomped away and out of the restaurant, he yelled, "Don't worry, I won't!"

A few customers were looking at him as they overheard the conversation. He turned back to the bar and asked Todd for a Jack Daniels on the rocks. He definitely needed a drink! Mark came up behind him.

"Way to go, Mike!" he said angrily. Mike turned to his brother. "What?"

"You mean to tell me you don't know? She walked right by you!"

He shook his head, "Know what? And who walk right by me?"

"Jenna is here with some of her college friends, and she saw you with Heather hanging all over you!"

"What? How long has she been here? And she saw me with Heather? Damn!"

The bartender delivered Mike's drink, and he took and downed it. He could feel the burn all the way down.

"She had dinner with her friends in the lanai, and now they are going to a club to let loose one of the girls said."

"Do you know what club they are going to?" asked Mike.

Mark was just about to tell him when Mike saw Jenna and her friends coming out of the lanai and heading out the door of the restaurant. Jenna wouldn't look at him. Who was that guy that had his arm and hand on her bare back? He clenched his fists. With anger in his eyes, he looked at Mark.

"Tell me where they are going."

"They're headed for the Rock Inn. They just put in a new club. I've heard it can get a little wild in there."

Mike started walking, but Mark grabbed his arm.

"Don't do anything stupid. I don't want to see you hauled off to jail."

"I promise to just talk."

Mark let go of his arm.

"Okay, but please remember they are all just friends."

Mike nodded and left the restaurant. Zack came up to Mark.

"What's with Mike tonight? First, I heard him yell at some blonde beauty, and now he looks like he's ready to kill somebody."

"Jenna."

Zack had a surprised look on his face. Mark put his hand on Zack's shoulder.

"Come on, let me buy you a drink, and I'll tell you all about it."

At the club, a table opened up that could seat the five of them. As they followed the hostess, Jenna looked around the club. The tables were done in monkey pod, and tropical rattan chairs were placed around the table. Flame lighting was all around the room, and it had a lighted dance floor. The music was from the 80s, and crowds of people danced out on the floor. It wasn't long before a waitress came up and asked for their drink order.

After they ordered, Kenny pulled Jenna up out of her seat.

"Come on, let's dance!"

As they danced to the music of "Dancing Queen," Jenna started to relax and feel the music. Just what she needed to forget seeing Mike with that blonde! It hurt to think he might be dating someone else. She was just starting to feel that maybe he was attracted to her. She was certainly attracted to him. Maybe she was getting mixed signals. The music stopped, and Kenny and her headed back to their table and found their drinks had arrived. Jenna took a long drink of her wine. It was so hot in here!

At the entrance to the club, Mike stood and watched Jenna and that guy she was with out on the dance floor. Just watching Jenna made his heart go faster and his thoughts run wild! She had perfect rhythm, and when she swayed her hips around, it just did things to him! They went back to their table, and he saw her take a big draw on her glass of wine. If she wasn't careful, she would be drunk before long. Another round was served. She finished off her wine and took another drink from her second glass. The music slowed, and Jenna and the man she was with got up to dance. Oh, this is not happening! Mike moved on to the dance floor. As Kenny took her into his arms, Mike tapped him on his shoulder.

"May I cut in?"

Kenny looked at him and said, "Sorry man, this is my dance."

Mike gave him a look that could kill. "I think not." Kenny looked at Jenna. She had a shocked look on her face and then he looked at Mike. *This must be the guy,* Kenny thought.

"She's all yours," said Kenny.

"Kenny!" Jenna cried.

As he walked off, Mike grabbed her hand and pulled her into his arms. Jenna struggled to get free, but he held on.

"I don't want to dance with you!" He placed his hand on her bare back. He took her left hand and placed it on his shoulder and took her right hand in his, and pulled her close. She tried to resist but he held her tight.

"But I want to dance with you."

"Why? And who was that blonde you were with tonight? Are you dating her? You could have told me!"

Mike pulled her even closer and looked deep into her eyes.

"Dance with me, Jenna."

Suddenly she couldn't resist him. She didn't know if it was all the wine she drank or just being close to him. She relaxed and let him lead her around the dance floor. They were perfect together.

At the table all eyes were on Jenna and Mike.

"What happened, Kenny?"

Kenny looked exasperated.

"I am assuming that the man Jenna is dancing with is Mike. When he wanted to cut in, I wasn't going to let him, but if looks could kill, I wasn't going to argue with him!"

"He's as handsome as Jenna said," sighed Sasha. "And she was right. After meeting Mark tonight, they are identical!"

"I wonder how she tells them apart?" asked Barb.

"Chemistry, Barb, chemistry!" she said, "Just look at them!"

They watched them dance, and it was unmistakable. If they were any closer, they would be one!

Mike, with his head bent down by Jenna's ear, felt like he was in heaven. Her skin was so soft, and her scent was mind blowing.

"I'm not seeing anyone."

Jenna looked up at him.

"You're not? Then why was she hanging all over you?"

Mike took a deep breath.

"She was an old flame that I broke off a while ago. I happened to run into her at the International Market Place while I was out running errands for the restaurant. She wanted to get back together, but I told her I was seeing someone else."

"You did?"

"I did."

She smiled up at him.

"And who is this person you are seeing?"

He smiled down at her, "You Jenna, I know we've only known each other for less than a week, but I'm feeling something powerful here, and I hope you are feeling it, too."

She gazed into his eyes and felt this pull, this attraction she felt for him since the day she met him.

"I am."

"Shall we see where this goes?"

"I'd like that."

He pushed her back and twirled her and brought her back to him. Then ever so lightly, he brushed his lips over hers. Jenna thought she was going to melt right there on the dance floor. The music stopped, and he raised his head to look at her.

"Have I told you, you look beautiful tonight?"

She grinned at him.

"Not yet, but I wouldn't mind hearing it."

"You're beautiful Jenna," he said softly.

She blushed.

"Thank you. Would you like to come and meet my friends?" she asked.

"I'll have a quick drink with you and your friends and then I have to get back to the restaurant to help Mark close," he grinned, "I kinda left him in a hurry."

She took his hand and led him to their table and introduced him to her college friends.

Chapter 9

*M*ike stayed for an hour and excused himself to head back to the restaurant. When he got up to leave, he took Jenna's hand and led her out into the lobby of the hotel.

"I like your friends."

"I'm pretty sure they like you, too."

Mike turned her to face him and took her hands in his.

"What time do you get off work tomorrow night?"

"It's probably going to be late. It's my night to work till closing. Why?"

"I want to pick you up and make sure you get home safe." He had this feeling inside of him that he needed to protect her.

"Mike, it really isn't necessary. I don't want to take you from your work. I'm used to walking home."

"You are not taking me away from work. I don't like the thought of you walking home late at night. Anything could happen to you. I asked Mark for your phone number. I hope that's okay." She nodded her head. "I will text you my number when I get back to the restaurant. Will you please text me when you are 20 minutes from leaving the Bistro?"

Jenna was about to refuse him, but the look he gave her said he wasn't going to take no for an answer.

"Okay."

"Promise?" he asked.

"I promise." Mike took her in his arms and held her close. Jenna hugged him back. If felt so good to be held in his arms. It felt like home. When they broke apart, Mike moved his hands down her arms and took her hands again. He gave them a gentle squeeze. "Well, good night," she whispered.

He gazed deep into her eyes. "Good night, Jenna. I'll see you tomorrow."

She stood and watched him leave. She thought about the butterfly kiss he gave her out on the dance floor. It made her feel warm and tingly inside. She wondered when he kissed her again, would it turn into the passion that she hungered for? And yet she was so not experienced in an intimate relationship. But she so wanted to explore these feelings she had for him. Would she be able to satisfy his hunger when it happened? He was such a powerful man. And so experienced compared to her. She headed back into the club to re-join her friends. Only time with him would tell.

Mike arrived back at the restaurant shortly after 10:00. He found Mark was just finishing up taking the money trays out of the registers and printing out the reports to take back to the safe in Mark's office. He looked up as Mike came through the door.

"Hey! I didn't expect you back tonight. Did you find Jenna and her friends?"

"Yes."

"How did it go down?" ask Mark.

"Well, when I first got there, I wanted to bash the guy who was dancing with her." Mark gave him an angry look and put his hands on his hips ready to give his brother hell. Mike raised his hands, palms up towards his brother. "But I controlled myself and calmly cut in, sort of."

"Don't tell me you punched him!"

"No, nothing like that, I just gave him a little encouragement to get off the dance floor!" Mark chuckled. "Jenna and I are good." With a gleam in his eyes, he thought about her body moving to the rhythm of the music. When she was in his arms, they fit together perfectly as they glided across the dance floor. "She's a great dancer." He remembered the kiss he had given her. The next time he takes her in his arms and kisses her, she will know the passion that can be between them. Mark was saying something to him. "What, bro?"

"Boy, when you tune out, you don't hear anything!"

"Sorry, what did you say?"

"Zack mentioned when he was here tonight that he has all the equipment but the cameras, and he will pick those up tomorrow. We should be ready to install everything after we close tomorrow night. How about helping me take care of this, then we'll lock up and go home? It's going to be a long day and night tomorrow."

"Right!" said Mike. Mike helped him put the cash trays and reports in the safe and called it a night. When they left the restaurant, Mike smiled and thought of only one special woman on his drive home.

Saturday morning came with lots of sunshine. Jenna busied herself with cleaning her apartment and catching up on her laundry. Sasha was studying at the campus library and would be home later this afternoon.

Cuddles needed a little playtime, so while she waited for the dryer, she sat on the floor while her cat chased a toy mouse on a string around the lanai. She laughed when Cuddles jumped and pounced on the mouse. She heard the dryer buzz and got up to fold and take care of her laundry. She had a couple of hours left before she had to be at work and decided to get started on the dessert she had been wanting to make. She took the ingredients out of the cupboard and refrigerator. Grabbed a pencil and paper and went to work.

She made the peanut butter cookies, and while they were cooling, she started on the Hawaiian sauce. In a sauce pan, she took fresh pineapple, strawberries, and one kiwi fruit. She added some brown sugar and simmered it until it thickened. She set it aside to cool. She took one of the cookies and set it in the bottom of a bowl, added one scoop of vanilla ice cream and poured the warm mixture over the top. She sprinkled one tablespoon of chopped pecans over the top and took a bite. It was good, but it needed something. She took another bite and looked at the clock. It was almost 3:00! This would have to wait. She finished eating the dessert and decided to ask Sasha what she thought when she saw her tonight. Jenna hurried and put everything away and went to get ready for work. When she was ready, she made sure Cuddles had food and water. She bent to pet her and told her she would be home soon. Jenna picked up her purse and out the door she went!

Mike was busy at the restaurant going over the reservations for tonight. He had one of the girls get a table ready for Lieutenant Fillmore and his family in the Hawaiian Room. Everyone was busy getting ready for their customers. Four o'clock came, and the door was opened. They were so busy, the night flew by.

Lieutenant Fillmore came in with his family shortly after 6:00. Mike met them at the front of the restaurant. He shook the Lieutenant's hand.

"Hi Ray, hi Maggie." He looked down at Lieutenant Fillmore's daughters. "And how are you two young ladies tonight?"

"Good!" they both replied.

Mike got down on his haunches and looked at the girls.

"Let me guess, you're Tracy!"

"Nope, I'm Stacy!"

"You girls! I can never tell you apart!"

Mark came up behind his brother as Mike stood up. The girls jumped up and down.

"Can we guess your names?"

Everybody grinned.

"Sure, you can! Go for it!"

"Let's see, you're Mark!" Stacy pointed to Mike. "And you're Mike!" Tracy pointed to Mark. "I think we all have the same problem! We can't tell each other apart!"

They all laughed. Mike picked up the girls.

"Let's get you two girls and your parents to your table." Mark shook hands with Ray. "Hey, I'll be back to help you guys get set up. I don't have anything on the radar for tomorrow, so I'll see you around midnight."

"Thanks Ray. It sure is appreciated! Enjoy your dinner, and the tab is on us!"

"Thanks!" he replied.

Mike took them into the Hawaiian Room. As they crossed the bridge, the girls squealed, "Look at all the fish!" Mike put the girls down on the bridge. "Can we touch them?"

"No, girls," said their dad. "They are only for watching. Come along, time to go to our table and have dinner."

Mike got them seated. Ray caught Mike's arm before he sat down.

"I mentioned to your brother that I would be here to help tonight."

Mike put his hand on his shoulder.

"Thanks, Ray." Mike turned to Maggie and the girls. "Enjoy your evening, and if you need anything, just let your waitress know, and she will come and let me know."

"Can we feed the fish?" the girls yelled out.

Mike laughed, "No, I'm afraid they have already been fed!"

With that, he gave them a wave and went to attend to other customers.

The night finally came to a close. Mike checked his phone. Jenna hadn't sent a text. She promised she would. He helped Mark close up for the night and still no text from her.

"Hey bro, I'm going to go check on Jenna. She hasn't texted me yet, and I want to make sure she didn't decide to walk home."

"No problem. Get going."

"Thanks." Just as he was pulling out of the parking lot, his phone dinged. He checked the message.

> Sorry this is late. We were slammed tonight and we are in the process of cleaning up. I should be ready to go in 20 minutes.

He smiled and took off for the Bistro.

Jenna finished her clean up duties and was getting ready to walk out the door when she heard Lilly call out. She turned back.

"Have a good time tomorrow. I'll be looking forward to all the deets!"

She smiled and waved, "Goodnight!" She turned to open the door and ran into a hard chest! She looked up at Mike and blushed. She was sure he heard everything that Lilly said. "I'm sorry. It seems I'm always running into you!"

"I'm glad it's you who keeps running into me!" he said with a wink and a grin. "Are you ready to go?"

"I am."

Lilly watched them leave and sighed. Jenna was one lucky gal, to have one of the most handsome men on the island escort her home!

Mike opened the door of his corvette for her, and she slid in. He came around the front of the car and got behind the wheel. He looked over at her. She was so pretty, even with her hair coming loose from her pony tail. He pulled out of the parking lot into the traffic.

"So, the Bistro was busy tonight?"

"Super busy, I'm exhausted! Looking forward to just putting my feet up when I get home. How about you?" she asked.

"Same, it was non-stop until around 9:30." He looked over at her and saw she had her eyes closed. He smiled and shook his head. He drove the short distance to her apartment and pulled up in front of her door.

She opened her eyes when the car stopped. She smiled when she looked over at him.

"Thank you, Mike. I'm sorry I'm not much of a conversationalist tonight."

"No worries, you look like you need to go straight to bed." And he wouldn't mind putting her there. Just the thought aroused him! He got out of the car and came around to open the door for her. He put his hand out to help her out of the car. With his arm around her, he walked her to the door. She turned to face him. With that sexy grin of his and a glint of mischief in his eyes, he asked, "Would you like me to carry you to bed?" and wiggled his eyebrows.

"Michael TreVaine! Are you trying to seduce me?"

He had a look of surprise on his face. He hadn't expected that response!

"Would you want me to?"

"Hmm… If I wasn't so tired, maybe." She looked into his eyes to see if he was serious and saw the hunger there. Her woman parts went into overdrive! "I think I'd better go in. Are we still on for hiking tomorrow?"

"I'll be here at 1:00!"

"Okay, I will see you then. Goodnight, Mike."

"Goodnight Jenna." He watched her go in and sighed. He

hoped the guys and he could get this security system up and running quickly, or he wouldn't be up for anything tomorrow, let alone hiking! He got in his car and headed for the restaurant.

When he arrived back at the restaurant, Zack, Ray, and Mark were having a beer and discussing where they should start to install the equipment. Mike grabbed a beer from the cooler and sat down at the table.

Mark was looking at the cameras.

"These are really small. Will they cover the whole storeroom?"

"We are going to place two in the storeroom," said Zack. "One above the entrance to the storeroom, and one towards the back of the room. It should give you enough coverage to let you know who's in there and if any liquor is being taken out. These two will be placed at the front and back entrances of the restaurant, and this other one can be placed anywhere in the restaurant. Do you two have any place in particular you'd like this one?"

Mark and Mike looked around the restaurant. Mike turned to his brother.

"What about behind the bar, where the cash register is?" asked Mike.

"Excellent. That would be the best place. That way we could see if anyone is tampering with the register," said Mark.

"Now," said Zack. "This equipment has a security app where it will be installed on your cell phones rather than on a monitor. That way, you both will be the only ones to view anything going on inside and outside your restaurant."

"Perfect!" said Mark.

"If you both are in agreement," said Ray, "Zack and I will go and canvas the parking lot and both front and back entrances. If all is clear, we'll get started on the installation."

"Good, just let us know what you want us to do," said Mike.

They all got up from the table and went to work. It was 3:00 when they finished. Zack checked out how everything was working. He then showed both Mark and Mike how to access the cameras through the app on their phones.

"This is pretty slick Zack," Mike said, smiling.

"Yeah, now maybe we can catch whoever it is doing the stealing!" said Mark.

"Well, men, I'm heading out. Hopefully the girls will let me sleep in this morning," said Ray. "Good luck with that!" said Zack. Mike and Mark walked them to the door to let them out. They shook hands.

"Thanks again and be safe going home," said Mark. With a quick wave they left. Mark turned to his brother, "I don't know about you, bro, but I feel better."

"So do I, Mark, so do I," said Mike. Mike went and shut off all the lights. As they walked out together, Mark asked, "Do you have any plans for today?"

"I'm going hiking with Jenna, but not until this afternoon."

"Hiking huh? Are you taking her to the cave?"

Mike looked at his brother and grinned.

"Maybe... You have a safe trip home."

"You too, bro." said Mark. He watched Mike get in his car and drive off. He shook his head and chuckled. *This should be interesting.*

Chapter 10

Jenna sat in church and enjoyed Pastor Kingsley's sermon for today. It was all about trust. Trusting in Him who gives us the strength to get through anything life brings us, the good and the bad. She sang the last hymn with her church family and then proceeded to the door where Pastor Kingsley was shaking hands with everyone as they left the church. It was a beautiful church. She looked around the sanctuary. The high ceilings and stained-glass windows with the sun coming in softened the room. As she looked at the cross at the altar, it always reminded her of what our Savior sacrificed for us on the cross. Whenever she came here, she could feel His presence with her.

Jenna was next to shake hands with the Pastor.

"Ah Jenna, it's so good to see you this morning!"

"Thank you, Pastor Kingsley. I enjoyed your sermon this morning. I definitely need to do a little more trusting and not depend on me to figure out everything in my life!"

"We all have a tendency to do just that. We must remember that our Lord knows all. Even the next step we take."

"Thank you, Pastor Kingsley, I will remember that. Have a wonderful day! I'll see you next Sunday!"

"That you will, Jenna! You have a wonderful day as well."

As Jenna left the church, Pastor Kingsley thought, *Such a nice young woman. The man who wins her heart will be a lucky man indeed!* He turned back to greet the rest of his congregation. He had a busy day ahead of him, and he and his wife were looking forward to Mrs. Wilkins pot roast for dinner!

Jenna rushed home when she noticed the time. She had only 20 minutes to get ready for her hiking trip with Mike. She got all jittery just thinking about being with him today! She rushed into her apartment and into her bedroom. She changed out of her dress into a pair of dark brown shorts and a tan tank top that hugged her body. She took out a pair of thick socks to wear with her hiking boots. No sense in getting blisters on her feet!

She came out of her bedroom, and her cat was coming towards her meowing something fierce!

"Cuddles, what's wrong?" Then she remembered. "Oh! I forgot to feed you this morning, didn't I?" She picked up her cat and gave her a hug. "I think your mama's brain is starting to malfunction with everything going on in her life!" She put her cat down on the floor and gave her something to eat. She checked her water, and her cat was all set. She walked by the counter and noticed a note from Sasha.

I will be back late tonight. Don't wait up! - Sasha.

Jenna read the note and put it back on the counter. It was a little after 1:00, and Mike should be here any minute. She went to get her backpack to put a few items in it for their trip. She got her cooler out to put a couple cans of coke and a few bottles of water in it, then added some ice. After that was done, she put on her boots and waited. It was 15 after. She decided to wait 10 minutes, then she would text him.

Mike had a hell of a time getting to sleep after he got home this morning. He kept thinking about where he was going to take Jenna on their hike and what he wanted to do with her. He was so aroused, he couldn't sleep. He must have dozed off around 6:00. When he woke up it was 12:15! He flew out of bed and into the shower. It must have been the fastest shower on record! He looked at himself in the mirror and decided he didn't have time to shave. He threw on a pair of dark green twill shorts and a t-shirt. He got a pair of socks out of the drawer and grabbed his boots. When he was ready to go, he looked at his watch.

"Damn!" There was no time to pack some items he wanted to take on their trip in his back pack! There wasn't even time to make a pot of coffee! "I am going to be so late!"

It was already well after 1:00! He sent a text to Jenna as he headed out the door.

> Sorry I am running late, will explain when I get there. Can you please put on a pot of coffee for me?

Jenna sent back a thumbs-up sign. Mike got into his SUV and headed for Jenna's apartment.

Jenna started the coffee pot and took out the thermos in the cupboard. After reading his text, she had a feeling he was going to need it. She filled the thermos with the first pot and started another. She decided to pack some sandwiches just in case they got hungry. You can burn a lot of calories hiking up the mountain. Just as the coffee finished brewing, the doorbell rang. She ran to the door with Cuddles right behind her!

"Oh no, you don't!" She picked her cat up and opened the door. Jenna stood still as she took in the rugged sexy man that stood outside her door. He was dressed in a navy t-shirt that hugged his broad chest and showed off every muscle in his arms and abs. His twill shorts showed his strong muscular legs. His hair was still wet from his shower, and she could tell he hadn't shaved. Her heart was racing, and suddenly she needed to sit down! Mike was looking at what she was holding in her arms.

"You have a cat!"

She came out of her shock at seeing him.

"What?"

"You have a cat!" he repeated.

"Oh yes! Come on in, so I can put her down." Cuddles was already trying to wiggle out of her arms. Mike stepped in and she closed the door behind him. She went up to Mike to introduce him to her cat. "This is Cuddles. Whenever the doorbell rings, she likes to try and escape. Can you say hi to Mike?"

As if on cue, her cat looked at him and meowed! Mike grinned and gave her some scratching behind the ears. She closed her pretty green eyes. *I agree,* Jenna thought, *I'd like that strong hand stroking me!*

Jenna put her cat down, and since she wasn't able to escape, Cuddles decided it was time to take a nap. She jumped up on the chair, curled up and promptly fell asleep!

"Come into the kitchen, I have coffee ready for you."

"It smells good! I didn't have time to brew a pot before I left. You're a life saver!"

Jenna poured coffee in two of her mugs. "You take cream, right?"

"Right." He couldn't think of anything else to say at the moment. He couldn't stop watching her. When she stretched to reach for the mugs out of the cupboard, he noticed her back and then his eyes slid down to that cute bottom of hers. When she poured the coffee, he saw her firm breasts in that tight fitting tank she was wearing. She went to the refrigerator to get the cream, and all he could think about was taking his hands and feeling those beautiful tan legs. Hell, he could skip the hiking and hold her close all day!

Mike shook himself. Why did this woman have such a hold on him! He thought he knew the answer but didn't want to think about it. He wasn't ready.

Jenna handed him his coffee. He brushed her hand with his as he took the mug from her. Jenna had a chill go through her. He looked into those beautiful brown eyes and took a sip of his coffee. He closed his eyes.

"This is so good! It hits the spot!"

Jenna didn't realize she was holding her breath while he took his first sip. She let out a breath.

"Oh, I'm so glad! I never know if I get it right for someone else besides me. I hope you don't mind. I filled a thermos with coffee and packed ham and cheese sandwiches with some cold drinks in the cooler for our trip. It gets pretty hot up in the mountain this time of day."

"Jenna, you're a Godsend. I wanted to pack some things in my backpack but didn't want to take the time. Thank you for doing all this."

"It was my pleasure. I enjoyed fixing it." She noticed he finished his coffee and poured him another cup. "Can I get you something to eat before we go? I have some bagels and cream cheese. I might even have some strawberry jam!" She smiled as she looked up at him. He smiled back.

His eyes gleamed when he said, "That sounds great. I am hungry!" While she went to get the food ready, Mike looked around the apartment. "Did you do the decorating or was it a joint effort with your roommate?"

He liked the paintings and water color landscapes of the island on the walls. There were sea shells and different figurines placed on the end tables and a remarkable drift wood piece centered on the coffee table.

"I collected most of it. When I first moved to the island, I liked to go exploring and collected a lot of the shells. That driftwood, I found on Waikiki beach my first year here. Sasha has added a few things. She likes the modern look. I like contemporary with a mix of rustic thrown in."

"I like it." He turned back to see she already had two bagels with cream cheese on one plate and one on another plate. She set the jam and a knife in the center. She refilled his coffee and poured herself another one. She came around and sat next to him. She opened the jam and offered it to him. "Ladies first!" he chuckled. She laughed and spread some jam over her bagel. He did the same and took a bite. "Hmm, this is good." They finished off their bagels and he sighed. "I was starving, thank you!"

"You're welcome."

Jenna got up and Mike followed her into the kitchen.

"Can I help?" asked Mike.

"No, you're my guest!"

"Jenna, you prepared all of this for me let me do something!"

"I got this. It will only take a minute." She hurried and put everything in the dishwasher and turned the coffee pot off all while he watched her. *He makes me so nervous when he does that! Maybe, I should have let him help me,* she thought. "Do you need to use the restroom before we go?" she asked.

He was still watching her. "I think I will. I put down a lot of coffee."

"There is a half bath off the kitchen on your left."

When he left, she went to use the one in her bedroom. She looked at herself in the mirror to make sure she wasn't 10 shades of red. He seemed to be able to do that to her on a regular basis. When she came out, Mike was staring down at her cat. Mike wasn't particularly fond of cats, but he thought he could get used to this one.

He bent down and placed his hand on her head to pet her, and she immediately woke up, grabbed his hand with her paws and bit him all while pounding his arm with her back legs!

"Ouch!" He drew back and untangled his hand from her. Cuddles looked at him with fire in her eyes for disturbing her sleep! Jenna came up behind him.

"I should have warned you. She gets a little feisty when someone wakes her from her nap." Her cat looked at both of them, then curled back up and went to sleep.

Mike turned to Jenna.

"Feisty, you say! She bit my finger!"

She looked at his finger and didn't see any broken skin.

"Aww, it doesn't look like she hurt you to bad." She took his finger and placed a kiss where Cuddles bit him. "Does this make it better?" She looked up into smoldering eyes. He took a deep breath.

"If we don't get out of here now, we are never leaving this apartment!"

With that look in his eyes, she hurried to get what they would be taking on their trip. She grabbed the cooler and back pack and headed for the door. Mike stopped her.

"Let me take these, you get the door." And then they were off.

Mike held the door for her and stored the cooler and backpack in the back seat.

"This is nice," said Jenna. When they were on the road, Jenna was curious about what happened after he dropped her off last night. "Did you have a rough night?" she asked him.

Mike turned his head briefly to look at her.

"You could say that. I meant to explain when I arrived at your apartment why I was so late, but I was having a caffeine withdrawal, and then your cat attacked me!"

They looked at each other and burst out laughing!

When he caught his breath, he started to explain his night to her.

"After I dropped you off, I met Mark, Zack, and Lieutenant Fillmore back at the restaurant to install security equipment."

"Wow! That was quick!" she said.

"After the incident on Friday, we thought the sooner the better."

"The incident?" she asked.

"Oh, I'm sorry, you don't know. After our meeting with Zack Friday morning, Mark went back to the restaurant, only to find the entrance door unlocked. When he first went in, he didn't see or hear anyone, and there were no lights on. He went to his office and then heard a loud noise. He called Zack. Mark then went to see if he could catch whoever was in the restaurant. By the time he got to the storeroom, whoever was in there was gone. Mark found a whole case of Jack Daniels on the floor of the storeroom and only a couple of bottles survived."

"Oh, my, gosh!" she exclaimed. "They tried to take a whole case in broad daylight!"

"Yep, anyway, Zack was able to get everything we needed, and we were there until 3:00 this morning installing. I have to say I feel a lot better now that it's done," he said.

"I hope this will catch the person doing this!" she said.

"Me too, Jenna, me too," he said

They arrived at the parking lot, and Mike paid the entrance fee and parked the car. There were several trails that would take you to the crater from this point. Mike got out of the SUV and came around to open Jenna's door but found her already out and getting in the back seat of the SUV.

"Should we put everything that's in the cooler in the backpack?"

"Sounds good!" he said. They transferred everything to the backpack and locked the car. Mike put the back pack on as they headed over to a large map of trails leading up to the crater.

"Which one are we taking?" asked Jenna.

Mike looked at several different trails and knew which one he wanted to take. It was a little more intense, but the views of the island were worth it.

"Let's take this one." He pointed to the trail on the map.

Jenna had never taken that trail. She looked at him, "Is it safe?"

Mike grinned at her. "I'll keep you safe."

Suddenly Pastor Kingsley's sermon came to mind: trust. He held out his hand to her, and she took it.

They started up the trail, and it wasn't long before the heat took its toll. Half way up to the crater, the trail became narrower, and they had to let go of each other. Mike went ahead of her, as he knew where he was going. He stopped every so often to make sure she was okay. She was such a little trooper!

"How are you doing?"

She was a little out of breath.

"I'm doing great. This trail is a little more challenging than what I'm used to though."

"There's a cave just up ahead. We'll take a break and have our sandwiches and something to drink there. The views from that area are breathtaking."

"Lead the way, kind sir!"

Mike laughed, and they headed up to the cave. When they approached the cave, Jenna looked around. Mike was right. The view from up here was breathtaking! You could see the deep blue ocean with the sun glistening on it for miles! Looking down the mountain, the array of colors in the hills and valleys were magnificent! She took her phone and started taking pictures. Mike came up beside her and was taking it all in. She turned and looked up at him.

"You were right, it's beautiful up here!"

Mike smiled down at her.

"Are you ready to have something to eat? I'm famished! There's a nice rock we can sit on just inside the cave."

"It's not too far in, is it?"

"Nooo! Come, I'll show you."

She reluctantly followed him to the mouth of the cave. She didn't like going into places she wasn't sure about, especially dark places. He showed her where the rock was, and she thought she could handle it. She could still see the sun. He opened the backpack, and they sat and ate their sandwiches and had a Coke. She felt much better after she had eaten.

Mike stood up and looked around the cave.

"Let's go exploring!"

Jenna just stared at him.

"Uh, it's dark in there!"

"Come on, Jenna, where's your sense of adventure?"

"It flew out the window when we came in here!" she said a little angrily.

Mike held out his hand.

"Do you trust me?"

There was that word again. Trust. Could she trust him? *Dear Lord, you know how scared I am in unfamiliar places, especially dark places! What do I do? I don't want him to think that I don't trust him to keep me safe.*

Mike could see she was apprehensive by the look on her face. But then she got up off the rock and took his hand.

Mike took his cell phone out and turned on the light, and they started moving forward. Jenna stops him.

"What if there are snakes in here?"

"There are no snakes on the island." She heard that once. They went a little further. She pulled on his hand.

"What if there are wild boar in here? I happen to know that wild boar live on the island!"

"Let's hope there's none in here!" Mike chuckled.

"Mike! This is not funny!" she said angrily.

"Jenna, I have been in this cave many times and I have not run into any wild boars!"

"Okay." They walked farther in. Jenna started to shake. Mike could feel her shaking and wondered if he should turn back. "Don't let go of me."

He smiled down at her. "I won't let go." She heard a noise at the back of the cave.

"What was that?" Mike shone the light towards the sound. Jenna saw something fluttering. "Mike! Is that, is that a bat?" As it came towards them, Jenna started screaming. It flew right past them and out the cave entrance. Jenna followed suit and ran screaming out of the cave. Mike caught up with her. She was so distraught, Mike had to shake her.

"Jenna! Jenna, it was only a bat!"

She looked up at him with tears in her eyes, "It was only a bat? Are you freaking kidding me right now? I'm scared to death of bats and dark places." She was literally crying now. She beat her fists on his chest. "Why would you take me in there?"

Mike felt terrible. He should have turned back when he felt her shaking.

"I'm sorry, Jenna. Stop beating me and look at me." She calmed down enough to look into his eyes. She could see he felt terrible and wasn't aware of her fear.

She laid her head on his shoulder and let the tears come. She put her arms around his mid-section as Mike put his arms around her and pulled her close. He let her cry, and when she was all cried out, he took her chin in his hand and lifted her head up to press his lips next to hers.

The kiss started out gentle and then he couldn't hold back any longer. He kissed her with a passion he didn't know he possessed. Jenna had never in her life been kissed so passionately. She matched him kiss for kiss. It seemed to go on forever. She moved her arms up around his neck and hung on for dear life. She felt weak as he continued to kiss her. When he lifted his head, he gazed into her eyes.

"I've been, wanting to kiss you like this since the first day I laid eyes on you."

"Really?" she asked.

"Really," he said. He took her face in his hands and brushed the tears from her cheeks with his thumbs. "I'm so sorry, Jenna. If I'd known about your fear, I would never have taken you in there."

"I forgive you. I should have told you about my fear." He bent his head and kissed her again. His hands started exploring. She was so soft against him. He wanted to touch every inch of her. He lifted his head for a brief moment. "Jenna, open your mouth for me, I want to taste you."

She opened her mouth for him, and he couldn't get enough of her. She tasted so good and her scent was intoxicating. Jenna held on. She felt weak and exhilarated at the same time. She tightened her arms around his neck and gave her tongue over to him. His hands were moving over her body and when he reached her breast, she moaned.

She thought she heard voices, and Mike must have heard it, too, because he broke the kiss and slid his hand around her waist. They looked down the trail and saw two couples coming up fast!

"Are you two okay? We heard someone screaming their lungs out and thought someone might be hurt!"

Jenna and Mike looked at each other and started laughing. They couldn't stop!

One of the gentlemen looked at his wife and said, "Well,

Martha. It looks like they're fine. Come on, everyone. Let's go on up to the crater."

Mike and Jenna finally caught their breath as they walked by them.

"Hey! Thanks for checking on us!"

"Yes," said Jenna, "Thank you, but it was only a bat!"

Mike took one look at her and kissed her again!

"Let's leave these two love birds alone," said Martha.

As Mike continued to kiss her, the group headed out. He lifted his head, took her hand, and went back towards the cave. She stopped him.

"I'm not going back in there," she said stubbornly.

"I am just going to go and get your backpack, little one. And what would you say if we head back down the trail and have some dinner?"

Her eyes lit up!

"Yes!" We could grill some steaks! We'll need to stop at the market and pick up some things. Oh! And I have a dessert you can try!" Jenna was all excited about the prospects of them cooking dinner together. Mike bent his head and kissed her sweet lips.

"You are all the dessert I want." His eyes were intense as he gazed at her. She melted and blushed at the same time. He picked up the backpack without letting go of her hand and led her back down the trail.

Chapter 11

They stopped at a market that Jenna was familiar with on the island. They both decided that they were hungry for steak, among other things. Jenna wanted to make kabobs out of the steak, so Mike went to pick out the meat while Jenna collected the vegetables they would need. On his way to the meat counter, Mike walked by a display of flowers and decided to pick out a bouquet of flowers for Jenna. He went on to pick up the meat and grabbed a bottle of their best red wine for dinner. They met up at the checkout counter, and he handed her the flowers.

"Oh Mike! They're beautiful!" said Jenna surprised by the gesture.

"Beautiful flowers for a beautiful woman!" he said seductively.

Jenna smiled up at him. "Are you trying to seduce me again?"

"Is it working?" he grinned.

She laughed.

"Hmm, we'll see."

The clerk asked them if they were ready to check out. Mike and Jenna looked at the clerk and then at each other.

"Do we have everything we need?" asked Mike. Jenna looked down into their cart and checked the items.

"It looks like it."

"Then let's go!" said Mike

Mike paid for all their groceries, and they headed back to her apartment. When they arrived, Jenna unlocked her door but was careful to make sure Cuddles wasn't waiting by the door. When it was safe, Mike brought all the groceries in and set them on the counter. After they took everything out of the bags, Jenna took the flowers and put them in a vase and set them on the table. Such an array of beautiful colors! She went up to him to give him a quick kiss.

"Thank you!"

He pulled her close.

"You're welcome, little one," he said and proceeded to kiss her senseless. He lifted his head and brought his hands up to her face to brush the stray hair from her face. He reached and pulled out the elastic band that tied her hair up in a ponytail and watched it fall. As he ran his fingers through her hair, "Wear it down for me, Jenna. I love the way it flows down your back and shoulders."

Jenna was mesmerized. She couldn't move. He kissed her again with that same passion he showed her earlier, their tongues tangling to the music of their own hearts beating. Jenna wrapped her arms around his neck and pulled him closer. Mike responded with a kiss that went deeper. He was so lost to his senses that this woman made him feel. He wanted her in a way he has never wanted a woman before. His hands started to explore again as if they had a mind of their own. He lifted her tank top, so he could feel her skin on his hands and wanted to kiss every inch that was exposed. He lifted his mouth from her lips and started down her neck. Jenna moaned and felt the sensation going through her body. Just as he went to pull her bra up and taste one of those beautiful nipples of hers, Jenna came to with a start.

"Mike!" Jenna said breathlessly. She pressed her hands against his chest. "I can't."

"You can't or you won't?" Mike looked into her eyes and was just a little frustrated at this point. Jenna could see a smoldering fire in his eyes. She was shaking now. She wanted him, but it was too early in their relationship. Jenna placed her hands on his face.

"Mike, I have never had a man affect me the way you do. Can we take it a little slower?"

Mike searched her eyes and could see she was apprehensive about going too far.

"Okay, we'll slow down, just a little." He put her bra back in place and pulled her shirt down. "How about we get started on dinner?"

"I think that is an excellent idea," said Jenna.

"Do you have a cork screw?" he asked.

"I do." She went to the drawer, all the while thinking about how she was going to tell him she had never had a relationship with a man. Would he laugh or walk away, only wanting to be with a more experienced woman who could pleasure him more? She found the cork screw and handed it to him. She pulled two wine glasses out of the cupboard and Mike poured them each a glass of wine. She lifted her glass and tasted it.

"Mmm, this is really good. Just, the right amount of sweetness!" Mike took a sip and with an amused look he said, "I had a feeling you liked your wine on the sweet side."

"You were right! Do you mind if I go freshen up before we start dinner?" she asked.

"Actually I'd like to do the same."

"Sure. I'll meet you back in the kitchen in a few minutes." Mike thought he might need more than a few minutes.

Jenna hurried off to her bedroom and looked at herself in the mirror. Her face was all red from his beard where he had kissed her. Thankfully she hadn't put on a lot of makeup this morning, or she would have really looked bad after her crying jag outside the cave.

She used the restroom, washed her hands, and splashed her face with some warm water. She ran a brush through her hair and touched her lips off with some lip gloss and headed back to the kitchen.

Mike was already in the kitchen, sipping on his wine. It appeared he had also washed up. He was so handsome. He looked up when she came in.

"What would you like me to do to help with dinner?' he asked.

"Well," said Jenna, "if you could cut the steak, I'll cut the vegetables, and we'll put them on these spears. I'll make my Hawaiian sauce, and we can take them out and put them on the grill," she said. "Sounds like a plan!" he grinned. They worked side by side putting the kabobs together sharing what types of foods they liked and disliked. When they finished, they took the kabobs out to the patio. Mike started the grill and placed them on the grate. Jenna handed him her sauce for basting and left him to cook while she went and finished putting their meal together.

Inside, she took some red potatoes, washed and quartered them and put them in a microwave dish. She wouldn't have time to bake them as she normally would. She chopped an onion and added it to the potatoes. She then poured garlic butter over the potatoes and onion and set it in the microwave. She set the timer for five minutes. She hurried and put two salads together and set them on the table. She picked up the wine bottle and went to check to see how Mike was doing with the kabobs.

"How's it going?" Jenna topped off Mike's wine glass and smiled up at him.

"Good! If you like your steak done on the medium side, they are almost done."

"Perfect! I'll go and finish up the potatoes." Jenna went inside and checked the potatoes. They needed a bit more time. She sprinkled some cheddar cheese on top and set the microwave for two more minutes and turned it on. While the potatoes were cooking, she took out her Hawaiian placemats and placed them on the table along with silverware and napkins.

Jenna was just putting the potatoes on the table when Mike came through the door. She lit the candle in the centerpiece as he sat the kabobs down on the table.

"Wow!" Mike said with a surprised look.

"You did all this while I was grilling?"

She gave him a big smile, "I'm a woman of many talents!"

"So I see!" he chuckled.

"Shall we sit?" asked Jenna.

"You don't have to ask me twice. Everything looks delicious!"

They sat down at the table and Mike topped off their wine. Jenna turned to him and asked, "Do you mind if I say grace?"

"No, not at all!" said Mike. He caught her eyes as she took his hand in hers. She bowed her head and said a prayer of thankfulness. When she looked up, he was still watching her. Mike thought he must be the luckiest man alive to be sitting here with the most passionate, beautiful, caring person he has ever met. He squeezed her hand.

"Thank you for all of this."

"You're welcome, although I had a little help from the grill master," she chuckled. "Let's eat, I'm starved!"

Mike cut into his steak.

"Mmm, this is excellent! You'll have to share your recipe for your Hawaiian sauce, because this is really good!"

"Thank you," said Jenna. "I will."

"How many classes are you taking besides the internship this semester?" he asked.

"I only have the one class which is my last class before I graduate in June. I also have to have 120 hours put in for the internship to receive my BA degree. I will be glad when I'm done. It's been a long five years."

"Five years?" asked Mike.

"Yes, after I graduated high school, I attended a junior college before I went to State. Then towards the end of that year, I was given the opportunity to study at the University here on the island. Due to some of the courses I took, when I arrived at the University, I started my sophomore year." explained Jenna.

"And that's where you met Sasha?"

"Yes, and we have become close friends ever since. How about you? Did you ever attend college?" she asked.

"I have an Associate's Degree in Business Administration. I took the courses online. When I was discharged from the Air Force, my focus was on investing in a restaurant, so I haven't been able to go back and get my BA degree. But you know what, Jenna? I've never felt that a person had to have a college degree to become a success in life," he said with conviction. "Now Mark, he did the same and took online courses and received his BA Degree in Marketing with a minor in Accounting. He is a whiz when it comes to numbers, as you are, I'm sure," he said smiling.

"I agree with you Mike, about not having to get a degree to become successful. Some people have that gift of taking something small and becoming a giant success! You and your brother have certainly done that!"

"Thank you, it was hard at first, but it's definitely paying off."

They finished eating, and Jenna asked him if he would like dessert. With that sexy grin of his and eyes that wanted to devour her, he asked, "Shall we go to your bed or would you prefer the couch?" he asked wiggling his eyebrows.

Her eyes got big.

"Mike! Not that kind of dessert!"

"Are you sure? Because I am so ready to have you!" he growled at her.

Jenna could feel the blush as it rose up from her neck. Mike chuckled as he watched her face turn a bright red.

"I will fix you my dessert that I have been creating and see if it isn't better than what you're thinking about," she said grinning. Mike watched her as she put the dessert together and wondered if he was ever going to get her to bed. He wanted to feel her luscious body next to his and ravish her. She wanted to take it slow, but he wanted to go full steam ahead!

Jenna brought the dessert over and set it in front of him.

"I need your opinion. I think I'm missing an ingredient that I can't put my finger on."

"So, I'm to be the guinea pig?"

Jenna laughed. "Will you just try it?"

He smiled up at her and took her finger and dipped it into the ice cream. He focused his eyes on her as he put her finger in his mouth to get her reaction.

"Mmm, perfect!" Every nerve in her body was set on fire as he licked all the ice cream off her finger. "I think all it needs is your finger, so I can lick off every bite!" he said seductively.

She slapped him on his shoulder.

"Mike!"

He laughed. He took a spoon and dug into the dessert. She watched him as he took his second bite, for real this time.

"Oh, this is really good!"

"You don't think it's missing anything?"

"Just you!" he said, wiggling his eyebrows again.

"Mike, be serious!"

"Okay." He finished off the dessert and looked over at her. "Jenna, it's good just the way you prepared it!"

She sighed, "I still think it's missing something."

Just like a woman, he thought. His mom did the same thing. She tried a new recipe, and it was never quite right even though it tasted delicious.

Jenna started clearing the dishes off the table when Mike caught her by the waist and pulled her down onto his lap.

"Your dessert was good, little one, but it's not as good as the dessert I've been wanting all day long." He nuzzled her neck and started kissing her there. When he touched the sensitive spot behind her ear with his tongue, she moaned.

"Mike, I..."

He worked his way from her ear to her cheek and finally to her soft lips. His tongue traced her upper and then her lower lip and she opened for him. Their tongues tangled, and Jenna felt the strength go right out of her as he took possession of her mouth. She felt his hand slide up her leg and to her waist as she pressed her chest to his. When he explored her stomach, it set her hormones into overdrive. His hand reached under her shirt and captured one of her breasts. Oh, it felt so good to have his hand there. She didn't want him to stop, but a little voice in the back of her head said, *You need to stop this. He's going to find out you have never been intimate with a man.* She just told him she wanted them to slow down, and now, she wanted to shut that voice off—but she kept hearing it.

Mike couldn't get enough of her. She felt so good in his arms. Her response to his touch was overpowering him. Her firm breast fit perfectly in his hand. He wanted to feel her skin against his. He wanted to taste every inch of her and feel her under him and show her the passion that two people could feel for each other. His lips traveled back to her ear, "Jenna, sweetheart, where do you want me to take you? I want you now!" Jenna sat up and tried to get off his lap as she realized where this was going. Mike held on. "Jenna, what is it?" Mike didn't understand. He thought she was with him on this.

"Mike, I, we hardly know each other. I'm not ready for an intimate relationship. I'm sorry."

Mike sighed. He put his head on hers and closed his eyes. He was so aroused, he hurt. He wasn't happy about not being able to take her to bed and showing her how it could be between them. He hasn't been with a woman in a while now. He wanted this woman beyond measure. But he would respect her wishes.

Jenna hoped he understood. She didn't want to lose him before they even got started. She loved the way he kissed her. The way his hands touched her body left her wanting for more. But she couldn't let him take her to bed. She was scared of not knowing what it was like. Of course, she heard her friends talk about it. These feelings between them were escalating way too fast. She needed time. Mike lifted his head and searched those beautiful brown eyes. He gave her a tender kiss.

"Okay, little one, we'll wait. But one day soon I will have you."

Jenna gazed into his eyes and saw the hunger, and knew he meant it. When the time was right, she wanted to be ready. She gave him a kiss.

"I just need some time."

Jenna got up from his lap and started clearing the table. Mike sat there for a few minutes to come down a bit before he went to help her. They worked together putting leftovers away and filling the dishwasher. When they were done, Mike took her in his arms. They gazed at each other, not knowing what was next.

"Would you like some coffee?" asked Jenna. "We could have it in the living room. Maybe watch a movie?"

"As wonderful as that sounds, I think I'd better go. After last night, I'm feeling it."

"It is getting late. I have a class in the morning. But I'll see you tomorrow at the restaurant?"

"Yes, I'll be in later in the day. I have a few meetings in the morning and one with a new vendor in the afternoon. Thank you again for making our dinner and putting everything together for our trip. Next time, I will make you dinner," he said smiling.

"Hmm, that sounds nice."

He bent and gave her a searing kiss and the promise of what was to come. He lifted his head and felt he needed to get out of there now or he would want to just keep on kissing her. He seemed to be out of control when it came to her. He took her hand and led her to the door. He raised his hands and placed them on either side of her pretty face. His blue eyes gazed into hers.

"I enjoyed our day together," he said.

"So did I." Her brown eyes smiled into his. He gave her a gentle kiss.

"Goodnight, Jenna."

"Goodnight, Mike." He opened the door and left.

Jenna stared at the door and prayed he wasn't too upset at how the night turned out. Cuddles came out of her bedroom and rubbed up against her legs. Jenna picked her up and held her close.

"What do you think Cuddles? He's a pretty nice guy, and so hot!" Her cat meowed at her. "But you weren't very nice when you bit his finger this afternoon!" Jenna gave her head a scratch and put her down. "Come on, let's get you a snack." Her cat followed her into the kitchen excited to get her snack while Jenna had only one thought on her mind, Mike.

While Mike was driving home, he thought about his day with Jenna. She was so hot when she responded to his kisses and his touch. Then she suddenly ran cold. Could she be innocent? She must be what, 23? She had to know what it was like between a man and a woman. He sighed. If he had to wait until she was ready, he would wait. She is one woman that will be well worth it!

In a small home on Koiolu Street, Tonya brought her mother her dinner on a tray and hoped she would be able to eat a little of it. Her mother, Ruthann Forest, lay in bed as she was dying of cancer. The doctors were not able to do anything else for her mother. She had very little time left and Nathan, her stepbrother, and her would have to call in hospice soon.

Tonya and Nathan both gave up their apartments to stay and take care of her mother when she wasn't able to do things for herself anymore. When she was working at the Hawaiian Lanai, her friends volunteered to watch her if Nathan couldn't be here. They worked out a schedule and took turns caring for her.

"Hi, Mom," Tonya said cheerfully. "How are you feeling? I brought you your dinner and a good book we can read together." Her mother loved to read, but her sight wasn't very good, and she was too weak to sit up for very long. Tonya put the tray down on the table beside her bed and raised the hospital bed, so she could sit up better. She adjusted the pillows behind her back and asked if she needed to use the bedpan. Her mom nodded yes. Once that was done and taken care of, she set the tray of food on her mother's lap. Her mom could only eat soft food, as it was so hard for her to swallow. There was some blended chicken noodle soup, applesauce, raspberry yogurt, and a steaming cup of black tea on her tray.

"Would you like me to help you eat tonight?" Her mother nodded yes. It was hard for her to have a conversation with someone. She seemed to grow weaker by the day.

As she fed her mom, Ruthann ate as much as she could, which wasn't much. Her mother thanked her and said she'd had enough, but to leave the tea. Tonya did as she was asked. She helped her mom take a drink of tea. She had her medicine in a cup, which helped with the pain, and some supplements to give her the nutrients she needed since her appetite had diminished. Her mom took her pills and lay back down on her pillows. Tonya helped her to get comfortable. She took the tray from the room and into the kitchen.

When she came back in to her room, her mother appeared to be asleep. She drew the covers up over her mom, and her eyes opened.

"Read," she said weakly. Tonya settled down into the easy chair next to the bed and started reading one of her mom's favorite books. She hadn't finished the first chapter before her mom fell asleep. She gave her mom a kiss on the cheek and turned off the light.

She was just coming out of the room when Nathan walked through the door.

"How's Mom doing?"

"Not good. I think we should call hospice in soon. She's hardly going to the bathroom, and she's not eating much."

Nathan sighed and nodded his head.

"I'll call them in the morning. I have the day off tomorrow, so I'll make all the arrangements."

Nathan was older than her. Mom's first husband was an abuser. She divorced him when Nathan was five and married Tonya's father, William Forest, a year later. He was an honorable man and was every bit of a loving father to both of them. He died suddenly in a car accident four years ago, and their mother was never the same. When she found out she had cancer six months ago, she refused treatment. The doctors did all that they could, but Ruthann just wanted to go home to be with her husband, Bill, in heaven.

"Okay, I've got Sonya coming over tomorrow night to help with dinner and feeding her while I'm at work. She's so frail, Nathan. I don't think she is going to be with us much longer."

Nathan came over and gave her a hug.

"I know, sis. It will be hard losing her, but we'll get through this together."

They broke apart. Tonya looked at her step brother and asked, "What are we going to do about the money we owe the loan shark?"

"Well, with this week's checks from the restaurant and the money we have from selling the liquor, we're a couple hundred short. We have 10 days before that asshole comes looking for us. I'll think of something. Don't worry."

"I'm trying not to, Nathan, but the bills just keep piling up and her Social Security isn't covering everything. We've got to put an end to this!"

"We will, sis, we will. If worst comes to worst, we'll go to the police, and then to Mike and Mark."

Tonya was scared about going to the police. She didn't want to go to jail in the midst of all that was happening in their lives. What would their mother think? She could only pray that they could get the rest of the money needed to cover the $2,000 owed and be done with this. But since the last encounter with the loan shark's minion, she had a bad feeling in her gut.

Chapter 12

Jenna was in her office at the restaurant checking out All-in-One POS software for Mark. She had three companies she was comparing cost and the timeline to install the system. She was just printing out the report when Mark came into her office.

"Hey Jenna, how are you coming along with the new software estimates?"

"I'm just printing off the report. I have three companies that you and Mike should look at. All three have high ratings for their software. It would come down to cost and how much you want to spend. I'm sure anyone of these would save your restaurant money over time."

She got up from her desk and went over to the printer. She put the report together and placed it in a folder that she already had marked and handed it to him.

"Thanks for putting this together for me. I'll look this over and get with Mike on it. Now, I would like you to go over last week's sales and inventory reports and compare them with the manual inventory sheets that I have been taking since last Thursday." He handed her the reports. Mark looked tired today.

"Is everything okay? You look worn out!"

Mark sighed, "It was a long weekend. As you know, we installed a security system after we closed on Saturday, and I didn't get much sleep before Sherry dropped our son Cameron off at noon on Sunday. He kept me going the rest of the day!"

"Kids that age definitely have a lot of energy. I have several nieces and nephews that seem to never run out of it!"

"So, you come from a large family?"

"Yes, I'm the youngest of six children. My parents are dairy farmers. I do miss them. I'm hoping they will be able to come to my graduation along with some of my siblings."

"When do you graduate?" he asked.

"June 5."

"Well, you can count on Mike and me to be there! Say, I need to give you a key to the restaurant in case I am not available to let you in. There should be a key in the top drawer of the desk. When I first found out my soon-to-be ex-wife was having an affair, I sort of lost it and fell into a depression. Mike had to hire someone to handle the books until I was able to return." Mark went around to the desk and opened the drawer while Jenna waited. He looked around for the key but didn't find it. "Hmm, that's strange. She said she put it in here." He looked through the other drawers and didn't see it. "I'll get with Mike and see if he took it and put it with the extra keys."

It suddenly dawned on Jenna that she failed to mention to both Mark and Mike about a woman that came out of her office last week.

"Mark, I just remembered something that happened last Wednesday when I left your office. There was a woman coming out of my office, and she looked upset about something. When I asked her if I could help her, she said she was looking for Mike. She said he wasn't in his office, so she thought she would look in mine. When she left, I went in to check the computer screens, and it didn't appear like they were disturbed," she said with concern.

"Did she say who she was?" he asked.

"No, I'm sorry; she didn't, and I failed to ask. But she had red hair. She was a little taller than me and slender. I didn't know if she was one of your waitresses or a hostess."

"That might be Tonya. She's one of our hostesses. She's a good worker. I'll check with Mike to see if she ever caught up with him and what she wanted. Thanks for letting me know. In any event, I'll make sure Mike gives you a key," he said as he came back around the desk. "Let me know if you find anything in those reports I gave you."

"Will do, boss!" Jenna grinned. Mark grinned back and left to go to his office.

Jenna worked on the reports till it was almost time to go home. She had a few more pages to get through, but she didn't see anything suspicious other than the incident on Friday. She went through the last three pages, which were Saturday's sales. Man! Were they busy! She checked the sales to inventory report and then compared it to Mark's manual report, which he took this morning. There were two cases missing! This time, it was a case of their most expensive wine and a case of Johnny Walker Red!

How is this person doing it? she wondered. *The restaurant has lost a lot of revenue in the past several months. I sure hope their security system will show who it is and soon!* She'd better show these to Mark.

She came out of her office and went directly to Mark's, but he wasn't there. She checked Mike's office, but he wasn't there either. Come to think of it, she hadn't seen him all day. She thought about the day they spent together and smiled. They did have fun, except for the cave. She especially liked it when he held her in his arms and kissed her with a passion that left her wanting. It gave her goosebumps just remembering.

"Are you looking for me, little one?" Jenna almost jumped out of her skin! She turned around and faced the man she was just dreaming about!

"Mike, you're back! You scared me!"

Mike grinned at her.

"Do you know you're adorable when you get worked up?"

"Ha, ha!" she chided. "I was actually looking for your brother. He wasn't in his office, so I thought he might be with you."

"How you disappoint me, my little one!" He put his hands on her waist and pulled her close. "I've missed you," he whispered. He bent his head and gave her a seductive kiss. Jenna moaned and kissed him back. She missed him, too!

"Hey you two!" said Mark coming up behind them. Mike and Jenna broke apart. Jenna was blushing and ran a hand through her hair.

"Hey bro!" said Mike.

"Are you just getting back from your meetings?" asked Mark.

"Yes, it's been a long day."

"How did it go with the new vendor?"

"Good!" said Mike. "They have quite a few items to offer the restaurant. Particularly some fresh organic fruit and vegetables I want to try."

"Sounds good," Mark turned to Jenna. "Did you want to see me?"

"Oh yes! I was just coming to find you!" she exclaimed.

Mark grinned, "It looks like you were side-tracked!"

Jenna blushed again. It seemed like she was doing a lot of that lately. Mike was watching her with an amused look on his face.

"Uh, yes, um, I wanted to go over with you what I found in these reports. Actually, Mike, you should look at this, too."

Mike gave Jenna a wink and smiled, "Let's go into my office and we'll take a look."

Mike took a seat behind his desk. Jenna and Mark took the two in front. Jenna spread the reports across the desk, so they could both see. She pointed out the two missing cases of wine and liquor taken on Saturday. Mike and Mark looked at each other. Mike leaned back in his chair. He put his hand to his chin.

"How does this person get two cases out of this restaurant with so many of the staff around?" he asked with concern in his voice.

"Well," said Jenna. "Looking at these reports, you were extremely busy that night. It's possible he or she could have taken a few at a time while the staff was busy serving."

"It's possible. I am so glad we put the security system in when we did, and not a moment too soon!" said Mark.

"I totally agree." Mike was watching Jenna. He couldn't wait to get back to her today. She was like a drug, consuming him. He got out of his thoughts and focused back on what Mark was saying.

"By the way, did you happen to pull the key out of the desk drawer when Anna left?" Mike shook his head.

"No, I never thought about it."

Mark looked at Jenna and back at Mike.

"It's missing." Mike sat forward.

"What?"

"It's missing. Last Wednesday, Jenna saw a woman with red hair come out of her office. When Jenna asked if she could help her, her reply was she was looking for you. I'm thinking its Tonya. Did she approach you about anything?"

Mike thought back to that night.

"I don't remember even talking to her that night."

"I don't want to accuse her, but she could have taken the key, which would explain why the door was unlocked when I came in on Friday."

Mike looked confused.

"It's hard to believe it would be her. She always shows up for work on time, and I've never had a complaint on her work ethics."

Jenna listened to the conversation and felt she had to say something.

"Mike, when she was looking for you, she seemed nervous or agitated when she came out of my office. When I told her that you may be out on the floor, she couldn't get out of the office fast enough."

"Is Tonya on the schedule for tonight?" asked Mark.

Mike signed into his computer and pulled up the schedule.

"Yep, she should be here right now."

"Jenna, do you think if you saw Tonya, you could verify it was her that came out of your office?" asked Mark.

"Sure." Mike looked over at Jenna. "Tell you what, let me buy you dinner. It's already after 6:00, and you can tell me if it was her you saw."

"Okay, what do you want me to do with these reports?"

"I'll take them," said Mark. "I'll put them with the others. If you don't mind, I'll stay and have a bite with you two, and then I'll have to run."

Mike shrugged his shoulders.

"Fine with me," he said. "What about you, Jenna?"

"Oh yes! Please join us!"

She said that a little too fast, Mike thought. He got up from his chair. "Let's go, I need to check on what's happening out on the floor."

"I'll just take care of these reports and check my emails and be with you shortly," said Mark.

Jenna got up and looked at Mike.

"I need to sign out and lock my office. I'll only be a minute."

Mike walked out with her and locked his door. He waited by the main door while she signed out and locked up. She smiled up at Mike as he took her arm and led her out into the restaurant and into the bar area. The restaurant was half full of customers with people coming in to be seated. He took her to a booth in the corner of the bar, so they would have more privacy. Jenna slid in. Mike with his hands on the table leaned down as she looked up at him and brushed his lips over hers. He lifted his head and smiled down at her.

"Mike!" She looked around. "We shouldn't be doing this in front of customers!"

"I can't help it. I can't resist you. Your lips just ask to be kissed!" Jenna blushed. Mike chuckled. "I'll send Megan over to you. Order me a Jack Daniels on the rocks while I go and check on things."

He kissed her again and left to see what needed to be done.

Kalea was standing by the hostess station, watching the exchange between Mike and Jenna, and was growing more upset by the minute. This rule around here was keeping Mike and her apart. *He should be mine! I've got to find a way to stop this!* Her eyes shot daggers at them both, especially Jenna. Some customers came up to her to let her know how many were in their party. She switched her facial expression from anger to warm and friendly as she greeted them and took them to their table.

Mark sat down across from Jenna as Megan came to their booth with menus and silverware.

"What can I get the both of you to drink?"

Jenna just wanted water with lemon. Mark ordered a beer. She was just about to leave when Jenna asked, "Megan?"

"Yes?"

"Mike would like a Jack Daniels on the rocks."

"No problem" I'll have your drinks right out to you."

"Thank you," said Jenna.

Mark watched Megan leave. She was definitely a hot little package. Jenna was watching Mark and his expression crossing his face.

She knew that look. She saw it in Mike all the time when he looked at her. Mark turned back to her.

"What are you hungry for, Jenna?"

She picked up her menu and scanned the items offered.

"I don't know. Everything looks good. I tried your Hawaiian steak last Friday and it was excellent."

"Yes, that is one of our favorite items on the menu. We get a lot of requests for it."

"What do you recommend, Mark?"

"Well, if you're asking me, I would prefer just a big old fashion cheeseburger and fries."

"You know, that sounds really good!" she exclaimed.

Megan brought their drinks and sat them down in front of them.

"Did you want to wait for Mike?" Jenna looked at Mark.

"Yes, oh, here he comes now." Mike came up behind Megan and slid in the seat beside Jenna. "Have you ordered yet?"

"Not yet, we were waiting for you," said Mark.

"What do you all want?"

"Cheeseburgers!" said Mark and Jenna at the same time.

"Cheeseburgers?" asked Mike. They all chuckled.

"It sounds really good," said Jenna.

"Then cheeseburgers it is!"

Megan asked how each of them wanted theirs done and what they wanted on them.

"Oh, and Megan, bring us a big plate of fries, and we'll share them."

"Sure thing!" she said.

Megan picked up the menus, gave them a big smile and left to turn in their order. Mark returned her smile as he watched her go.

We need to re-think this rule of dating employees, he sighed. Mark turned to his brother, "Everything in order?" he asked.

"So far, but the night is young," he commented.

"True."

Jenna listened as the two brothers conversed. Mike sat so close to her, she could feel the energy between them. She watched his hands and remembered those hands on her body and the way his touch made her feel. She shivered. Mike turned toward Jenna and was asking her something. She came out of her thoughts.

"I'm sorry, what did you ask me?"

"Tonya is over at the hostess station. Is she the woman you saw coming out of your office?"

Jenna looked over to where Mike said she was. There was a pretty red headed woman getting ready to seat a group of people.

"That's her. That's the woman who came out of my office."

All three looked over at Tonya at the same time she looked over at the three of them and caught Mike's eyes. She quickly looked away and took the group to their table. Mike sighed. He was hoping it wasn't her. She was so good with the customers. Their food came, and Megan asked if they needed anything else. Mike looked at Mark and Jenna as they shook their heads no.

"I think we're all set Megan, thanks," said Mike.

When they started eating, Tonya came from the Hawaiian room and looked over at her bosses and the new intern. She had a bad feeling inside. She hoped that they didn't find that the key to the restaurant was missing. She and her stepbrother had to put a stop to this. She'd have a talk with Nathan when she gets home tonight.

"That was the best cheeseburger I've had in a while!" exclaimed Jenna.

Mike smiled and winked at Jenna.

"I must agree. You and Mark made a good choice."

Jenna smiled back, and they seemed to get lost in each other. Mike couldn't help himself. He leaned down and brushed his lips next to hers. He seemed to be always on fire for her every time he was near her. Didn't matter where they were; it always seemed like it was just the two of them in their own little world. Jenna couldn't believe she was kissing him in a public place. He always drew her in, and she was mindless of nothing else but him.

Mark watched the two of them. His brother was falling hard for Jenna. And he was pretty sure Jenna is feeling the same. He cleared his throat. Jenna was the first to break away. She wished she would stop blushing! Mike continued to gaze into her eyes. He gave her a quick kiss and took her hand in his. He placed it on his thigh as he turned back to his brother. He wanted to stay connected to her at all times. Jenna relaxed as she felt his thumb brushing back and forth over her hand. Mark was just about to say something when Megan came back to their table to take the dishes and ask if they wanted dessert. Mark looked at the two of them, and they all agreed that they were full. Mark smiled up at Megan.

"Thank you, Megan, but you can bring us the check."

"I'll have it right out for you."

When she left, Mark looked at both Mike and Jenna.

"Now that we know it was Tonya coming out of Jenna's office, what do you think the next step should be?"

"Well, we can't really come out and accuse her since we don't actually know if she did indeed take the key. Now that the security system is in place, let's watch the camera feed each night. If it is her, she's bound to strike again. I find it hard to believe if she is stealing that she would be working it alone."

"I think you might be right, bro. It saddens me that it could be her. She is one of our best employees." Mark sighed. He looked out over the bar area. Tonya was at the hostess station, staring right at them. You could tell by the expression on her face she was nervous about something. Mark turned back to the two lovebirds.

"Okay, let's wait this out and see what comes down over the next few days. I'm going to take off. It's been a hell of a day." He got up out of the booth, threw some bills on the table, said his good-byes, and walked right up to Tonya.

"Hi, Tonya!" he said with a smile.

"Uh, hi, Mark," she said nervously. Mark could tell she was apprehensive about talking to him. He'd keep things light.

"How are you doing tonight?"

"Oh, fine, everything is fine," she replied. She kept looking away.

"How is your mom doing?"

Tonya had a surprised look on her face when he asked her that question. She had no idea he was aware of her mother's condition.

"She's not doing so well. She's been sick for a long time now."

"Oh, I'm so sorry to hear that," he said with concern in his voice. "If there is anything we can do to help, just let us know. And I mean that, Tonya," he said with sincerity.

Tonya almost broke into tears.

"Thank you, Mark, I appreciate the offer, but there is not much anyone can do at this point." Mark could see she was torn.

He smiled, "Don't be afraid to ask Tonya. We're always here to help. You have a good night."

He turned and left the building. Tonya was stunned and didn't know what to think as she watched her boss leave the restaurant. But one thing was for sure: she couldn't keep this up for much longer.

Mike and Jenna watched the interaction between Tonya and Mark. It wasn't long before Mark left the restaurant, and Tonya greeted a couple and took them to their table.

"What do you think, Mike?" Jenna asked, curious to know what he thought.

He turned his head towards her.

"When Mark first went up to her and started talking to her, she seemed a little nervous, but then suddenly she looked a little taken aback, like he said something that surprised her."

"That was my impression, too."

"I'll call Mark after we close, but, I'll check the camera feed before, to see what he said to her."

"Okay," she said. "Let me know if there is anything else I can help you with."

Mike put his arm around her and squeezed her body next to his. As he looked at her, he had a mischievous glint in those blue eyes of his.

"Honey, if we weren't sitting here in this booth with a crowd of people all around us, I could show you lots of things you could help me with!" He grinned.

"Mike! You are incorrigible, do you know that?" She slapped him on his leg.

"Ouch!"

"Oh, like that hurt! You know I didn't mean it that way!"

Mike laughed. "You are so cute when you get riled up! I love teasing you."

She laughed with him.

"Do you have the time?" she asked.

He looked at his watch. "It is almost 8:00."

"Mike, I need to go. I have a paper that is due on Wednesday, and I wanted to get started on it."

"Do you have everything you need to get started on it here? It's starting to get dark out, and I don't want you walking home. You can work in my office until we close and then I'll drive you home."

She thought a minute.

"I do have my notebook and iPad. I guess I could. Let me text

Sasha to let her know I will be home late and see if she'll feed Cuddles for me."

"You mean your attack cat from hell?"

She looked up from her text to see the expression on his handsome face, and it was priceless! She laughed.

"She just gets a little upset when someone wakes her up from her nap. She's really a good cat."

"Uh-huh," he said. Jenna sent her text and received a thumbs-up response. "Okay, boss. Show me the way!"

Mike slid out of the booth and took Jenna's hand to help her out. They walked to the office, and Mike unlocked the main door and the door to his office.

"Are you sure you want me in your office? I don't want to take up your space if you need it."

"It's fine Jenna. I won't be back until after we close, so you will have all the privacy you need to start your report."

"Okay, boss!" Jenna put her notebook and iPad on the desk. She felt two powerful hands on her waist as he turned her around. When she searched his eyes, they looked like they could devour her at any second.

"What are you going to do for me for setting up this fine accommodation for you?"

"Say thank you?"

"You can do better than that, you little minx!" His mouth came down hard on hers as he crushed her to him. Jenna couldn't breathe. She could feel every part of him as his kiss became more demanding. The emotions running through her body was earth-shattering. "Open for me, sweetheart."

She did as he asked. When his tongue met hers, they tangled to a dance of their own design. Jenna was lost to the feelings this man created in her. She wrapped her arms around his neck and ran her fingers through his hair and pulled him closer to her if that was even possible. Mike wanted to consume her and ravage her at the same time. He tried to slow it down with her, but every time he came near her it was always the same. He couldn't stop himself. His hand moved around to her side and up under her breast. His thumb massaged her hard nipple, and he moaned. More than anything, he wanted to make love to her. When Jenna felt his hand on her breast, she broke the kiss.

"Mike, what if someone comes in?"

"What, sweetheart?" He was so enticed by her. He started kissing her neck. Jenna wanted more than anything to let herself go, but this wasn't the time or place for making love.

"Mike," she groaned and pushed out a little from his chest. "You are bound and determined not to let me get any work done on my paper."

It was like a splash of cold water in his face. He shook his head.

"You're right, I need to get back out on the floor and you need to get to work." He didn't want to leave her. He felt like every part of him was on fire for her. He reluctantly let her go. "I'll lock the outer office door, so no one will disturb you. I will be back after we close."

"Okay," she whispered. She looked at his broad chest, his tousled hair and blue eyes that ached for her. She ached for him, too.

"Jenna, please don't look at me like that, or I won't be responsible for what happens next!"

"Sorry, I'll just get started on my paper." She scooted behind the desk to give them some space, or neither one of them would get any work done.

"I will be back in a few hours." He gave her one last agonizing look before he left the office.

Jenna sat down at the desk. She was shaking from the emotions he awakened in her. He knew exactly what to do with his hands and lips to leave her wanting him with a passion she has never before felt in her life! *You need to get a grip, Jenna!* she told herself. She shook herself and started to get to work on her paper. As if she could even concentrate on it!

She worked till it was almost 10:00. Mike would be coming back soon. For the last half hour, her eyes were heavy, and she could hardly stay awake. Mike had a couch in his office and she wondered, should she? She went over to the couch and lay her head down on one of the pillows. She didn't even remember falling asleep.

The night finally came to a close, and when the last employee left for the night, he locked up and headed back to his office. When he came in, he found Jenna sound asleep on his couch. He smiled. His heart melted as he watched her sleep. He was pretty sure he was falling for her. He went up to her and brushed some of her hair away from her pretty face. She moved a little. He bent down and kissed her cheek. She opened her eyes.

"Oh my, gosh!" she said. "I didn't mean to fall asleep!"

She tried to get up, but he held her back. He gave her a tender kiss. In one swift move, he pulled her up, sat down and pulled her with him onto his lap. With his arms wrapped around her he said, "You can fall asleep on my couch any time you would like, little one."

She smiled up at him. "I didn't realize how tired I was until I laid my head down. What time is it?"

"Close to 11:00," he said.

"Oh Mike, I need to get home."

He would have liked nothing better than to take her to his home and make love to her through the night. Jenna saw that look in his eyes, and if they didn't leave soon, she may not be able to stop him. He was a powerful force that continued to overwhelm her.

Mike brought his hand up and ran his fingers through her long hair as he bent to give her a kiss that scorched her. She couldn't help herself. She matched his kiss with a passion that made her soar. His hand went from her hair down to her waist and up to the buttons on her blouse. She trembled at his touch. The blouse came open, and he unclasped her bra. He moved the fabric away from her breast and explored her soft skin under his hand. She had beautiful breasts. They filled his hand as he went from one to the other and traced her nipples with his thumb. She moaned and arched her body to give him more access. He kissed her and then followed down her neck and latched onto one of her nipples and then the other. If one could get lost in the shear magic of her body, it was him.

Jenna shivered. The sensations that rocketed throughout her body when he took her breast in his mouth was mind blowing. He eased her down on the couch, so that they were both lying down. Somehow both Jenna's bra and blouse were lying on the floor. Mike continued to kiss and work his hands over her body. She was barely aware of him taking her slacks off and was left only in her cotton panties. Mike took his shirt off and finally felt her soft skin against his. It was total heaven. He kissed her with a need inside him that burned.

Jenna was barely aware that she was naked except for her cotton briefs. She felt his skin against hers and her hands explored his broad chest and back. She pulled him closer to her as his hand slid down to her center. He worked his fingers inside her till she cried out.

"Sweetheart, I am going to need to get a condom." He finished undressing, pulled a condom out of his wallet and slid it on. Jenna had never seen a man completely naked before. He was magnificent. She wasn't even embarrassed as she watched him. She better let him know she wasn't experienced at intimate relationships. When he lay back down beside her, she tried to tell him. "Mike, I..."

"Shh.. Jenna, please don't tell me to stop. I've wanted you since that first day I saw you."

"But I..." she groaned as he started to kiss her swollen lips. His hands moved sensually over her breasts, down her stomach and finally to her center where he brought her to her second climax. "Mike! I need you now!"

Mike took her leg to open her for him.

"Put your leg over my hip, honey." He eased into her. She was so tight. He wondered, "Jenna, sweetheart, is this your first time with a man?"

Her eyes told the story. She nodded her head yes. Mike was torn. He could have her right here, right now. But he didn't want her first time to be here. He wanted it to be special.

"I'm sorry, Mike. I'm scared. I've never let a man touch me like this before. I seem to lose my head every time I'm near you."

He pulled away from her delectable body and brought her up with him and pulled her close. His eyes searched hers and he could see the want and confusion in them. Mike sighed, "As much as I want you, little one, I am going to give you more time to make sure this is what you want. Entering into a relationship is a choice that only you or I can make. Do you understand?"

Mike saw the tears building up in her pretty brown eyes.

"I'm so sorry. I just don't want to disappoint you. I have no idea of what I'm doing or how to please you." And then the tears came.

"Oh Jenna," he whispered, "Please don't cry." He pulled her closer to him and let her cry. When there were no more tears left, he took her chin in his hand and lifted her head and looked directly into her eyes.

"Jenna, you make me feel things that no other woman in my life time has ever done. You could never disappoint me. I just want you to be sure." She could see in his eyes that he meant what he said. He could have taken her, and she would have let him, but he didn't. She realized without a doubt she was falling for this incredible man looking down at her. She put her arms around him and hugged him tight. When she let go of him, he touched her sweet face and gave her a tender kiss. "Let's get you home little one."

"Okay," she whispered.

They dressed, and Jenna gathered up her things. Once they locked up the office and the restaurant, they headed to Mike's corvette. As they left the parking lot, there was a man sitting in a car watching them leave.

Chapter 13

When Mike dropped her off at her apartment it was after midnight. Thankfully Sasha was sleeping. In the kitchen, Jenna made some hot chocolate. It always calmed her when things seemed to be spiraling out of control. While she sipped on her hot cocoa, she thought back to what almost happened tonight. She almost lost her virginity. Here she was, a 23-year-old woman, and still a virgin! That might be one for the history books!

Mike was one experienced lover. He knew just where to touch to make her body soar to heights that she never dreamed possible in all her fantasies. He knew she wanted him and yet he stopped things from going any further. Next time, Jenna thought, she was going to be ready to give him everything because isn't that what you do when you love someone with your whole heart? Jenna stopped herself short!

Wait a minute. You've only known him over a week! Could you really fall in love that fast? Jenna knew the answer to that, and it was yes! She was totally, heart-stoppingly, madly in love with Michael James TreVaine! But did he feel the same? Or did he want to only have a sexual relationship with her. He said he wanted her to be sure before they entered into a relationship. Is that all he would want? Jenna knew that she wanted more than just the sex. She wanted all of it. The sharing, giving of each other, to be able to discuss anything that life has to offer. Yes, she wanted the happily ever after!

When she started college after high school, she promised to devote herself to her studies and not let anyone or anything get in the way. She was going to get her degree, work a couple of years to establish her career, and then find someone, get married, and raise a family in that order! Now, only a couple of months from getting her BA she suddenly finds herself in love with a man who she doesn't know if he wants the same things.

She finished her hot cocoa and decided to get to bed. Maybe she would talk to Sasha about what's happening with her and Mike. Or, she would go and talk to Pastor Kingsley. She was just too tired to think about it anymore. She rinsed her cup out and put it in the dishwasher and went to get ready for bed. Hopefully she would be able to sleep.

Mike walked in the door of his home and felt lost. Here he was in this big beautiful home, and he was completely alone. Before he met Jenna, he never really thought about being alone. He had a busy life. He could take or leave it when it came to relationships. He thought he was happy. He had everything he has ever dreamed about having. After his breakup with Selena, he decided he was through getting close to someone and was never going to do matrimony. Then Jenna walked into the office, and suddenly everything was turned upside down. His attraction to her was over powering. He went into the kitchen and made himself a hot tea. When he finished making it, he sat at the counter and thought about tonight when he held her in his arms. She was soft and wanting. He wanted to possess her with every fiber of his being. Finding out she was still a virgin stunned him. A virgin! He smiled. When it was the right time, and she was sure about what she wanted, he was going to claim her as his own.

The thoughts of making love to her and showing her all the ways they could pleasure each other already had him aroused. He could see her here, living with him, filling the house up with children. Did Jenna want children? He didn't know. He's only known her a little over a week. But he knew in his heart he was falling for her. She was such a caring, loving person. He wanted to get to know every part of her. He wanted to marry her!

Whoa! Did I just think that? Would she even consider marrying me when we've only known each other a short while? Mike, you need to slow down here! He needed to take his time with her and get to know her on every level. He finished his tea and decided to hit the sheets. As if he could even sleep.

Nathan came in through the door of his mother's home. He found Tonya asleep on the couch in the living room. He went to wake her.

"Tonya, wake up." He gave her a little shake. She opened her eyes.

"Nathan you're home. I was waiting up for you. You weren't home when I came in from work. Where have you been?" she asked.

"I was at the restaurant waiting for Mike to leave. It was midnight before he and the new intern left. I was able to take another case and a half of liquor out of the store room. Should be enough to bring the extra money we need to pay off the loan," he said.

"This is going to be it, right? No more stealing. Mark came up to me this evening as he was leaving the restaurant and out of the blue, asked how our mother was doing. Said if there was anything they could do for me, don't hesitate to ask. Oh Nathan! I feel so guilty! We should have never done this. Mark and Mike are two of the best bosses we have ever had! What if we get caught! What will they think of us!"

"Tonya! Slow down! Everything is going to be alright. I promise you, I am done with all this. I will sell the liquor in the morning before I go in to work," he said.

"What about all the past-due bills? How are we going to pay them when all our money is going to the loan shark?" she asked.

"I don't know Tonya," he sighed. "Maybe we could go to the bank and consolidate them down to one payment."

Tonya looked at her brother as if he had grown two heads.

"With our credit history?" she asked. "Not likely."

"Well, it was worth a shot," he said, sounding as down as he felt. "How was mom today?"

"The same, hospice will be here in the morning."

"Okay. It's late, let's get some sleep, sis. Maybe things will look better in the morning." Nathan got up off the couch and headed for his room. Tonya just sat there and couldn't see how things would ever look better in the morning. If anything, she was sure it would be worse!

The next morning, Mark was in the store room doing inventory. He noticed when he took the inventory yesterday morning that there was a case of Bacardi Rum that was at the back of the store room on a shelf, and now it was gone. He decided to finish the rest of the inventory and then he would check the camera feed to see who might have been in here. When he finished, he took the inventory sheets to his office, so he could compare them to the sales. Too bad Jenna wasn't working today. She was good at finding the problem with the liquor theft quickly. *I wonder if Mike had a chance to look at the camera feed from last night.* As he sat down at his desk, he decided he needed to get to work and get to the bottom of all this.

It took him over an hour to see that two bottles of their Crown Royal was missing along with the case of Bacardi. He brought up the app for the security system and took a look. There were the usual bartenders that worked last night going in and out of the store room, but he didn't see any of them take a whole case out. After 10:00, there was no activity.

Huh, Mark said to himself, *I'll wait until Mike comes in and see what time he left the restaurant. Maybe together we can shed some light on the situation.* He went to get the cash trays out of the safe and got started on counting cash and change to get ready for the bank deposit. The morning flew by, and it wasn't long before Mike came into his office.

"Hey bro, how are things going today?" asked Mike.

Mark looked up at his brother, "Have a seat."

Mike sat down in the chair in front of the desk, "You sound pretty grim this morning, what's going on?"

"When I took inventory this morning, I noticed right away that a case of our Bacardi Rum was missing. And then, I caught two bottles of our Crown Royal missing when I compared the reports. What time did you leave last night?"

"Jenna and I left a little after midnight."

"Jenna was with you?" he asked. "Yes, it was after 8:00 when we finished dinner, and I didn't want her to walk home, so I let her use my office to start a paper she needed to have done by tomorrow."

"Did you see anyone around in the parking lot when you left?" Mark asked.

"No, but I'll admit, I wasn't really looking."

"You're in to her, aren't you?"

"I'm afraid so. Even though I've only known her a short time I can't stop thinking about her. I want to be with her every second of every day. I feel lost when she's not around. Do you think this is crazy?" he asked his brother.

"Do you believe in love at first sight? Because I could tell just by watching you with her, that you have fallen, pretty hard, bro, and I'm pretty sure she feels the same way," said Mark.

"I hope so. I found out last night she has never been with a man."

"A virgin, how do you get so lucky?"

Mike chuckled, "I don't know, bro, but I'm going to back off for a bit and give her some time. I want her to be sure before we start a relationship."

"Is it just a relationship you want or do you want the whole enchilada and marry the girl?" he asked.

"I can't believe I am saying this, but I am pretty sure I want the whole enchilada. I can't imagine a life without her."

"Well, for what it's worth, I think you're doing the right thing by giving it some time. Now, getting back to the problem at hand, can you pull up the security app, and let's take a look at the entrance camera at the time you and Jenna left the restaurant. You said it was around midnight?"

"Yes," said Mike. Mike pulled up the app on his phone and took a look. He saw when they came out of the restaurant to go to his car. As he watched the film, a few minutes later a man came up to the door, looked around, put a key in the door and came into the building. It looked like Nathan. Mark looked up at Mike.

"Can you believe this? Our head bartender! Nathan!" exclaimed Mark! "A most trusted employee, stealing from us!"

Mike had a disgusted look when he glanced back at Mark. "No, I can't. Let's take a look at the storeroom camera to make sure." They switched back to the storeroom camera, and there he was, taking the case of Bacardi and then taking the two bottles of Crown Royal out of the storeroom. Mike sits back in his chair and shakes his head. "If, I didn't see this for myself, I would never have believed that it would be Nathan that would steal from us. Let's get a hold of Zack and see how we should approach him without scaring him off."

Mark looked at his brother.

"What about Tonya? Somehow Nathan had a key. I'm guessing they are in this together."

"You're right. I'll get a hold of Zack and see if he has time to come in, or if we should come down to the station." Mark thought about it for a moment.

"Maybe it would be best to meet at the station. We need to devise a plan, so we can get at the truth. After talking with Tonya last night, something isn't right. She told me her mother has been sick for a long time. Call Zack and let's see how we can get to the bottom of all this. I need to finish up these reports and make a bank deposit. Then get back with me."

"Okay, I'll give him a call." Mike got up to leave. "I'll let you know what time, and if you need anything else from me, I will be in my office."

"Thanks Mike, the sooner we find out why Nathan is compelled to steal from us the better."

Mike nodded his head and went to his office. He sat down at his desk. He pulled up Zack's number and pressed the call button. He waited for Zack to answer, but only got his voice mail. He left a message for him to call him as soon as possible. He decided to check Nathan's and Tonya's work schedule to see what day they were both on the schedule. It looked like they were both on for Thursday. *It might be best to have Zack here, then,so we could all sit down in my office to get to the bottom of all this and why.* He sighed and looked out of his office window. He never thought he would ever have a problem with one of his employees of this magnitude, let alone two! He turned back to his computer and pulled up the monthly reports he needed to go over before the auditor came to check to make sure all account receivables were entered correctly while he waited for Zack's call.

Jenna hardly slept last night as she tossed and turned over thoughts of Mike. She really needed to talk to someone. Cuddles, was at the end of her bed sleeping. She must have gotten tired of the bed shaking with Jenna moving around all night. She usually slept right beside her. Jenna got up out of bed and did her morning routine and went into the kitchen. She was surprised to see Sasha in the kitchen making an egg and cheese sandwich.

"Good morning, Sasha, I'm surprised to see you here this morning."

"My class was cancelled for this morning. I just made a fresh pot of coffee. Would you like me to make you a sandwich? You look a little like death warmed over," Sasha said with concern. Jenna went to pour herself a cup of coffee. "That sounds really good. And to go with your comment, I feel like death warmed over. I wasn't able to sleep much last night."

Sasha fixed their sandwiches and poured herself a cup of coffee and sat at the counter with her best friend.

As they ate, Jenna said, "This is really good Sasha, I appreciate this."

"You're welcome, now tell me what's going on," she prodded.

Jenna didn't know where to begin.

"Well, you know, Mike and I have been seeing each other almost since the first day I met him."

"Uh huh, go on," Sasha urged.

"He makes me feel so special Sasha. He's warm and tender. He kisses me with a passion I have never felt before in my life! Last night, when we were together, we almost made love in his office. But when he found out I haven't been with a man, he stopped."

Sasha looked at Jenna shocked!

"Wait a minute. You have never had sex before?"

"I'm a little embarrassed to admit it, but no, I have never had sex before, and quite frankly, I'm a little scared of the whole thing. I've heard you girls talk about it, but I don't really know what it feels like other than when Mike touched me in places that sent me reeling and wanting more."

"Well, I can tell you," Sasha said softly. "The first time can be a little painful. But after that, it can be the most exciting feeling you may ever know. You will know when you are ready to take that first step. When do you see him again?"

"He hasn't texted me yet, but I assume tonight after work. He said he wants to give me time. I already know that I want him desperately, and I've fallen in love with him. Do you think this is too fast? We've only known each other a little over a week!"

Sasha smiled, "Jenna, when I saw you and Mike dancing together at the club, I knew you two were goners. I only hope that one day I will find a man that looks at me the way Mike looks at you."

Jenna sighed, "Thank you, Sasha, it helps to talk about these things."

"You're welcome. Now let's get this mess cleaned up and go for a walk. I could use some sun."

Jenna felt so much better after she talked things through. They hurried and got ready to get out in the beautiful Hawaiian sun.

Mark opened the door to Mike's office. Mike looked up from his computer.

"Hey bro, were you able to get ahold of Zack?"

"Come on in and shut the door." Mark closed the door and sat down in front of Mike's desk. "I wasn't able to get ahold of him. I left a message. He may be out today or working on a case, just waiting for a call back. I checked Nathan and Tonya's schedule, and they are both working Thursday night. What would you think about having Zack here a half hour before they come in, and we bring them into the office and discuss the theft?"

Mark thought a moment.

"Do you think we should wait that long?" he asked.

"Well, I don't think Nathan would be stupid enough to take anymore liquor out of here since last night. And I think it would be better to talk to them both at the same time, so we can get to the bottom of how him getting the key plays into this."

"I think you're right. If it works into Zack's schedule, let's plan on Thursday then," said Mark. "I'm off to make a bank deposit and pick up a few things for the office. Let me know when you here from Zack."

"Will do," said Mike. When his brother left his office, Mike sat back in his chair with his hand on his chin. He hated waiting. He likes to get things done and not leave problems hanging. He could only hope he would hear from Zack soon. He thought of Jenna. She was working at the Bistro tonight. He sent her a text to let her know he would be picking her up. Mike focused back on the reports he was working on and tried to forget the turmoil going through his head. But Jenna, she was always in the back of his mind.

That night, business at the restaurant started out slow, but picked up around 6:00. Mike had his hands full making sure everything was running smoothly. Zack came into the restaurant a little after 6:00. He was a little over six feet tall, black hair that was cut short. His brown eyes shone against his olive skin, but they could look like steel when he was interrogating someone. When he walked in a room, he turned heads. Dressed in dark dress slacks and a light blue shirt with the collar unbuttoned, he was striking. Zack looked around the restaurant and saw Mike with some customers in the bar. He headed in that direction and took a seat at the bar. Nathan came up to him and greeted him.

"What can I get you, Zack?"

"Hey Nathan," he said. "I'll have a Michelob on draft."

"Coming right up!" said Nathan.

When Nathan went to get his beer, Mike came up and sat down beside him.

"Hi, Zack, did you get my message?"

"I did, but I was tied up all day on a case." Nathan came back with his beer and sat it down in front of him.

"Are you going to have something to eat?" asked Mike.

"I was thinking about it," said Zack.

"Let's go over to the booth. I haven't had dinner yet, and we can sit and catch up."

Mike got up and led the way. Zack threw some bills on the bar, grabbed his beer, and followed him to the booth. Tammy, one of their waitresses, came with a couple of menus and asked if she could get them anything. She was a tall slender woman with brown hair and hazel eyes. She wasn't a beauty, but she was pretty in her own special way. Mike knew she had a little girl at home to support. Her husband left her when her little girl was only two.

"Hi Tammy," Mike greeted her with a smile. "Could you bring me a Corona on draft?"

He looked over at Zack.

"Oh, I'm all set."

He gave Tammy a brilliant smile. She blushed and smiled back and went to get Mike's beer. Zack turned to Mike.

"What's going on?"

Mike looked around to make sure no one was listening.

"We know who's been stealing. Mark discovered another case missing plus two other bottles. We watched the camera feed, and it's our head bartender Nathan." Zack looked a little perplexed. "And that's not all, we are pretty sure Tonya is involved."

"Tonya?" Zack felt instantly deflated. He secretly had a crush on her. She was so pretty with her voluptuous curves and gorgeous red hair. She had a smile that sent his heart into overdrive. He didn't even want to think about arresting her.

"Mike are you sure Tonya is involved?" he asked.

"Well, it's not written in stone yet, but somehow, Nathan has a key. Jenna saw Tonya coming out of her office one night and seemed extremely agitated. There was a key in Jenna's desk drawer that was put there when Anna left and it's missing."

Zack shook his head.

"So, what are your thoughts on how you want to proceed?" asked Zack.

Tammy came back with Mike's beer and asked if they would like to order something to eat. Zack looked up at Tammy, "I'll try your fried Halibut and fries."

"Mike?"

"You know, I'll have the same, only bring me a salad with the Hawaiian dressing on the side."

"Did you want another beer, Zack?"

"Yes, a Michelob."

"Thank you, Tammy," said Mike. She smiled, picked up the menus and went to put their order in.

Mike and Zack faced each other. Mike took another look around to make sure no one could over hear. In a low voice, "Hear are my thoughts. Both Tonya and Nathan are working on Thursday night. If it works into your schedule, I would like you to be here a half hour before they are scheduled to come in. I will pull them off the floor and bring them into my office where Mark and you will be waiting. You will have time to review the camera feed before we come in. This way we can talk to them both and get their take on why they needed to steal from us," said Mike.

"Are you thinking about pressing charges?" asked Zack.

"I don't know. We haven't discussed that possibility."

Their food came, and as they started to dig in, a figure caught the corner of Zack's eye. He turned his head and saw a man that the Police Department has tried to indict him on several charges of drug trafficking, loansharking, and he was sure he was connected to several homicides in the city. He owned a prestigious business in downtown Honolulu and worked his criminal business under cover. He was a big man with a balding head and beady black eyes. His name was Marco Manchez. Zack stared at the man as he walked over to their booth with a big breasted woman with blond hair and heavy makeup on, hanging on his arm.

"Detective, I'm surprised to see you here." He gave Zack a steely glare.

"Well, Marco, I do have to eat," said Zack returning his glare.

Mike was watching this exchange with a puzzled look on his face. Marco turned to Mike and put out his hand. Mike got up out of the booth and shook his hand.

"Marco, how are you and your lovely wife doing tonight?"

"Very well, thank you. Do you always allow this trash in your restaurant?"

Mike looked at him in surprise. With his hands on his hips, he said, "Well, Marco, I refer to Zack as a friend and not as trash. He is welcome in my establishment, as well as you and your lovely wife. Let me bring Kalea over to seat you at your table in the Hawaiian Room."

Mike left to get Kalea. Marco's look was threatening as he turned to Zack.

"I am watching you detective."

"As I am you Marco," Zack said with certainty.

Kalea came up behind the couple. "Mr. Manchez, may I show you and your wife to your table?"

He turned to Kalea.

"Yes, Kalea, you may." With one last look at Zack, him and his wife followed Kalea into the Hawaiian Room.

Mike sat down and looked at Zack.

"Do you mind telling me what the hell that was all about?"

"It's a long story. Sometime when we have more time, I will tell you about Mr. Marco Manchez." They finished eating, and Zack took out his phone to check his calendar for Thursday. "It looks like I can be here. What time are the two scheduled to work?"

"One comes in at 3:00 and the other one at 3:30."

"Okay, I will be here at quarter to three. Listen, I need to go. How much do I owe for my meal? It was very good by the way."

"I got this," said Mike.

"Mike, you don't have to do this. I can pay for it."

Mike smiled, "Listen, Mark and I appreciate what you and the police department do for our community. And you certainly don't get the recognition that you and the police force deserve. Let me get this."

They both came up out of the booth. Zack shook Mike's hand.

"Thanks, man, I'll see you later this week."

"That you will," said Mike. Zack took off, and as he was leaving the restaurant, his only thought was how he was going to catch Mr. Marco Manchez and put him behind bars!

The night finally passed, and Mike was on his way to pick up Jenna. He was running a little late, but she said she would wait. He pulled up in front of the Bistro and found her waiting outside. He flew out of the car, came up to her and pulled her in his arms.

"Sorry I'm late, I didn't mean for you to be waiting outside. It's been a hell of a day."

"No worries, I haven't been waiting long."

He gave her a quick kiss and escorted her to his car. On the way to her apartment, they were both quiet. He pulled up to her door and shut the engine off. He turned to look at her and brought his hand up to her pretty face and brushed some strands of hair back behind her ear. Jenna closed her eyes.

"I missed you today my little one," he said gently. Jenna searched his eyes and saw the longing, but she also saw how tired he was. She felt the same. It was a rough night. And with very little sleep last night she was ready to crash.

"You look like you could use a cup of coffee. Would you like to come in? I'll brew us a pot."

"That actually sounds good."

He got out of the car and came around to help Jenna out. Jenna opened the door of her apartment carefully to make sure her cat didn't come running out. As soon as they came in, Mike sat down on her couch while Jenna went and made the coffee. He was so tired. He didn't get a whole lot of sleep after last night. He laid his head back against the couch and closed his eyes. When she came back out to the living room with their coffee, she found Mike asleep. He looked so peaceful. She hated to wake him. She put the mugs of coffee on the table and sat down next to him. He woke and put his arms around her.

"Would you like a sip of your coffee?" she whispered.

"Yes please." She reached down to pick up his coffee mug and handed it to him. He took a sip.

"Good," he said and lay back against the couch. She took his mug from him and put it back on the table. He pulled her closer to him, and she laid her head on his chest. He felt so good. She closed her eyes and fell instantly to sleep.

A short time later, Sasha came in and found Jenna and Mike sound asleep on the couch. She smiled and went to get a blanket. She covered them and they hardly moved. She saw the two mugs of coffee on the table and decided she better take them to the kitchen. She poured out the coffee, rinsed the cups and placed them in the dishwasher. She turned and shut the coffee pot off. As she walked by the sleeping couple, she noticed that they went from a sitting position to lying down with their arms wrapped around each other in the time it took to take care of the mugs. She shook her head, turned out the lights and went to bed.

Chapter 14

Mike was dreaming he was holding Jenna in his arms, and she was brushing her hand over his forehead. She put her hand on his cheek, and it felt a little rough. Actually, it didn't feel like a hand at all. He opened his eyes and the cat from hell was staring down at him with her green eyes full of curiosity. She put her paw out and touched his forehead again. He pushed her off the arm of the sofa and looked around. He barely remembered having some coffee and pulling Jenna close before he crashed into oblivion. He looked at his watch. It was almost 6:00 in the morning! He couldn't believe he slept that long. Jenna was still asleep in his arms. Her soft body was half draped across his, and her hair was all over him as she rested her head on his chest. He took his hand and ran his fingers through her long dark strands and brought it back along her face and neck. She shifted a little and snuggled up closer to his neck. He brought her up and moved her body, so he was on his side and she was crushed between him and the back of the couch. He brought his lips next to hers and began a slow kiss. He knew the instant when she responded, and he deepened the kiss. She started moving her hands over his chest and back. He moaned, as his hands moved over her sweet ass and up around her back and down again. He pulled her shirt up, so he could touch her soft skin. The bra came away, so he could take her firm breast in his hand. Her nipple was already hard from his touch.

Jenna was in a wonderful dream with Mike kissing and touching her in all the right places. She arched her body, so he could have more access to her breasts. He squeezed her right breast and the sensation went throughout her body. She moaned from the pleasure he was giving her. She wanted to give it back. She ran her hand up and under his shirt, so she could explore his muscular chest and run her thumb over his hard nipple. Mike reacted and crushed her to him. He bit her lower lip and worked his tongue inside her mouth. He tasted her and went deeper. Jenna responded, and he was fast losing control. He ran his hand down her side and shifted her so he could unbutton her slacks and get his hand to her center. He sent gentle kisses down her neck as he worked his fingers inside her.

Jenna cried out as she felt her body respond and explode as the climax hit her. He suddenly remembered that Sasha was down the hall and Jenna's cries could wake her. He covered her lips with his to quiet her. He gently removed his hand from her center as he continued to devour her mouth. Suddenly, he lifted his head, his breathing ragged. Jenna wanted to drag him back down to her, but he took her hand from around his neck.

"Jenna, sweetheart, you are driving me mad. I want you more than life itself, but I can't have you here. We seem to always end up on the couch when we're making out."

Jenna searched his eyes and saw the hunger and knew he wanted her as much as she wanted him. She could feel his arousal this close to him.

"Oh, Mike, I want you in the worst way," she whispered. "But you're right, Sasha, could be getting up at any time." She smiled. "Do you know you are very comfortable to sleep on?"

He chuckled, "Did you know you fit perfectly on me?"

She snuggled back onto his chest and sighed. She could stay like this forever. She felt something else coming up on the side of her and sit down. Jenna looked at the same time Mike did. Her cat meowed at them and her green eyes were curious as to what was going on. They both chuckled and Mike reached out to scratch behind her ears. She closed her eyes and bent her head to further enjoy his scratching.

"Sorry, Cuddles, for pushing you off the couch."

Jenna sat up a little. "You pushed my cat off the couch?" A look of shock that he would do that!

"She woke me up with her paw in my face, and it took me by surprise! But look at her. I'm making it up to her right now." That he was. Her cat was enjoying every minute of it. Jenna lay back down on his chest.

"I suppose we should get up," she said. "I'll make us a pot of coffee and some breakfast before you have to go."

"As much as I would like nothing better than to hold you like this all day, I suppose we should." Mike sat up and pulled Jenna up. Cuddles jumped off the couch and headed for the kitchen. They got up, and Mike buttoned her slacks back up and straightened her shirt. They both needed to use the bathroom and headed that way.

Jenna decided to get out of her work clothes and put on her yoga capris and a clean t-shirt. She said the heck with the bra and did her morning routine then headed back to the kitchen. She had an extra toothbrush and toothpaste for Mike if he wanted to use it. When she came in, he already had the coffee going. He gave her a slow appraisal as she walked up to him and gave him a quick kiss.

"I brought you a toothbrush if you would like to use it."

"Umm, in a minute," he noticed she ditched the bra. He put his hands on her sides and drew the shirt up over her breasts. He stood and admired those pretty full breasts and rosebud nipples that fit perfectly in his hands.

"Mike, Sasha could walk in any minute."

He sighed. Pulled her close and gave her a sweet kiss. He lifted his head, pulled her shirt back down and asked, "Where's the toothbrush?"

"I put it in the half bath for you."

He gave her a quick kiss. "I'll be right back."

Jenna went to get a couple of mugs out of the cupboard and poured them each a cup of coffee. She was putting cream and sugar for her when Mike came back into the kitchen. She put cream in his coffee and handed it to him. They both took a sip.

"This is good, Mike, thank you for making it."

As he looked at her, his smile reached up to his eyes, "You're welcome little one."

"Would you like scrambled eggs and bacon for breakfast?"

"That would be perfect. What can I do to help?"

"How are you at frying bacon?" she asked.

"I'm the best bacon fryer this side of the island!" He stood with his arms up showing off those nice muscles of his and a silly grin on his face. She laughed.

She set about getting the frying pans out and went to get the bacon out of the fridge. She handed it to him and went to get what she needed. She scrambled up enough eggs for the three of them and started the toast while Mike finished up the bacon.

"Good morning you two," Sasha said as she entered the kitchen. They both turned and said good morning back. "Something smells really good!" she said.

"We're making scrambled eggs and bacon. It will be ready in just a few minutes. Coffee's ready if you would like a cup," said Jenna.

"Thanks, I could really use a cup!"

While Sasha went to get her coffee, Mike and Jenna put everything out on the table. They picked up their mugs and sat down at the table. Jenna said grace.

"Everything looks delicious!" said Sasha. Jenna smiled. They helped themselves and began eating. "Who cooked the bacon?"

"Mike."

Sasha looked at Mike and smiled, "Great job!"

He smiled back and looked over at Jenna, "See, I told you I was the best bacon fryer this side of the island!" They all laughed. "Hey Sasha, what are you majoring in?" asked Mike.

"After I finish my undergraduate degree, I will go on to graduate school and then on to medical school. I plan on being a doctor specializing in natural healing. I want to stay away from prescription drugs as much as possible."

"Wow, how long will it take to complete your studies?" he asked.

"Ten years total."

"That's a long time, but when you finish, I will be your first patient," he said smiling. He glanced at Jenna and gave her a wink.

"Jenna tells me you love to body surf," Sasha said to Mike.

"And she is absolutely right. I took it up when I was in the service and fell in love with it. I'm usually out on the waves two to three times a week, but something else has taken up my time lately." He looked over at Jenna and gave her another wink. Jenna blushed.

"Did you ever compete in the body surfing competitions?" asked Sasha.

"No, I never really had time to compete. I just enjoy being out there in the waves."

They finished eating, and Mike got up from the table and brought the coffee pot over and filled their coffee cups.

"You make a great waiter!" Jenna smiled up at him.

"I've had a lot of practice. What time is your class this morning?" he asked Jenna.

"Nine o'clock, speaking of which I will need to get ready soon."

She gave Mike a longing look. She wanted this to last. Mike caught her gaze, and the thought of leaving her made his insides hurt. Sasha felt like she needed to excuse herself and leave them alone.

"Well, you two, I need to get ready for my class that starts at 8:30." She picked up her dishes and put them in the sink.

"Just leave those Sasha, I'll help Jenna with the dishes before I leave," said Mike.

"Okay, I'll just go and get ready."

Jenna was still watching Mike. He sat the coffee pot down on the counter and pulled her up out of her chair. She went willingly into his arms, and when her lips touched his, she was lost; lost to the feelings he stirred inside of her. The passion he brought out of her. The love that was growing with each day she spent with him. Mike knew he shouldn't be kissing her again. It was getting harder to leave her. He wanted to hold her and love her till he was spent. He finally broke the kiss and reached up to put his hands on the sides of her face and then gently ran his fingers through her hair.

He gazed into her eyes, "Well, little one, I think we better work on getting this mess cleaned up, so you can get ready for your class, and I can go home and take a shower."

"Will I see you this afternoon?" she whispered.

"You can count on it," he smiled. He gave her a quick kiss. They gathered up the dishes and cleaned up the kitchen. After he said goodbye, Jenna went in her room to get ready for her class.

The morning flew by, and she was walking up to the restaurant. She let herself in with the key Mike had given her. The kitchen lights were on and she thought Mark would be in the storeroom taking inventory. She went to let him know that she was here.

"Mark? Are you here?" Mark came out of the storeroom followed by Palani.

"Oh, I thought I heard two voices," said Jenna.

"Hi, Jenna," said Palani, "it's nice to see you again."

"You too! I enjoyed your Hawaiian steak the other night. It was very good. And the cheeseburger I had on Monday, were the best!" exclaimed Jenna.

"Thank you, but I still need to fix you something special. Will you be here for dinner tonight?"

"I'm not sure, but I will let you know later on."

"Please do," he said. Jenna looked at Mark.

"I'm headed to the office. Is there anything in particular you would like me to focus on today?"

"Yes, but I will be heading that way as soon as I finish here and I will get you started."

"Okay, boss!" she chuckled and went to her office. Mark watched her leave. Today Jenna looked pretty in her black dress jeans and light blue blouse that fit her perfectly. *Mike is one lucky guy,* Mark thought.

Jenna unlocked her office and sat down at her desk. She opened her computer and waited for Mark to come in and let her know what he wanted her to work on today. A few minutes later, Mark walked in.

"Hey Jenna, have you ever requisitioned a bank statement?" he asked.

"Yes, I do it all the time with my own, but I've only done a mock business bank statement in class. Should be pretty easy."

"I have the last two months that need to be done. If you could work on those today that would help me out," he said. He showed her how to get into the bank statements, and then the reports she would need to correlate to the bank statement. "Let me know if you have any problems or questions. It can be overwhelming the first time you do one."

She looked at her screen and felt she could handle it.

"I will let you know, Mark, if I have any issues."

"Okay, I'll leave you to it," and he went to his office.

Jenna pulled up the first bank statement. *Wow,* she thought, *This is a little more than what I did in class.* She decided to print off the report and then match the debits and credits with what was entered on the bank statement. This one statement took her over three hours! She was surprised that it balanced. There was so much information here. She decided she needed to get up and walk after sitting so long. She printed the reports out for Mark, signed out, and went out into the restaurant to the restroom. She was just freshening up and was ready to head back to her office when Kalea stepped in.

"Oh, Kalea, how are you?" Jenna said with a smile.

"Fine," Kalea said curtly. Jenna wondered what she ever did to this woman who has been rude to her ever since her first day at the restaurant. "I see you and Mike are getting a little chummy lately."

Well, if looks could kill...

"I beg your pardon?" asked Jenna. "Look, I just want to warn you that Mike loves to start a relationship with women, and after he grows tired of them, he drops them and goes on to his next conquest. I've seen him do it over and over again."

"Well, for your FYI," Jenna said just as curtly. She wasn't going to let this woman intimidate her. "Mike and I are just friends, and if we do decide to have a relationship, I'm sure it will last more than a few months!"

"I hope you're right, Jenna, because if you're not, you are in for one big surprise!" With that, Kalea opened the door and stomped out.

Jenna stood there, not knowing what to think. She looked at herself and saw the color had drained from her face. Was Mike only trying to get what he wanted? What if and when she gave herself over to him, it wasn't good enough? Would he just leave? She wanted to think they had something different, something solid they were creating together. Now, she didn't know. She was so insecure when it came to men that it left her doubting her feelings for Mike. Was it all about sex? Is that what all this chemistry was about between the two of them? She got herself under control and went back to the office.

Mike came into Mark's office and asked if he had seen Jenna.

Mark looked up, "She wasn't in her office?"

"No," said Mike.

"She must have stepped out for a minute. I'm sure she'll be back. Did Zack ever get back to you?"

"Oh, sorry, bro, I meant to text you. Zack came in and had dinner last night. He said he would be here on Thursday at quarter to 3:00. I sat and had dinner with him when Marco Manchez came in with his wife. He walked up to our table and you could feel the tension between him and Zack."

"I wonder why? He has an established business in downtown Honolulu."

"I don't know. He said it was a long story." Mark shrugged his shoulders, "It's not our concern."

"You're right. I'm going to check on Jenna." He left Mark's office and found Jenna at her desk. "There you are, my little one!" he said smiling down at her. "I've been looking for you."

Mike knew the instant she looked up at him that something was wrong. She sat back in her chair and crossed her arms.

"Have you? Is this all a game to you Mike?" Mike went and shut the door to her office. He came back and crossed his arms and stood looking down at her.

"What are you talking about?" he asked.

"You, me, us." she answered curtly. "When you get what you want are you going to up and leave just like all the others?" she asked sarcastically.

Mike had no idea where this was coming from, but he had his suspicions. Mike leaned down and put his hands on the desk. She saw anger in his expression.

"Who has been talking to you?" Jenna was a little taken aback. She had never seen him angry. "I, uh, ran into Kalea in the restroom." He raised himself back up. He thought it might be her. She has had a crush on him since day one. She has been shooting daggers at Jenna ever since she arrived. Mike walked around the desk, pulled Jenna out of her chair, sat down with her in his arms. She struggled to get free. He tightened his hold on her.

"Jenna, you are going to listen to me."

"Maybe I don't want to listen," she said angrily. He took her chin and turned her face towards him, "Please."

His deep blue eyes pleaded with her. As she looked at him, she started to relax.

"Okay, explain." He sighed. He didn't know where to start, so he started at the beginning.

"When I was in high school, I fell in love with a girl who was one year younger than me. We were very close all of my senior year. When I enlisted into the Air Force, we wrote back and forth for a year. When I came home from leave, we couldn't stand to be apart. She graduated and went off to college, and the letters became less frequent. I was starting to get anxious about the thought of losing her. When I got the Dear John letter from her, I sort of lost it. My brother, Mark, and my buddies in the service helped me to see she wasn't worth it. 'There are lots of women in the sea,' they would say. I swore I would never let another woman take my heart. So, I dated a lot of women, and yes, I had relationships with some of them. But then you walked in the office that first day and turned my life inside out. I have never felt what I feel for you, with any woman, not even my first love. You, Jenna Hathaway, make me feel." He brushed his hand over her face and ran his fingers through her hair and held her while he bent his head and showed her just how much she meant to him. Jenna returned his kiss and felt the tears sliding down her cheeks. When he raised his head, "What's this?" he brushed the tears from her face.

"I'm so sorry, it seems if I'm not laughing, I am always crying when I am with you."

He smiled and laid her head on his chest and held her for a while. She sat up and looked directly into his eyes, "Thank you for sharing. Kalea made it sound like this is what you do on a regular basis."

"Kalea has had a crush on me since she started here. Mark and I do not date employees. Our relationship is strictly business." he said. "Now, my sweetheart, is there anything else you want to know?"

She loved it when he called her that, especially when they were making out. She smiled and thought for a moment.

"What is your favorite color?" she asked. He laughed and hugged her tight.

"Yellow, what's yours?"

"Blue, like your eyes," she said. He gave her a quick kiss.

"Okay, little one, I need to let you get back to work or Mark will have both our heads!" She got up off his lap and he came out of her chair. He placed his hands on her waist and pulled her close, "Will you have dinner with me tonight?"

She smiled up at him, "I will, but it might be a while. I'm working on this last bank statement. It took me three hours on the first one!"

He chuckled, "Okay, I'll let you get to it."

As he was leaving her office, "Mike?"

He turned back toward her, "Yes?"

"Don't fire her."

He smiled and walked out the door.

It was after 6:00 when she finished the requisition. She printed out the reports and put them in a folder for Mark. She walked to his office but found the door locked. She took the reports back to her office and locked them in a file drawer. She locked her office and went in search of Mike.

She looked out over the restaurant and found him seating a group of people into the Lanai. Mark was at the hostess station getting ready to seat a group as well. She had awful feeling he let Kalea go. Oh, she didn't want him to do that! She wasn't sure what she should do. She went into the bar area and took a seat at the bar. She remembered meeting Todd, one of the bartenders who came up to her and asked if she wanted anything to drink.

"I'll have a glass of white Mascato."

"Sure thing, I'll be right back with your wine."

She looked around for Mike but didn't see him. He must be with some customers, she thought. A very good-looking man came up to the bar and sat next to her. Todd set her glass of wine down in front of her and turned to the man.

"Hi Zack! What can I get you?"

"Just a Mick on draft," he said.

When Todd left to go get his beer, Jenna turned to the man and asked, "Are you Detective Williams?"

Zack looked at the very attractive woman sitting beside him and wondered if he could land a date with her. She had beautiful brown eyes and a perfect figure, what he could see of it sitting in a bar stool.

"Yes, and you are?" he asked giving her his look that drew most women in. He was very charming Jenna thought. I bet he could have just about any woman he chose.

She put her hand out to shake, "I'm Jenna Hathaway."

Well, that totally deflated him, Mike's woman. He shook hands with her, and he could see why Mike was so in to her. Mike came up behind Jenna and put his hands on her shoulders. Jenna placed a hand on one of his and smiled up at him. She gave his hand a squeeze when she saw the look on his face when he looked at Zack.

"I see you have met Zack," Mike said curtly.

"Yes, I caught his name when Todd got his beer and connected him to the detective you and Mark are working with. I felt I should introduce myself."

Zack took a drink of his beer and looked up at Mike.

"You have a very charming woman here, Mike. I am totally jealous!"

Mike had a sly glint in his eyes when he replied, "She is more than just charming, she is incredible in all the right ways."

Jenna gave his hand another squeeze only this time a little harder. Mike got the hint. He smiled back at his friend.

"Jenna and I are just about to have dinner. Would you like to join us?"

Zack looked surprised by the offer.

"Not on your life!" he answered with a grin on his face.

Mike bent down to Zack's shoulder and said so only he could hear, "Smart man!" Mike gazed down at Jenna, "I have a table out in the lanai for us."

She picked up her glass of wine and slid out of the bar stool and turned back to Zack, "It was very nice meeting you, Zack," she said smiling.

"Same here," he said. Zack watched them go into the lanai. Yep, she was put together in all the right places. Mike was one lucky guy. He finished his beer, threw some bills on the bar and left.

Mike pulled out Jenna's chair for her and sat down across from her. Carol came up to them and asked if she could get them something to drink. Mike looked at Jenna.

"I will have a glass of water with lemon, please."

"Just a coffee with cream," said Mike.

When she left to get their drinks, Jenna took a sip of her wine and wanted to know what happened to Kalea.

"Mike, I haven't seen Kalea, you didn't fire her, did you?"

He shrugged his shoulders. "She quit!"

"Mike, I didn't mean for this to happen. I never should have told you it was Kalea."

"I didn't give you a choice. I had a talk with her about interfering in relationships. She exploded on me and walked out. End of story," he said irritably. "As far as I'm concerned, it's for the best."

Jenna sighed, "I feel bad that it came to this."

"Jenna," he said calmly. "An employee is supposed to be loyal and not make problems for others. She should not have come to you and discussed my private life. I realize it was done out of jealousy, but it was still wrong."

Carol came back with their drinks and asked if they would like to order something to eat.

"Thank you, Carol, but Palani is making our dinner. He should be bringing it out shortly. But could you bring out some dinner rolls with some cinnamon butter for us?"

"Sure thing," she said. "I'll be right back with them."

Jenna looked at Mike and realized he did the right thing by confronting her.

"You're right, now I understand why she was so rude to me whenever I approached her."

"I noticed her reaction to you as well." Mike reflected on his talk with Kalea. When he approached her, she was shocked that Jenna said something to him. When he told her he forced it out of her because Jenna was so upset, she went off on him and told him she quit and was never coming in this restaurant again! When he asked her for the key to the restaurant, she stormed into the locker room, came out and threw the key at him.

"You have a nice life, Mike!" Then she left. Actually, Mike was relieved she was gone. It wasn't the first time she tried to interfere with one or two of his relationships.

Mike looked over at Jenna. He could see the concern over Kalea leaving was upsetting her.

"Let's not let this spoil our dinner. What's done is done. And it wasn't your fault. So put that out of your pretty head."

"But won't her being gone put extra work on you and Mark?" she asked. "Yes, for a little while. But we'll hire and train someone. It's part of owning a restaurant. It's nothing we haven't dealt with before," he said. "If there is anything I can do, or even come in and help when I can just let me know," she said with sincerity. Mike's eyes softened as he took in this incredible woman who has so much on her plate already.

"Thank you, I'm sure we will be fine. You have enough to do."

"Just know that I am here if you need me."

Mike got that glint in his eyes and a smile spread across that handsome face of his.

"Oh, I need you, but in a much different way. Soon my little one you will satisfy this need I have for you." Jenna blushed.

Thankfully, Palani came out with their dinner followed by Carol. Palani set two main dishes in front of Mike and her. It looked delicious! Sitting on a bed of cooked cabbage leaves was a mound of Kalua pork. He turned to Carol, and she handed him the side dishes. He placed cooked rice and pineapple wedges next to the main course. Jenna looked up at Palani.

"Palani, it looks wonderful."

Palani smiled down at her, "This is one of Hawaii's traditional cuisines, enjoy. I will be back later with your dessert."

After he left, she looked over at Mike. He had been watching her exchange with his head chef.

"What?" she asked.

He smiled and gazed at her lovingly.

"Nothing, let's eat."

Jenna tasted her pork. It was so tender it almost melted in her mouth.

"Mmm, this is so good!" She looked up at Mike. He hadn't touched his food and was still watching her. "What?" she asked again.

He chuckled, "You're adorable, did you know that?"

She didn't know what brought all this on. She laughed, which showed in her eyes as she leaned forward, "Of course!"

He laughed with her and dug into his pork. As they were eating, she asked, "How do they make this dish in the restaurant? I heard it's usually prepared in an imu."

Jenna had never been to a luau, where they prepare the pig and bake it underground for up to nine hours.

"Yes, traditionally it is baked in an imu, but we don't have the space for a pit large enough to roast a full-size pig. So Palani lays the butt roast on foil, prepares it with some Hawaiian salt and smoke sauce, wraps the foil around it and places it in a deep roasting pan. He cooks it in a slow oven for eight to nine hours. You can easily get the same results with this method as with the imu. Have you ever been to a luau?" he asked.

"No, I've never been. I've wanted to go, but could never find the time."

"One day, I will take you to one. They are quite entertaining."

"When I graduate in June, I would love to go."

He paused, laid his fork down and asked, "What are your plans after you graduate?"

She looked into his blue eyes, "Well, I hope to get a full-time job in an accounting firm," she answered. "Will it be here on the island?"

"I like it here, so I would definitely look here first."

"What about marriage and a family?" He knew he was asking her a lot of questions, but he had to know what her thoughts were on having children. Something he never even considered, but looking at Jenna, he suddenly had a desire for having lots of them.

"Yes, someday I want to marry and would like children, but when I started college, my focus was to finish and start a career before I married."

He gazed intently at her. As she returned his gaze, suddenly her plans she set for her life didn't seem as important to her. She loved this man, and if he asked her to marry him, she would in an instant.

"How about you?" she asked. "What are your thoughts on marriage and children?"

"To be honest, I never even thought about it until now." Carol came up to their table and asked how everything was. "It's great Carol." He looked over at Jenna. "Would you care for anything else, Jenna?"

"Yes." She looked up at Carol, "A cup of coffee with cream please."

When she left, they finished up with the main course and Jenna felt she couldn't eat another bite. Carol brought her coffee to her and refilled Mike's. She removed the empty plates from the table and hurried off to the kitchen.

"I don't know about you Mike, but I don't think I have room for dessert."

"You will break Palani's heart if you don't try his dessert that he will be bringing out shortly."

"Well, I wouldn't want to do that!" She took a sip of her coffee and looked around the lanai. It was getting dark, and the bus boy was lighting the tiki torches. The soft glow from the light was relaxing and the warm breeze from the ocean brushed across her arms. A slow song was playing through the speakers. Mike got up and stretched out his hand to her.

"Dance with me."

"Out here?"

"It's my restaurant. I can do whatever I want. Dance with me."

She took his hand, came up from the table and into his arms. Mike held her close as they moved to the music. Jenna felt relaxed in his arms as she laid her head on his chest. The music stopped, and Mike took his hand from hers and placed it under her chin. He lifted her head as he bent down to give her a gentle kiss. They were interrupted when Palani brought out their dessert.

Mike broke the kiss and whispered, "There will be more of this later."

"Hmm, I can't wait." They sat back down at the table and Palani set two slices of what appeared to be chocolate pie with whip cream and little bits of pineapple sprinkled on top. "Oh my gosh! Palani! I love chocolate pie!"

"Well, this is different. It's called Haupie pie. It is made with coconut milk and cocoa. It's a real treat here on the island."

"Thank you, Palani. It looks delicious! And your Kalua pork was excellent!"

"Thank you! Enjoy." He bowed, turned back and headed for the kitchen.

Jenna took a bite of her pie and closed her eyes, "Oh my, this is heavenly."

"Palani makes the best Haupie pie. Customers rave over it."

"I can see why," she said. They finished their pie and Carol brought over some more coffee. "Will you need to close tonight? I see Mark is still here."

"Do you need to get home?" he asked.

"I really should. There are some things to get done at the apartment, and I want to get up early to go jogging. As much food as I have had tonight, I feel like I've gained five pounds."

Mike chuckled, "Let me go see what Mark wants to do, he normally doesn't work on Wednesday nights, so he might want get out of here." He got up and went to find his brother. He found him at the bar talking to Todd.

"Hey bro, would you mind if I run Jenna home?"

"No, I don't mind. Listen, it's almost closing time, I'll close. You and Jenna go and enjoy the rest of your evening."

"Are you sure?" asked Mike.

"I got this. Go on and get out of here."

Mike grinned. "Thanks, bro, I owe you one." Mike caught up with Carol and paid their bill. He went back out into the lanai only to find Jenna wasn't there. His heart stopped. Where was she?

"Are you looking for me?" He turned around and caught her smile. He smiled back and let out a breath.

"I am. Mark said he would close, so if you're ready to go, I'll take you home."

"I just need to get my purse out of office." They walked back to the office and Jenna hurried and picked up her purse and re-locked her office. She just remembered something she needed to tell Mark. She looked up at Mike, "Can we stop and let Mark know that his bank requisitions are in my desk file drawer?"

"Sure."

They found Mark and let him know where to find the reports, and they were soon on their way to her apartment.

When they arrived, Mike killed the engine. Jenna looked over at Mike as he turned to her.

"What does your day look like tomorrow?" she asked.

"Normally it's my day off, but I will need to go in and make some changes to the schedule to accommodate Kalea leaving. I haven't told you yet, but we found out who has been taking liquor out of the storeroom."

"Who is it?"

"Nathan," he said.

"Nathan? Are you sure?"

"Mark found another case of liquor taken plus two other bottles Tuesday morning. We checked the camera feed and saw Nathan come into the building after we left Monday night. The storeroom camera was further proof it was him. I have Zack coming in tomorrow afternoon just before they come in and we will get to the bottom of why he needed to steal from us. Tonya will also be brought in at the same time due to the missing key."

"Oh Mike, you and Mark have your hands full. Are you thinking about prosecuting?"

"We haven't discussed it yet. We just want to know why at this point. Then we'll go from there. There will have to be some kind of restitution."

She put her hand on his arm. "Again, if you and Mark need me to help, till you figure this all out, just let me know."

Mike took her hand and placed it in his.

"Thanks little one. I appreciate the offer. Now, let's get you inside." Mike came around the car and helped Jenna out. Jenna let them into her apartment mindful of Cuddles. Mike shut the door behind them and instantly pulled her in his arms. He needed to hold her and kiss those sweet lips. Jenna pulled him closer. As the kiss grew more demanding, Jenna wrapped her arms around his neck and held on. A sound came from beside them.

"Hey if you two need to get a room, the bedroom is that way!"

Jenna broke away from Mike and was embarrassed to see Sasha standing there.

"Sorry, Sasha, I wasn't sure you were home."

"Well, here I am!"

"Hey," said Mike, "I need to get going anyway. It was good seeing you again, Sasha." Mike took her hand and led her back towards the door. "I will see you tomorrow night after work."

"Mike, you don't have to...." She let the sentence fall. One look and she knew she wasn't going to get anywhere with him. "Okay, I'll see you tomorrow night." He gave her a quick kiss, opened the door and left.

Jenna closed the door and looked at Sasha.

"Sorry."

"Hey you have nothing to be sorry about. I can see you are one step away from falling into bed with him."

"You know I would never have sex in the apartment. We made that rule in the beginning. When he kisses me, I seem to lose all control of myself." Sasha watched her friend and knew her feelings for Mike were all new to her. She went and gave Jenna a big hug.

"No worries." She looked at her friend and wiggled her eyebrows. "You know, he has that big beautiful home that would be perfect for your first time!"

"Sasha!" she laughed. "You know, you're right! Let's go make a cup of hot cocoa and relax before we go to bed."

"Sounds like a plan!" They made their cocoa and sat on the couch to catch up on each other's lives. A couple of hours later, Jenna said goodnight to her friend and went to bed. When she laid her head down on her pillow, do you think she could sleep? She tossed and turned most of the night, thinking about Mike and what he and his brother were going to face tomorrow. She wished with all her heart she could hold him and tell him whatever they decide it would all work out. She finally fell asleep in the early morning hours only to awake several hours later.

On his way home Mike was disappointed that their time together was cut short. It seemed his need for her only gets stronger with each passing day. It was good to know that she wanted marriage and a family, but could he wait till she was able to get established in her career? It seemed like a long time to him. He would marry her tomorrow if he could. He shook his head and smiled. He had to wonder how he got from not wanting to marry to wanting it so badly. In his heart, he knew. He was so in love with Jenna that he thought he would burst. Tomorrow is going to be a hard one for him and his brother. His main focus was to get at the truth and then they would go from there. Tomorrow couldn't come soon enough.

Chapter 15

*J*enna pulled herself out of bed. She couldn't get back to sleep, so she might as well get up. She went into the kitchen and made herself a pot of coffee. It was after 8:00, and she must have got, what, four hours sleep? Hopefully this coffee would revive her. She knew Sasha had an early morning class and was already gone for the day. Her cat came into the kitchen and wanted to be fed. She fixed her up with her favorite cat food and settled down at the counter to enjoy her coffee. Today, Mike and Mark were going to confront Nathan and Tonya. She worried over the outcome. *I know our Lord says not to worry about what we face in life and trust Him, but sometimes it was hard, especially when you care about the people you love.* She sent up a prayer for things to work out for everyone concerned. She got up and made herself some toast and decided she would go for that jog this morning.

When she left, she felt compelled to follow the trail to Hanauma Bay. When she approached the Bay, she saw him, sitting on a beach towel looking out over the blue waters of the Pacific Ocean. He was still wet from coming in from the surf. She walked up and placed a hand on his shoulder. He jumped and looked up at the same time. When he saw who it was, he relaxed and smiled up at her.

"Hi," she smiled back. "May I join you?"

He reached up for her hand, "Please." He pulled her down next to him and put his arm around her. He was a little wet but she didn't care. She took her shoes off and put her feet in the warm white sand. "What brings you out this way, my little one?"

"I had this urge to take the trail here. I was hoping I would find you here. We didn't have much time together after we arrived back at my apartment." He pulled her closer to him. He brought his hand up to her soft face and gave her a tender kiss. She could taste the salt from the ocean on his lips.

When he lifted his head, he said, "Maybe we can make up for it this morning."

"Hmm, I'd like that." He kissed her again with more passion this time. She put her arm up around his neck and placed her hand behind his head and drew him closer to her. She didn't want to let go of this moment. When he lifted his head, they were both breathing hard. Mike's heart was racing. He wanted this woman, and not just for sex; he wanted all of her. Her wants, her dreams. "Come back to the house with me."

The passion in his eyes sent chills down her spine. She wanted more than anything to give him the pleasure he was seeking.

"Okay," she whispered. Jenna brushed off the sand and put her shoes back on. Mike put his sandals on and shook out the beach towel. He took her hand and they walked to his home. "Do you have any thoughts about today?" she asked.

"I'm trying to wrap my brain around all of it. I honestly don't know until Mark and I talk to them. Then we will make our decision."

"Well, for what it's worth I sent up a prayer for everything to work out as it should."

He stopped and faced her.

"Thank you, Jenna. I haven't prayed in a long time. That means a lot to me." He gave her a sweet kiss. He took her hand, and it wasn't long before they reached his home. He opened the door for her and they went inside. He closed the door and turned to her. "I'm going to take a quick shower to rinse the salt off, and I'll be right back."

"Would you like me to put coffee on?" she asked.

"That would be great!" When he left, she hurried and put coffee grounds and water in the coffee maker and pushed start. Then went in to the hall bathroom and freshened up a bit. She hurried back out and took a seat at the counter while she waited for Mike.

When he came out to the kitchen, he was dress in only his shorts. She was glad she was sitting down! Looking at his broad tan chest and his hair still wet from his shower sent butterflies right down to her center. She watched him get two mugs out of the cupboard and fill them with coffee. He knew what she liked and preceded to fix her coffee and his. He handed her the mug and came around and sat next to her. She took a sip, "Hmm, just right." He smiled and took a drink of his own coffee.

"Jenna, may I ask you something?"

"Sure, what would you like to know?" When she looked into his blue eyes, she could see concern there. "What do you see in your near future?" he asked. She thought she might have answered that question last night, but thought she might know what he was getting at.

"I see a very tall handsome man with sandy blond hair and incredible blue eyes, living together, maybe having a couple of kids, letting me work in the career I majored in. How about you? What do you feel is in the near future for you?"

"I see a beautiful brunette, with big brown eyes, the perfect figure, living together in my home, maybe having a bunch of kids, standing by my side through thick and thin, loving each other till death do us part." Wow, she could see in his eyes he meant every word. "Do you think we are going too fast?" she asked. He took her hands in his and looked deep into her eyes. "Jenna, I've fallen for you in a big way. Maybe it is a little fast, but I know what I feel."

"I've fallen for you, too, Mike, but I'm scared. I have never felt this way with any man. I hadn't really even kissed a man until I met you." Mike got out of his chair and lifted Jenna in his arms and carried her back to his bedroom. He gently laid her on his bed. With the hunger, passion, and love all rolled into one in his eyes, she knew she wasn't going to resist him.

"Sweetheart, let me show you what it will be like between us." She held out her arms and he gladly went into them. He started with her lips, and worked his way over to that sensitive spot behind her ear. She moaned. Mike traveled down her neck and kissed her breasts through her shirt. He slid his hands underneath and pulled the shirt up over her head and unclasped her bra. He gently removed it and caressed each one of her beautiful breasts, then bent down and suckled each one until Jenna cried out. Jenna was lost to the magic he created inside her. Mike was working his hands on her body. He removed her shorts and panties with one swift move. Jenna was a little shy as he admired every part of her body while his hands caressed every inch of her. Jenna started to get a little bolder and moved her hands over his chest and back down to his waist. Mike brought his hand down to her center and started to work his fingers inside her. Jenna moved with the pace he was keeping and cried out when she climaxed. Mike took off his shorts and boxers and slid on a condom. He spread her legs and eased into her.

"Sweetheart, this first time may hurt, I will try and make it easy for you."

She gazed into his incredible blue eyes and nodded her head.

"Okay, I'm ready, just show me what you want me to do, so I can give you the same pleasure." He slowly eased into her giving her time to adjust. She was so tight. He had never taken a virgin before. With one quick thrust, he went deep inside her. Jenna cried out and arched her body.

"Oh baby, I'm sorry," he whispered. He kissed her until she relaxed. "I promise you will only feel pleasure from now on." When he started to move, she moved with him. Jenna's hands moved up and down his back, hips, and chest. Mike thought he was going to lose control but held on until he could bring Jenna with him.

He was right, all Jenna could feel was a mind-blowing explosion deep within her as he moved slowly inside her. She dug her nails into his back and bit his shoulder trying to hang on a little longer. She cried out, "Mike!"

"Sweetheart, stay with me just a little longer." He kissed her neck and traveled up to her lips. He traced his tongue over her lower lip and she opened for him. He went in and their tongues tangled. Her taste was intoxicating. He went deep inside her and increased his pace. Jenna had never experienced an orgasm. She held on till she knew she couldn't.

"Mike please!" she cried. Mike lost all control and took them both on a ride to supreme ecstasy! Mike shuddered and came down on Jenna before he could relax. They were both sweating from the experience. Mike came up on his arms and brushed the hair from her face. He gently kissed her, "Jenna, my love, you have given me the most incredible gift a man could ever want."

She gazed into his eyes, "I never knew it could ever be like this. It was so powerful." She started to caress his chest, arms, back, and down over his hips. She came around and felt where they were one and Mike could feel himself getting hard again. She saw the smoldering fire in his eyes as he started to move inside her again. He brought them both up to an earth-shattering orgasm that left them both exhausted. This last time, he watched Jenna and saw all the emotions cross over her face, and it was mind blowing. He has never experienced anything like this before in his life. This feeling of being fulfilled! The awesome power of becoming one with her! He lifted his head and took a deep breath. He smiled down at her and gave her a quick kiss.

"I need to get up and get rid of this condom. Don't move." When he got up to take care of himself, Jenna thought she couldn't move even if she wanted to. Mike was an excellent lover. He sent her skyrocketing into a kaleidoscope of bursting color that she could have never imagined in her wildest dreams. Mike came back to bed and pulled down the covers. He helped Jenna get under them and he snuggled down underneath pulling her close to him. They had a few hours before they needed to go to work. Mike closed his eyes. He was content to just lay here and hold her in his arms.

"Mike?"

"What my love?"

She had to ask, "Did I please you?"

Mike pulled her even closer to him, "Oh, Jenna, sweetheart, more than you will ever know."

When she looked up at him, he gave her a sweet kiss. She laid her head on his chest and felt her eyes getting heavy.

"Does having sex make you sleepy?"

Mike chuckled, "Yes, my love."

It wasn't long before they had both fallen asleep.

Jenna woke up with a start. She was still in Mike's arms, and he was watching her.

"Oh, my gosh! What time is it?"

Mike checked his watch, "It's quarter to two."

"Mike, I have to go!"

She tried to get up but he pulled her back down and placed her on top of him with her legs straddling him. With a grin, he said to her, "Did you know that you snore?"

"What! I do not snore!"

He laughed, "Oh, yes, you do, my little one."

She tried to get up off of him, but he held her. His hands started to move relentlessly over her body, and she relaxed as she let the feelings engulf her. He reached over for a condom and slipped it on. He lifted her and eased into her. They both started moving together, and it wasn't long before they exploded on another orgasm. Jenna came down and put her head on Mike's chest.

"Will it always be like this between us?"

He knew the answer as sure as he knew his own heart.

"Yes, my love, it will. Now as much as I would like to take you again, we must get up. Do you want to take a shower before you go?"

"I think that might be a good idea." That way she could change into her work clothes when she got home.

She eased off of him and gathered her clothes and headed for the shower. She turned on the water, and when it was warm, she walked in. *Wow! This is huge!* Mike happened to have one of those rain showerheads, and it was heavenly. She felt a warm body move in next to her. Mike took the soap and started to lather her body. When he finished, he gave her the soap, and she did the same for him. He kissed her under the shower. When he broke the kiss, they both rinsed off. Mike tuned the water off and pulled a towel off the shower stall and toweled her dry. His gentle rubbing was erotic to her skin. He handed her the towel when he was done, and she dried him off. He bent and kissed her again and pressed her body to him. Mike wanted to take her again. He couldn't get enough of her. He knew they didn't have the time. He was already late going into the restaurant. He lifted his head and held her tight.

"We are going to have to continue this later my little one."

Jenna looking up with longing in her eyes wanting more than anything to stay with him and forget about the world. Mike sighed and pulled away from her. "Come on, before I change my mind and have you right here."

When they were dressed, Jenna decided to jog it back because it would be faster. She would have just enough time to change and head to the Bistro. She gave him a quick kiss and told him she would see him tonight.

Back at her apartment, she hurried to change. She took a quick look in the mirror to see if she looked any different. After all, losing her virginity was a big deal to her. She came to the conclusion that she didn't look any different other than she was a little sore. Mike was quite the lover! She grinned, gathered up her things, made sure her cat was taken care of, and headed out to the Bistro.

Mike was so late. He rushed into Mark's office only to find him not there. Then he remembered they were to meet in his office. He went directly in and both Mark and Zack were there studying the camera feed. Mark and Zack both looked up as Mike came in through the door.

"Where the hell have you been, Mike? I expected you here around 2:00."

"Sorry, something came up that I needed to take care of."

Mike sat down and glanced over at Zack. He was still a little pissed at him for flirting with Jenna. As of this morning, she was officially his and only his. He knew he was going to have to let it go. They needed Zack on this case. "After looking at the camera feed, what action do you think we should take once we bring them in to question them?"

Zack studied Mike. He sensed he was still upset with him when he came on to his woman. He would settle this misunderstanding later. Now down to business.

"I see from the feed that it is indeed Nathan. Whether Tonya is involved is yet to be determined. Depending on their story, it will be up to you and Mark to decide if you want to press charges. When you bring them back, let me do the questioning."

"Okay." He turned to his brother. "Did you happen to rework the schedule for tonight?"

"I did. I called in Cindy to hostess tonight in Kalea's place. She's had some experience in the past in that position. She was glad to help out."

"Good, we'll post the opening for the hostess position on the board first to see if anyone is interested, before I run an ad." He checked the time. "Both of them should be here, so I will go and get them and be right back."

When he left, Mark glanced at Zack.

"I feel some tension between you and Mike."

Zack looked surprised. He didn't think he gave off any bad vibes.

"What makes you say that?"

"Mike and I have this telepathy. Being identical, we feel each other's emotions. When Mike broke his leg playing football, I felt the same pain he did until the leg was set. I couldn't walk on that leg for hours."

"Man, I never knew that happened between twins," he said.

"So, what's got him all riled up at you?" asked Mark.

"Well, if you must know, I accidentally made a pass at Jenna last night not knowing who she was at the time."

Mark chuckled, "He's a little possessive when it comes to her. He'll get over it."

Just then, the door opened and Nathan, Tonya, and Mike walked in.

Mark and Zack greeted the two.

"Have a seat," said Mark. Mike notice Mark had already brought in extra chairs, so they were all able to sit down. "I suppose you are wondering what we have called you both into the office for." Mark had a steel look in his eyes as he glanced from Nathan to Tonya. His brother could be a bad ass when he wanted to. Tonya sat ridged in her chair while Nathan was nervous as a cat.

"Did we do something wrong?" asked Nathan.

"I want to show you something and then you can tell me."

Mark pulled up the app on his phone and started the film. He then gave it to Nathan to look at. The color drained from Nathan as he saw himself taking the case of liquor out of the storeroom. He showed it to Tonya and she thought she was going to pass out.

"Is that you Nathan?" asked Zack. Zack watched them both and knew this is not what they had expected when they came in here.

"Yes."

"We know you had a key to get in. How were you able to come across one?"

Tonya knew that they were sunk. Tears came rolling down her face, "I'm so sorry. I took the key out of your intern's office and gave the key to Nathan."

Nathan took control of the situation. He didn't want his step-sister going to jail.

"Listen. Don't put any of the blame on Tonya. I asked her to see if she could find a key. This was all my doing. If anybody goes to jail, I want it to be me."

"Well, that may be what will happen," said Zack. "But I'm pretty sure your employers want to know why you two would do such a thing." Mark handed Tonya a tissue. Nathan turned to his stepsister, and she nodded her head. He took a deep breath. "Our mom has been sick for a long time. She has cancer, and we recently called in hospice. They told us she may only have a week."

"Wait a minute," said Mike. "You and Tonya are brother and sister?"

"Stepbrother and -sister. We have the same mom, different father."

"Well, that explains why I never would have caught the connection when I did the background check," he said exasperated.

"We still need to know why you and Tonya chose to steal the liquor from here. My guess is you sold it?" Zack asked sternly.

"Yes, but keep Tonya out of this. To back up a bit, between our checks and mom's social security, we didn't have enough money to pay all of mom's medical bills. We were feeling kind of low one night and decided to go have a drink at a local bar in downtown Honolulu to discuss what we could do to make some extra money to pay the bills," Nathan explained.

"So that's when you decided to steal from your employers and turn around and sell it!" Zack said in a raised voice.

"No! Not at first!" Tonya's phone kept vibrating in her pocket, but she was afraid to get up and answer it. She hoped their mom was okay.

Nathan continued, "A guy came up to us, said he heard us talk about needing money, said that his boss could help us out and could give us a loan to pay off the medical bills. He asked how much we needed, and he said he could have it for us the next day. So, we met him outside the same bar that afternoon. We signed a simple contract and he gave us the $1000 we needed. Told us we could make payments. The next thing we knew, every time we made a payment, he upped the interest. He made it impossible to make the payments on time. That's when I started taking the liquor out of the restaurant and selling it. This was going to be the last time I swear."

"So you borrowed money from a loan shark?" asked Zack.

"Yes."

"How much do you owe him?"

"It's now $2000. We paid the principal back but we now owe that again and an extra $1,000!"

"Do you know who the loan shark is?" Zack asked in anticipation. He prayed it was Manchez. He wanted to nail that guy.

"No, but his thug's name is Ralph."

Zack got up and started pacing. Tonya's phone was still vibrating. She was just about to excuse herself when there was a knock on the door.

"Come in," said Mike.

The door opened and Cindy came in.

"I hate to interrupt, but Sonya has been trying to get a hold of Tonya. It's your mom. You need to go home now." Tonya started to sway, and Zack came around the desk and caught her just before she hit the floor. He put her head between her knees to bring her out of the fainting spell. She came to, and tears poured down her cheeks. He wanted to hold her but knew he couldn't. Mark looked at his brother. He nodded. "You two get going. We will discuss this at another time. But know you are not out of the woods on this matter."

Nathan helped his sister up, and they left the office.

Mike saw the concerned look on Zack's face when he caught Tonya before she fell. He wondered if there wasn't something there between the two.

"What do you think, Mike?" asked Mark.

"I'm having a rough time with it! I wonder why they just couldn't come to us. We would have given them the loan and not charged them interest."

Zack put his foot up on the chair and leaned his arm on his leg, glancing both at Mark and Mike.

"It's hard for an employee to go to their employer to ask for money. It can be an embarrassment for them. But whatever the reason, they borrowed from a loan shark. They can get rough when it comes to getting their money. Some have even been killed over it.

We need to be on the alert for anyone looking for them. My guess is he will come to the back of the restaurant."

Both Mike and Mark leaned forward.

"Are you serious?" Mike asked with concern.

"I'm very serious. You asked me the other night about Manchez. The Police Department has been trying to put him behind bars for drug trafficking, loan sharking, and we are pretty sure he's connected to some homicides in the city, all under the cover of his business down town. We've been trailing him for a while now. He covers his tracks. Usually works through his thugs. When we get close, they usually end up dead behind an alley," explained Zack.

"Well, that's just great Zack! This man and his wife have been coming into our restaurant on a regular basis. I never would have suspected him of these crimes!" exclaimed Mike.

"Mike, you need to calm down," said Mark.

"Mark, we now have God knows who, coming to our restaurant to collect his money from two of our employees! I don't want something to happen to them or God forbid any of our other employees, and we don't even know when he will show up!"

"Mike." Mike turned to Zack. He could see the anger and worry when he looked at him.

"The police department and I are going to get to the bottom of this. I'm not sure what your decision is going to be as far as prosecuting Nathan and Tonya, but I need to talk to them further to get a description of this Ralph character and when they are to meet with him next. Can you give me addresses and phone numbers, and I will get right on it tomorrow. With what's happening with their mom I don't want to upset them further."

"I agree," said Mark. "I'll get their employment papers for you."

There was another knock on the door.

"Come in," Mike said curtly. Cindy stepped in.

"I hate to bother you again, but I have been on the phone trying to reach Todd and Bill to see if they could fill in for Nathan with no luck. Also, we are short a hostess. It's starting to get busy out there. What do you want me to do?"

Mark looked at Mike.

"Oh no, Mark I haven't bar backed since I worked at the Officer's Club!"

"You are the only choice. I don't know a damned thing about mixing drinks!" he exclaimed. "Cindy, tell Jeff Mike will be out shortly, and I will be out to help you as soon as I get some paperwork for Detective Williams."

When she left, Mike stood up and put his hands on his hips and gave his brother a glare that even hell would freeze over!

"Oh, this should be good, bro! Hopefully I won't wind up poisoning our customers!" Mike took off his suit coat and threw it over the back of the chair and stormed out of the office. Mark glanced at Zack and got a shit ass grin on his face, "This should be good!"

"I'll be sure to sit at the bar and harass him before I leave," he chuckled. Mark went to get the paperwork for Zack. He put it in a folder and handed it to him.

"I'll put this in my car and be right back. I can't wait to see this!" They both left the office laughing.

Mark got started helping Cindy seat customers. He glanced over at Mike, who looked pretty good behind the bar. There were already a couple of women sitting at the bar, eyeing him. He grinned and got to work.

When Mike came behind the bar, he rolled up his sleeves and had Jeff give him a quick rundown of where everything was located. He was a little nervous at first but found it all came back to him pretty quickly. There were a couple of young women at the bar laughing and ogling him. *I certainly don't need this tonight,* he thought. He sent Jeff over to wait on them while he waited on two couples seated at the far end of the bar. He put their drinks together and took their cash. *Now what?* He's never worked the cash register behind the bar. This was totally different than the main register. He called Jeff over to show him how it was done. He heard a voice behind him, "Having fun, bro?"

He turned and glared at his brother as he laughed and walked away to greet some more customers. He saw Zack sitting at the bar next to the two women. He had a grin on his face as he yelled, "Hey bartender! I need a drink over here!"

Mike put the cash in the drawer and gave the change to the couples. Mike walked up to Zack with a sly grin. *Two can play this game...* He leaned down and placed his arms on the bar,

"What can I get you Detective Williams?" He gave him a name of some weird beer. Mike yelled down to Jeff.

"Hey Jeff, do we have any Snicker Doddle beer?" Jeff looked at him like he was nuts and shook his head no. Mike turned back to Zack.

"Nope, don't have that brand."

Zack burst out laughing.

"I'll have a Mick on draft, and whatever these two lovely ladies would like." Zack looked over at them and saw they were staring at Mike. Oh, brother, he could always get the women. Mike turned to the ladies who were actually quite attractive, but not as beautiful as his Jenna.

"What can I get for you lovely ladies tonight?"

"I'll have another glass of Chablis," she said giggling.

"I'd like a Royal Crown and seven," said the other one.

"Coming right up," he said. Mike went to get their drinks. When he set them down, Zack took out his wallet. Mike shook his head, "I started a tab for you. Did you want to order something to eat?"

"In a little bit, I'll just enjoy my beer," said Zack. Mike glanced out over the restaurant and saw Marco and his wife at the hostess station waiting to be seated.

"Don't look now," Mike said in a low voice, "But Manchez and his wife just walked in."

Mark came up and greeted Marco and his wife. Knowing the information that Zack had given him and his brother tonight left him feeling a little uncomfortable. He tried to be nonchalant.

"Good evening, Marco. How are you and your lovely wife doing tonight?"

"Fine, fine, what's Mike doing behind the bar?" Marco was looking over at Mike. Good thing he knew how to tell them apart. He caught himself several times mistaking one for the other.

"Oh," Mark glanced over at the bar, "We had two people call in sick tonight. It happens. He's just helping out," he chuckled, "He hasn't bar backed since he worked at the Officer's Club. He looks pretty good back there, don't you think?"

Marco chuckled, "Indeed!"

"Would you like a table in the Hawaiian Room?" asked Mark.

"Perfect." Mark led them to a secluded table that he knew they enjoyed. "Enjoy your meal."

"Thank you. Say, Mark. Have Mike make our drinks."

"Sure, what would you like?"

"I will have an Old Fashioned made with Crown Royal, and my wife will have a dry Martini."

"I'll be right back."

Mike was busy getting drinks ready for one of the waitresses. Mark came up to the bar and motioned to Mike. Mike walked over to his brother, "What's up?"

"Marco wants you to make his drinks."

Mike shrugged, "What are they having?"

"Old Fashioned with Crown Royal and a dry Martini."

"As soon as I get this order ready, I'll bring it right out."

"Just so we are on the same page, I told him two employees called in sick." Mike gave his brother a thumbs-up and went back to work. He finished up the order and made Marco's drinks. He put them on a tray and told Jeff he'd be right back.

When he placed the drinks in front of Marco and his wife he said, "Good evening Marco, Millie. It's been a while since I made these, how about giving them a taste to make sure their right."

They took a sip.

"Excellent!" said Marco.

"Yes, very good Mike," Millie smiled.

"I heard about your dilemma. So, you bar backed at the Officer's Club."

"It was a long time ago, when I was in the service. But I'm finding it's all coming back."

"Yes, as I can see in these drinks you made."

"I don't mean to cut this short, but I need to get back or Jeff will have my head," said Mike grinning.

"Enjoy your dinner."

"Thank you, I'm sure we will." Mike turned and walked back to the bar. Even though they were regular customers of his, after talking with Zack this afternoon, he needed to find more about what Manchez did in the business world. If he needed to go behind bars, then somehow, he would help to make that happen.

The night flew by. People were still in the bar, including the two women he served earlier. Mike told Jeff he was on his own the rest of the night and went to find Mark. He found him sitting with some customers out in the lanai.

"Sorry to interrupt," he looked at his brother, "I need to leave. Can you handle things till I get back?" he asked.

"Of course!" said Mark.

"Thanks.

Mike arrived at the Bistro just before they closed. He was starving. He saw Jenna wiping down the counter.

"May I get some service around here?" Jenna whirled around to see Mike grinning at her.

"Hey there, you're early."

"I had to get out of the restaurant. What can you make me that would be quick and simple?"

"Hmm, how about a Hawaiian pizza?" she asked.

"Perfect. What time are you going to be finished?"

"I was just about to text you, should be done in 15 minutes. I'll put your order in to go if you like."

"That would be great, Jenna."

"Would you like coffee while you wait?" she asked.

"Please."

"Have a seat and I'll bring it over." He took a seat in one of the booths by the window. Jenna brought his coffee and set it down in front of him. "You look like you've been put through the ringer. Is everything okay?"

He sighed, "It's been a night. You know we called Nathan and Tonya in."

She sat down across from him.

"Yes, how did it go?" she asked.

"They admitted to stealing the liquor. They are also involved with a loan shark."

"A loan shark! That could be dangerous. I've heard they can be brutal when they don't get their money on time."

"Zack informed us of the same. While we were in the meeting, Nathan and Tonya had to leave. Their mother is dying of cancer. So, nothing has been resolved." he said. Jenna looked puzzled.

"How are they related?"

"Stepbrother and -sister," he said.

"That must be really hard on the both of them. It wouldn't be easy to lose a parent."

"No, it wouldn't. I don't know, Jenna, we are at a standstill. Zack is going to try and find out when they are supposed to meet up with one of the loan shark's thugs. I'm telling you this because I want you to be aware, if someone comes around the restaurant that looks suspicious or is looking for them. This needs to be kept strictly confidential until we can get this resolved."

"I understand."

One of her co-workers brought Mike's pizza out. Mike took his wallet out and paid her.

"Keep the change," he said with a smile. "Let me see if anything else needs to be done and clock out. I'll be right back." Five minutes later she was ready to leave.

On the ride to her apartment, Jenna asked, "If Nathan and Tonya's mother dies, will you need help while they're gone?"

"When I get back to the restaurant, I'll check the schedule to see who I can bring in to help out this weekend. I know where you are going. We will be fine. You are working to much as it is," he said sternly.

"Okay, but if you find you are short staffed after making phone calls, I'm here." Mike took a deep breath.

"Jenna, sweetheart, you are one of a kind." He pulled up in front of her apartment. When he walked her to her door, he took her hands in his. "I have to go, but I want you to know our time together this morning meant a lot to me."

He gazed at her with longing as he lifted her hands and kissed each one. Jenna blushed as she thought about this morning and her giving herself to this man.

"Are you sure you can't come in and at least eat your pizza?"

"No, I must get back. Mark and I need to talk. Will I see you tomorrow?"

"If I get a chance, I'll come by the restaurant," she said smiling up at him.

"I'll look forward to seeing you my love."

He placed her arms up around his neck and pulled her close. When his lips covered hers, he gave in to the passion and desire he felt for this woman. Jenna's body pulsed with desire as she returned his kiss. She couldn't believe after this morning that she was ready to make love to him again. She wanted him so badly. When they broke apart, they were both breathing hard, hearts beating wildly. His eyes blazed with wanting her.

"I need to let you go, or I will never leave."

"Be careful," she said. He gave her one last kiss and headed for his car. As he pulled out onto the main road, his thoughts turned back to how his brother and he were going to deal with the problems they are facing with the two employees involved and a loan shark!

Chapter 16

Mike walked into the restaurant and found Mark sitting at the bar drinking a beer.

"Hey, do you want to share a pizza with me?" Mark turned to his brother.

"Oh man would I ever! I'm starving!"

"Let me go warm this up, and I'll be right out."

Mike saw his brother come in from locking the door when he came back from the kitchen. The last of their customers had left. Jeff was still cleaning up. He sat their pizza in one of the booths and went to grab two beers out of the cooler and some napkins. When he sat down, he opened the box and they both dug in.

"Thanks, bro, this is really good. I didn't have a chance to eat a bite all night. Is this from the Bistro where Jenna works?"

"Yes, you have her to thank for suggesting it."

They ate their pizza and drank their beers in silence. Jeff came up and said goodnight.

After they finished, Mike asked, "What do you think we should do about Nathan and Tonya?"

Mark leaned over, his arms on the table.

"At first, I felt we should prosecute. After thinking about it, I don't think that is the way we should go. It was still wrong to take the liquor, and there needs to be restitution, but sending them to jail isn't the answer."

"I have to agree. But my concern is we are not only dealing with theft, but them borrowing money with a loan shark. If Manchez is involved with loaning money and charging astronomical interest, then we need to help put him behind bars. Have you heard what business he's into at his downtown location?" asked Mike.

"Your guess is as good as mine. I have never asked him what he did for a living. He always comes off as a successful businessman."

"Me either. I guess this is going to be a waiting game. Waiting for Tonya and Nathan to get back to us about their mom, and Zack getting more information on them, and you know how I hate to wait."

"Yes, bro, I do. What do you say we close up this place and head home? We can't do much else tonight. Zack should have some information for us tomorrow."

"You're right, bro, no sense stewing about it," he said. Mark always had a way in calming him down when he was frustrated or stressed out. They both got up and worked together to close out the two main registers. They locked the cash and reports in the safe, checked the dining areas and kitchen, and it wasn't long before they were on their way home.

In the little house on Koiolu Street, Nathan and Tonya sat on each side of the bed, each holding their mother's hands. Hospice just left and said it could be any day now. Her breathing was very shallow. Tonya squeezed her hand and she shifted a little. She barely opened her eyes as she tried to speak. She looked over at Nathan and was trying to tell him something.

"Pa...pers," Ruthann barely got it out.

"Mom don't try to talk, everything is going to be fine."

"Pa...pers." Nathan shook his head at Tonya. He didn't understand. Tonya leaned down close to her mom.

"Mom, what are you trying to tell us?" She turned her head towards Tonya's voice.

"Papers in desk," she said faintly. Tonya could barely hear her. She closed her eyes.

"Try to rest, Mom."

Ruthann drifted off.

"Could you understand her?" asked Nathan.

"She didn't make much sense, something about the desk," replied Tonya.

"Have you thought about how we are going to pay for mom's funeral?" asked Tonya.

"I have no idea. I'm not sure she has a life insurance policy. I know Dad did. Mom used it to take care of Dad's funeral expenses. I have no idea if any money was left over. Mom was pretty private about it," he sighed.

"She was never the same after Dad died. We seemed to have lost them both that day. Let's try and get some sleep. It's going to be a long night," said Tonya.

The next morning, hospice arrived to check on Ruthann. Friends stopped by to bring a favorite dish for them and to see how Ruthann was doing. Neither one felt like eating but appreciated how everyone came together to care for them.

The nurse came out of Ruthann's room after checking her vitals. She approached Nathan.

"Your mother hasn't got long. She has no vital signs, and her heart rate is very faint and rapid. You both need to go in and say goodbye."

Nathan and Tonya approached Ruthann's bed. With tears in their eyes, both Nathan and Tonya bent and gave their mom a kiss on the cheek. Tonya moved her head by her mom's ear,

"Mom, it's time to go home to be with Dad. Nate and I will be just fine."

At that time, Ruthann breathed her last breath. Nate and Tonya hugged and cried over their mother's passing. The nurse came in and confirmed Ruthann had passed. She came up to Nate and Tonya and sighed, "So sorry for your loss. I did not know her very long, but could tell she was a warm, loving woman. She had a long battle and now she is at peace. Let me know if there is anything else I could do for you both."

"Thank you Nancy," said Nathan. "Both Tonya and I appreciate all you have done for our mom."

Nate went and called the funeral home. While they waited, both of them sat by their mom's side until they arrived. When they took her body from the home, Tonya burst into tears as she felt the loss of her mother. Nate held her with tears of his own.

"We'll get through this, sis. Somehow we'll get through this together."

Mike got out of bed the next morning and felt like he had been hit by a semi. He hadn't slept much the last two nights, and his body was screaming at him. It was still early, and he tried to go back to sleep but to no avail. He decided to get up and make coffee.

Once the coffee was made, he sat down at the counter and tried to come to grips with what was going on at his and his brother's restaurant. He hated waiting. He wanted to get this resolved. Just then his phone rang. It was his brother.

"Hey bro, what's up?"

"I just got a phone call from Nathan, their mother just past an hour ago. They are meeting with the funeral director this afternoon to make the arrangements. They asked to be off until after the funeral was over. You'll need to re-arrange the schedule until they get back," said Mark.

"Do you know what day the funeral will take place?"

"Not until they talk to the funeral director. He said he would call back and let us know the details."

"Okay, I'll be into the restaurant by 2:00 and start working out the schedule," said Mike.

"Right, I will see you there."

Mike decided he would work out to relieve some of the tension in his body. He had set up a weight room in one of the spare bedrooms. As he lifted the weights, he could feel the release. When he was done, he jumped in the shower and felt a lot better.

When he looked at the clock, it was almost noon. Mike fixed himself a sandwich and pulled a coke out of the fridge. As he ate his sandwich, he thought about yesterday morning when he and Jenna made love. He never felt anything this powerful in his life! He missed her. He picked up his phone and sent a text to her.

I miss you.

It wasn't long before he received a text back:

I miss you too!

He smiled and sent back:

See you tonight?

Have a lot of catching up to do at home, but will try to come in some time tonight.

Can't wait.

Mike got up and cleaned up the kitchen. He decided he would get dressed and go in to work. He suddenly hated being here alone. He wanted her with him for all time. Another thought occurred to him. Once he married her, would she want to bring the cat from hell with her? He thought he knew the answer to that question. He'd better get used to having a pet around. He shook his head as he headed to his bedroom.

You're getting way ahead of yourself Mike. You haven't even asked her to marry you yet!

When he was dressed and heading out the door, he decided to visit a little shop in downtown Honolulu before he went into the restaurant.

After class, Jenna came home to start catching up with homework for the class she was taking. She was a little behind after spending so much time with Mike this week. She smiled when she received the text he sent her. She thought about their lovemaking yesterday morning. Actually, she had thought of nothing else but being in his arms. She shivered. He was such an experienced lover. Remembering how his hands caressed her body and him inside her sent her hormones into overdrive again! She shook herself.

Jenna, you need to focus and get this done!

She worked on her paper for the next couple of hours. When she finished, she cleaned up the apartment and played with Cuddles for a little while. She looked at the clock. It was almost five. She wanted to see Mike. She went to her bedroom and pulled out a pretty floral dress out of her closet. She quickly showered and dressed. The dress fit her body to a tee and hung down just above her knee. The floral colors looked pretty against her tanned skin. There was a small slit in the back of the dress that showed off her pretty legs when she walked. She decided on her wedge sandals as they were the most comfortable. Just in case they needed help tonight. She knew Mike would never ask her, but she could always offer. She put on a little makeup and fixed her hair, and she was ready to go.

She arrived at the restaurant around 6:30. The place was packed. People were waiting in line to be seated. She could see Mark and one of the other hostesses running around, but she didn't see Mike. She looked over in the bar area, and there he was. Behind the bar was the most heart stopping man she has ever met. He wore a white dress shirt with his sleeves rolled up, his shirt collar unbuttoned, and it looked like he hadn't shaved this morning except around his cheeks and neck. The lighting over the bar enhanced the highlights in his hair from the sun. He was busy mixing drinks and conversing with the customers. She hoped she wasn't drooling all over the place.

"Hi Jenna!" She jumped to see Zack standing next to her. He smiled, "He looks pretty good back there, doesn't he?" He noticed when he came in, she couldn't stop staring at him. She nodded her head yes. "Hey, it looks like there are two chairs available at the bar. Let's go give him a hard time."

They moved towards the bar chairs; at the same moment, Mike saw Jenna with Zack coming up behind her. Zack had a smile on his face as he watched the emotions cross over Mike's face. First, he looked in awe when he first saw Jenna. Then when he saw Zack, he looked as if he could murder him at any moment.

Jenna and Zack took the two chairs at the bar. Jenna couldn't stop looking at him. She needed to snap out of it. He came up to her and he saw she only had eyes for him. He leaned down on the bar with his lips just inches from her.

He grinned, "Hi sweetheart, you look gorgeous tonight. What can I get you?"

She swallowed, "You."

"If you don't stop looking at me with longing in those beautiful brown eyes of yours, I am going to haul you over this bar, take you back to my office, and have my way with you," he said seductively. Jenna felt the tingles going throughout her body. This man could turn her to mush when he looked at her that way.

She smiled demurely and asked, "When?"

He chuckled and bent to give her a seductive kiss. When he broke the kiss, his eyes were blazing.

"Soon," he said.

She heard someone at the bar yell, "Get a room already!"

Jenna looked around and was embarrassed to see people were watching their exchange.

"I'll have a glass of white Mascato please."

He turned and smiled at his friend.

"Zack, what can I get for you?" *Other than a punch in the face...* He was so jealous. He didn't like the idea of Zack sitting next to his woman.

"I'll have my usual." *Man,* thought Zack, *he is not a happy camper.*

He leaned down with his arm on the bar and looked him straight in the eyes and said quite loudly, "Oh, you mean that Snicker Doodle beer you wanted last night? Sorry, we still don't have that brand."

Zack fired back, "Well, if I can't have my favorite beer, then give me a Mick on draft!"

Jenna, watching the two, knew something was going on. She jumped in, "Is there really a Snicker Doodle beer because I would really like to try that!" The two men looked at her like she had two heads. "What?" she asked.

They burst out laughing at the expression on her face. Mike went to get their drinks and placed them in front of them. Jeff was giving him the eye.

"I'll be back in a bit."

Jenna looked around the bar and across to the hostess station. People were still lined up out to the door. As she sipped her wine, she wondered if there was anything she could do to help. Zack was talking to a gentleman seated next to him. She touched his arm and told him to tell Mike she would be back in a little bit. She couldn't just sit here and watch Mike throughout the night all hot and sexy, it would drive her crazy! She slid off the stool and went to see what she could do to help.

Jenna caught up with Mark, "Hey Mark, is there anything I can do to help out? You look like you and your hostess could use some." Mark smiled. *They looked so much alike,* Jenna thought.

"Hi, Jenna. I would love some help, but Mike will have my head if he sees you out here working."

"Well, Mike will just have to deal. What can I do to help?"

He grinned, "Mike is going to ream me out good, but I could sure use the help. Okay, can you go check the Hawaiian Room and see if any tables are available and report back to me?"

"Sure."

She went to check the dining room and found they were just clearing off three tables in one of the pagodas. She went back to Mark and told him what was available. Some customers were asking for more coffee, so she took the coffee around and filled all their cups. She was busy going from the Hawaiian Room to the lanai helping out where she could. The time seemed to fly. A customer asked if she could get him a drink. She hesitated. She didn't know if she wanted to confront Mike with a drink order. She noticed him watching her as she went from one room to the other all night. She would ask Jeff.

"What would you like?" He gave her his drink order. She went up to the bar to ask Jeff if he could fix it for her. While she waited, she looked around the bar and didn't see Mike. Whew, maybe she was safe. He didn't look happy when he glanced at her throughout the night.

"Jenna!" She jumped. She turned around to a pair of angry eyes and a grim look. "What do you think you are doing?"

Well, she was not going to stand here and let him preach to her about what she should do and not do!

"Listen, Mike, I saw that you were shorthanded, and I went to your brother and offered to help. Now if that bothers you, I'm sorry, but I am not going to stop!" With that she took the drink that Jeff made for her and went back to the customer who ordered it. Mike stood there for a moment and stared after her. She could be a little firecracker when she wanted to be. He got a gleam in his eyes. He kinda liked that in her. He watched her hips going back and forth with determination. He took a deep breath and couldn't wait for the night to end. He had plans with that high spirited brunette. He'd make sure he sent them both soaring before the night was through! He went back behind the bar and wished he could close the restaurant and get the hell out. He hated waiting!

Jenna was a little peeved at Mike. She loved him, but she didn't want to be controlled. She had a mind of her own. She would make that clear after they closed the restaurant and she could talk to him. Mark came up to her a little while later.

"Thanks, Jenna, I really appreciated your help tonight. Mike wasn't able to bring any extra help in tonight. They all had plans. But we are all set for the rest of the week until Nate and Tonya can come back to work."

"Did their mother pass?"

"Yes, this morning. The funeral is set for Wednesday at 11:00."

"Are you and Mark planning on attending?"

"One of us will be there. I'm not sure which one of us it will be until we check our schedules."

"If there is anything I can do for them, maybe make a dish for them to eat, please let me know," she said sincerely.

"I sure will, Jenna, but I have a feeling it's going to take more than that," he sighed. She watched him leave to go attend to some customers and wondered what he meant.

The night was fast coming to an end and customers were leaving. Mike came up to her and told her he had something to eat for them and his brother. He bent down and gave her a wink.

"Your favorite. Cheeseburgers!"

She smiled up at him, "Lead the way!"

Mike motioned to his brother. He took them to the booth where the food was waiting. Mark and Jenna took a seat.

"What would you like to drink?"

"Just a Coke, Mike," said Jenna.

"A beer," said Mark. Mike went and grabbed two beers and a Coke out of the cooler and slid in next to Jenna. They were all hungry after the night they put in. There wasn't much said until all the food was gone.

"Oh that was good! Thank you!" she said.

"You're welcome little one." He leaned down and gave her a quick kiss.

"Why don't you two go and get out of here. I can close up." Mike looked at his brother. He looked tired. He hasn't taken his usual day off, for a while now. "What would you say to let's closing up the restaurant together? You have put in some long weeks here lately since we found the theft. Better yet, Jenna and I will close the restaurant."

"Thanks, bro, but I'll stay and help. It will go faster."

Mike looked at Jenna and smiled.

"Just tell me what to do."

They got up from the table. Jenna picked up the dishes and put them in the kitchen. When she came back, Mike showed her how to cash out the registers. She gave the trays and receipts to Mark to put in the safe while Mike went and checked the dining rooms to make sure they were set up for tomorrow and turned the lights out. It wasn't long before they were ready to leave.

As they were walking out the door, Mark asked, "Hey Mike, I saw Zack sitting at the bar, was he able to find out any more about the case?"

Mike shook his head, "No, he said with Nathan and Tonya having to deal with the funeral arrangements, he didn't think it appropriate to interrogate them, so, he said he would get with them before the funeral to see what he could find out."

"Okay, drive safe going home," said Mark.

"Thanks, you too, bro!" said Mike.

Mike took Jenna's hand and led her to his corvette. As they headed to her apartment, Mike got a vibe that he was in trouble. She was a little distant towards him since she reared up and let him have it!

"I sense something is bothering you little one, tell me what it is." As if he didn't know.

She looked over at him. This may be their first real argument.

"Mike, you know I care for you deeply, but I don't want to be with someone who wants to control my life."

Mike gripped the wheel till his knuckles showed white, he hadn't expected that.

"Okay, how am I controlling you?"

"I understand when I asked you if you needed any help, you kept insisting that you and Mark would be fine. But when I came to the restaurant tonight and you were behind the bar—that left me all hot and bothered by the way—and Mark running around like a crazy man, I felt I should go and offer my help. I noticed that you were not happy about it, and when you came up to me and asked me what I was doing I got defensive. I like helping, and I don't want to be told that I can't."

Mike relaxed a little. He took a deep breath.

"Jenna, I don't want you to ever think that I would control you. I wouldn't. It's just that you work so hard and have very little time to enjoy yourself. I wanted you to relax and have fun. Maybe I'm a little selfish. I wanted you to be near me. When I saw you working, I was angry." He pulled up in front of her apartment and cut the engine. He turned and caught her eyes in the dim light. "I'm sorry. I did not mean to come off as controlling. Will you forgive me?"

When she gazed into his eyes, she knew she would forgive him. How could she not?

"Yes, I forgive you. Maybe I overreacted just a bit." She reached out and put her hand along his cheek. It felt rough against her hand. He took her hand in his and kissed her palm. He bent to give her a tender kiss that soon turned into hard and passionate. He lifted his head.

"Come home with me." Jenna sat back in her seat. She had never stayed with a man overnight. "I won't do anything you don't want me to. I just want to hold you. I sleep better when you are with me." She was having a hard time with this. How many other women had he ask to come home with him? Mike could see the emotions running across her face. "Jenna, if you're wondering if I have brought other women to my home, the answer is no. You are the only one I want in my home."

She searched his eyes. *How did he know...?* she wondered. "Okay, just let me get a few things and make sure Cuddles is taken care of."

When they entered her apartment, Mike sat down on the couch and waited while Jenna went to change and put some things together. The cat from hell came waltzing out of the kitchen and jumped up on the couch. Mike and the cat had a stare down until Cuddles decided it was okay to crawl up on his lap. He started to very carefully pet the top of her head and down her back.

"You know, you are going to have to get used to me because I am going to be around a lot. One day, you may be moving in with me, so we need to get along." She meowed at him and lay down fully across his lap. He continued to pet her as she began her soft purring.

"Are you talking to my cat?" Mike turned and noticed she had changed into a faded pair of skinny jeans and a deep blue t-shirt.

"Yes, Cuddles and I have had a nice conversation. Haven't we, Cuddles?" Jenna sat down next to him. "I need to get her fed and the litter box cleaned, and I'll be ready to go. Sasha isn't home, so I'll leave a note for her as well. Be right back." Jenna got up and took care of everything that needed to be done. She came back out and could see her cat was still enjoying Mike petting her. "You better be careful, you will spoil her." Just at that moment, Cuddles turned on her back, put her paws around Mike's wrist, and starting biting his hand in a playful gesture. "Or she might want to play with you," she laughed.

"You call this playing?" he said in astonishment. "She's biting my hand off!"

"Oh please." Jenna went to rescue him. She picked her cat up and set her down on the floor. She scampered off to play with one of her cat toys. Jenna looked over at Mike and grinned. "She can be…"

"A little feisty, I know!" he finished the sentence for her. He took Jenna's hand and pulled her down on his lap. "Just like her mistress."

She was just about to say, "I am not…," when he covered her lips with his own in a hot passionate kiss. When he lifted his head, she whispered, "feisty."

He chuckled, "I think I will give you a new pet name, 'feisty one.'" Jenna slapped him on the chest and tried to get up. He held her close to him. "Give me a kiss, and I will let you up." She gave him a quick kiss. "Not good enough." She gave him a sly look and proceeded to move her lips over his in a hard and passionate kiss that left them both wanting more. "We need to go," said Mike.

Back at his home, Mike took Jenna's things back to his bathroom. When he came back, Jenna was in the kitchen, putting water in the tea kettle. She looked up as he came in.

"Would you like some tea? I noticed you have a selection in this jar on your counter."

"I would love some, thank you." He sat at the counter and watched her prepare their tea. He loved watching her.

"Do you take sugar in your tea?" she asked.

"No thanks." She handed him his tea and came around the counter to sit next to him.

While they drank their tea, Jenna wondered what Mark and he decided. She turned to look at Mike.

"Mark told me Tonya and Nathan's mom passed this morning."

"Yes, the funeral is on Wednesday."

"Have you and Mark come to a decision on what action you will be taking with Nathan and Tonya after the funeral?"

"Mark and I talked, and we both decided not to prosecute. Our main concern, even though they stole quite a bit of liquor out of the restaurant, is that they borrowed money from a loan shark, which put them in the predicament they're in. Once Zack has found out more about their situation, we will know what to do. In the meantime, we wait. They need to get through the loss of their mom before we can proceed."

"I agree. I'm glad you are not going to prosecute. Do you know if they have money to pay for the funeral?"

"Unless their mother had a life insurance policy, I would say the odds are no. The reason they borrowed the money in the first place was to pay for some of her medical bills that her insurance didn't cover," he said.

"I have a little money in my savings I could give it to them. Better yet, if we find out she didn't have an insurance policy we could set up a Go Fund Me account. I bet lots of people would help out!"

Mike sat there amazed how this woman's heart was as big as a mountain. She always thought of others and never herself. His love for her grew with each passing day as he continued to get to know her. He reached over and ran his fingers through her hair and placed it behind her ear.

"Do you know that you are one incredible woman, you give so much of yourself without asking for anything in return." His eyes shone with what he was feeling for her.

"I don't know how else to be. I watched my parents helping others in their community when they were in need. I admired them giving when they may not have had the resources to give," she said.

"When we know more, we'll see what course we should follow. Right now, I'm beat," he said. Jenna got up from her chair and went to put their cups in the sink. When she started to rinse them, Mike came around and shut the water off. "Leave them." His eyes told her what he wanted. He picked her up and carried her back to his bedroom. He gently laid her on his bed and came down next to her.

"This seems to becoming a habit. I thought you said you were tired," she said smiling. She wrapped her arms around his neck and pulled him close.

"Sweetheart, I'm never too tired to make love to you. Now that we've started, I don't ever want to stop."

His eyes were like molten lava as his lips came down on hers. His tongue traced her lower lip and she opened for him. His kiss deepened as his hand moved down her body and back up underneath her shirt. He unclasped her bra and brought his hand around to her breast. Jenna melted under his touch. She brought her hands down to his chest and started working the buttons on his shirt. She wasn't very good at it but managed to get part of his shirt opened, so she could feel his skin against her hands. Mike sat up and finished unbuttoning and took his shirt off. He pulled Jenna's shirt up over her head and brushed away her bra, leaving her full breasts exposed to him. He bent to take one and then the other in his mouth.

Jenna moaned as she felt the pleasure building inside her. Jenna could feel the roughness of his beard as he moved over her soft skin. She slowly moved her hands over his tanned chest, back, and arms. Somehow, Mike had removed her jeans and panties and was moving his fingers over her inner thigh, to her center and down the other thigh. He went back and found her center while he kissed her stomach, moving up to her breasts, then up her neck to her tender lips. She could feel herself reaching her climax when she cried out, "Mike, I need you now!"

He didn't stop and brought her to the edge as she cried out for release. Mike got up and finished undressing. He pulled a condom out of the drawer and slipped it on and settled on top of her. Mike pulled her arms up over her head. He began to slowly kiss her upper body till she wanted to scream.

"Mike, honey, you're driving me mad. I need you inside me now!"

He came back up and kissed her swollen lips. He raised himself up. His eyes were on fire.

"Jenna, love, I want to take you hard and fast." She could feel his rapid heartbeat pressed up against hers. Her eyes told him what he needed to know.

"Whatever you want, darling, just come inside me. Please! Mike entered her slowly. With each thrust he went in deeper. He released her hands and placed his under her hips. Jenna's nails were digging into his back as he kept up the slow rhythm. She was about to explode. "Mike, please!" she whispered. There were tears in her eyes as she tried to hold on.

"Jenna, love, wrap your legs around me and hold on."

She did as he asked and then he was lost to the shear magic that went through him as he thrust hard and deep inside her. They both cried out as they came to an earth-shattering orgasm that left them both shaking in the aftermath. Jenna held him tight to her. She never felt anything so mind blowing in her life!

Mike raised himself up and brushed her hair away from her face and neck. He gazed into her eyes, "My God love, what you do to me!" He had never felt so on fire with any other woman. "Sweetheart, did I hurt you?" His lovemaking was pretty intense.

"No." She reached up and touched his face. She blushed, "I liked it!" She pulled him down to her and gave him a passionate kiss. "You are an amazing lover. I never knew it could be this way." He returned her kiss and rolled her, so she was on top. Jenna sat up and watched him as she moved her hands over his chest then down his sides. Their eyes locked as she began to move over him. She sensed a power that came over her as she continued to caress his muscular body. When he groaned and said her name, she knew she was pleasing him.

Mike started moving with her. He'd let her take control. He put his hands on her firm breasts and sensuously caressed every inch of her. Jenna came down on his chest and stated to rub her breasts over him. She whispered to him and kissed his neck. "How am I doing so far?"

Mike flipped her over and took control.

"Oh, baby, you are like a wildflower blooming before my very eyes. Oh, Jenna, you feel so good!" He took possession of her and brought them soaring on new heights. When they were able to come back down and their breathing slowed, Mike kissed her behind her ear and whispered, "Sweetheart, you are one incredible woman. I can never get enough of you."

"Oh, Mike!" She wrapped her arms around him and pulled him as close as she could. She loved him so much! She wanted to tell him but was afraid of what he might think. It was all happening so fast!

"I don't want to leave you, but I need to get up. I'll be right back."

When he left, she got up and slipped under the covers. His love-making left her feeling warm inside. She felt her eyes getting heavy and closed her eyes. When Mike came out of the bathroom, he thought Jenna might have fallen asleep. He shut the lights out and crawled under the covers. He wrapped his arm around her pulling her close. She snuggled against him, and she was out. Mike smiled. He needed to make this permanent. He didn't want to go a day without her in his life. He thought about the ring he purchased today. When the time was right, he was going to ask her to marry him. He pulled her closer to him and closed his eyes.

Chapter 17

Jenna woke up to the smells of coffee and sausage cooking. She looked at the clock. It was after 10:00. She laid there and remembered their night together. Mike woke her sometime in the night and made love to her again. When she didn't think it could get any better, it just did! He was magnificent. He showed her how they could please each other in so many ways. She shivered just thinking about him. She got up and decided to take a quick shower.

After she was dressed, she went into the kitchen to see Mike standing in front of the stove.

"What smells so good?"

Mike looked over at her and gave her a wink, "How does sausage and French toast sound?"

She came up to him and took a peek at what he was cooking.

"It looks wonderful! I'm starving!"

He bent to give her a kiss. He gazed at her intently. He noticed she had taken a shower. She smelled like tropical fruits.

"You look wonderful," he said seductively. She gave him a kiss back.

"What can I do to help?"

"How about pouring us a cup of coffee, breakfast is almost ready."

"You don't need to ask me twice." She went over by the coffee pot, reached into the cupboard for the mugs and poured them each a cup. She fixed up their coffee and took Mike's cup over to him. He was just flipping the toast. She handed him his coffee and he took a sip.

"Mmm, good!" He sat his cup on the counter and took hers from her hand and placed it beside his. Mike pulled her in his arms and gave her a searing kiss. "Good morning, my little one!" he whispered.

"Good morning!" she whispered back.

"How are you this morning?" He hoped she wasn't too sore after their night of lovemaking.

"I'm fine, better than fine, but if you're not careful you are going to burn the toast!" He pulled away and checked the toast. Just in time; any longer, and it would have been inedible. He placed the toast and sausage on their plates and took them to the island counter. Jenna grabbed their coffee, some forks and napkins, and placed them beside their plates. Mike already had the maple syrup out. When they finally sat down, Jenna was about to take a bite when Mike took her hand and he surprised her by saying, "Wait, are we going to say grace?" He was smiling when she looked over at him.

She smiled back and said, "Thank you, would you like to do the honor?"

He surprised her again and bowed his head and gave a prayer of thanks. He squeezed her hand and grinned, "Let's eat!"

"This is good, Mike!"

"Thanks. I couldn't decide on omelets or this. I didn't want to wake you to ask because you were so out and snoring away!" There was a glimmer in his eyes as he watched for her reaction. She slapped him across the leg.

"I do not snore!"

"Oh, yes, you do, honey. Like a chainsaw!"

"Michael James TreVaine! You are the most madding man I have ever met!" She picked up her plate.

"Where are you going?"

"As far away from you as possible!" she stormed. She sat down at the table and finished her breakfast, which really wasn't that far from him. He watched her. *Boy, she gets a little sensitive. I'll have to make it up to her.* He decided to let her cool off and finished his breakfast at the island.

When Jenna finished eating, she picked up her plate and put it in the sink. Mike was watching her every step. She picked up her mug and refilled her coffee. She was still mad at him. She turned around and took a glance at him. Those blue eyes bore into her. She felt herself starting to get nervous under that watchful gaze. He got up off his chair and walked up to her, his gaze never leaving her. He took her mug out of her hand and set it on the counter. He placed each hand on either side of her, so she couldn't escape.

"I'm sorry I made fun of your snoring." She stood up. She knew he wasn't going to let her go. She pinched his side for all she was worth! "Ouch! Dammit that hurt! Is this what I get for apologizing?" He took both her hands and placed them above her head with her back against the counter. Jenna knew she made him mad and regretted it when his eyes shot arrows at her. He slammed his mouth hard against hers in a punishing kiss. She responded to his brutal hold on her mouth and gave it back to him. She didn't know when it became more tender and passionate. Before long, she was clinging to him.

When they finally broke apart, she said, "Mike, I'm sorry. You just made me so mad! I don't know what came over me."

"Trust me, Jenna, I will never tease you about it again!"

"I'm sorry I hurt you." Tears sprang into her eyes. She had never hurt anybody in her life! What was wrong with her? She clung to him as the tears ran down her face. He held her tight as she repeatedly told him she was sorry. When the tears stopped, he lifted her head and touched his lips to hers. Mike wondered if he was going way too fast for her. He had to remember that she had never been in a relationship, and her emotions were running high. Maybe he needed to back off a little to give her time.

"I think I need to get you home, little one. We both have a full day and night to get through."

She nodded her head, "Yeah, I think that would be best. I'll just go get my things." She left him in the kitchen.

When she came back, she went to the door and told him she was ready to go. He came up to her, took her hand, and led her through the laundry room into the garage. She had forgotten they had come in that way last night. When he dropped her off, he had given her a light kiss and told her he would see her tonight after work. She walked into her apartment and Cuddles greeted her, rubbing up against her legs. Jenna picked her up and gave her a hug.

"What am I doing, Cuddles? This just doesn't feel right." She put her down and headed back to her bedroom. Maybe she just needed to rest. She hadn't slept much for the last several days. She lay down on her bed and tried to go to sleep.

Several hours later, Sasha came in to their apartment and found Jenna's bag by the front door. *That's odd, she never leaves anything lying around much less her overnight bag.* She went to check on her. She found Jenna asleep and went to wake her.

"Hey Jenna, it's time to get up."

Jenna opened her eyes to see her friend sitting beside her on the bed. "What time is it?"

"It's after 2:00. Is everything okay?" Sasha asked with concern in her voice.

Jenna sat up and looked at her friend.

"I don't know, Sasha. Everything was fine until I blew up at Mike this morning."

"What did you blow up at him about?"

"He told me I snore like a chain saw!"

"More like a freight train," Sasha commented.

"I do not snore!"

"Oh, yes, Jenna. You do. I can sometimes here you in my bedroom!"

"Really?" she asked.

"Jenna, I'm sure he was only teasing you. I can't believe that was the only reason you blew up."

She sighed, "You're right Sasha. When we sat down to breakfast, I went to take a bite, and he stopped me and asked if we were going to say grace. And it hit me. Sasha, we have only known each other a couple of weeks and I've already had mind blowing sex and spent the night with him! Every time we are together, we seem to combust! I think I was mad at myself and took it out on him."

"Wow! Let me ask you this, do you love him?" asked Sasha.

Tears were starting to form in her eyes as she said, "With all my heart."

"Would you marry him tomorrow if he asked?"

"In a heartbeat, but don't you think this is just too fast?" asked Jenna.

"Maybe it is a little, but when two people know that they are the one they want to spend the rest of their lives with, I don't think it matters. I told you once before that when Mike looks at you, he only sees you and no one else."

"Do you think I should talk to Pastor Kingsley about my situation?"

"Jenna, that's totally up to you. If it would make you feel better, then I would."

"Thank you, Sasha, you are a good friend. So, I really do snore?"

"Like a freight train!" They both started laughing. She gave her friend a hug and got ready for work.

Mike was feeling kind of down all night. He was worried about Jenna and whether or not she was regretting them having sex. He should have waited and taken his time with her. But when he was near her, he couldn't stop himself. The restaurant was super busy again tonight, but the night just dragged. When it finally slowed down, Mark came up to him and took him over to a booth and sat him down. Mark sat across from him.

"Okay, bro, spill it."

"Spill what?"

"Mike you have been down in the dumps ever since you stepped into this restaurant this afternoon. Tell me what's bothering you."

He sighed. They never were able to keep anything from each other. They just knew when one or the other was upset.

"I think I jumped the gun with Jenna."

"What do you mean?" asked Mark.

"Well as you know we have only known each other for a couple of weeks, but Mark, I know deep in my soul that I love her with all my heart. I've even bought an engagement ring yesterday. Every time we are together, I find that I can't keep my hands off her. We had sex. The kind that only men dream about, and I'm afraid she is starting to regret it. I should have waited and given us time to get to know each other better. When she blew up at me over my comment about her snoring, I had no idea she was so sensitive. I was only teasing her, Mark!"

"You two spent the night together?" ask Mark.

"Yes, and I want to spend the rest of my life with her. I hope I haven't blown it. She's special, Mark. She is so giving and caring of others," he said.

"I can't tell you what to do, bro, but I can tell you this. You two are head over heels in love with each other, and I knew the first day you met Jenna you were a goner. Your sexual relationship might have been a little fast, but Jenna will come to terms with it. You are not going to lose her over it. Back up a little bit, and let her have some space. Get to know her without the sex," said Mark.

"Thanks, bro. I had the same thoughts. It helps to talk about it. I will close the restaurant tonight. You go home and get some rest."

"Are you sure? Don't you have to pick up Jenna tonight?" asked Mark.

"She texted me just before we sat down to let me know some of her friends stopped in at the Bistro and were going to stay and walk her home. I sent a text back to let me know when she was home."

"Okay, Sherry's bringing Cameron by the house at 10:00 in the morning. It will give me more time to get some things done before he arrives."

"Have you and Sherry made any headway on custody?" asked Mike.

"Not much, I've been so busy here at the restaurant, I haven't pressed it."

"Everything will work out in time, bro," said Mike.

"Back atcha, bro, be safe going home."

"Thanks, you too."

When Mike came into his home after closing the restaurant, it just plain felt empty. God, he missed her! She texted him around 10:30 to let him know she was home. Was he being controlling by wanting her to let him know she was safe? He didn't know. Maybe she did think it was controlling. He was so confused. He needed to talk to her about what she was feeling.

He knew he wasn't going to be able to sleep and decided to take a walk along the beach. He changed into some sweats and a t-shirt and headed out the door. The night had cooled down, and the breeze off the ocean calmed his nerves. While he walked along the beach, he saw couples walking hand in hand or making out beside one of the palm trees. There was a group of students having a bond fire, laughing and having a good time. He stopped and looked out over the ocean. The moon was shining over the waves as the surf came rushing on to the beach. All he could think about was having Jenna next to him, holding her hand and kissing her under the stars. He kept walking. He didn't know how far he had walked before he turned around and headed for home. By the time he walked in the door, he felt calm enough that he thought he could sleep. He sure hadn't had much of it lately. When he hit the bed, thoughts of Jenna and their night together came rushing back to him. His last thought was he was holding Jenna close in his arms when he finally fell asleep.

Chapter 18

*J*enna was up early and was jogging on Waikiki beach. She wanted to stay as far away from Hanauma Bay as possible. She tossed and turned all night, thinking about how she went off on Mike and wondering what he must be thinking. She wanted to talk to Mike, but she needed time to sort out all these feelings she was having. She decided to talk to Pastor Kingsley this morning if he had time for her after church. She kept on going till she realized she had passed the restaurant. She slowed down and walked till her breathing slowed. Something caught her eye when she went by, so she turned around and started back. When she was even with the restaurant, she looked over and saw a man in a dark suit, wearing a cowboy hat. He looked to be over six feet and quite attractive. He glanced over at Jenna and smiled. She quickly turned away and headed back to her apartment. She wondered what he was doing there. The restaurant was closed today. Well, she couldn't worry about it. She had enough of her own. When she arrived back at her apartment, she hurried to dress for church. By the time she got there, she was so rattled that she didn't know if she could even talk to the Pastor. She went in and took a seat in one of the pews.

Mike came in after going out and body surfing this morning. He checked his phone, still no message from Jenna. He had texted her this morning to ask how she was doing and that he missed her. He felt deflated. He checked his phone messages and found that Zack had left a message this morning while he was out. He listened to his message and called him back.

When he answered, Zack began, "Hey Mike thanks for calling me back."

"What's going on?" asked Mike.

"I took the liberty of arranging an FBI agent from Waco, Texas, to meet at your restaurant hoping that you or Mark could meet us there."

"What time?"

"In an hour," he said.

"Mark is tied up today, but I can be there."

"Good, I'll see you in an hour." He hung up. Mike looked at his phone and wondered. Maybe he was able to talk with Nathan and Tonya. But what did an FBI agent from Texas have to do with it? He went to shower and dress and was soon walking up to the door of his and his brother's restaurant.

He was met by a tall Texan in a dark suit. He had one of those black Stetson hats on his head. Mike saw Zack pulling in to the side parking lot and waited for him to come and introduce them before he opened the door. They sized each other up. He wasn't much taller than Mike, about the same build. His eyes were a steel gray, and he had a full beard that he kept trimmed. Zack came up to them and shook hands with the Texan.

"Hi Jason, glad you could make it to our island to help us out." He turned to Mike, "Mike, this is Special Agent Jason Hague. Jason this is Mike TreVaine, he and his brother Mark own the Hawaiian Lanai." They shook hands and greeted each other.

"Let's go inside to my office and you can tell me what this is all about," said Mike.

When they entered his office, Mike sat behind his desk while

Zack and Jason sat in the two chairs in front. Zack proceeded to fill him in.

"Mike, we discussed a few days ago how the Police Department has been trying to get Manchez on several crimes in the city." He turned to Jason, "Manchez is a frequent patron of this restaurant, and that's why I wanted to have Mike sit in on our discussion. Mark couldn't be here, so Mike will clue him in when we are done." He turned back to Mike. "We hope to nail this guy on drug trafficking, loan sharking, and some homicides we feel he is connected to in the city."

"Are you hoping to connect Nathan and Tonya's case to Manchez?" asked Mike.

"I'm hoping we can. Manchez covers his tracks, and it may take a while to get him," said Zack.

"Have you been able to talk to either one of them yet?"

"Jason and I are going to their mother's house in the morning and get more details about this Ralph character and when they meet with him. What did you and Mark decide about pressing charges?" asked Zack.

"Mark and I discussed it, and considering what they have been dealing with over the last several months, prosecuting them isn't the answer. There will be restitution, of course, on their part, but my concern is that no one gets hurt in the process," Mike said with determination.

Jason spoke up for the first time, "Mike, we are going to do everything we can to make sure that doesn't happen. I work in a special division of the FBI where I go undercover to work in a person's business that we suspect is doing criminal activities and using their business as a cover up. Zack informed me that this Manchez knows most of the detectives and police officers in the Police Department. That is why they called me in."

"So, they don't suspect you as a cop?" Mike inquired.

"Yes. When we interview Tonya and Nathan tomorrow, we will get the information we need to form a plan for me to get inside. I know Zack is hoping it will be Manchez, but I will need to form a friendship with this Ralph guy to lead us to the main loan shark."

Mike looked at Jason with concern as he asked, "How long do you think this will take?"

"At this point, I really can't tell you. It may take several months. What I am hoping is that depending on the circumstances we can get Nathan and Tonya out of the picture and keep the enforcer away from your restaurant."

Mike relaxed a little.

"Jason, if you and Zack can accomplish that, Mark and I will be forever grateful. Mark and I have always kept up our self-defense skills since leaving the service. If we can help in any way please let us know."

Jason grinned, "I'll keep that in mind. What part of the military did you serve in?"

"Air Force," replied Mike.

"Special Ops in the Army," said Jason.

Mike sat forward, "My older brother Peyton is an Army Ranger in the special ops division! He's currently on tour. We are hoping it is his last."

"How long has he been in?" he asked.

"A little over 12 years now," said Mike.

"I was in for 14."

They all started talking and reminiscing about their military days, and the hours passed.

"Well, men," said Zack, "As much fun as this has been I need to get Jason settled in his rental. We have a big day ahead of us."

"I'll let you out, I need to get some work done, and it might be better if we are not all seen coming out of the restaurant at the same time."

"I like how you think, Mike!" said Jason. They shook hands at the door.

When Zack shook Mike's hand, he said, "I will keep you and Mark informed as we progress in the case."

"Thanks, Zack, we would appreciate it," said Mike.

Mike went back into his office and turned on his computer. *Might as well go over these reports while I'm here,* he sighed. He worked a couple of hours, but his mind kept wandering back to Jenna. He wondered what she was doing. Should he stop by her apartment? Would she want to see him? He turned his computer off and decided to go see Mark. He needed to let him know what was going on. And seeing Cameron would lift his spirits.

Jenna waited until everyone left the church to shake hands with Pastor Kingsley.

"Ah, Jenna, good to see you this morning," he said.

"Thank you, Pastor Kingsley. I was wondering if you had a few minutes to talk with me?"

"Why yes, I don't have to be anywhere for the next hour. Will that give you enough time?"

"Oh, yes, that would be great." He led her into his office and sat down behind his desk. "Have a seat." Jenna sat in the chair in front of his desk. "What can I help you with Jenna?"

Jenna took a few minutes to get her thoughts together.

"I've met a wonderful man," she smiled. "We have this chemistry between us that explodes every time we are near each other. But I have only known him for a little over two weeks! We started an intimate relationship, and I'm wondering if we are going way too fast. Do you think a person call fall in love with some one that quickly?"

Pastor Kingsley smiled.

"Jenna, when I first saw my wife many years ago, I knew she was the one I was going to marry. I'm not sure we had the chemistry that you are talking about," he laughed, "Maybe it took a little more wooing on my part, but when you know that special person is the one, yes, I believe you can fall in love very quickly. Tell me Jenna, do you love him?"

"Yes."

"Can you see yourself spending the rest of your life with him?"

"Oh, yes, I want to be with him all the time."

"Well, I can't tell you what to do, but I can give you a little advice. Get to know him without the intimacy. If he loves you, he will respect your wishes. Then if you both still feel you can't live without each other, then he will want to put a ring on your finger."

"Thank you, Pastor Kingsley. You have been very helpful." She got up from her chair and shook his hand. "If he is willing, see if you can encourage him to come to church. I would very much like to meet him."

"I will try, but he said it wasn't for him."

"As you know Jenna it is wise to be equally yoked as a couple. If you're not, it can be troubling in a marriage. You're a lovely young woman, Jenna, keep working on him, he'll come one day. What is the young man's name?"

"Mike," she said.

"I will put you both in my prayers."

"Thank you again, Pastor Kingsley, and I will try to get him to come."

"I know you will, and you are welcome, Jenna. Anytime you need to talk, I am here."

Mike sat in the living room at Mark's home. The Monopoly game was spread out on the coffee table, and Mark and he were getting totally beat by a seven-year-old boy! Cameron was a towhead, and the spitting image of Mark. He had the same deep blue eyes as both of us. He took his turn with the dice and stopped on the only one of Mike's houses.

"I think I am going to buy your house, Uncle Mike!"

"No, Cameron! That's my last house!"

He laughed, "Sorry, Uncle Mike!"

"Sure, you are. Well, I'm out."

They all laughed.

"Hey Cameron," said Mark. "Let's put the game away, and you get started on your homework. We're going to eat dinner soon, and I need to talk to your Uncle Mike about something."

"Okay, Dad."

When the game was put away and Cameron left to go to his room Mark turned to Mike and asked, "What's going on?"

Mike cued him in on the conversation he had with Zack and the FBI agent, concluding, "Zack said he would keep us informed as the case progresses."

"What time are they meeting with Nathan and Tonya tomorrow?" asked Mark.

"Around 10:30 in the morning," he said. "I'll be anxious to know what kind of game plan they come up with. If they need any muscle power, I'm on it!"

Mike chuckled, "I let them know if they need our services to let us know!"

"Good! Hey, do you want to stay for dinner? We're just having burgers and hot dogs on the grill."

Mike shrugged his shoulders.

"Sure. What can I do to help?"

"You can help me get the burgers ready."

They went into the kitchen, and Mike helped his brother prepare the hamburgers. Mark got chips and salsa out, so the two men could munch on the chips while the burgers and dogs were grilling.

"Would you like a beer, bro?" asked Mark.

"Sure, but I can get it." Mike went to the refrigerator and took out two beers and handed one to his brother.

"Have you heard from Jenna today?"

"No, I sent her a text this morning and haven't heard from her. I want to go see her. What do you think, bro?"

"That's up to you, Mike, but if it were up to me, I'd give her some space. If she gets in touch with you and wants to see you, then by all means go. In any event, she will be in the office tomorrow."

"If she doesn't call or text, I'll wait, but I just miss her! How did I fall so fast, bro?"

Mark could feel all the emotions going through his brother. If Mike was down, he was down. If Mike was nervous, he was nervous, and vice versa. It was part of being identical twins.

"It happens. Take it one day at a time. It will all work out. I'll get these burgers and dogs off the grill. Cameron and I went to the store earlier and picked up some potato salad and coleslaw. If you could pull those out of the fridge, we can eat. I'm starving." Mike went to get the food out of the fridge, grabbed a couple more beers and called Cameron to the table. They all sat down and enjoyed a hearty meal, and the time they spent together as a family felt good.

That evening, Jenna sat in the lanai and tried to study for an exam tomorrow. Thoughts of Mike came back to her and how she treated him yesterday. She needed to talk to him. Should she call him or wait until tomorrow when she would see him at the restaurant? He texted her this morning and said he missed her. She missed him, too. She missed his arms around her and his passionate kisses. She decided to send him a text.

Mike, I miss you. Can we talk?

She pushed send and waited.

Mike was trying to watch a game on TV. He sat and stared at the screen. He didn't know who was playing or what the score was. His interest just wasn't there. He shut it off and went into the kitchen to make a pot of coffee. While he waited for it to finish brewing, he heard his phone ding with and incoming text, his heart starting beating faster as he read the text. He breathed a sigh of relief. He shot a text back.

Yes, when?

He pushed send.

Jenna heard her phone and read his message. Sasha was out for the evening.

Tonight, here at my apartment?

She waited and his text was instant.

I'll be right there.

Jenna went in to put a pot of coffee on. She paced back and forth while she waited. She was so nervous. She just needed to relax. She wished she knew what he was thinking. Ten minutes later, the doorbell rang. Cuddles came running out of her bedroom. Jenna picked her up and opened the door. Mike stood in the doorway, and his eyes drank her in. In a pair of sweat pants and an oversized shirt, she couldn't be more adorable.

"Hi," he breathed.

"Hi, come on in," she smiled. He came in and closed the door so she could put her cat down. "I just made a pot of coffee. Would you like some?"

"Yes, I will take a cup." They went into the kitchen, and Jenna took two mugs out of the cupboard while Mike got the cream out of the fridge. They fixed their coffee, and Jenna led them into the living room and sat down on the couch. Mike sat at the far end, so he wouldn't be tempted to pull her in his arms before they could talk. They took a sip of their coffee, and Mike set his down on the coffee table. He leaned forward with his arms on his thighs as he gazed at her intently. They both started talking at the same time.

"I'm sorry, Mike, you go first."

"No, Jenna, you go."

She took a breath.

"Okay, I want to explain why I reacted the way I did yesterday. I needed a little time to sort out my feelings." Mike's heart beat faster, afraid of what she was about to tell him. "Mike, I want you to know that I don't regret when we made love together. It was the most beautiful experience of my life. You know I have never had a relationship with a man before, and that morning when we had breakfast together, it hit me that this relationship was going way too fast for me. I started feeling guilt about my actions. Would you consider slowing down and getting to know each other without the sex?"

Mike watched her while she talked and looked deep into her eyes. He loved her so much! He was relieved she wasn't going to boot him out the door.

"Jenna, I had a feeling that morning when we argued that you might be regretting what had happened between us, and I am so glad to hear you have no regrets. I am more than willing to just date and get to know each other better on an intellectual level as long as we can hold each other and do a little necking?" He smiled. "I miss having you in my arms."

"Oh, Mike, I would like that. I miss being in your arms."

"Can we start now?" he asked. Jenna grinned and nodded her head yes. She put her coffee down and scooted over next to him. He folded his arms around her and held her tight against him. She laid her head on his chest and felt her body relax against him.

They held each other for a long time not saying anything. Mike felt the tension leaving him as he held her close to him.

"Jenna, sweetheart," he placed his hand under her chin and raised her head to look at him.

She gazed into his eyes. "Yes?"

"I love you and I would do anything to win your heart."

"Oh, Mike, you already have it! I love you so much!" He bent his head and touched his lips to hers in a kiss that showed all the love he had for her. It soon turned to passion, and Mike had to restrain himself before things got out of hand. He broke the kiss and laid her head on his chest. They both had to slow their breathing. Mike laid his head back against the couch and closed his eyes. He was happy to just hold her. He should probably go before he fell asleep. He was feeling it with only having a few hours of sleep last night. He waited and held her for just a few more minutes before he would get up to leave. When he tried to move, Jenna held on and snuggled deeper against him. He looked down, and she was fast asleep. He adjusted them in a lying position and soon found himself falling asleep. It seemed the only way he could sleep is with Jenna in his arms.

Sasha walked into the apartment a little after midnight. She found Mike and Jenna sound asleep again on the couch. This was getting to be a habit. She smiled. She knew Jenna was upset about what happened yesterday, and it looked like they were able to sort things out. She picked up the coffee cups and took them in the kitchen. When she covered them and turned out the lights, they didn't even budge. Sasha had a feeling there would soon be wedding bells in the near future.

Chapter 19

*M*ike woke and found Jenna still in his arms her cat sprawled across his chest. He needed to get up and get home before he was tempted to take things too far. He shook her, and Cuddles woke and stretched. Her back and front claws dug into his chest. He picked her up with one hand and placed her on the floor. He hoped he would get used to a cat sleeping with them. He shook Jenna again.

"Hey sleepy head," he kissed her on the cheek. "It's time to wake up!"

"Hmm?"

"I need to get going." Jenna lifted herself and asked what time it was. "It's close to 7:00."

"Oh my, how did we sleep so long?" He chuckled. "I think we sleep better when we are together." Jenna yawed, "I think you are right." Mike sat up and pulled Jenna up with him.

"Would you like me to make some coffee before you leave?"

"That would be great!" They both went to use the restroom. Jenna changed, brushed her teeth, and went into the kitchen to make the coffee. Mike came in behind her and pulled her back against him. He held her for a few minutes before he turned her around to face him. "What would you like me to do?"

"Kiss me."

He smiled, "I mean with breakfast."

She put on a sad face, and he couldn't resist. He lowered his head and gently kissed her lips. He deepened the kiss and thought he was going to lose his mind trying to keep his hands from touching her body. Jenna wrapped her arms around his neck and brought him closer to her. Mike broke the kiss and pulled away.

"Jenna, I'm having trouble resisting temptation. I will always want you whenever I am near you. What do you say we make some breakfast?"

"Okay," she shivered as she stepped back out of his arms. His kisses always left her wanting him. Jenna went to the fridge and pulled some eggs while Mike started the coffee. They sat down and had a quick breakfast of scrambled eggs and toast. Mike helped her clean up the kitchen and told her he needed to get going. Jenna walked him to the door. He turned and gave her a quick kiss.

"I'll see you later this afternoon."

"Okay, this afternoon."

When he left, Jenna leaned against the door. How was she ever going to keep from wanting to make love to him! This was going to prove harder than she thought.

In the little house on Koiolu Street, Zack and Jason sat at the kitchen table with Nathan and Tonya. Zack introduced Jason to them and explained why he was with him.

"I know this is a hard time for both of you, and I wouldn't be here if it wasn't important to get the necessary information pertaining to your case. Before we get started, I want to say how sorry I am about the loss of your mother," Zack said sincerely.

Tonya with tears in her eyes said, "Thank you."

"Let's start from the beginning. When I interviewed you at the restaurant, Nathan, you said you and Tonya were having trouble paying your mother's medical bills and were at a bar discussing how you could make some extra money when a man came up to you and said he could help you out is that correct?"

"Yes, He said he worked for a man who was in the finance business, and he could get us the money the next day," said Nathan.

"Did he mention at all the name of the finance company that he worked for?" asked Zack.

"No, not that I remember."

"You said you signed a simple contract. Do you have a copy of that?"

"No, he never gave us a copy." Nathan looked over at Tonya to make sure she was doing okay. Zack also looked at Tonya and could tell she was nervous. Jason sat in the background and watched their body chemistry to make sure they were telling the truth. He could tell a lot just by watching facial expression.

Tonya spoke. Her voice was a little shaky when she said, "I do remember seeing 'MM Finance Company' on the top of the contract when we signed. I don't remember seeing an address on it."

Zack took down the information as they answered each question.

"So, he gave you the money and you started making payments," said Zack.

"Yes, and we were doing okay until we had half of it paid off. Then we weren't able to pay our electric bill and had to use the money that was going towards the loan to pay the bill, so it wouldn't get shut off. That's when things got complicated. He doubled our interest rate, and we were never able to get the loan paid down."

"When did you start taking liquor out of the restaurant and selling it?" asked Zack.

"A few months ago, we wanted to get the total loan paid off and be done with it. I know it was wrong, but we both felt trapped. I will take the consequences for my actions. Please leave my sister out of this."

Tonya put her hand on her brother's arm. She met her brother's eyes and said with conviction, "We are both in this together, and we will both take whatever punishment we deserve." She looked back at Zack. "Are Mike and Mark going to prosecute us?" asked Tonya.

"That is something you will have to discuss with them." Zack admired Tonya for stepping up and not letting her brother take all the heat. He hated not telling them of the owners' decision. "When are you supposed to meet with this Ralph character?"

"We are supposed to meet with him on Wednesday this week, but with the funeral that day, I don't know how we can," said Tonya.

"What time were you supposed to meet?"

"Four-thirty," said Nathan. "Do you have the money to give him?"

"We did have, but we gave it to the funeral director as a down payment on mom's funeral."

Zack sighed.

"She didn't have a life insurance policy?"

"We don't know for sure. She tried to tell us something before she died. Something about the desk, we went through it except for the drawer that is locked. We have hunted and turned this house upside down for the key and can't find it. She was a very private woman about her finances," Tonya said in frustration.

Zack looked over at Jason and grinned. Jason pulled out a small leather pouch that looked like a wallet. Inside he took out a lock pick, walked over to the desk drawer, and opened it. Tonya and Nathan got up from the table amazed how fast he had it opened. They looked inside and there was their mother's living will.

Nathan took it out of the drawer. He turned to Tonya, "Let's hope she had enough to pay her funeral expenses."

They sat down at the table and opened the folder.

Nathan looked over the will and discovered their mom did, indeed, have a paid-up life insurance policy, insurance on the mortgage and a bank account totaling over $100,000! Nathan looked at Tonya, "Why didn't mother ever tell us about this? Her own kids! It could have saved us from the mess we are now in!"

"I'm sure your guess is as good as mine!" They looked over at the detectives.

"We will pay back anything I have taken from the restaurant and the loan, but what are we going to do about the loan shark? After he roughed us up the last time, I don't think he is going to let this go, even when we pay him off!" Nathan said in a concerned voice.

Jason and Zack stood watching the two in shock over their mother's estate. They took one look at each other and sat back down at the table.

"Nathan, with you and Tonya's help, Jason and I along with the Police Department have come up with a plan to get you and Tonya out of the picture and Jason to go undercover inside the loan shark's business," said Zack.

"We're listening."

Jenna was going over the financial reports for last week. When she finished, she started the cost analysis and inventory reports. As she studied each day's reports there were no shortages for the last week. This was good news. She printed all the reports for Mark and placed them in the appropriate folder. Jenna knocked on Mark's door.

"Come in." Jenna stepped into his office.

"Hi, Mark, I finished up all the reports you wanted me to do. Is there anything else you would like me to go over?"

Mark took the folders from Jenna and gave them a brief glance.

"This looks good Jenna." He glanced up and gave her a smile. "No, it's almost 4:30. This was a big help. On Wednesday, I will show you how to do the daily reports on what we take in each night, fill out a bank deposit, and run a credit card report. Mike and I will be attending Nathan and Tonya's mother's funeral, but should be back here no later than 12:30 that day."

"Would you like me to get started on the cost analysis and inventory report before you get back?" asked Jenna.

"Sure, that would be great."

"Okay, have a nice night Mark"

"You too, Jenna!"

Jenna went back to her office, signed out, and shut down her computer. She checked her phone. Still no messages from Mike. She hadn't seen him since this morning when he left her apartment. She locked her door and went to see if he was in his office. She knocked, but he didn't answer. When she tried the door, it was still locked. She sent him a text.

> On my way out of the office and going back to my apartment, will I see you tonight?

She pushed send as she was walking out into the restaurant. She bumped into a hard chest. She was still looking down at her phone when she said, "Sorry."

When she looked up, a handsome man with deep blue eyes said, "Do you always text and walk at the same time?"

"Mike! I just texted you!" she said. His phone dinged.

"That must be you!" he said, grinning.

"I was just about to take off for my apartment. I finished a little early today."

"Come into my office. I want to run something by you first."

Jenna followed him into his office. He put his briefcase on the floor next to his desk and led her over to his couch. When he sat down, he pulled Jenna onto his lap. He gave her a sweet and gentle kiss.

"Do you have any plans for tomorrow morning?" he asked.

"No, why?"

"Would you like to go to breakfast with me? And then I would like to take you to one of our popular waterfalls on the island, if you're up for it."

She smiled, "I would love that." Her eyes just sparkled whenever she smiled, he thought. "What time?"

"I'll pick you up at 8:00 and make sure you bring a swimsuit."

"Um, did I tell you I am not a strong swimmer?"

"I think you mentioned that once."

"Well, I might have stretched the truth a little. I can float, but I absolutely cannot swim. I'm sorry."

He chuckled, "I will absolutely teach you."

"Just so you know, I panic whenever I am not able to touch the bottom."

He tightened his arms around her.

"Don't worry, I will keep you safe."

"Promise?" she asked.

"I promise." He gazed into her eyes. "I love you, Jenna."

She brought her hand up to the side of his face and whispered, "I love you, Michael James TreVaine."

He showed how much he loved her in a kiss that overwhelmed their senses. Softly and then grew more demanding. He traced her lower lip with his tongue to get entrance inside her mouth. When she opened for him, he tangled with hers in a powerful kiss that left them both breathless. Suddenly, Mike broke the kiss. If he didn't stop now, he knew he wouldn't be able to.

"Jenna," he gave her a quick kiss. "Do you want to have dinner before you go?"

She thought about it for a moment. She really needed to get some studying done.

"I'd better go I need to study if I'm going to spend most of the day with you tomorrow." She gave him a kiss back. It was silent for a long time.

When they finally broke apart, Mike said, "I need to get to work, sweetheart."

"I know." She hated to leave him. She got up off his lap. He rose and led her to the door. She stopped and gave him one last kiss. "See you in the morning."

"Yes, you will, my love."

As he closed the door, Mike didn't know how much longer he would be able to keep himself from making love to her. If he was going to keep his promise to her, he needed a distraction, something to keep his mind busy and off her luscious body. He straightened his tie, took his suit coat off, and went out on the floor. He let himself get caught up in the night's activities. It worked till he was home when he found himself alone with only thoughts of Jenna whirling around in his head.

Chapter 20

*M*ike was at Jenna's door promptly at 8:00 the next morning. When she opened the door, he saw Jenna with her hair up in a ponytail, khaki shorts, and a pretty blue tank top. She had no makeup on but some lip gloss on those pretty pink lips of hers. He braced himself. *Okay, we are going to breakfast, have some fun at the waterfall and get to know each other better, in that order. Maybe a kiss or two and nothing else,* he told himself sternly.

"Hi, come in. I will just be a moment." Cuddles came running out of the bedroom and brushed her body up against Mike's ankles. He picked her up and scratched behind her ears. She closed her eyes and enjoyed his fingers going back and forth in her thick fur. "I think she is beginning to get used to you coming to the apartment. She likes you Mike!"

He smiled down at her cat and placed her back down on the floor. When he looked at Jenna, he kept his gaze neutral.

"Are you ready to go?"

"Yes, I just need to grab my backpack."

"Did you remember to pack a swimsuit?"

She grinned at him. "I'm wearing it! I thought it would be easier. I wasn't sure there was a place to change at the water fall."

"Smart girl! There are restrooms, but I have no idea if there are changing rooms." He wore his suit under his shorts as well.

Mike opened the door of his SUV for her and stowed the backpack in the back seat. He took her to a quaint little restaurant not far from the falls.

"Would you like to sit outdoors?" he asked.

"I would love that!" The hostess led them to a table near the shrubbery. Jenna looked around, and it resembled a small tropical garden with tables weaving in and out of the colorful flowers. Umbrellas were opened over the tables to shade them from the warm Hawaiian sun. The lush green shrubbery enclosed the lanai. It felt cozy and warm. "This is so beautiful, Mike, how did you come across it?"

"I had a meeting with a restaurant owner in this area. After the meeting, I was driving by, and it drew me in. They have excellent food. Their omelets are out of this world." Mike watched her as she looked over the menu. He wondered again if she would marry him with only knowing each other for such a short time. He shook his head; time would soon tell. Their waitress came over and they both choose the Hawaiian omelet and coffee.

While they waited Jenna asked, "Tell me about your days in the Air Force. Was it hard to stay in for four years or was there a possibility you would have re-enlisted?"

He grinned, "When my brother and I first went in, we both thought it was going to be a long four years. After basic training, we were stationed here on the island and served our time at Joint Base Pearl Harbor-Hickam. We started out in maintenance and found that it was definitely not for us." He told her about the major mishaps he and his brother had fixing aircraft, and she laughed until tears came streaming down her face.

"That must have been awful!"

"It wasn't pleasant at the time, that's for sure!" he chuckled. Their breakfast came, and they both dove in. She didn't realize how hungry she was. "How did you get out of maintenance?" she asked.

"We both were able to get into administration and worked in the message center where I met General McCall and became his aid for the rest of my tour. He was quite the general. He was tough when he needed to be but was down to earth and became a good friend to me when I got out of the service. During my time serving under him, I was able to go on several top secret missions with him. We flew in an aircraft that could climb so high, you could see the circumference of the Earth. It was a thrill of a lifetime. If he hadn't retired, I would have considered staying in another four years. But it all worked out. I followed my dream of owning a restaurant, and here I am today. Sitting here with a beautiful woman, enjoying her company, and wondering why I'm so lucky."

Jenna blushed.

"Wow! I'm glad you didn't stay in. We might not be sitting here today. Do you ever wonder how your life may be different if you chose another path?" she asked.

"No, I think everything works out the way it should."

They finished their breakfast and asked for the check.

When they were back on the road, Mike asked, "What about you Jenna? Do you ever wonder how your life might be if you chose a different career?"

She thought a moment, "No, I think you are right. I feel like our Lord guides us on our path. If we make the wrong decision, he closes that door and opens up another door. Sometimes I have a rough time wondering if I'm on the path that He wants me to be. I try to put my trust in Him, even though we can't see Him. In my heart, I believe that we were meant to meet and be together."

She looked over at him to see his reaction to her words. He

reached over and took her hand and raised it to his lips. He kissed her hand tenderly and gave it a gentle squeeze.

"You know, Jenna, I believe in a higher power, someone who directs us in life. God, if you will. I'm not sure about Christianity. Do you really need to believe in the Son to believe in God?" he asked.

"I became a Christian when I was 15. When I asked him to be my Savior, I had the most extraordinary feeling come over me. It was like He came inside me. To answer your question, yes, for me it was to believe that Jesus is my Savior, and He is the son of God. There are all kinds of religion out there, and everyone has a choice to worship whatever or whoever that is. I chose the living God."

Mike was pulling up to the parking lot and eased into a space. He shut the engine off and turned toward her.

"Thank you, Jenna, you gave me something to think about. Shall we get out and go find this waterfall?"

She gave him a big smile, "We shall!" As she got out of the SUV, she hoped she didn't overstep. You never knew how people were going to react concerning religion.

Mike grabbed their backpacks and a couple of poles out of the back of his SUV. He handed one of the poles to Jenna.

"These are in case the trail is muddy or rocky. It will help keep our balance. Follow me!"

Jenna followed Mike on the narrow trail. She was glad she had the pole. There were places where you could slide and fall without it. The trail took you through the rain forest with tall bamboo trees, palm trees, tropical plants, and vivid flowers in an array of color. They came to a place where there was an opening above the trees where the sun came in and shafts of light came through. It was breathtaking. They finally reached Waimea Falls. She was amazed at how the water cascaded down a wall of rock formation

50 feet high into a pool of water. Green vegetation and small trees were on either side of the falls, and it was just magnificent. The water was clear, and you could see the bottom. Mike watched her taking it all in.

"Are you ready to jump in?" he grinned.

"As ready as I will ever be," she grinned back.

They shed their clothes and stepped in. Jenna jumped back.

"It's a little cold don't you think?"

"Here's what you need to do. You need to rush right in and take a dive, and it will be over quickly. If you ease in a little at a time, it will be pure torture!"

Mike took off and dove straight for the middle of the pool. When he came up yelling how good that felt, she was a little optimistic.

"You know, I think you are forgetting something," she yelled.

"Oh, yeah," he laughed, "What's that, little one?"

"I can't swim, remember?" He chuckled and swam closer to her. "Okay, I'm right here to pull you up when you come in."

She was still skeptical. She gazed into those blue eyes of his as he encouraged her to come in. She took a deep breath. She ran and dove in and almost lost her breath it was so cold! He pulled her up next to him.

"See, that wasn't so bad!" he laughed.

"Mike it is freezing in here!" She put her hands on his shoulders. "Are we over our head here?"

"Yes, little one, but I've got you." He had his arms tightly around her as he treaded water.

"Please don't let go of me." She was starting to shiver and looking down into the water.

"I won't let go of you until you can relax. Jenna, look at me." She looked up into his eyes as he bent to kiss her lips that were quivering. Jenna started to relax as she wrapped her arms around his neck and snuggled closer to his warm body. If you could call it warm; it felt cold in the water, but his lips were warming her as he continued to kiss her passionately. She stopped shivering as her body began to adjust to the temperature. Mike lifted his head, his breathing a little unsteady.

"That's better, little one. Are you ready for your first swim lesson?"

"Oh, okay," she said, shaking. "Now take your arms from around my neck and place your hands in mine." She did as she was told and eased away from him into the water holding on to his hands. "Very good, can you see my legs kicking in the water?"

She looked down in the water, "Yes."

"Good, now I want you to relax and do the same thing. Gently kick your legs back and forth." He watched as she followed what he told her. "That's it, Jenna, you're doing great. I'm going to let go so you can move your arms in the water." She looked at him with fear in her eyes and shook her head no. "Okay, little one, let's try another way. Keep kicking your legs and just relax. I'll take one hand away and hold on to you with the other.

"Okay."

He let go of her hand and was beside her treading water.

"Move your free arm back and forth over the water as you continue to relax and kick your legs." Jenna could feel herself getting more comfortable as she continued to follow Mike's instructions. He came around in front of her. "Are you feeling up to doing it on your own?"

"As long as you catch me if I panic."

"You're not going to panic. The key is to stay relaxed. Take some deep breaths and continue kicking and moving your arms." He let go of her hand. Jenna started moving her other arm and found she was actually treading water!

"Oh, Mike, honey, I'm doing it! I'm treading water!"

It was pure joy to watch her master this technique in the water. He was so proud of her! "Are you comfortable enough to try and swim?" She looked questioningly at him. "Okay, let me show you and then you try. I won't go far." She watched him as he swam out a little way from her. He stopped and turned back around to her. "Okay, remember to stay relaxed, keep kicking your legs and move your arms as if you were paddling."

Jenna started paddling, all the while telling herself to relax. She swam up to Mike, and couldn't believe she did it! Mike pulled her up and wrapped his arms around her.

"Oh, sweetheart, you did it! I'm so proud of you!"

"Oh, Mike, thank you! You are the best swim teacher ever!"

He gazed into her pretty brown eyes and asked, "Is that all I am to you, little one?"

Jenna wrapped her arms around his neck and smiled as she gazed back into his eyes.

"You, Michael TreVaine, are the most handsome man I have ever met. You're loving and caring, and I trust you with all my heart."

"That's all I needed to hear."

Their lips met in a slow and loving kiss that made Jenna's heart pound. Mike wanted to hold on to this magic that they always seemed to bring when they are together. He knew it was getting late but wanted to feel her body next to his just a little longer. When they finally broke apart, he placed his forehead on hers and asked, "Are you ready to swim back to shore?" She nodded her head yes. "Just remember to stay relaxed, I will be right beside you."

They started off, and Jenna found it was easier each time she did it.

They came up on shore and toweled off and dressed. When they headed towards the trail, Mike took her hand in his.

"This is the most fun I have had in a long time."

Jenna grinned up at him, "Me too, thank you for bringing me here. I shall always remember being here with you."

He bent his head and gave her a kiss worth remembering. They walked back to his SUV, and it wasn't long before they were pulling up in front of her apartment. He cut the engine. He turned and looked at her mischievously and asked, "Would you like me to pick you up after work?"

She looked surprised.

"Oh, are you asking me now?"

He chuckled, "Maybe I have been coming on a bit too strong. I just want to know you are home safe."

She gave him a dazzling smile.

"I would love for you to pick me up, as long as it doesn't take you away from your work. I will be working till close, so I may not get out until 11:00."

"Perfect. Just text me when you are close to leaving."

"Will do, boss!" she laughed. He grinned as he got out of his SUV and helped Jenna with her backpack.

He gave her a quick kiss.

"I will see you later."

She watched him back out of the drive. When he waved, she thought she must be one of the luckiest girls on the island to have such a wonderful man care so much for her.

While Mike drove back to his house, he reminisced about the day with Jenna. He loved watching her eyes light up when she accomplished each swim technique. Having her gorgeous body next to his was an added plus. He thought about what she said about becoming a Christian. Maybe he should look into it. He could look up Pastor Kingsley online and set up a meeting with him. Get his thoughts on marriage. He pulled into his garage and felt a lot better.

He had a lightness to his step that he never felt before. He would set his plan in motion.

Chapter 21

Nathan and Tonya greeted family members and friends as they came to pay their last respects to their mother Ruthann Suzanne Forest. The service was simple, just like their mother would have wanted, with Pastor Kingsley presiding over the service. There was a luncheon after the service in the fellowship hall of the church. People gathered to share their favorite stories about Ruthann, which lifted Tonya's and Nate's spirit during this difficult time.

Tonya was having trouble focusing at times as her mind kept returning to the meeting that was coming up with the lone shark's enforcer Ralph this afternoon. She was nervous about their plan that they set up with Zack and Jason. She hoped that they could pull this off. They were to meet at the police station at three to go over the game plan.

Mike and Mark walked up to Tonya. They each gave her a hug.

"So sorry for your loss" said Mike.

"If there is anything we can do, please let us know," said Mark.

In a low voice, Mike added, "Zack filled us in last night and we will be there when this goes down. Don't worry about anything, just concentrate on getting through this."

"I'm just so scared," said Tonya.

"Jason will be right with you. He won't let anything happen to you or your brother. If he needs backup, Mark and I will be there.

We will go over the game plan when you and your brother arrive at the police station at 3:00."

Nathan walked up to them and shook hands with Mike and Mark.

"Thank you for coming, Tonya and I appreciate it." Mark pulled out an envelope out of his breast pocket and handed it to Nathan.

"This is for you and Tonya to use as you want. I hope you don't mind, Zack told us of your mom's estate, and we are thankful you will be able to cover your mom's funeral expenses."

Nathan stepped up and said in a low voice, "We will also be paying back all the liquor I took out of your restaurant."

"We will discuss this at another time when you get through this," said Mark. He looked around to make sure no one was listening. "Just so you know, we won't be pressing charges. We just wished you would have come to us instead of borrowing the money, not knowing he was a loan shark at the time."

"I am so sorry for what I did. If we had known about our mom's estate, we wouldn't be in this mess. We didn't even know she had a will! She kept to herself about her and dad's finances," explained Nathan.

"Once you both get through this we'll talk. I need to get back to the restaurant, are you coming, bro?" asked Mark.

Mike was looking over at a couple talking with Pastor Kingsley, "I'll meet you back there, bro, I want to talk to Pastor Kingsley before I go."

Mark shrugged his shoulders when he looked at his brother. "Okay, I'll see you back at the restaurant." When he left, Mark wondered what in the world he wanted to talk to the Pastor about. Well, he knew it would eventually come out. It was only a matter of time.

"If you'll excuse me, I will see you both this afternoon." Mike went over to the Pastor and waited for him to finish his conversation with the couple he was talking to. This was as good a time as any to try and make an appointment with him. The Pastor shook hands with the couple and turned to Mike. Mike shook hands with him and introduced himself.

"Hello, I'm Mike TreVaine, I wondered if you had a minute to speak with me?" he asked.

"Why yes, Mike. You wouldn't be Jenna's Mike, would you?" asked Pastor Kingsley.

Mike felt himself blush, which he almost never did, wondering what Jenna might have told him.

"I'm afraid I am. I would like to know if I could set an appointment up with you for sometime next week if you are available."

"I am sure that it would be possible. Let me give you my card. Just call the office. My secretary has my schedule, and she can set up a time when we can meet." He handed Mike his card.

Mike smiled, "I won't keep you. I know you're busy. Thank you for spending this time with me. I look forward to when we can meet next week."

"You are welcome, Mike," he said. Mike shook his hand again and left to head back to the restaurant. Pastor Kingsley watched him go. He smiled; prayer was a powerful thing!

Jenna was sitting at her desk going over the inventory and cost analysis report when Mark came into her office.

"Hi Jenna," he said. She looked up from the report.

"Hi Mark, how are Tonya and Nathan doing?"

"They are doing well. It was a nice service," he said.

"Good, I heard Pastor Kingsley presided at her funeral. He's a very good minister."

"Yes, he is. He did a good job. Are you just about finished with that report?" asked Mark.

"Actually, I was just finishing up." She pushed print and went over to the printer to put the report in the folder for him.

"Good, come into my office, and we will get started on counting the cash drawers, setting up for the next day, and running the credit card report."

"Okay, sounds good!" Mark showed her what to do with each drawer and how to fill out a bank deposit slip. This kept her busy for the next several hours. Mark then showed her how to process the credit card report. It was quarter to 3:00, and Mark excused himself to attend a meeting down at the police station. Jenna knew they were getting ready to meet with this Ralph character and setting up a plan to release Tonya and Nathan from this loan shark. She hoped it worked!

Back in the conference room at the Police Department there were seven people sitting around the table discussing what was going down this afternoon. Zack explained to Tonya and Nathan that, "Jason's undercover name is going to be Mick Southerland. He's all set up in the system as a former enforcer out of Dallas, Texas. His former boss was arrested for loan sharking, and Mick walked away without getting caught. Mick is a friend of the family, and you will introduce him as such. Let the rest play out. And make sure you don't let this guy get to you. He will sense something is up."

Lieutenant Fillmore spoke up, "We have a wire on Jason through his watch, so Zack, who will be in a dark blue Chevy van, can hear the conversation. Mark and Mike will be with Zack in the van if Jason needs back up. The man we are really after knows most of the men in the police department. So, we don't want any police around if we can help it. Do you have any questions?"

"No," said Tonya, "I'm just nervous and hope I don't start shaking when we talk to him."

"Just act like you have in the past when dealing with him," said Zack. "You will do fine."

"Take deep breaths and relax before you meet with him," said Mike.

"Okay, it's almost 4:00. You three head over to the restaurant and follow the same routine as you usually do. Mike, Mark, and I will head over in the van and park in the back parking lot where we can see you," said Zack.

"Are we all ready to go?" asked Lieutenant Fillmore.

"As ready as we will ever be," said Nathan.

With a gleam in his eyes, Zack said, "Let's do this!"

It was almost 4:00 when Jenna finished processing the credit card report. She needed to get up and stretch. She saw Mark's trash can was full, and she was pretty sure hers might be over flowing. She picked up his can and went to get hers. She would check Mike's but knew his door was locked. She dumped Mark's into hers and headed for the kitchen. The dumpster, she knew was just a little way out the back door. She set a wedge in between the door, so it wouldn't close on her. She went and dumped the trash and was heading back into the restaurant when she saw a man pacing back and forth a little way from the back of the restaurant talking to himself. She wondered if this was Ralph. He was a little early. He looked to be about six feet tall, a little on the pudgy side. His hair was shoulder length and looked like he hadn't washed it in weeks! He had a certain evil about him. He stopped and looked over at Jenna.

"What the hell do you want bitch!"

"I was just about to ask you the same question."

Zack was pulling up to the parking lot when Mike looked out the windshield and saw Jenna out talking to a man who had seen better days. He was walking up to her, and Mike wanted out of the van. Mark grabbed his arm.

"Mike, wait!" he said.

With storm clouds in his eyes, he shot a look at his brother.

"I am not sitting here in this van when Jenna may be in danger! What the hell is this guy doing here so early? I thought they were supposed to meet at 4:30!" he yelled.

"He must be getting impatient. The door is propped open, Jenna will be able to get inside if he tries anything," said Zack. They watched and waited. Mike with his heart in his throat and clenched fists was ready to flee the van if he had to.

"What is it that you want?" asked Jenna.

"I'm waiting to meet with two people who work at this restaurant."

He was one disgusting dude, Jenna thought.

"Maybe I can help you. Can you tell me who you are to meet?" she asked.

"It's none of your business, bitch!" he yelled.

Jenna was really getting put out with being called a bitch every time he spoke.

"Look, I work here, and the two people you are meeting with may not even be on the schedule for tonight." Her heart started racing as he started to walk towards her. Maybe she went a little too far. He got right in Jenna's face. She tried to stay calm.

"Okay bitch! I'm looking for Tonya and Nate. Now tell me if they are here!"

Jenna backed up towards the door. She almost gagged, he smelled so bad!

"Well, I'm pretty sure I saw them on the schedule for tonight. You know it might be a good idea to take a bath once in a while. You reek something awful!" Jenna was not normally a rude person, but this guy was disgusting! When he pulled back his arm to hit her, she almost lost it. Palani opened the door. The man backed off.

"Are you alright, Jenna? I was coming out of the storeroom and heard voices and noticed the door propped open," he said with concern. She smiled up at Palani, then turned, and gave the man a weathering look.

"Oh, I'm fine, Palani, just some smelly asshole trying to sell me something."

With that, she walked back into the restaurant. She was shaking from the encounter with him. Palani gave him a disgusting look and told him they didn't allow solicitors to come to the back door.

"And by the looks of you, you wouldn't be allowed in the restaurant!" The man gave him the finger and walked off. Jenna picked up her trash can. Palani, concerned, asked, "Are you sure you are alright?"

"I'm fine, Palani, no worries."

He watched her go. She was pretty shaken. He would let Mike know when he came in.

She was shaking when she got back to her office where she was going to stay put until Mike came and got her!

In the van, Mike grabbed the door handle as the guy drew back his arm to hit Jenna when Palani opened the door. The man backed off and Jenna went inside. Mike breathed a sigh of relief. She was safe. If he would have hit her, he would have killed him!

"Good, Jenna is inside." Even both Zack and Mark were holding their breath. "It won't be long now," said Zack.

Five minutes later, Tonya, Nathan, and Mick came out the back door. Ralph had gone to the side of the building. When it was time to meet, he came around and stood in front of the three of them.

Mick took one look at him and thought this guy is a real piece of work! He wondered who in the hell would hire him to work his business.

Ralph was studying this guy that was with Nate and Tonya and was cautious. He glanced at Nate.

"Who in the hell is this guy?" he shifted his head towards Mick.

"He is a friend of the family," replied Nate.

"What's he doing here?" He gave Mick a steely glare.

"Mick, this is Ralph, Ralph this is Mick."

With his arms crossed and feet apart he stood and looked at Ralph with eyes that could burn right through you, Mick nodded his head. Ralph walked up to Nate and stood inches from his face.

"I asked you what he was doing here. My business is with you and Tonya, you asshole! Not him!" he yelled.

"Do you mind stepping back? You reek! Don't you believe in taking a shower?"

That earned him a punch in the gut. Nate was sent back a couple of paces. He clutched his stomach and groaned. Ralph was getting a little tired of people telling him he needed to take a shower or a bath! He was just fine the way he was!

Tonya started to get pissed. Nervousness gone! She looked back at her brother to make sure he was okay.

"Look Ralph," said Tonya, "we have your money, but we had to borrow it from Mick. The money we had for you went to the funeral home to put towards our mom's funeral expenses. Our mother passed and her funeral was today!" she said with force.

Ralph stepped back.

"Well, I'm sorry about your mom, but where is my money?"

Mick walked up to Ralph. Mick stood a good six inches taller than him, and Ralph wasn't quite sure he wanted to mess with him. He waited while Mick pulled out a money clip with a wad of bills that made his eyes pop out! He counted out $2,000 and handed it to Ralph.

"Here's your $2,000. The loan was just transferred to me. I'm sure your boss won't have a problem with that, right Ralph?" asked Mick.

"Well, it's not usually done this way."

"Doesn't matter how it's done! You got your money. Now you go and tell your boss that the debt is paid in full. If he gives you any shit, he can come and see me. Better yet I would like to meet this boss of yours. We work in the same circles. I can help him out if you know what I mean."

Mick's eyes bore into Ralph. He could tell he was a sleazebag. It wouldn't surprise him if he skimmed off the top and pocketed the money. Good reason for his boss to kill him if he ever got caught. And Nathan was right; he stunk to high heaven! He wasn't sure he would be able to work with this guy.

Ralph was trying to figure out if he could trust this guy. He had an evil glint in his eyes as he thought about all the money that was in Mick's pocket. He decided he would get to know this guy, and if he checked out, he would introduce him to his boss. If it didn't work out, he'd knock him off and take all his money!

Ralph looked at Tonya and Nate.

"Okay, you two are off the hook, and you can make your payments to him. Mick, my friend, you and I have some discussing to do. How about we go to my favorite bar down town, and I'll buy you a drink."

"How about I meet you down there, just tell me where it is."

Mick knew this worthless piece of shit may try to steal his money. He would watch his back and see what he could do to get rid of him through Ralph's boss. They both walked out into the parking lot and Ralph gave him directions to the bar. Mick decided to take his time and let this asshole stew a bit.

Chapter 22

Zack, Mike, and Mark watched Tonya and Nathan go into the restaurant while Mick and Ralph walked to their cars. As they listened, Ralph was giving directions to a bar in downtown Honolulu.

Mike turned to Zack, "Is Mick in?"

"Not yet, but it's a start. He needs to establish a relationship with him and then he will be checked out to see if his story matches what we have in the system."

They watched Ralph leave, and Mick get into his car. Mick called Zack's cell phone.

"Did you get all that?"

"Yes. Are you heading down to the bar?"

"Yes, I want him to sit for a few minutes before I get there," said Mick.

"Right, I will follow you down with the van. I got your back," said Zack.

"Thanks," said Mick.

"Do you need one of us to go with you?" asked Mike.

"No, we'll take it from here. Thanks for volunteering to be back up. I appreciate it," said Zack.

"No problem. Actually, it was exciting except for the part when Jenna was talking to that piece of shit! And speaking of Jenna, I need to go to her. I'm sure she is wondering what happened," said Mike. Mark and Mike got out of the van, waved to Zack, and entered the restaurant through the back entrance. Palani stopped Mike and had a quick word with him.

Mark went to check with the hostess to see how things were going. After talking with Palani, Mike went directly to Jenna's office. When Mike walked in, he found her with her head bent down pacing back and forth. She looked up when Mike entered her office. She rushed into his arms.

"Oh, Mike, honey, I was so worried!" She pulled away from him. "Are you alright? How did it go? Was Tonya and Nathan released from the loan shark? Are they alright? How about the undercover cop, did he make it in?"

"Whoa, slow down a little." Mike took her over to her chair, sat down, and pulled Jenna onto his lap and wrapped his arms around her. "I will answer all of your questions, but first I want a kiss." She gave him a quick peck on the lips. "Jenna, sweetheart," he said sternly.

"Yes?"

"I need more than that from you."

She gazed into his eyes and saw something she hadn't seen before. Was it fear? She pressed her lips against his in a long searching kiss which turned into heated passion.

When he lifted his head, he asked, "Do you have any idea how scared I was when I saw you out standing in front of the back door talking to that sleazebag of a man who was about to hit you?"

"You saw that?" she asked.

"Mark and I were with Zack in the van and saw everything. Thank heaven Palani came out when he did, because if he had hit you, he may not be living today. What were you doing out there?"

"Well, I needed to get up and stretch. I saw that the trash can in Mark's office needed emptying, and mine, too. It was still early, so I hurried and went to the dumpster. When I went to go back into the restaurant, I saw a man pacing back and forth and thought it might be Ralph. He saw me and asked what the hell I wanted. He called me a bitch, Mike! Several times! Well, that got my hackles up, and I proceeded to ask him what he was doing out here. I'm afraid I got him angry with questioning him. That's when he came up to me. Mike, he smelled so bad. When I mentioned he needed to take a bath once in a while, he brought his arm back at the same time Palani came out to check to see what was going on."

Mike could not believe what he was hearing.

"Jenna, you could have been seriously hurt!"

"I'm sorry, Mike, but he made me so mad! I even called him an asshole before I went inside the restaurant! And I never swear!" Mike watched the expression on her face while she was explaining and he had to smile.

"You, my little one, are one feisty lady! I am definitely going to have to change your pet name. Jenna, I am so thankful that nothing happened to you." He bent and kissed her hard. It was a long time before they broke apart. "Jenna, sweetheart, I need to go see what is happening out on the floor."

She sat up.

"But you haven't told me how it all went down!"

"Tell you what, let's go see if Mark needs any help, then we'll have dinner, and I'll tell you everything." Jenna got up off his lap, and Mike followed her out of the office. She locked her office and Mark's. Mike took Jenna's hand, and they walked out into the restaurant.

Mark was seating a group, and there was a line up at the door.

"What do you want me to do?" she asked. He looked around and saw Kristy, the new hostess, was on tonight.

"Could you check with Kristy at the hostess station and see if she needs help. She's new, and she looks to be overwhelmed."

"Okay, boss!" she smiled. Mike smiled and shook his head as he went to check on the dining rooms to see if any tables were available. Jenna walked up to Kristy and asked how she could help. Kristy looked relieved and gave her a notepad and a pen and asked if she could take names.

"How long is the wait time?" asked Jenna.

"About an hour," said Kristy. Jenna got to work and the rest of the night flew by as the demands of the restaurant overtook them. They were finally able to sit down to dinner around 9:00 when it slowed down.

Mike had ordered the Hawaiian chicken with rice and salad. He had Megan bring an assortment of dressings for the salads. He wasn't sure what Jenna preferred. When they sat down in a corner booth in the bar area, Megan came up to see what they wanted to drink. When their order was in, Mike put his arm around Jenna.

"Thanks for helping tonight."

"You're welcome, I was glad I could help."

Mark joined them.

"I took the liberty of ordering you a beer," said Mike.

"Thanks, bro. Is it me, or is this place getting busier by the day?" asked Mark.

"It has been crazy lately. We may have to hire more staff if this continues. They are overloaded trying to keep up," said Mike. Mark took this opportunity and said, "What would you think about hiring a general manager? We could use a break from working out on the floor every night and focus on other aspects of the business. I'll be honest, I am fast approaching burn out. I can't seem to slow down enough to relax and have a life!"

Mike listened to his brother and knew he was right. Both of them were stretched to the max, especially Mark, who handled all the bookkeeping and helped out on the floor when needed, which had been a lot more lately.

"You're right, bro, we are both feeling it. I'll place an ad on Monday and start the interview process the following week. And while we are discussing staff, how about someone to help with the financial end?" asked Mike.

Mark looked over at Jenna and smiled. He looked back at his brother and said, "Jenna has been doing a great job on the reports and learning all the aspects of what I do. She catches on fast." He glanced back at Jenna, "You have been a big help to me, Jenna. I appreciate all that you have accomplished and in helping find the shortages, which led us to the people who were taking the liquor," said Mark.

"You're welcome. I find that I am learning a lot. I like the work," replied Jenna.

"Maybe you would consider a job here at the restaurant after you graduate?" asked Mark.

Jenna looked surprised by the offer. Mike was watching her reaction hoping she would consider the job. She looked at Mike and back at Mark, "I would very much consider working here."

Megan brought out their drinks and shortly after their food.

"Would there be anything else I can get you?" she asked.

Mark looked up, gave Megan a wink, "I think we are all set, Megan, thank you."

Megan smiled and blushed at the same time. When she left the table, she couldn't help feeling flutters in her stomach when Mark winked at her. He was gorgeous. She needed to forget about him because she knew he wouldn't date her. Maybe when she finished her online schooling and landed a job, maybe there would be a chance to get to know each other. She could only hope!

Jenna took a bite of her Hawaiian chicken and raved over Palani's skill at producing such tender mouthwatering dishes. He had an excellent staff under him that worked together to accomplish the four-star rating this restaurant deserved. She thought about the job offer, and it would be an honor to work in such a highly rated establishment. Mike and Mark were discussing possibly expanding the restaurant or maybe building another one on the other side of the island. Jenna was content to just listen and enjoy her meal. She still wanted to know how it went down today with Tonya and Nate, but she could wait. After they finished eating would be a perfect opportunity.

Megan came and took the empty dishes. All three ordered coffee. When she returned with the coffee Jenna piped up and finally asked how it went with Nathan and Tonya. Mike took her hand and placed it on his thigh. He smiled down at her.

"You have been pretty patient, my feisty one!"

She smiled back at him, "I have, and now I want all the details!"

"Well, you already met Ralph. Which by the way, I don't ever want to go through that again!" said Mike.

"You gave us all a scare!" said Mark.

"I gave myself a scare! When he walked up to me, I wasn't sure what to do. I tried to remain calm. I was glad Palani came out when he did!" Jenna exclaimed. Mike squeezed her hand and continued explaining.

"When Tonya, Nathan, and Mick came out the back entrance, Ralph came around the side of the building and met with them. We could hear the conversation through Mick's wire in his watch." Ralph was upset with Mick being there and wanted to know what he was doing in their business. Nathan got a punch in the gut when he told him he reeked."

"Is he alright?" asked Jenna.

"He's fine. Tonya took it from there and gave him the story about giving the money to the funeral home, and they had to borrow the money from Mick, who was a friend of the family. Mick took out a money clip with a wad of bills and handed it to Ralph. The loan was passed off, and Tonya and Nate are out of it," explained Mike.

"So, this undercover agent got in?" asked Jenna.

Mark spoke up, "Zack explained that it was a start. If he could establish a relationship with Ralph and Mick's story checks out, there's a good chance he will get inside the loan shark's business."

"Wow, I hope it works. Too many people are taken advantage of, especially when they are struggling with their finances. Did you find out if their mother had life insurance?" she asked.

"Yes, she did. So, you don't have to set up a Go Fund Me account, little one." Mike beamed down at her.

"That must have been such a relief for them."

"It was. Now what do you say we close up shop and head home?" asked Mike.

"I'm all for it," said Mark, "I'm beat!"

In downtown Honolulu, Mick was having trouble stomaching being around Ralph. Even his appearance was embarrassing, let alone the stench. Ralph was starting to slur his words since he had four shots of whiskey to his two bottles of beer. He ordered another shot and asked if Mick needed another beer. Mick shook his head no.

"Are you sure? 'Cause I'm buying!"

"No thanks, Ralph, I'm driving."

"That never stopped me, I have an in with the sheriff's department. I never get caught."

"Well Ralph, I'm new in town and don't need a ticket for drunk driving."

Ralph's drink came, and he chugged it down in one gulp. He wiped his mouth with the back of his hand and looked at Mick.

"I like you, Mick. If what you told me about working for Ray Lopez checks out I'll introduce you to my boss. He has a few openings in his line of business. I'll put in a good word for you."

"Thanks, Ralph, I would appreciate it. I need a job and bad. The money's getting low."

Not from what I seen, thought Ralph. Ralph ordered another drink.

"Don't you think you should go easy on that stuff?" asked Mick.

"Nah, I do it all the time!"

With any luck, Ralph will end up with sclerosis of the liver and eliminate himself, Mick thought. "Hey, you mentioned you know a cop that works for the sheriff's department. How did you get in with him?"

Ralph huffed, "He owed the boss some serious money and couldn't pay him back. The boss offered him a deal. He would clear the loan if he would check out the men he hired into his business to make sure they weren't an undercover cop." Ralph was really slurring his words.

"What all does your boss, deal in?" asked Mick.

"Oh, he's into a little bit of everything." He shrugged his shoulders. "Drug trafficking, loan sharking, I even heard he may be into human trafficking. You didn't hear that last part from me."

"Didn't hear a thing, Ralph, didn't hear a thing."

"I got a go take a leak." He slid off the bar stool and stumbled to the restroom, running into people as he went.

Mick was ready for a reprieve. He took a look around the bar and saw a pretty young woman with long straight black hair, dark eyes, and olive skin. Her lips were a pale pink, just right for kissing. She glanced up at him and their eyes locked. She looked away and turned to listen to what one of her friends were saying. She laughed and the whole bar lit up with her smile. He wondered how he could ditch Ralph, so he could go over and introduce himself. Ralph came back out of the restroom and slid back on the bar stool. He ordered one more whiskey and guzzled it down. He took one look at Mick and said he was leaving. Thank God for small miracles! He watched Ralph weave and stumble his way out the door and realized Ralph stuck him with the bar bill. What an asshole! He turned back to the table where the pretty lady and her friends were sitting, and they were gone! Damn! He so wanted to meet her! There was something about her that drew him. Maybe he'd run into her again. A pretty blonde woman waltzed up to him and introduced herself to him. He pushed a button on his watch. Zack didn't need to hear this conversation. She looked like she was up for some action tonight so who was he to argue.

"Hi, I'm Mick Southerland. Can I buy you a drink?"

Zack, sitting out in the van, followed the conversation. He was curious who in the sheriff's department was working for Ralph's boss. He was also shocked to hear that Ralph's boss could possibly be into human trafficking, another crime to pin on him. God, he hoped it was Manchez! He really wanted to put that guy away for a long time. It sounded like Jason may soon get inside. He thought he had heard a woman in the background before he turned his watch off. Maybe Jason would get lucky tonight. He thought of Tonya. One day he was going to get brave enough to ask her out. He was relieved that everything had worked out for her and her brother. He saw Ralph come out of the bar and stumble to his car. He had called a patrol car from the police department to be ready to follow Ralph and arrest him for drunk driving. He wasn't going to get out of this one. The patrol car was sitting a way back from his van, and he radioed him to be ready. When Ralph pulled out of the parking lot, the patrol car pulled out onto the road and sped up behind him. The officer pulled him over, got out of the car, and walked up to his window.

"Sir, may I see your driver's license and registration please?"

Ralph took one look at the officer and slurring his words said, "Do you work for the Sheriff's Department?"

"No, sir, I don't. Officer Beck, from the Police Department, your registration and driver's license please."

Ralph bent down to the glove box and pulled out the registration. He was having a rough time getting his driver's license out of his wallet. When he finally got it out and handed it to the officer, he said, "Can I ask you why you stopped me?"

"Sir, you were weaving all over the road, and I can smell your breath a mile away. I stopped you because you are under the influence of alcohol, and you shouldn't be driving. I will be right back."

While Ralph sat in the car, he swore, wondering how in the hell this happened. He never got caught. Officer Beck got back in his car and ran a check. He radioed Zack, "This guy has several warrants out for his arrest. Call for back up, this guy may run."

Zack got on the radio and called in back up. He watched officer Beck get out of his car and walk back up to Ralph's window. He gave him back his license and registration.

"Sir, I am going to have to ask you to step out of the car, I am placing you under arrest for driving under the influence of alcohol and several warrants for parking tickets you haven't paid."

"Like hell you will!" Ralph punched the gas pedal and took off!

The officer flew to his car and sped down the road in a high-speed chase on Kalakaua Avenue in downtown Honolulu. Zack followed behind in the van. He watched as Ralph took a turn down an alley. Zack sped by and took a right on 10th Avenue to try and block him from coming out of the alley. As he approached, Ralph sped out and took a right turn on 10th. Zack got on the radio and gave his location. It wasn't long before they had Ralph cornered. Ralph tried to take a right turn on to 11th Street but failed and hit a light pole.

Police cars surrounded Ralph's car. Officers filed out of their patrol cars with their guns pulled as they approached his vehicle. When they asked him to step out of his car with his hands up, Ralph knew he was in trouble, not only with the police, but with his boss. He hoped his new friend Mick could help him out.

Chapter 23

*T*he next morning, Jason showed up at the Police Department when he got a call last night from Ralph saying that he was arrested on drunk driving charges and not paying his parking tickets. Zack met him in the lobby and led him back to his office.

"Have a seat," said Zack.

Jason took a chair in front of the desk.

"So, Ralph gave you a call?"

"Yeah, right in the middle of entertaining a pretty blonde I hooked up with last night. I thought it could wait until this morning," said Jason.

"Good call, but I've got to tell you, according to the officers on duty last night he's been a real pain in the ass. His stench is so bad, they could hardly stand to go back to his cell," said Zack.

"Tell me about it! Zack, I'm not sure I will be able to stomach working with this guy!" Zack leaned forward and placed his folded hands on his desk. "I've given this some thought and maybe you could use this to your advantage."

"I'm listening," said Jason.

Zack grinned and explained how he could manipulate Ralph and be able to stand being around him.

Jason was led back to Ralph's cell. When Ralph saw Mick coming back the first words out of his mouth was, "What the hell took you so long? I called you last night!"

"Well Ralph, you caught me in a rendezvous with a beautiful blonde woman, and I wasn't going to leave her to come bail you out! I do have a life," he said curtly.

"Sorry, can you get me out of this joint?"

"Why didn't you bail your own self out? The bail was set for $2000 plus what you owe for the parking tickets. Now, Ralph, I know you had the two grand since I gave that to you last evening," said Mick.

"What the hell was I supposed to do, Mick? If I went back to my boss and didn't have the money, he would have me killed! And if he finds out I was arrested, he still may have me killed! You gotta help me, Mick!"

Mick was giving him the eye and then a sly smile broke out across his face. That look left Ralph wondering what was going to come out of his mouth.

"Okay, Ralph, I will get you out of here on two conditions."

"What's that?" he asked cautiously.

"Number one, that you clean yourself up, put on some clean clothes, and get a haircut."

"Why do I need to do that? I look and smell just fine!" he said.

Mick shook his head. *Is this guy for real?* "Number two, you introduce me to your boss."

Ralph thought it over, "I'll agree to number two, but not to number one. I don't need a bath!"

"Either you accept both, or you can bail yourself out or sit here until your court date. Which is it going to be Ralph?"

Ralph was mulling it over. He couldn't give up the money to bail himself out, and he couldn't wait for a court date; maybe when Mick got him out he'd try to ditch him so he wouldn't have to take a bath. He hated baths.

"Okay, Mick, you have a deal, now get me out of here!"

"In due time, Ralph. I need your clothes size and shoe size."

"What do you need that for?"

Mick grinned, "Well, Ralph, you're not leaving here until you have showered and changed clothes. Are we still in agreement?"

Ralph started to pace in his cell. Dammit! It didn't look like he was going to get out of this, he thought. He turned and faced Mick with a steely glare, "Okay you got me, but I don't have to like it!" Mick was relieved. Ralph gave him his sizes, and Mick left to acquire said clothes.

Mick and Ralph came out of the police station and walked across the street. Ralph fought the shower, and it took two police officers to make sure he scrubbed down.

"That wasn't so bad, now was it?" asked Mick.

"It wasn't fun!"

"What do you have against taking a bath or a shower?"

"When I was young, my mom used to scrub me so hard, it made my skin raw, and when I got older, I refused to take them. When she tried to make me, I hauled off and cuffed her. She never asked me again."

"You beat your mother?" asked Mick.

"Once, and that's all it took."

Mick could feel his muscles getting tense and clenched his fists. What a low life! He couldn't believe anyone would beat their mother for any reason, much less a bath.

They were walking in front of the shops on Kalakaua Avenue and took a right into a barber shop. Ralph stopped.

"Are you really going to make me get a haircut?" he asked angrily.

"That was part of the deal, unless you want me to take you back to jail," said Mick.

He glared at Mick and walked in.

When they came out of the barber shop, Ralph looked like a new man. He had it cropped short, and when the barber was done, he couldn't believe the change it made in his appearance. Maybe this wasn't a bad thing after all. He actually felt pretty good!

Mick put his hand on his shoulder.

"Now, Ralph, my friend," said Mick, "how about introducing me to your boss?"

"His office is just around the corner on 10th Avenue. I need to turn this money in, so this would be as good a time as any," said Ralph. "Let's go!"

Mick and Ralph arrived at the high rise and were in the elevator heading up to the 25th floor.

Ralph turned to Mick, "Let me do the talking, and I'll see if I can get you in."

Mick wasn't sure he trusted Ralph, but he was in it now and had to go with it. The elevator door opened, and they walked out. Ralph went up to the receptionist and asked to see Mr. Manchez. Mick instantly became alert that that was the man Zack and the Honolulu Police Department were trying to bring down. Ralph turned to Mick.

"I will need to go in first, take care of business and then I will come out and get you."

"No, I will go in with you," Mick said sternly.

"Hey Mick, don't you trust me?"

"Should I?" asked Mick.

Just then the receptionist looked up, "Mr. Manchez will see you now."

Ralph opened the door. The two men walked in.

Marco Manchez was sitting behind a large mahogany desk in the middle of his office. Two leather chairs were set in front of the desk. As Mick looked around the room, there was a conference table with six chairs placed around it in front of tall windows on one side and a small round table with two leather chairs placed in front of the windows on the other side. The expensive art work and paintings that adorned the walls brought about an air of the man sitting behind the desk. *Very impressive,* thought Mick, *but at what price?* How much money did his criminal activity go towards purchasing these fine relics? He turned back to look at Manchez, he was staring at Ralph with unbelieving eyes.

Ralph walked up to Manchez and the look he gave Ralph was of shock!

"Ralph, is that you?" asked Manchez.

"I'm afraid so. Hell, I know you would prefer the old me, but I was forced to take a look at myself and make some changes."

Manchez looked up at Mick who was standing behind the chair with his arms crossed and legs apart. He gave Mick a steely glare. He glared back at Ralph.

"Who the hell is this guy and what's he doing here?" he yelled. Ralph looked over at Mick and turned back to Manchez.

"I ran in to him when I collected on a loan for Nathan McDaniels and Tonya Forest."

Mick was watching Ralph as he tried to explain why he was here. Mick took over the conversation. Mick walked up to Manchez's desk and extended his hand.

"Mick Southerland." Manchez shook his hand cautiously while eyeing him at the same time. "I am sorry to intrude. I'm a friend of the family of Nathan and Tonya. Their mother just passed away. I loaned them the money to pay back this loan as their money went to funeral expenses. I am here to make sure the loan is cleared. They kept a record of their payments and the interest you charged, and after looking at the original money borrowed, this loan has been more than paid back." Mick's eyes bore into Manchez.

Marco sat back in his chair mulling over what Mick said and trying to read this guy. He sat forward and glared at Ralph.

"Is he telling the truth?"

Ralph stared back.

"Yes. He was with Tonya and Nate and handed over the cash when I went to collect the money."

Marco looked back at Mick.

"Have a seat." Mick took the seat next to Ralph. Marco's beady eyes stared into Mick's.

"What line of work are you in Mick to have that kind of cash on hand?" Mick smiled as he stared back at Manchez.

"I was working for a guy by the name of Ray Lopez. Have you heard of him?" asked Mick.

Marco leaned back in his chair again and thought for a moment.

"The name sounds familiar. Wasn't he the guy who got caught for loan sharking over in Dallas?"

"The very one," replied Mick.

"If you were working for him, how was it that you didn't get caught with him?"

"I was out of town when it came down. I certainly wasn't going to turn myself in. When I got the call that Nate and Tonya's mother passed, I saw this as an opportunity for a fresh start as well as paying my condolences to them. When they told me about their dilemma, I offered to help them out. What are friends for, after all, and with what I've seen of the island, I could very well make it my home here. But I'm going to need a job. I came here with Ralph, not only to make sure the loan was clear, but to see if you have any openings available since I've worked in the same circle as Ralph here."

"What makes you think I would hire someone straight out of Dallas?" asked Marco.

Mick shrugged his shoulders, "I don't, but if you would consider it, I could make it worth your while."

Marco studied him and asked, "What other business dealings was Mr. Lopez involved in?"

"The police got him on loan sharking and drug trafficking. Those were the only two I was involved in."

Marco leaned forward and pulled a file drawer out from his desk. He pulled a file with Tonya and Nate's paperwork in it. He placed it on his desk and took a rubber stamp and marked paid on the loan papers.

"The loan is paid. Now if you will excuse us Mick, I need to discuss some business with Ralph here. I will get back to you if and when I decide there is an opening."

Mick got out of the chair and handed him his card, "I would appreciate it. You can call me anytime." He left the office wondering if he had made a good enough impression on Manchez to get him in the door.

Marco looked at Ralph, "You have the money?"

"Yes." Ralph pulled out his wallet and handed the wad of bills over to Marco. He watched nervously as he counted out the full $2,000. When he was done, Marco looked straight into Ralph's eyes. "Do you think this guy is on the level?"

"Yeah, I do. But there is only one way to be sure." Ralph stared back at Marco.

"Call the informer and see if his story checks out," said Marco.

"We could use a guy like him in my business. Go out and see if you can get any more loans." Ralph got up and was ready to leave when Marco said, "Oh, and Ralph," Ralph looked back, "Nice improvement on your hygiene. Stay that way!" he said sternly.

Shit, thought Ralph. *Now, thanks to Mick, I'm going to have to bathe on a regular basis! The hell if this doesn't suck!*

Zack and Craig Jenson, another detective who was working the case with him, sat in the van and heard every word that was said. Zack jumped up and down in his seat when he heard Manchez first talking to Ralph.

"Sounds like Jason has a good chance of getting in," said Craig.

"Hell yes, he does," said Zack. "Let's head back to the office, make sure his story lines up with what we have in the system. Whoever the informer is, he may be checking it soon," said Zack.

"This case is getting bigger. We need to send in another undercover agent to find out who the informer is," said Craig.

"We'll talk to Lieutenant Fillmore when we get back to the station," said Zack. "See who we could send in."

As they headed back, Zack felt more optimistic that this case would soon be wrapped up.

Chapter 24

*J*enna slept in this morning. When Mike drove her home last night, he came in, and they sat and talked until after one in the morning. When he left, she was bone tired and fell instantly asleep when she hit the bed. She enjoyed spending time with him. She looked at the clock. It was 9:30! She was supposed to meet him at one of her favorite coffee shops not too far from her apartment in an hour! She sprang out of bed and into the shower. She dressed in a pair of blue jeans and a soft, yellow knit, sleeveless sweater. She slid into some yellow flip flops to match her sweater, and was soon heading in the direction of the coffee shop.

She was a little late. She saw Mike sitting outside at one of the tables in the lanai. She waved and walked into the restaurant and out into the lanai where he was sitting. He rose and gave her a kiss.

"Hi gorgeous!" he grinned.

"Hi handsome!" she grinned back.

"I took the liberty of ordering you your coffee. Have you eaten anything this morning?" he asked. "No, have you?"

"Just a roll, but I could eat some breakfast." Jenna took a sip of her coffee. This coffee shop had great coffee. Jenna looked over at Mike. "I have never had any of their food. What do you recommend?" She only stopped here for coffee in the morning before she went to class.

"They have a great breakfast menu. When I've come here in the past, I usually get their waffle with fruit. It's excellent!" he said.

Jenna was looking over the menu and thought what he suggested sounded good.

"Okay, I'll have that." Their waitress came up and filled Mike's coffee and asked if they were ready to order. Mike gave her their order and turned back to Jenna when she left.

He gazed intently into her brown eyes. She didn't have a lot of makeup on. She was beautiful without it. Her long dark hair flowed down her back. The slight breeze brought some tendrils onto her cheek. He took his hand and brushed them behind her ear. Oh, how he wished he could take her home and make love to her. But he made a promise to her, and he would keep it. She would have to make the next move.

Jenna felt herself tingling as Mike caressed her skin and tucked her hair behind her ear. His blue eyes shone as he gazed into her eyes.

"Have you heard any word from your parents if they will be able to make it to your graduation?" he asked.

"Not yet, I left a message with them on the date and time of the commencement, but still no word. I know they are busy with the planting season but should be finished in time for my graduation. I haven't talked to my mom in a couple of weeks. I'll try calling her a little later today."

Their waitress brought their waffles out. They were huge with a mixture of strawberries, blueberries, and pineapple on top. Whip cream was put around the fruit and looked simply delicious. Jenna took a bite and thought she was in heaven. She caught Mike's eyes. "This is amazing, thank you for recommending it!"

He gave her an appreciative grin, "You're welcome, little one. What would you like to do this morning?"

She hadn't really thought about it. She needed to get some studying done for her class in the morning before she went into work.

"Well, I need to study before I go into work later today, why?"

"Would you like to take a walk down Kalakaua Avenue? Maybe go into some of the shops at the mall?" He wanted to spend as much time as he could with her. He wanted to know everything about her. Jenna looked at her watch.

"Do you think we could be back by 1:30?"

"I think we could manage it, what do you say?"

She knew the mall wasn't far from there, so she said, "Sure, I would love to go." She gave him a radiant smile. He smiled back. She brought such joy into his heart. They finished up their waffles, paid their bill, and started out walking to the mall.

He held her hand while they walked down Kalakaua Avenue looking into windows and seeing displays of what the stores had to offer. He found that they had a lot in common as they discussed different topics along the way. They entered the mall and came across a store Jenna wanted to go in to. She saw a necklace that was displayed in the window. She went ahead of him to see if there were any in the display case inside. A clerk came up to them and asked if he could help them.

"I saw a necklace in your display window outside your store and wondered if you had one inside to look at," enquired Jenna.

"Do you see anyone of these that matches it?" he asked.

She looked around the display case and didn't see a one.

"No, is there any way you could pull the one in the window?"

"Sure, just show me which one it is," he replied. Jenna took him out and showed him the necklace while Mike stayed back and waited. The clerk and Jenna came back in. He pulled the necklace from the window and took it to the display case where Jenna and Mike waited. He handed it to Jenna. It was beautiful. The necklace was a cross made in white gold with a quarter karat diamond in the center on a thin, white gold chain. The diamond sparkled under the lights in the jewelry store. She looked at the price tag and knew she would have to put this on her wish list. It was way too expensive on her budget.

Mike was watching her and saw the emotions crossing her face. He knew she wanted it but handed it back to the clerk. Mike intercepted and took the necklace from her. He looked over at the clerk, "Could she try it on?"

Jenna looked at Mike in surprise.

"Mike no, I can't really afford it right now."

Mike ignored her. He took the necklace out of the box. Jenna pulled her hair up, so he could place it around her neck. Jenna tingled as she felt his fingers grazed along her neck. He turned her around, so he could see. It looked perfect against her tan skin. He noticed that when she wore any jewelry, it was always simple, nothing gaudy. Mike pulled out his wallet and handed the clerk his credit card.

"We'll take it," said Mike. The clerk took one look at his credit card and smiled.

"Yes sir, Mr. TreVaine." The clerk turned back to Jenna, "Do you wish to wear it or would you like me to put it back in the box so you can take it home?"

Jenna was speechless. Mike gazed down into questioning eyes. "Mike, I…"

"She'll wear it," said Mike, still gazing into her eyes.

"I'll be right back with your receipt," said the clerk.

Jenna was overwhelmed. She didn't know what to say.

"Mike, I can't accept this, it's too much!"

"It's too late, it's already been done. Jenna, the necklace was made for you. It looks perfect around your neck. I want to buy this for you. Think of it as an early graduation gift." And he was thinking it would go perfect with the diamond ring he bought for her.

The clerk came back with his credit card and receipt. Jenna watched him put his credit card and receipt back in his wallet. When she caught his eyes, she reached up with her hands on either side of his face and kissed him right there in the store. She broke the kiss and slightly pulled away, "Thank you, but I still think it's too much."

Mike pulled her in his arms and kissed her with the love that he was feeling for this woman. The clerk walked away thinking, *Jeez, go get a room already!*

When they broke apart, he replied, "It's not too much for the woman I love."

Jenna's heart melted; she loved him so much. He took her hand and walked her out of the store.

They walked around the mall but didn't see anything that enticed them to have a look. Time went by, and it was soon time to head back. When he walked her up to her apartment door, she was curious, "When will Tonya and Nathan be back to work?"

"Tomorrow," he said.

She opened her door, careful of Cuddles. She closed the door quickly when she saw her cat heading for the door. Mike picked her up and gently scratched behind her ears. He held her for a few minutes and gently put her down. She scampered off in the direction of the kitchen.

"Would you like some coffee if I put it on?" she asked.

"That would be great, I'd love a cup." They went into the kitchen and her cat was looking and meowing at her like, 'Did you forget me this morning?'

Mike, watching, asked, "What's the matter with her?"

Jenna sighed, "I completely forgot to feed her this morning!"

"Tell you what," said Mike, "I'll put the coffee on while you get her fed."

"Okay." Jenna set about getting Cuddles food and filling her water dish with fresh water and her cat was soon feasting off her favorite food. Mike had the coffee on, and it was almost done brewing. Jenna took the cream out of the fridge and set it on the counter.

Mike came up behind Jenna while she was pouring the coffee into mugs. He took her hair and pulled it away from her neck, so he could shower kisses down her neck and back up to that sensitive spot behind her ear. Jenna was feeling goose bumps all the way down to her toes. She turned around to face him as he pressed his lips down on hers all while pulling her body close to his. Jenna wrapped her arms around his neck and kissed him back. Mike wanted desperately to explore her delicious body but held back. When he lifted his head, they were both breathless.

"Our coffee's getting cold," she whispered. Jenna pulled him back to her for another passionate kiss. She wanted him. It was getting harder for her to resist the temptation to make love with him. She wanted to feel his hands and lips all over her body again. She started moving her hands over his chest and back. She went to pull his shirt up, so she could feel his skin on her hands. Mike grabbed her hands and broke the kiss. He put his forehead on hers.

"Jenna," he groaned, "You're making this hard for me. If we were at my home, I would pick you up and haul you off to bed, but we're not." He searched her eyes and saw the longing and hunger there. He placed his hands on each side of her face and ran his fingers through her hair. He took a deep breath. "Jenna, love, I want desperately to make love to you again, but you have to be sure it's what you want. If we start again, I am not going to stop. Do you understand?"

She looked deep into his eyes and nodded her head, "Yes, I understand. When we do make love again, I won't stop you ever."

He pulled her in his arms and just held her. They were still holding each other when Sasha walked in.

"Hi, you two, I smell coffee, is there any left?" she asked. Mike started to pull away, but Jenna held on and laid her head on his chest.

She looked over at Sasha, "It might be cold."

Sasha went over and checked it out.

"Well, thank goodness we have a microwave! Can I warm yours up?"

Jenna reluctantly let Mike go. She felt the loss. She immediately took his hand, looked up at Mike, he nodded and she said, "Sure."

Sasha went to get their cups and poured one for her. When they were warmed back up, she handed the mugs to them to fix up the way they liked. When they were all seated at the counter, Sasha asked, "So what have you two been up to today?"

Jenna kept Mike's hand in hers. She wanted to stay connected to him.

"We had breakfast at the coffee shop where I get coffee before class. They have great waffles there. Then we walked to the mall," she looked at Mike and smiled, "Mike bought me this necklace."

Sasha picked up the cross that was lying on her chest.

"Oh, Jenna, it's gorgeous! It's perfect for you!" She looked over at Mike. "You have excellent taste," said Sasha.

Mike smiled, "Actually, Jenna picked it out, and you are right," his eyes shone as he looked at Jenna, "She does have excellent taste!"

Jenna smiled back at Mike. She wished they were alone. She wasn't finished talking to him, or kissing him for that matter.

"Are you home for the day?" Jenna asked Sasha.

"Yes, I have a lot of studying to do tonight. Say, aren't you supposed to be getting ready for work?"

Jenna shook her head, "It's only 2:00."

"Uh, you better look at the clock. It's almost 3:00," said Sasha.

She looked up at the clock. Oh, why can't she keep her time straight! She was supposed to get some study time in! Mike squeezed her hand.

"Hey, go get ready, and I will drive you over to the Bistro. I can pick up a sandwich while I am there for dinner. I need to get some work done at home, so it will work out perfect." He leaned down and gave her a quick kiss. "Get going!"

Jenna got up from her chair and went to rinse her cup. She set it in the sink.

"I'll be back in just a bit," she said to Mike. She changed into her work clothes and put her hair up in a ponytail. She applied some makeup and she was ready to go. When she came from her bedroom, Mike and Sasha were discussing where Sasha wanted to apply for medical school.

"I'm looking at a couple of schools in Waco, Texas."

"Waco, Texas! Sasha, that's so far! When will we see each other?" cried Jenna.

Sasha glanced at Jenna, "Well, it's not written in stone, but they have excellent medical schools there. No worries, I'm applying closer to home as well. We'll see where I get accepted and then I'll make my decision."

"I hope it's closer to home, I want to be able to see you."

Sasha came up to her and gave her a hug.

"Where ever I end up, we will always make it a point to see each other. There's always Facetime, and we will get together when we can. You will always be my good friend. We won't ever lose touch. Now, don't worry, after all, I do have to graduate first!" she laughed.

Jenna smiled and was sad at the same time. She knew Sasha would be moving on to medical school. Everything was just moving too fast. It was only a couple of months till graduation. She hugged her friend back with tears in her eyes. She didn't want to think about it.

Mike was watching the two of them. His heart went out to them. There would be a lot of changes for them in their immediate future. He would make sure to be there when it happens. He got off his chair and walked up to Jenna.

"We'd better go or you will be late."

Jenna glanced up at Mike and said, "Okay, I just need to get my purse." She went over to the desk where she put it when they came in. Mike took her hand and led her to the door. She turned back to Sasha, "I will see you after work."

"Okay, I'll be here burning the midnight candle!" she grinned.

After Mike dropped Jenna off and ordered his dinner, he went home to get some much-needed work done at his home. This was the first day off he has had in a while, and his yard was showing it. He ate his sandwich and got busy. He needed to be back at the Bistro in a few short hours. While he worked, thoughts of Jenna never left his mind. She wanted him this afternoon. Was she ready to make a commitment to their relationship? He hoped so. He wanted to hold her and love her long into the night.

Chapter 25

When Jenna came in after Mike dropped her off, she found Sasha in the lanai still studying.

"Hey, how's it going?" asked Jenna. Sasha looked up as Jenna came into the lanai.

"Hey Jenna," she sighed. "It's going, I am so ready to graduate. I'm looking forward to summer break before medical school when I'll probably have my nose stuck in a book 24/7!"

Jenna laughed, "You are probably right! Mark offered me a job in the accounting department at the restaurant after I graduate."

Sasha sat forward in her chair.

"That's wonderful Jenna! Are you going to take it?"

Jenna sat down in the chair next to the table, "I'm leaning towards it. I still have a lot to learn, but I have to admit, I enjoy the work." She stared at her friend. "Are you really thinking about going to Waco, Texas, for medical school?" asked Jenna.

"I really am. There are several good schools in the area, one in particular in the field of alternative medicine, which I want to pursue. I've already sent my application in to see if they will accept me as a student."

Jenna sighed. She knew this day would come when they both went out to pursue their career in the field that they chose.

"I'll miss you. I don't like the thought of you being that far away, but I understand you need to do what's best for you to become a doctor in the field of medicine of your choice. Promise me when you get that degree, you'll come back and practice medicine here on the island."

"I shall try Jenna. But I hope you and Mike will come visit me, and I will come back to the island when I can. We will stay in touch. You will probably get sick of me Facetiming you all the time," chuckled Sasha.

"Never!" replied Jenna. "Hey, do you mind if I study out here with you? I have a quiz tomorrow morning."

"No, I'd love the company," said Sasha.

Jenna got up and went to get her books. They spent a quiet evening studying and relaxing in each other's company. *I am so going to miss this,* thought Jenna.

The next morning, Jenna decided to stay after class in the commons area to get a jump start on some charts she needed to do for her class on Monday. Her phone dinged. She took it out of her pocket and read the text. It was from Mike.

> Hey pretty lady, are you finished with class?

Jenna replied:

> Yes, stayed after to work on some charts for class. It's nice and quiet here. I should be able to finish them.

Mike replied back:

> Will I see you tonight?

She sent back:

I'm planning on it. Around 7:30?

Perfect! See you then, love you!

Love you too!

Jenna smiled; this past week they had spent a lot of time talking and getting to know each other better. Her favorite time with him so far was at the waterfall. He was so patient with her, showing her how to swim and not be afraid. Something her brothers could never do. They were too impatient with her. Being the youngest, they never had much time for her other than teasing and giving her a hard time when she was growing up. The necklace Mike bought her was over the top. She placed her fingers on the cross she wore around her neck. It was beautiful. She remembered their kiss later. He was so good at bringing out the passion she felt inside for him, and she so wanted him. Next time, she was afraid she wouldn't be able to hold back. She shook herself. *Stop daydreaming! You need to get this done!* She worked the next several hours and finished up the charts. Now she could relax this weekend, knowing she was ready for her class on Monday.

Back at her apartment, Jenna decided she had plenty of time to get some laundry done and take a jog along the beach before she had to get ready to meet Mike. She threw some clothes in the washer and went to change into her jogging shorts and a tank top. She pulled her hair up in a ponytail and put a cap on her head to keep the sun from getting in her eyes.

It was a warm day, and it didn't take long to work up a sweat as she jogged Waikiki Beach. The ocean breeze helped cool her as it blew softly across her skin. She jogged past the restaurant and wondered if Mike was there yet. She was looking forward to seeing him tonight. Her heart beat a little faster just thinking about him. She went a little farther down the beach before she decided to head back. She slowed her steps to cool down. She walked past a bench where a very attractive man was sitting and drinking his water. He looked very familiar to her. Where had she seen him? He raised his water bottle to her and flashed a smile her way. She tentatively smiled and waved back. She picked up her speed again and quickly jogged back to her apartment.

Jason, sitting on the bench, admired the pretty woman that past him. He remembered her jogging on this beach last Sunday when he met with Zack and Mike. If they ran into each other again, maybe he would introduce himself. He also wondered about the black-haired beauty he saw the other night at the bar. She intrigued him. Maybe he would go there tonight on the chance that she would be there. He got up and started jogging back to his rental. It was a little home tucked in some other small homes with tropical plants and palm trees in between the houses. It had a beautiful view of the ocean and the beach. It was a little piece of paradise. He felt like he was on vacation instead of working on a major case. When he reached home, he quickly took a shower and made himself something to eat. He was looking forward to checking out the night life in Honolulu.

Jenna came back into her apartment and threw her clothes in the dryer. She went into the kitchen and downed a glass of water. Sasha came in while she was standing by the sink.

"Hey Jenna, what are you up to tonight?"

"Hey, I'm meeting Mike at the restaurant at 7:30, why?" she asked.

"I was wondering if you would go to a bar with me tonight. It's one of the popular ones that just opened up in downtown Honolulu a few months ago. Barb, Kenny, and I went there the other night and had a blast! There was also a very sexy, handsome man that I locked eyes with that gave me a zing right down my spine! I'm hoping he will be there tonight, so I can meet him."

"Sasha," said Jenna, "I'm sure Mike is not going to want me to go to a bar when we are planning to have dinner together. That's why I'm meeting him later in the evening, so he will have time to sit down. And if we did go, what if he doesn't come in? It would be a waste of time."

"But what if he does? I so want to meet him! Please, Jenna?" Sasha pleaded.

Jenna hated to turn her down. "Can't Kenny or Barb go with you?"

"No, they have plans."

"What about Bruce?" she asked.

"No, he has plans, too. Besides I don't want to walk in with a guy, he'll think I'm dating him. Please?" she pleaded again.

Jenna looked at her friend and thought for a moment. She didn't know how Mike was going to take this.

"Okay, tell you what, let's go get changed, and we'll have dinner with Mike. Maybe he would join us later. I would feel better knowing he would be with us."

Sasha jumped up and down with excitement.

"Oh, thank you Jenna. You're a gem!"

"Well, I don't know about that Sasha," Jenna said sighing. "I hope I'm not going to live to regret this."

"Oh, you won't, Jenna, I promise." Jenna still had mixed feelings as they went to shower and get changed to meet Mike for dinner.

The restaurant was packed as usual for a Friday night. She hoped Mike would have time to join them. It was just after 7:00. She didn't see Mike, but Mark saw them and came up to say hi.

"Hi Mark, is Mike around?"

"He's out on the lanai seating a group of people. Can I get you two seated?"

"Yes, do you have anything in the bar area?"

"Let me check." He came back and said there was a booth that just opened along the windows. She looked over at Sasha, and she nodded her head.

Jenna turned back to Mark and said, "Perfect!" Mark led them to the booth at the same time Mike was coming in from the lanai. When he saw Jenna, he came and lifted her up and swung her around. "Mike! Put me down!"

"Not till you kiss me," he said with a grin.

She gave him a quick kiss and slid down his muscular body. She blushed and whispered up to him, "There are too many people around." She felt like everyone was staring at them. Mike laughed, put his arm around her, and followed them over to the booth. Mark left them with menus and went back to seat more customers.

Mike slid in next to Jenna. He glanced across at Sasha.

"Hi Sasha, how are you tonight?"

"I'm great."

"Are you joining us for dinner?" he asked.

"If you don't mind," she said.

"Of course not, you're more than welcome."

For now, Jenna thought. *Wait till I tell him where we're going later. I hope he doesn't blow a nut!*

He turned to Jenna and drank her in. In a pair of black skinny jeans and aqua knit sweater, they showed off her figure perfectly. The diamond in her necklace glittered as she moved about in the booth. He lifted his hand and brushed her hair behind her ear.

"It's going to be a while before I can join you. Can I get you both a drink?"

"Yes, a glass of white Moscato," said Jenna.

Mike looked over at Sasha.

"A glass of chardonnay, please."

He turned back to Jenna and kissed her sweet lips. He whispered in her ear, "Can't wait to get you alone." His eyes glittered with anticipation. Would he still feel this way after she told him where Sasha and she were going later? He gave her another quick kiss before he got up to put their drink order in.

A few minutes later, Tammy set their wine on the table in front of them.

"Can I get you two an appetizer to start with?"

Jenna looked at their list on the table.

"Sasha, what do you think? Should we have potato skins or nachos?" asked Jenna.

"Let's get an order of potato skins."

"Sounds good," said Jenna. Jenna glanced up at Tammy, "We'll have an order of those."

"I'll put that right in for you ladies."

"Thank you," said Jenna.

When Tammy left to put their order in, Jenna took a glance around the bar and saw Nathan and Todd were attending bar tonight. She noticed Tonya was also seating people in the Hawaiian room. She was happy to see them back to work. She would have to ask Mike how it went in their meeting this afternoon. She glanced over at Sasha, who was studying the dinner menu. She picked up hers and asked, "What are you thinking about ordering?"

"They have a Cajun sword fish on the menu for their special tonight. I'm leaning towards having that."

"Hmm, I've never had sword fish, is it good?" asked Jenna.

"If it's prepared right, it's excellent."

"Maybe I'll try that, too."

Their appetizer came, and Tammy set it down on the table with small plates and napkins. It was huge! Potatoes sliced in half were baked to perfection. Tomatoes, onion, and bits of pineapple were sprinkled over the top. Sour cream was served on the side along with some sweet salsa.

"I'm not sure I'll want dinner after eating this!" exclaimed Sasha.

Jenna smiled, "It might be a while before we order. I'm not sure how long Mike will be so eat up!"

Jenna was just about to take a bite when Mike slid into the booth, took it from her and put it in his mouth.

"Hey! That was mine!"

As he was chewing, he stopped and gave her a kiss.

"Sorry, hungry." He got up and was off.

"That man! He ate the whole thing!" she chuckled. Sasha watched them and wished she had someone who cared for her as deeply as Mike did for Jenna. She shouldn't be thinking like this, she had another four more years of intense studying ahead of her, but still...

"You are so lucky, Jenna, to have someone like Mike in your life," said Sasha.

Jenna looked across at her friend, "I know, I didn't plan it, it just happened. He just waltzed right in and took my heart. I can't imagine my life without him in it. Someday it will happen to you, too."

"Hopefully not until I have my medical degree. Speaking of degrees, have you ordered your cap and gown yet?" asked Sasha.

"No, not yet. It's on my to-do list. It seems to be getting longer by the day. How about you?" she asked.

"Yep, all done. My family wants to take me out to dinner after graduation. Were you able to get a hold of your parents?" asked Sasha.

"No, I meant to call them yesterday and didn't get to it. With the time change it's hard to know when it's the best time to call. Sundays they relax more and are not out in the fields as much. I'll try then." They finished up their appetizer and were sipping on their wine when Mike came and joined them.

He slid in the booth, put his arm around Jenna and pulled her close. He gave her a short, sweet kiss. He nuzzled her neck and whispered something in her ear. She blushed and had goose bumps at the same time. Sasha sighed. Mike heard and remembered they were not alone.

"Sorry, Sasha, are you beautiful ladies ready to order some dinner?"

"Are you going to be able to join us?" asked Jenna. The restaurant was still busy with customers waiting at the door.

"I'm going to try, what are you two having?"

"Sasha, are you still getting the Cajun sword fish?" asked Jenna.

"Yes, I am."

"Make that two," she said to Mike.

"Excellent choice," he said and motioned for Tammy. She came up to their booth and Mike gave them their order. Tammy asked what sides they would like.

"Would either of you like another glass of wine?"

"No, just coffee with cream for me," said Jenna.

"I'll have another glass," said Sasha.

Mike turned to Tammy, "You can bring me a cup of coffee with cream with dinner. Thank you, Tammy."

Mike turned back to Jenna and her friend.

"What are your plans after dinner?" he asked out of the blue. Jenna stiffened and looked over at Sasha. Sasha looked back at Jenna and then over at Mike.

"We were planning to go to a new bar over on Kalakaua Avenue. Sort of a girl's night out," she said hesitantly.

"You mean the the H-Bar & Grill that just opened up?" asked Mike.

"Yes, that's the one. I was there the other night and wanted to take Jenna with me. We haven't had a chance to go out together in a while," said Sasha.

"I've heard they serve good food there," said Mike.

Jenna was hesitant when she looked in Mike's eyes, "Do you mind if I go with her?"

Mike searched her eyes. Yes, he did mind! He didn't want her to go out to a bar! It could be dangerous after certain hours! His heart pounded with the thoughts of something happening to her. But if he said no, would she think he was trying to control her? Anger started to brew in him, and he tried not to let it show. He took a deep breath.

"If you promise to text me when you arrive and when you are home safe then who am I to stop you from going."

Jenna let out a sigh, "I promise, but I was hoping you would join us later after you close."

Mike looked over at Sasha, she nodded her head in response, and he turned back to Jenna.

"I will text you when I am on my way if you're sure you want me there. I wouldn't want to intrude on your ladies' night out," he said curtly. Jenna heard the tone in his voice, he wasn't happy. She wasn't happy either. She didn't have a good feeling about this whole situation.

"Please?" she pleaded with him. He stared into her eyes and got a vibe that she wasn't too crazy about going to this bar, but was doing it for Sasha, whatever that reason may be.

"Okay," he said reluctantly, "I'll come after work, but if you run into trouble, text me and call 911." Jenna drew a sigh of relief. She wasn't sure how Sasha was with all this, but she didn't care. She felt somewhat safer knowing he would join them later.

Their dinner came and the conversation went in other directions. Mike was interrupted several times to handle customers who wanted to see him. Jenna and Sasha finished their dinner, which was excellent. Tammy came up and asked if she could get them anything else as Mike came back to their booth.

"Could you warm up Mike's dinner? He's been up and down all night," she asked.

"Of course," said Tammy. When she left, Mike slid in for the third time tonight since he sat down to dinner. "I'm sorry, I'm afraid I haven't been much company to you both."

"No worries, Sasha and I probably should get going." She knew her friend was getting anxious to leave. It was getting close to 9:30. "I want to make sure you have eaten first before we go though." Tammy came back with his meal, and suddenly he wasn't hungry anymore.

"Listen, you don't have to wait for me, Mark put in an order and he will join me shortly." He came up out of the booth. He felt like he was on a merry-go-round with his world spinning all around him. Jenna looked up at him.

"We need to pay our bill..."

She was quickly interrupted.

"I got this, you two go on ahead, and I'll meet you later," he said curtly. Jenna stood before Mike when she got out of the booth. Sasha went to the door to wait for her friend. Jenna looked up at Mike with pleading eyes for him to understand.

"Can I get a hug?" she asked tentatively. He searched her eyes and he couldn't help himself. He slammed her body against him in a hug that left her breathless.

He whispered to her, "Please be careful."

When he released her, she placed her hands on either side of his face and kissed him desperately. She didn't care if anyone was watching. When she released him, she whispered, "I will," with her heart pounding she left him.

Mike watched her go and prayed nothing would happen to either one of them. He wanted to go after her, to tell her to wait for him, but knew he had to trust their judgment that they would stay safe. He slid back down in the booth with his heart pounding in his ribs and tried to relax just as Mark came up to join him.

Mark sat in the booth across from Mike.

"What a night! Did Jenna and her friend leave?"

"Yes, they're going to that new bar in downtown Honolulu," said Mike sighing.

"I can tell you're not happy about it."

"No, I'm not!" He sat there stewing. His night wasn't going as planned. He and Jenna were going to have dinner together, and after they closed, he would take her back to his home and entice her back into his bed. Now she's off to a bar with her friend, and God knows what could happen to them! He ran his hands though his hair trying to get a grip on himself.

Mark watched his brother going through emotional hell right now.

"Listen, Mike, if it would ease your mind, go and be with them. It's almost closing time. I can handle closing tonight."

Mike looked back at his brother. He was torn. The restaurant was clearing out and their employees were setting up for the next day. But if he barreled into the bar just after they left, he wouldn't be showing Jenna that he trusted her. Mark's food came, and Mike asked Tammy if she would bring him a Jack D on the rocks. "Oh, and bring me the check for Jenna and her friend also."

She smiled, "I'll be right back."

"Thanks Tammy," said Mike.

Mark started eating and noticed Mike hadn't touched his food.

"You're not eating?" he asked.

"No, the food's been sitting out here and warmed up a couple of times. I'll catch something when I get home, or maybe at the bar."

Tammy came back with his drink and the check. She was about to leave when Mike said, "Hang on a minute Tammy." He pulled out his wallet, glanced at the check, threw some bills on the tray and handed it to her. "Keep the rest."

"Thank you," she smiled. He smiled in return and glanced back at his brother.

"I've decided to stay and help you close."

"Are you sure? Because you don't have to," said Mark. Mike took a drink of his Jack Daniels and felt the burn.

"I'm sure. As hard as this is for me, I need to let go and trust Jenna."

"Tell you what," said Mark, "I wouldn't mind checking out this bar, would you mind if I go with you?"

"No, bro, I would welcome the company." He would keep his nerves from fraying.

"Good, let me finish eating. We'll get this show on the road and be out of here in no time."

"Okay, you finish eating, and I will get started. The sooner we do get out of here the better."

Mike got up and did his nightly checks in the dining rooms and the kitchen. Palani and his crew were just finishing up with their kitchen duties. Mike went to cash out the main register and left the bar one open for the few that were left sitting at the bar. Todd had left for the night, leaving Nathan to finish up. He thought about the meeting with Tonya and Nathan and was glad they agreed to his and his brother's terms for staying employed at the restaurant. Both of them have proved to be good employees in the past, and he didn't want to lose them. What happened to them was unfortunate. But he was glad they were willing to pay back what they took at what Nathan sold the liquor for was a relief. Zack sat in on the meeting and suggested some community service that he would set up for them next week. Mark and he would not be pressing charges if they both were in agreement to the terms that were set up.

The last of their customers had left, and he saw that Mark was finishing up the bar register. When all the employees left and they were ready to lock up, it was almost 11:00. Mike and his brother walked out of the building, locked the door, and headed towards the parking lot behind the building.

Mark took one look at Mike's corvette and said, "Let's take my car, there's more room. I can bring you and Jenna back after we check out this bar."

Mike hesitated.

"Okay, let's go!"

Twenty minutes later, they were pulling up to the bar.

Jenna and Sasha arrived at the bar, and the place was packed with people. There was a country song playing over the speakers, and you could hardly hear yourself think, let alone talk. Jenna turned to her friend.

"Are you sure you want to stay? There doesn't seem to be a table available and it is so loud in here!" said Jenna. Sasha was looking around the bar area to see if the guy was here from the other night. She spotted him sitting next to a woman he was talking to on his left. There was a man sitting on his right who looked familiar to her. It couldn't be the same guy he was with the other night, was it? That guy was filthy. This guy was clean cut. Jenna nudged her friend. "Do you want to stay?"

Sasha turned back to her friend.

"The guy I want to meet is sitting at the bar, but he might be with someone. He's talking to a blonde woman right over there. She pointed over to where they were sitting. Jenna glanced over to where she was pointing. She looked at the guy and then the one on his right. She started to get the chills. He couldn't be Ralph, could he? If it was him, it was a cleaned-up version of him.

Sasha noticed a table opening up towards the far side of the bar where she would have a clear view of the guy she wanted desperately to meet. Maybe she could get his attention.

Jenna wanted to go. "Let's get out of here, Sasha!"

"No, Jenna, we came all the way over here, and the guy I want to meet is here. A table just opened up, let's go!" Jenna reluctantly followed her to the table she indicated and took a seat. A waitress came and cleared the table and asked if they wanted anything to drink. Sasha ordered a glass of wine, and Jenna ordered a coke.

Sasha looked at her friend, "You're not having a drink?"

Jenna turned back to her friend, clearly not happy about staying here, and said, "Somebody has to drive!"

When their drinks came, Sasha was trying to figure out how she was going to get the guy's attention.

"Oh, for heaven's sake!" said Jenna, "Why don't you just go up to him and introduce yourself!"

"I'm not going to do that! He might be with that blonde. I'm not going to embarrass myself!"

Jenna sighed. This night was proving to be one that she didn't want any part of. She wished Mike were here. Sasha tapped her arm and pointed to the bar. The blonde looked like she was getting up to leave.

Mick was glad Heather was leaving. She was fun the other night, but he didn't want another round. She was great in bed, but he could tell she was the clingy type, and he didn't need that. She handed him her phone number.

"If you want another night like the last one, give me a call. I am more than available." She gave him a sultry smile as she was leaving and ran her hand along his shoulders. He looked back at her and thought, *What a relief.* He put her phone number in his pocket intending to throw it away when he got home. When he turned back, he took a glance around the bar. His eyes caught a pair of dark eyes, and his heart started to beat faster. The black-haired beauty was here! She was with another woman. He took a quick glance, and his head started to swim. Both the women were here that he wanted to meet, and they were sitting together! How lucky could a man get in one night!

"Excuse me, Ralph, I need to get up for a while. He locked eyes with the black-haired beauty and walked up to their table. Ralph just huffed. All he wanted to do was drink. He ordered another whiskey on the rocks.

As the man walked up to their table, Jenna suddenly realized it was the same man who she saw at the restaurant last Sunday, and sitting on the bench today! He was definitely handsome, and Sasha was eating him up, she noticed. Sasha stared at the man coming up to their table. He was tall, broad shouldered, his hair was a dark brown, and he had steel gray eyes. He had a beard that he kept trimmed close to the face, and he wore a black Stetson hat on his head. He was by far the most ruggedly attractive man she was ever about to meet.

"Hi ladies!" he said, "Mick Southerland." He shook hands with each one, but noticed a zing went up his arm when he shook hands with the dark-haired beauty. He held on to her hand a little longer than necessary. She pulled her hand away.

"This is Jenna, and I'm Sasha," she said nervously.

"Glad to meet you both. Can I buy you lovely ladies a drink?"

"Oh, no thank you, I'm fine," said Jenna.

He looked back over to Sasha, who said, "I'm all set, but would you like to join us?"

"Don't mind if I do."

He took a seat next to Sasha. Jenna noticed he had a slight southern drawl. As Mick and Sasha started talking to each other, Jenna glanced around the bar while sipping her Coke. The inside looked like any other typical bar in Honolulu. Dark wood paneling, high tables with bar stools sitting around them, TVs hung down from the ceiling at different areas of the bar, so you could watch different sports on the screens. The loud music was over the top, and Jenna wished she was back at the apartment curled up in Mike's arms. She had her phone out on the table, but she didn't hear her phone ding with an incoming text.

Ralph, still sitting at the bar, wondered where Mick had run off to. He took a look around and saw him sitting with a couple of women laughing and having a good time. He huffed. *Must be nice,* he thought. He was lucky if he could get a woman to talk to him. He studied the woman on the left facing him. She looked familiar to him. She was a pretty little thing. *Wouldn't mind having a go with her,* he thought. Then he remembered. She was the bitch that called him a smelly asshole! Trying to get into his business too! He needed to teach that bitch a lesson, but maybe he would have a little fun with her first. He continued to watch her and thought, *Yeah, definitely going to have some fun.* He'd wait for the right moment. He ordered another drink.

Jenna needed to use the restroom and noticed that they were down the hall just to the left of where they were sitting. She nudged Sasha and told her where she was going. She gave her phone to her.

"If Mike sends a text, let him know where we are sitting." Mick picked up on the name.

"Are you talking about Mike TreVaine?" he asked.

"Yes, do you know him?" asked Jenna.

"I met him last Sunday at his restaurant."

Jenna suddenly started putting the pieces together. This was the undercover agent, and he was here with Ralph. She came around to him and whispered in his ear, if you could call it whispering. She didn't want Sasha to hear. "I won't blow your cover."

He had a surprised look on his face when she left to use the restroom. Sasha watched Jenna leave. She turned to Mick, "What was that all about?"

"Nothing to worry your pretty little head over," he grinned. Sasha wasn't so sure. She would ask Jenna as soon as they left for their apartment.

Ralph watched the pretty lady head to the restroom. This was his chance. He got up off his bar stool and headed down the hall. He stood on the other side of the door, so she wouldn't see him when she came out of the restroom.

Jenna finished up in the restroom and freshened up a bit in anticipation when Mike arrived. She looked at her watch. It was after 11:00. He should have texted by now. She would look at her phone when she got back to the table. She opened the door and left the restroom.

Someone came up behind her, grabbed her arm and shoved her up against the wall, pinning her there! Her heart started pounding when she saw who it was.

"Hey pretty, bitch! Remember me?" Jenna couldn't say anything as her mind was racing on how she was going to get out of this situation. She would scream, but she didn't think anyone would hear her over the loud music. He smelled a lot better except for the alcohol on his breath.

"What do you want?" she asked shaking.

"Well, I thought you and I could go have a good time since you owe me for being disrespectful to me. Maybe we should start right now?"

He ran his hand down the front of her as he bent his head to kiss her. She quickly turned her head. She thought she was going to be sick as he went down her neck instead. She felt his hands bruising her arms as she struggled to break free of him.

"Let me go!" she screamed at him.

"Quiet bitch!" he pulled her out and slammed her against the wall! She tried to see if anyone could help her. Then she saw him. Mike was headed her way with fire in his eyes.

Mike and Mark stood in the doorway, Mike trying to find out where the women were sitting. He saw Sasha sitting with a man at a table by the far wall. Where was Jenna? Mark nudged his brother.

"Mike! She's down the hall, she's in trouble!"

When Mike saw Jenna with the guy who looked similar to Ralph, the one who had attempted to hit her, running his hand down the front of her, his slimy mouth trailing down her neck, his blood started to boil. Mark grabbed his arm.

"Don't kill him I don't want you to go to prison."

"I'm not making any promises!" He jerked his arm out of his brother's grasp. Mike's adrenaline was coursing through his veins as he rushed through the bar and down the hall where Jenna was trapped.

Sasha was deep in a conversation with Mick. In the corner of her eye, she thought she saw Mike storming in the restaurant with Mark right behind him. She turned her head as they headed towards the restrooms. The look in his eyes told her something was terribly wrong! Mark came up to her and told her to stay put. He looked over at Mick, "You come with me. You may have to save your friend."

Mick got up and glanced over at the bar where Ralph was supposed to be sitting, only he wasn't there!

Shit! Shit! Shit! he said to himself. He went with Mark just as the shit was about to hit the fan.

Ralph felt a hand on his shoulder and stiffened. He looked to his right. He wondered who this jackass was and how fast he could take him down. He didn't like interruptions, especially when he's trying to get it on with a woman.

"What the hell do you want? Can't you see I'm busy?"

"Get your filthy hands off of her!" Mike roared. Mike pulled him off her and sent Ralph reeling backwards. Jenna ran to Mark with tears in her eyes, shaking. Mark held on to her.

"It's okay, Jenna, you're safe now. Mike will handle it from here."

"I don't want Mike to get hurt because of me!" she cried.

"Don't worry, Mike's an expert fighter, he's got this."

Sasha couldn't sit there any longer. She came around the corner to see Jenna in Mark's arms crying and shaking uncontrollably. When Mark saw her, he said, "I thought I told you to stay put!"

"I couldn't stand it, I heard Mike yelling and had to come and see if Jenna was alright." Sasha took in the scene. Mick was standing with his legs apart and arms crossed watching Mike and that sleazebag getting ready to go at it. Jenna looked on with fear in her eyes for Mike. Mark just smiled with a gleam in his eyes as he knew what was about to happen.

"Who in the hell do you think you are?" yelled Ralph, "I'm going to teach you a lesson that you will never forget! Nobody interrupts me when I'm trying to take a woman, nobody!"

Ralph lunged forward to take a swing at Mike. Mike caught his fist with his left arm and put his right fist in Ralph's jaw. Ralph went reeling back for the second time.

"You think you're tough, you just wait!" Ralph came at him, again swinging with his left fist. Mike caught it again with his right and giving him an upper cut with his left to the jaw sending him back onto the floor. Ralph shook his head as he tried to get up.

Mick, watching, warned, "Ralph, I wouldn't get up if I were you."

"You stay out of this, this is my fight!" Ralph slowly got up and started to stagger towards Mike. There was a crowd from the bar now watching what was taking place.

"If you know what's good for you, you will stop right there," Mike growled. Ralph kept coming. He brought his arm up, and in one slick move, Mike latched on twisted it behind his back and shoved him against the wall. "Before I put your lights out, you are going to hear what I have to say," he said with conviction, "You ever come near my woman or touch her in any way again, you will live to regret it! And furthermore, she is not a bitch! Do you understand?"

Ralph with his head pressed against the wall muffled, "Go to hell!"

With that, Mike pulled him away from the wall, punched him in the gut and with a right fist to the jaw and then a left, Ralph was on the floor, out cold! Mike shook his hands out and turned around to see Jenna with tears in her pretty brown eyes come running into his arms. He folded her in his embrace and just held her. Mike looked at his brother, and Mark nodded. He pulled Jenna away from him.

"Let's get out of here!"

Jenna searched his eyes.

"Mike, I was so scared, you didn't kill him, did you?"

Mike looked back; Mick was there getting Ralph to his feet as he came to.

"Nope, he's still moving! I need to get out of here. Come on, bro, take us back to my car.

"Wait," said Jenna. Jenna searched for her friend. Sasha was standing off to the side clearly upset. Jenna walked up to her and gave her a huge hug.

"Oh, Jenna," said Sasha tearfully, "I'm so sorry. I wished we had never come here. Can you forgive me?"

"There's nothing to forgive," she said giving her a slight smile, "At least you got to meet Mick. Are you okay to drive back to the apartment? I want to be with Mike, and I don't want to leave you here by yourself."

"I'll walk out with you. I'll go to our table and get our purses," said Sasha.

When they left the bar, they followed Sasha to her car. "Are you sure you're okay to drive?" asked Mark. "We can always leave it and come back for it in the morning."

"No, I will be fine. Just take care of Jenna. She gave me a pretty big scare!"

"She gave us all a scare! That dumb jerk hopefully learned his lesson!" he said. Sasha got into her car.

"Drive safe," he said.

"I will, thank you," said Sasha.

Mike and Jenna were waiting by Mark's car. Mark unlocked the doors, and Mike and Jenna slid into the back. Mark got in on the driver's side and started the engine. He pulled out onto the avenue and headed back to the restaurant. He looked back in his rearview mirror and could barely see his brother and Jenna snuggled up together lying back against the seat. Nothing was said until he pulled up next to Mike's car.

Mark glanced back at them, "I just want you to know, bro, I'm proud of you for not killing him when I know you wanted to. And Jenna, you held up really well under the circumstances."

"Give me time, Mark, the night's not over!"

They piled out of the car, and Mark came up to Mike to take a look at his hands since his were aching. Sometimes being a twin has its disadvantages.

"How's the hands, bro?" He held them out and stretched his fingers back and forth.

"There a little sore, but I'll be fine. No worries, bro."

"Good. Will you be alright to drive?" he asked.

"I'll be fine you go on home and get some rest." He gazed down at Jenna, "I have a feeling I will be well taken care of tonight."

She gazed back up at him. "Yes, you will."

"Goodnight then," said Mark.

"Goodnight," they both answered in return. Mark went to get into the driver's side and headed home. As he was driving, he chuckled. His brother was some badass when it came to fighting. Both he and his brother were at the boxing ring at least twice a month to work out. It definitely came in handy at times.

Back at the bar, Mick was helping Ralph out of the bar and into his car.

"Are you sure you don't want me to drive you to the hospital, Ralph? You look like it might be a good idea to get checked out by a doctor."

"No, I'll be fine. It's not the first time I've been in a fight." He rubbed his hand over his jaw. "Man, that guy could hit."

"You should have stayed down the first time you landed on the floor," said Mick.

Ralph glanced up at him. "I thought I could take him, I guess I was wrong."

"I guess you were." Mick hit the top of his car. "Careful going home Ralph."

Just as Mick headed back into the bar to pay his tab, he heard the sirens and lights flashing coming to a stop in front of the bar. Mick stood at the door when the police officers approached him.

"We got a call that there is a fight going on here at this bar. Came to investigate."

"Sorry boys, but it ended. The people involved have gone home," said Mick.

"We will still have to talk to the owner or the manager."

"Be my guest!" Mick followed the officers into the bar. When he went to pay his bill, the bartender asked if he was taking care of the guy's tab that was sitting next to him. Mick sighed and shook his head. "I guess I am." This was the second time he was stuck with his bill. He left the bar and thought, *What a night…* Just when he was getting to know Sasha, Ralph had to go after Mike's woman. He had to chuckle; Mike was one hell of a fighter. Maybe he would ask him where he worked out. He could use the practice himself.

Chapter 26

When Mike and Jenna arrived back at his home, Jenna sent Mike to the couch while she went to the kitchen to see if she could find anything to put on his hands. Mike took his suit coat and necktie off and laid them on the back of a chair. He flung himself on the couch and turned on the TV. Jenna found a couple of bags of corn in the freezer and thought, *Perfect!* She also found two cotton dish towels in one of the drawers and wrapped each bag in each cloth.

When she came out to the living area, Mike already had the TV on and was trying to find something to watch. He looked up when Jenna came up to him.

"I found some frozen corn in your freezer. Can you put your hands on your thighs?" Mike did as she asked. Jenna gently laid the frozen corn on his hands. "Oh, Mike, they're so swollen." Mike was watching her and saw the love and concern in her eyes. "Do you have any Ibuprofen?" she asked.

"In the medicine cabinet in my bathroom," he said.

She went to get the medicine and a glass of water. She came back and handed him two capsules and the water. He took them, washed them down and set the glass on the table. Jenna replaced the cold corn back on his hand. She turned to him.

"Are you hungry or would you like a cup of tea?" she asked.

He gave her a questioning look and raised his eyebrows, "I am hungry, and I would love a cup of tea, but you don't have to do all this. I can get up in a few minutes and help. Just sit with me," he coaxed.

"Let me do this for you. I'm a little hungry myself. It won't take me long. I'll be right back."

Mike watched her as she went into the kitchen. He should be holding her. She had to have been traumatized with that creep's hands all over her and his mouth running down her neck. His blood started boiling just thinking about it. He had held himself back from doing serious harm to the jerk. He continued watching her as she busied herself making sandwiches and tea. He had a feeling staying busy was a way that she coped when things went out of her control.

"What would you like on your sandwich?" she called from the kitchen.

"Just a little mustard," he answered.

Jenna came into the living area with his sandwich, some chips, his tea, and sat them down on the coffee table. She went back into the kitchen, picked hers up, and went to sit down next to him. She removed the frozen corn from his hands and saw they looked a lot better. But he definitely would have some bruising. She handed him his sandwich.

"Thank you." He took the sandwich from her and took a bite. "Mmm, good," he said.

He finished the sandwich so fast she had to wonder, "You didn't eat your dinner, did you?"

He shook his head and placed the empty dish on the table.

"No, I lost my appetite when you and Sasha left for the bar. I started the closing process, so I could get out of there." His eyes bore into her with the fear of seeing her being molested. "I was almost too late."

"Mike, honey, I want you to know that I never wanted to go to that bar tonight." She put her sandwich down on the table and gently took his hand in hers. "I only went because Sasha wanted to see if a guy she saw there a couple of nights ago would be there tonight. As it turns out, he happens to be the undercover agent working with Zack. I had no idea who he was until he mentioned that he met you at your restaurant."

Mike picked up the remote and shut the TV off.

"Come here, sweetheart." Jenna got up, and he pulled her across his lap. She laid her head on his shoulder. He held her while his hand went up and down her arm. She relaxed against him. "I want to know how you are doing," he asked softly. He felt her stiffen. He kissed the top of her head. "Tell me." He felt her start to shake. He gently took her chin and lifted her head so he could look into her eyes. "Tell me, love."

Her eyes filled with tears as she remembered the sick feeling she felt when he held her against her will and started running his hands and mouth over her. Tears were streaming down her face as she began to let it go and tell him what she was feeling.

"Mike, I never felt so scared in all my life!" He took one of the cloths from the frozen corn and gently wiped away her tears. "When I saw Ralph was at the bar, I tried to get Sasha to leave, but she insisted that we stay because the guy she wanted to meet was sitting next to him. I was miserable without you being there with me. The music was so loud, I didn't hear your text that you were on your way. The undercover agent noticed Sasha and came over and introduced himself. So, while they talked, I decided to use the restroom. When I came out, that's when Ralph grabbed me and pinned me against the wall. I panicked and wanted to throw up when he started to touch me and run his dirty mouth down my neck. No one came by to help me!" The tears kept coming. "I was never so glad to see you in all my life! Where did you learn to fight like that?" she sniffed.

He finished wiping the tears from her face before he answered.

"When Mark and I were in the service, we needed an outlet to relieve some of the stress that a person deals with while serving their country, so we took up boxing. We still work out in the ring a couple of times a month. It would have been nice to have a set of gloves on tonight," he said, looking at his knuckles. Jenna took his face in her hands.

"Thank you," she cried, "I don't want to think about what would have happened if you hadn't come when you did. I love you, Mike."

He placed his hands over hers and brought his lips to hers in a kiss so gentle it rocked her world. He lifted his head and said, "As long as I live, love, I will never let anything happen to you. I love you more than you will ever know." His arms went around her and Jenna's arms went up around his neck for an earth-shattering kiss that went on for a long time. When they broke apart, he whispered, "Do you want to go back to your apartment?"

"No," she whispered back.

He raised his eyebrows and asked, "The couch or the bed?"

She smiled and said, "The bed."

They got up off the couch, and Jenna started to pick up the dishes to take them in the kitchen. Mike stopped her.

"Just leave them; it can wait till morning."

"Can you eat the rest of my sandwich? I hate wasting it."

"I could probably put it down, bring it back with us." She picked it up along with a cup of tea and headed back to his bedroom. She set the plate and cup of tea on the table. She turned to him, "Do you have a shirt I could wear?"

He looked over her body seductively.

"It will just come off."

She blushed, "I think I will feel better if I start out with it on."

He chuckled and went to his drawer and handed her one of his t-shirts. She took it from him and headed in the bathroom to change and wash her face. When she looked in the mirror she groaned. Her mascara was smeared down her face and around her eyes, which were still red from crying. She took her clothes off and put Mike's shirt on. She cleaned up her face and ran a comb through her hair. She felt a little better.

She came out of the bathroom and saw Mike sitting at the table. He finished off the sandwich and was drinking the tea. He looked over at Jenna and caught his breath. She was the most beautiful and seductive woman he had ever met. She stood there in his shirt that hung down to her mid-thigh. When she walked toward him, his heart throbbed as he watched her breasts move with every step she took.

Jenna noticed he changed into a pair of shorts. His broad chest was exposed to her, and she hungered to feel his skin under her hands. He got up out of the chair, and she saw the hunger in his eyes that matched her own. He took her hands in his. His eyes traveled up to her eyes but not before he saw the bruises on her upper arms.

"Oh, sweetheart, I'm so sorry. This never would have happened if I had gone with you."

She placed her fingers on his lips, "Shh nobody could have known that Ralph would be there." She pulled him over to the bed. He pulled down the covers and eased her down on the bed. Neither one said a word as they kissed and touched and made love to each other long into the night.

When they were spent, Mike needed to get up. When he came back, he slid under the covers and wrapped Jenna up in his arms. He breathed in deeply. Jenna had her head resting on his chest and her arm tightly around him. He couldn't feel more content if he tried. When he felt her relax her hold on him, and her breathing slowed, he knew she had fallen asleep. He closed his eyes and felt relief that the night was over and his love was safe in his arms.

Jenna woke with Mike's arm around her, and his body snuggled up against her back. She needed to get up. When she tried to move, his arm tightened around her and pulled her closer to him moving his hand to her breast.

"Mike," she whispered. "I need to use your bathroom."

He groaned and lifted his arm from her. She turned toward him. His eyes were still closed. She kissed him on the cheek.

"Hurry back," he whispered gruffly.

She was up and out of his bed in a heartbeat. She hurried in to relieve herself and freshen up a bit. When she came back to bed, Mike opened his eyes and pulled her next to him. She snuggled into his embrace.

"How are you feeling this morning?" he asked softly.

"I'm fine. How are your hands?" He extended his arm and looked at one of his hands. She watched as he opened and closed it. "It's a little sore; otherwise, it's fine. No more talk, only lovemaking."

She put her arms around his neck and reached up and touched her lips to his.

"Mmm, sounds like a plan."

He returned her kiss, placing his hand on her hip then on her thigh to lift her leg over him. She could feel his arousal. His eyes were burning with desire. He explored her body with his mouth and his hands. He eased her on her back and reached for a condom on his night stand. He slipped it on and eased into her.

Jenna was spiraling in the emotions this man brought out in her. She kept pace with his steady rhythm until she thought she was going to lose her mind!

"Mike…" she whispered.

"Tell me what you want, love," he whispered back.

She gazed into his eyes.

"I want it the way you gave it to me our first night together."

He kissed her mouth, her neck. Then he placed his hands under her hips as she wrapped her legs around him. He kept up the steady pace until he could no longer hold back. He drove into her fast and furious until they both exploded on an orgasm that left them with their hearts beating wildly, and they were out of breath. They held on to each other until their breathing slowed. He brought himself up on his arms and smiled down at her.

She touched his face and smiled back, "You are one incredible lover, did you know that Michael TreVaine?"

He nuzzled her neck, "Only because I have the most beautiful woman to make love to. Sweetheart, you fulfill me like no other woman could. I love you."

"I love you so much," she said in return. She pressed her lips to his. "Do you know it is almost noon? I'm going to need to get back to my apartment to get ready for work sometime today."

He sighed, "Are you sure we can't just stay like this?"

She chuckled, "I'm a little hungry, aren't you?"

"Only for you, little one," he kissed her lips, her cheek, her neck.

"Mike, honey, we need to get up."

He lifted himself back up on his arms and brushed her hair back. He gazed into her brown eyes.

"Okay, you win this time. Let's go shower, and I will cook you something to eat before I take you back to your apartment."

They had some fun in the shower, and finally, they were dressed and in the kitchen. They didn't have time to cook, so Mike started the coffee while Jenna warmed up some pastries he had in the fridge. When they finished eating, Mike took her back to her apartment.

He gave her a quick kiss and said he'd see her tonight. Jenna walked into her apartment.

Sasha was sitting on the couch when she walked in.

"Hi, Sasha, you're not studying at the library today?"

"No. I've been waiting for you to come home." Jenna came over and sat down next to Sasha. "Do you have any idea how upset I was last night? I need to know what's going on, Jenna. Who was that guy who Mike beat up, and who is Mick? What's he really doing here? You whispered something to him before you went to the restroom, and he looked surprised. Now, tell me Jenna," she said curtly.

Jenna stared at her friend. She wasn't really sure she could tell her everything that's been going on.

"Sasha, I hope you are not going to be mad at me, but I am not at liberty to discuss what's been going on at Mike and Mark's restaurant. What happened last night at the bar has to do with those events that have taken place there."

"So you were attacked because of something that happened at their restaurant?" asked Sasha.

Oh boy, Jenna thought. How did she explain this without giving away Mick's cover?

"Yes. I saw him hanging out at the back of the restaurant when I took my trash out. He looked agitated. When he saw me, he asked me what I was doing. I asked him the same question. We got into an argument. I called him something not very nice, and when he saw me at the bar, he attacked me." Jenna hoped that was going to be enough information to satisfy her curiosity.

"Okay, but what about Mick? What does he have to do with all of this?"

"Mick's the guy's friend. Mark wanted to make sure Mike didn't kill him." Jenna thought back to last night when she watched Mike level the guy. *If Mike hadn't come when he did…*

Jenna shuddered. She didn't want to think about it.

Sasha was not happy with her friend's answers. She knew there was more to the story than what Jenna told her.

"Are you going to be okay to work tonight? What if that guy comes looking for you?"

Jenna looked taken aback. She hadn't thought of that. Ralph didn't know her other than consistently calling her a bitch! She would watch her back. Maybe she would take a self-defense class. Mike couldn't be with her 24/7, and she wouldn't want him to. Oh, why did Sasha have to put that into her head! Her heart started to beat faster. *Calm down, Jenna,* she said to herself. She took a deep breath.

"I'll be fine, Sasha. I'll make sure I keep an eye out. Mike is picking me up after work, and tomorrow we are spending the day together. Speaking of which, I need to get ready for work."

Jenna went to her bedroom with Sasha at her heels. Sasha grabbed her arm to turn her around.

"Hey, I'm sorry for giving you the third degree. I'm also glad you weren't seriously hurt." Sasha gave her friend a hug.

Jenna, with tears in her eyes, said, "I'm sorry, too, that I'm not able to tell you more. But when I am able, I will tell you everything."

"I will hold you to that," Sasha said smiling

The rest of the weekend flew by. On Sunday, Mike and Jenna enjoyed a quiet day together at his home. Mike cooked dinner, and they relaxed on the patio with a glass of wine, watching the fire burning in the outdoor fireplace. The sun had set, and it was getting late.

Mike refilled her glass.

"Stay the night with me?" he asked softly.

She gazed up at him. "I would love to, but I have class in the morning, and you said you have an appointment at ten tomorrow.

I didn't bring anything with me to wear, and my iPad is at the apartment, along with my homework."

"We could go back to your apartment, get what you need, and I could have you at your class by 8:55, sharp."

"You talk a good line TreVaine. But we never sleep."

"If I promise to let you sleep, will you stay?"

She studied him and knew in her heart that it wouldn't happen. He was just too irresistible.

"Okay, but you promise to let me sleep?"

He raised his hand, "Scouts honor."

She chuckled. "Okay, let's go."

They came into her apartment. Cuddles met them at the door. Jenna picked her up and gave her a hug while Mike closed the door. Jenna put her down, and she scooted into the kitchen.

"I'll need to feed her and take care of her litter box."

"Maybe I can help. Can you show me where you keep her cat food and I can feed her," he said.

"Are you sure?" she asked.

"Yes."

"Okay." She took him to the cupboard where the cat food was kept and handed him the litter scoop. She left him to take care of her cat while she gathered what she needed and packed her iPad and homework for morning. When she came back into the kitchen, Mike was bent down petting her cat while she ate. He stood up when he heard her come in.

"All set?"

"Yes. I just need to leave a note for Sasha." She wrote out the note and they were on their way.

When they were back at his home Jenna wanted to get into her pajamas, so she headed back to Mike's bathroom. She quickly changed, did her nightly routine, and she was ready. Mike stood in the doorway, wondering how he could convince her to move in with him until they were married. *Mike, you haven't even asked her to marry you yet,* he argued with himself.

Jenna saw him in the mirror. She turned to him.

"You're looking kind of serious there, Mike. What are you thinking?"

Mike shook his head. "Just how cute you look in your pajamas."

He came towards her and picked her up. Jenna put her arms around his neck.

"Honey, you promised we would sleep tonight." He carried her to his bed. She noticed that he already had the covers pulled down. He laid her down and covered her up. "And sleep you shall." He kissed the top of her head. "I'll be back in a bit. Get some sleep."

She looked at him with questioning eyes. "You're not going to join me?"

"No later."

She saw the fire in his eyes and didn't question him further.

"Goodnight then," she said.

"Goodnight, love."

He left his bedroom before he changed his mind and devoured her right there in his bed. Jenna didn't know what to think. She wanted him beside her.

Mike went into the kitchen and made himself a cup of tea. He had to restrain himself from making love to her. He promised her they would sleep. He took his tea in the living room and turned on the TV. He watched some mystery movie to kill time. When it was over, he turned it off, shut the lights off, and headed to his bedroom. When he came in, he glanced over at Jenna, and she appeared to be sleeping. He undressed down to his boxers and climbed into bed. He stayed on his side of the bed and closed his eyes. It wasn't long before he, too, fell asleep.

True to his word, Mike had Jenna at her class on time the next morning. Mike stopped at a coffee shop to kill some time before his appointment with Pastor Kingsley at 10:00. He ordered some coffee and took a seat in one of the booths. Zack walked in the coffee shop and saw Mike. He ordered a coffee and went to join him.

"Hey Mike! Mind if I join you?"

"Hey Zack! No not at all, have a seat." He slid into the booth.

"Jason filled me in on what happened Friday night. How is Jenna doing?" he asked.

"She was pretty shook up, but she's doing fine now. I just dropped her off at the university."

"Jason said Ralph was pretty messed up. Thought he should have gone to the hospital. I didn't realize you and your brother were expert fighters."

Mike shrugged his shoulders.

"Boxing was something we took up in the service. We still work out twice a month."

"Jason wanted to know where. He said he could use a little stress relief," said Zack. Mike pulled out his wallet and handed him a card. "He will need to call ahead to get in and apply for a membership. Tell him my brother and I would welcome a challenge. By the way, how is the case going?" asked Mike.

Zack looked around the coffee shop to make sure there was no one close to them before he answered.

"Jason has a good shot at getting inside. We found out that Ralph indeed works for Manchez."

Mike leaned forward.

"Is there anything we can do to help?" Mike asked.

"All we need you to do right now is act as if you know nothing when Manchez comes into your restaurant. Treat him the same as you always have. Manchez can sense if something is off and if anybody is getting close to his business. He's very cautious. I will keep you and Mark in the loop as the case progresses," said Zack.

"Okay," said Mike, "But just FYI. If Ralph comes near Jenna again, I won't hold back like I did Friday night."

"Well according to Jason, if that was holding back, I don't think I want to know what happens when you go full force!"

Mike smiled, "It won't be pretty."

Mike and Zack sat and talked until Mike had to go for his appointment.

"Sorry Zack, but I have to run." Mike stood up and shook Zack's hand and wished him a good day. Zack watched him leave. He hoped Ralph wouldn't be stupid. He already knew where Jenna worked. Maybe he would have a patrol car stop over on the days she worked, just as a precaution. He would talk to the Lieutenant about it. He needed Jason to get in. He was too close.

Mike walked into Pastor Kingsley's office.

"Good morning Pastor Kingsley." Mike shook his hand.

"Good morning, Mike. It's nice to see you again. Have a seat."

Mike sat down in the chair across from his desk.

"Thank you for taking the time to see me this morning," said Mike.

"You are most welcome. What can I be of assistance to you?" asked the Pastor.

Mike thought a moment.

"I'm not sure where to begin."

"Does this have to do with Jenna?"

Mike looked surprised.

"Yes, it does. How did you know?" he asked.

"Jenna mentioned you in a conversation we had."

"I see," said Mike. "Jenna and I have been seeing each other and I've fallen pretty hard for her. I want to marry her. I know it's been a short time since we started dating, but I can't see my life without her in it."

Pastor Kingsley smiled.

"How soon did you want to get married?" he asked.

"For me as soon as possible, but I haven't asked her yet. My guess is she will want to wait until her parents can be here," said Mike.

"Well, I think you need to ask her and go from there. If you want to know if it's too fast, then I would have to say if two people love each other and know for sure they want to spend the rest of their lives together, then no. It's not too fast. My recommendation is when you do propose and she accepts that you take classes here at the church before you marry. It's a four-week course. It will give you and Jenna a perspective on the importance of entering into matrimony. Here is a pamphlet to get started when you are ready."

Pastor Kingsley handed him the folder.

"Thank you," said Mike. "Also, Jenna mentioned in a conversation we had that she was a Christian. I am not. I wanted to know if you have any information about becoming one. I watch Jenna when she is with others. She is so compassionate and loving, such a giving person. I want what she has."

"You don't know how happy this makes me. Here is a book on Christianity. It's the New Testament. Read the first four books. Come to Church on Sunday if you can, and if you are ready, I will help you to become a new Christian in Christ."

Mike got up from the chair and shook his hand.

"Thank you, Pastor Kingsley. I'll get started tonight."

"You are most welcome. Hope to see you on Sunday," said Pastor Kingsley.

Chapter 27

Downtown Honolulu, Ralph walked into Manchez's office. "I have the information on Mick. His story checks out." Ralph sat down and put the report on his desk. Manchez looked into a face swollen and bruised.

"What the hell happened to you?" Ralph ran his hand over his jaw. It still hurt like hell.

"I got into a fight," he said.

"With who?" asked Manchez.

"Some guy at a bar Mick and I were at."

Manchez sat forward and placed his arms on the desk hands folded. He gave Ralph a steely glare.

"Why?"

Ralph started to get uncomfortable.

"I was trying to get it on with a woman. I didn't know she belonged to someone else. She came on to me!"

Manchez sat back in his chair. He wasn't sure he believed that story.

"You know, Ralph, you are not supposed to draw attention to yourself. Were the police involved?"

"No. We left before the police arrived," said Ralph.

"What about the guy who beat you?"

"He and his bitch left before Mick and I did."

Manchez was not happy. He needed to find out what really took place. He glared at Ralph.

"Keep a low profile until those bruises heal. I don't want you out collecting or getting loans for the next two weeks. Come back, and we'll talk."

Ralph looked taken aback.

"Hey Mr. Manchez, I can still do my job!"

Manchez sat forward.

"I said two weeks! Now get out of here. I've got work to do."

Ralph got up out of the chair and left the office. Manchez looked over the report Ralph sat on his desk. Looked like his story confirmed what was on the report. He opened his top desk drawer and pulled out a card.

He buzzed his secretary. Helen opened the door.

"You wanted to see me, Mr. Manchez?"

"Yes, Helen. Get ahold of Victor ASAP. I need to have a meeting with him."

"Yes, sir, right away, sir," she said and left the office. Manchez picked up the phone and dialed Mick's number.

Ralph came out of the building, wondering what the hell he was going to do for the next two weeks! How was he going to make any money! He started walking to his car. *It's all that bitch's fault,* he said to himself. He knew where she worked. He needed to find out where her boyfriend worked too. He would take care of the both of them. He needed to devise a plan. Yeah, nobody was going to screw with him. He needed to make a few phone calls. He reached his car and drove off.

Helen buzzed the intercom.

"Yes, Helen?"

"Victor is here to see you."

"Send him right in," said Manchez.

Victor opened the door.

"You wanted to see me, sir?"

"Yes, come in and have a seat." Victor came and sat in a chair in front of his desk. "I called you in here because I have a job for you to do. Ralph is slipping up. I want you to follow him and report back to me on his activities over the next two weeks. I don't want him drawing attention to our business. He dodged the police last Friday, and I want to make sure it stays that way. If he slips up at all and the police get involved, you know what to do." Manchez had a gleam in his eyes. "Do I make myself clear?"

Victor slowly smiled, "Yes, sir. Rest assured I will take care of any problems that occur."

"Good." Manchez leaned back in his chair. "I have a man coming in that I want to consider hiring. His name is Mick Southerland. He checks out. I am putting him in Ralph's place for the next two weeks. If he does well and can be trusted, I will hire him in permanently."

Helen buzzed the intercom again.

"Yes, Helen," he said gruffly.

"A Mick Southerland is here to see you. Does he have an appointment with you? It's not on my calendar," she said.

Boy, that was quick, he said to himself. "Yes, Helen, send him right in."

Mick opened the door and stepped in.

"Mick!" said Manchez. "Come in and have a seat."

Mick took the chair next to a man who looked like a Sumo wrestler. Big broad chest with bulging muscles on his arms and legs. His black hair was pulled back behind his thick neck. *Definitely going to have to get brushed up on his self-defense skills,* he thought.

Manchez introduced the two.

"Mick, this is Victor Kamaka. Victor, Mick Southerland." They shook hands. "Mick, I wanted to meet with you to discuss taking over for Ralph for the next couple of weeks. If you work out, we'll talk about a permanent position in the business."

Mick, surprised, sat forward with his elbows on the arms of the chair, hands folded.

"Thank you, Mr. Manchez. I appreciate the offer. It couldn't come at a better time."

"Ralph told me he was in a fight Friday night. He said you were with him. What's the story?"

Manchez's eyes bore into Mick's. Mick didn't waver.

"I happened to be talking to a beautiful young lady when I saw a man come storming into the restaurant and passed our table. I looked over at the bar to see if Ralph was still sitting at the bar. He wasn't. I got up, went down the hallway to find Ralph holding a woman against her will and mauling her. The guy was her boyfriend. He pulled Ralph off of her. Ralph got mad and came at him. The rest is history. Ralph didn't stand a chance against him," said Mick. "His face is pretty messed up."

"What about the police. Were they called?"

"Both Ralph and the couple left before the police arrived."

"Ralph said the woman hit on him," enquired Manchez.

"Mr. Manchez, do you really think any woman would come on to Ralph?" asked Mick.

He chuckled.

"You have a point," said Manchez. He looked over at Victor. "You have your instructions. I need to talk to Mick."

Victor rose from his chair, nodded his head and left.

Manchez pulled a file drawer open. Took out a folder and handed it to Mick. "Here are the names and addresses of the loans that are outstanding with the loan amounts and balances for each one. If they miss a payment, you are to raise the interest accordingly. There is a ledger to document and an interest chart for the loans.

I'll need an update towards the end of every day during the week. Do you have any questions?"

Mick was looking through the folder.

"It looks pretty straight forward. Shouldn't have a problem," said Mick. "I'll need to pick up a map of the city to learn my way around."

"Stop at Helen's desk. She'll have one."

Mick rose from his chair along with Mr. Manchez. Mick shook his hand.

"Thanks for the job. You won't regret it," said Mick.

Manchez's eyes glared into Mick's. "Just make sure you get my money. If you do well here, I have another area of business I would like to put you on."

Mick raised an eyebrow in question.

"May I ask what that might be?"

"I will let you know when the time comes." Mick nodded his head and left the office. He picked up a map from Helen and headed out.

Manchez sat back down in his chair. He had a gleam in his eyes. If Mick worked out like he thought he would, he'd move him in his drug trafficking runs. Ralph was another problem he would have to deal with. Their stories were the same, except for one minor detail. He didn't like men attacking women. He respected the opposite sex. If he slipped up again, Victor would know what to do.

Zack and Craig watched as Ralph came out of the building clearly agitated. Several minutes later, a big man in a dark suit entered the building. *Probably another one of Manchez's enforcers,* he thought. Fifteen minutes, later Jason entered the building.

"Here we go, Craig. Let's see if he gets in." They both listened to the conversation. They watched the big man called Victor come out and head to his car. Craig turned to Zack.

"I wonder what his instructions are."

"From the conversation, I have a feeling it's not going to go well for Ralph," said Zack. He would need to warn Mike and Jenna to be on the lookout over the next several weeks. Jason came out of the building and headed to the parking lot where his car was parked. He got in and pulled out. Zack's phone rang. He answered the call, "Hey, nice job getting in."

"Thanks. We could arrest him based on the evidence I have in my hand," said Jason.

"I know, but Manchez mentioned about putting you in another part of his business. We want to nail him for drug trafficking and other crimes tied to his business. I want to make sure he's put away for a long time. We are headed back to the police station. We'll be in touch," said Zack.

"Right, I'm on it," said Jason.

Chapter 28

Jenna hurried into the restaurant. She was running late. She had to catch up on some reports she wasn't able to finish on Monday. After she logged into her computer, she pulled up the reports. She was so engrossed in her work, she didn't hear Mark come in.

"Hey Jenna, how are the end of the month reports coming?"

Jenna, caught off guard, jumped. She looked up at Mark.

"Oh, hi, Mark, I'm just finishing up. I should have them to you within the hour."

"Great, bring them in my office when you finish."

She smiled, "Will do boss!"

Jenna went back to work. When she finished, she printed off the reports and slipped them into a folder. She knocked on Marks's door.

"Come in."

Jenna walked in.

"Here are your reports. Sorry it took me longer than expected. I had some trouble with two of the reports not balancing." Jenna pointed out which ones. Mark looked over the two she was talking about and instantly found the errors. He explained to her how they should be entered. "If you could go back in and make these changes, you'll see the report will balance." Jenna felt a little down. She should have caught those entries. Mark watched her emotions. He knew what she was feeling. "Jenna, you're doing a great job. This was your first time doing end of the month reports. I have the greatest confidence you will fly through it the next time." He gave her a smile.

"Thank you, Mark, I'll go make these changes and be right back."

Jenna, back in her office, pulled up the two reports. She made the changes, and sure enough, they balanced. What a relief! She printed them off and headed back to Mark's office bumping into a hard body. Strong arms came around her as demanding lips came down on hers. He lifted his head.

"Hi," he breathed.

"Hi," she sighed.

"How is your day going?" he asked.

"Much better now that you're here, how about you?" she asked.

"With you in my arms, it couldn't be more perfect." He pressed his lips to hers and kissed her passionately.

Jenna broke the kiss.

"Umm, I need to get these reports to your brother."

He sighed and let her go.

"If you must, come back to my office when you are through. I need to discuss something with you." Jenna's heart started to pound. That didn't sound good.

"Okay," she said hesitantly. "I'll be in shortly."

Jenna knocked on Mark's door. She entered when she heard the familiar, "Come in.'

"Here are the corrected reports." She laid them on his desk. "I was wondering if I could leave a little early today. That is, if you don't have anything else you need me to do today. I need to get over to the university to finish up some graduation details. The deadline is today to order my cap and gown." Mark took a brief look at the reports and placed them back on his desk.

"No everything looks good. We can start fresh on Monday, and I will show you how payroll works."

"Thank you, Mark, you have a good rest of your day," she said.

"You too Jenna," said Mark.

Jenna quickly went to log out and turn off her computer, picked up her purse, and locked her door. Her heart started pounding again when she walked over to Mike's office. The door was ajar so she walked in. He looked up when she came in. She took a seat across from him.

"You wanted to talk to me about something?" she asked nervously.

He gave her a warm smile and leaned back in his chair.

"Jenna, come over here." She stared back at him, not sure she wanted to. "Jenna, now, and close the door." She did as he asked. When she was beside him, he reached up and pulled her down on his lap. "You're shaking sweetheart, why?" he asked.

"You're making me nervous. What did you want to talk to me about?"

He chuckled, "Jenna, love, you need to relax. It's nothing bad." He pulled her against him and kissed the top of her head. "I just wanted to let you know that I will be going out of town for a few days and will be back Friday evening," he said. Jenna pushed away from his chest. She searched his eyes.

"When are you leaving?"

"Tomorrow morning. My flight leaves for Los Angeles at 8:00. I'm meeting with an investor who has taken an interest in franchising our restaurant."

"Oh, Mike, that's wonderful!" she was excited for them.

"Well, it's not written in stone, but both Mark and I felt it was worth taking a look at. Also, and I hope you won't be angry, but I made arrangements with Mark to pick you up from work and get you home safely."

"Mike, I could have a friend come and walk me home. Mark doesn't need to come and get me!"

"Jenna, love. Please don't be upset. After last Friday, I need to know that you are safe."

She took a deep breath. She really didn't think this was necessary, but if it would ease his mind... "Okay, if you're sure it isn't interfering with Mark's schedule," she said.

"It's fine. He said he would be glad to do it." He was relieved. He pulled her close to him and just held her.

"Mike, I need to get over to the university before 5:00."

"I'll take you," he said.

"No, I'll be fine, and then I'm going right back to my apartment. I will text you when I get home." He released her and let her get up from his lap. She went to get her purse, but he pulled her back. He embraced her and kissed her sweet lips. "Don't forget to text." She smiled. He was so protective. She liked that in him.

"I promise, I won't forget." She headed out of the office.

When she left the restaurant, Jenna was unaware of a man sitting in his car across from the restaurant, eating a sandwich. He watched as Jenna came out of the restaurant and started walking. He immediately got out of his car and followed her.

Jenna was home by 6:00. She sent a text off to Mike.

Home safe and sound, will I see you later?

It was a few minutes before he replied. They must be busy.

I'm sorry, have a boatload of things to get done before I leave in the morning. I will see you when I return on Friday, should be around 9:00. I will text you when I get in. I love you!

> Love you too!

She threw her phone down on the counter.

Two days! How am I going to manage without him for two days, she wondered. Cuddles came out from her bedroom meowing at her. She picked her up and snuggled with her. "Are you hungry?" She put her down and went to the cupboard. Cuddles was excited pacing all around Jenna waiting to get fed. Jenna laughed and filled her dish.

After she filled her water dish, she decided to get some work done around the apartment. Maybe she could talk Sasha into watching a movie with her later tonight. The night flew by. It was getting late. Sasha had not come home yet, so she decided to go to bed. She brought her phone back with her to put it on the charger. She did her nightly routine and climbed into bed. She was just about to sleep when her phone dinged.

> Are you awake?

She smiled and sent back:

> I am now
>
> Can I call you?
>
> Yes.

Mike called and they talked for over an hour. When they finally said goodnight, Jenna relaxed and fell asleep knowing it wouldn't be long before he would be home again.

Jenna was up early the next morning and took a jog along Waikiki Beach. She jogged past the restaurant a little way and decided to turn around. She noticed a man was jogging the same path when she passed him going back. She didn't think anything of it until she looked back and saw him turn around and jog behind her. Chills went down her spine. She calmed herself down and increased her speed. When she reached her apartment, she was out of breath. She hurried inside and shut the door. She looked out the window and didn't see the man pass her house. Maybe he turned off on another trail. She couldn't shake the feeling that he was following her.

"Jenna," Sasha said behind her.

Jenna jumped and spun around.

"Oh, Sasha, you scared me!"

"Are you alright?"

"I don't know. I just came in from a jog and could have sworn that a man was following me. He gave me the creeps, but I didn't see him pass the apartment. Maybe I'm getting paranoid with what happened last weekend."

"Well, it never hurts to be cautious," said Sasha. "I just put on a pot of coffee. Would you like some?" she asked.

"Sure. I would love a cup." They fixed up their coffee and took it out into the lanai. Jenna glanced over at Sasha.

"You came in awfully late last night," she said.

Sasha blushed, "I ran into Mick last night at the bar."

"You went to the bar by yourself?" Jenna asked in astonishment.

"Yes, but he saw me at the door and came right over. He never left my side, so I felt safe. Later, we went to his bungalow and talked. It was all very innocent, Jenna!" Jenna grinned at her friend. "Sounds like you two are getting to know each other. But be careful. I wouldn't want you to lose your heart with someone who may not be here for very long."

"He said he was considering making his home here."

"What about Waco, Texas, and medical school?" asked Jenna.

"We'll cross that bridge when we get there," she said.

"Okay if you say so. Say, aren't you supposed to be in class this morning?" "It was cancelled again. We still have lab at 10:00, which I probably should get ready for."

She finished her coffee and went to take a shower. Jenna sat there a little longer, trying to figure out if she should call the police department about this morning and hope they didn't think she was nuts. She decided to shrug it off. She would keep her eyes open and watch her back. If she saw him again, she would call the police.

Jenna had some time to kill, so she went to the International Market Place to pick up some groceries for tomorrow. She thought she would surprise Mike and make him dinner. She came back to her apartment and put everything away. She changed into her work clothes and started out for the Bistro. She hadn't gone far when that same feeling came over her. She looked behind her. She didn't see anyone. She started out again. She felt sure somebody was watching or following her. She stopped and looked again. No one was around except some tourists.

You're losing it, Jenna, she said to herself. She hurried off to the Bistro. It was the first time she was glad to be at work surrounded by the people she worked with. She felt a little safer.

The Bistro was busy all night. She texted Mark to let him know it was going to be 11:00 before she would be done. He texted back with a thumbs-up sign. This is one night she was glad Mike had arranged for Mark to pick her up. Her nerves were shot. She kept looking around and behind her all night!

Mark pulled up in front of the Bistro and watched a car go by. He tried to get the license number, but he went by too fast. He noticed him following him since he left the restaurant. He went into the Bistro to find Jenna waiting for him.

"Hi Jenna, are you ready to go?"

"I am more than ready. We were slammed tonight!"

He grinned, "Let's go!" When he grinned like that, he looked exactly like Mike. It was uncanny. She followed him out to his car, and she gave him directions to her apartment. Mark kept looking in the rearview mirror.

"Is there something wrong?" asked Jenna.

"I'm not sure, but the same car that followed me over here to the Bistro is behind me again. I can tell because of his headlights."

Goosebumps came out on Jenna's skin.

"Mark, earlier today I had this feeling that someone was following me when I was jogging and later today when I came to work. Do you think there's a connection?"

Mark thought a moment.

"Now, this might be out there, but if someone was following you, the person that's following me may think he's following Mike." He handed Jenna his phone. "Pull up Zack's number and dial it for me." Mark's car had sync, so he could talk hands free.

"Detective Williams," he answered.

"Zack, Mark here. I've had a car following me since I left the restaurant. After I picked Jenna up, the same car came up behind me and is following at a distance. Jenna also said she thought she was being followed this morning and later today when she went to work."

Zack listened. He was afraid of this. Ralph may be seeking revenge for being laid off for two weeks.

"I'll send an unmarked car over to Jenna's to keep watch tonight. Call me if he follows you to your home."

"Right," said Mark. Mark looked over at Jenna. "I feel better knowing the police will be there to watch over you and Sasha."

"Me too," she said.

Mark pulled up in front of her apartment. They sat in the car and watched the car following them drive by. It was the same car. He tried to get the license number again with no luck. Mark backed his car up to see if he could see his tail lights. Sure enough, he braked and turned down a side street. Mark pulled forward and shut the engine off.

"I hope you and Sasha want some company because I am not leaving until the police are here."

"We would welcome the company," exclaimed Jenna.

Jenna unlocked the door, and they went inside. Cuddles came running out to greet her. She picked her up while Mark closed the door and locked it. He turned back to Jenna. He grinned, "Is this the attack cat from hell?"

"I see you've been talking to Mike," she chuckled. "This is Cuddles."

Mark scratched behind her ears and received a greeting from her. He laughed, "I think Mike must have been exaggerating. You're just a softy."

"Can I make you some coffee while we wait?"

"Thank you, I could use a cup. I have a feeling it's going to be a long night."

Jenna went in the kitchen while Mark took a seat on the couch. Mark pulled up Zack's number and waited for him to answer.

"Hey Zack, I'm over here at Jenna's, I'm going to stay until the police show up. The car that was following us drove past, and I was able to see him brake and turn down a side street," said Mark.

"Officer Brown should be there soon. I gave him your cell number to let you know when he's out there."

"Good. Thanks, Zack."

"You bet. Let me know if you have any problems going home."

"Will do," said Mark.

Mark heard the front door open, and Sasha walked in.

"Mmm, I smell coffee. Oh, hi, Mike! How's it going?"

Mark grinned, "I'm Mark."

Sasha laughed in surprise. "Oh my gosh, I'm sorry! Is there something I should know?"

"Mark! What would you like in your coffee?" Jenna yelled from the kitchen.

"Just cream," he yelled back. Sasha went into the kitchen to see if she could help. Jenna was just getting mugs out of the cupboard to fill when she turned and saw Sasha coming up beside her.

"Can I help?" asked Sasha.

"Oh, hi, I didn't hear you come in. Yes, could you get the cream out of the fridge?"

"Sure." Jenna took another cup from the cupboard and poured the coffee. Sasha brought over the cream.

"May I ask what Mark is doing here?"

"It's a long story. Let's bring our coffee into the living room and we'll tell you all about it," said Jenna.

Jenna handed Mark his coffee. Jenna sat on the other end of the couch and Sasha sat down on the love seat. Jenna took a sip of her coffee. She knew Sasha was chomping at the bit, so she started explaining what happened when she went to work and when Mark brought her home.

"What do you think Mark? Could it be that guy that tried to molest Jenna last weekend?" Sasha asked with concern.

"It's possible. But until we find out 'who' it is, Zack has Officer Brown coming to watch the apartment. He should be getting here any minute." Just then, his phone rang. Mark rose from the couch and walked over to the door. "Hello, Mark TreVaine here," he answered. Mark listened to the officer telling him where he was parked outside the apartment building. Mark took a look out the front window and saw his car. He glanced around the surrounding area and didn't see the black sedan that had followed him. "Did you happen to see a black sedan in the vicinity when you pulled up?" asked Mark.

"No, sir, I did not. But I will keep a look out for one."

"Okay, thanks."

Mark came back into the living area to let the girls know the officer was on duty.

"I'm going to head out. If you need anything, don't be afraid to call," said Mark.

Jenna walked him to the door.

"Thank you, Mark, for staying until the police came."

"No problem, Jenna. Mike would have my head if I didn't keep both you and Sasha safe."

"Be careful going home," said Jenna.

"Thanks, goodnight."

"Goodnight."

Jenna came back into the living room and picked up the cups to take to the kitchen. Sasha had already gone back to her bedroom. She shut off all the lights and headed back to her bedroom. She hadn't heard from Mike today, so she checked her phone. There were over 10 messages from him. The last one said, "CALL ME!!!"

Jenna pulled his number up and pressed the call button.

He immediately answered. "Jenna, are you alright? I've been worried sick! Did Mark pick you up after work?"

"Mike, honey, slow down. I'm fine. In answer to your question, Mark did pick me up from work, and I'm home safe and sound. No worries." She hesitated in telling him what was going on. "How is your trip going? Did you meet with the investor?"

Mike breathed a sigh of relief. "Yes, for an hour today. We have a meeting in the morning to go over details on the franchise. I'm going to try to get on an earlier flight back to the island tomorrow. I miss you!" said Mike.

"I miss you so much," she said in return. They talked for a little while longer then said goodnight. Jenna went to get ready for bed. When she finished, she climbed into bed. She lay there wide-awake, listening for sounds. She thought she heard a noise outside her bedroom window. She got up to look. She couldn't see anyone. She checked to make sure it was locked. She decided to make sure all the windows and doors were locked. She knocked on Sasha's door. She didn't hear anything. She opened the door. Sasha was sound asleep. She went over to her window and found it unlocked. She hurried and locked it and went around the rest of the apartment. When she was done, she peeked out the front window and saw the officer sitting out in his car. What a relief! She was really getting spooked! She shook herself and headed back to bed. Cuddles came up and joined her. She petted her cat and felt herself start to relax. Her last thought before she drifted off to sleep was Mike. She couldn't wait for him to get home.

Mark took off for home. He had traveled five miles down the road. He was turning right on 12th Avenue when a car came up from behind him and slammed into the back of his car, pushing him into a light pole. The air bags deployed, and he couldn't see a thing for the powder that flew out of them. The car took off before Mark had a chance to see if it was the black sedan he saw following him earlier. He felt a sharp pain in the back of his neck. He called 911 and gave them his location. Then he called Zack. When Zack answered he could tell he had been asleep.

"Sorry to wake you, Zack, but I was just hit from behind on my way home. It threw my car into a light pole."

Zack was instantly alert.

"Are you alright, man?"

"Just shook up. The car came out of nowhere. One minute, there was no one behind me. The next, I was slammed from behind.

My neck is a little sore, but otherwise, I'm fine. The ambulance and police are on their way."

"Were you able to get a look at the car who hit you?"

"No. The airbags deployed, and I couldn't see a thing."

"What's your location?" asked Zack. "I'm at Honolulu Boulevard and 12th."

"I'll be right there."

Zack dressed and took off at high speed to the scene of the accident. When he pulled up the ambulance had arrived, and parmedics were checking Mark out. Several city police were at the scene, checking out the car and waiting to ask questions. Zack walked up to Mark. He had a neck brace around his neck. He shook Mark's hand.

"How are you doing?"

"I'm doing okay," said Mark. The EMT came up to Zack.

"He refuses to go to the hospital."

Zack looked at Mark.

"You should probably go to get checked out. Just to make sure there are no other injuries," said Zack with concern. Mark stared back at Zack.

"I'll go if you take me. I'm not going in an ambulance," he said with conviction. Zack studied him. He was pretty sure he wouldn't be able to convince him to go with the EMTs.

"Okay, I'll take you. Let me go talk to the officers first. They can question you in the morning."

Zack went over to the officers and explained he was a detective for the Police Department. He showed them his badge and told them he was taking Mark to the hospital. He handed the officers his card and told them to get a hold of him in the morning. Zack came up to Mark.

"Are you ready to go?"

Mark stood up from the back of the ambulance and followed Zack to his car.

On the way to the hospital, Mark spoke up.

"Zack, I think whoever hit me thought I was Mike. And he's not just after Mike, he's after Jenna, too. My gut tells me Ralph is involved."

"I have the same thought." Zack radioed Officer Brown and told him about the accident. "Be on the lookout for a black sedan with a dent in the front end. How's it looking over there?" asked Zack.

"So far, all is quiet."

"I'll check back around with you when I get Mark home."

"Roger, over and out," said Officer Brown.

It was after 4:00 in the morning before Zack dropped Mark at home. He was pretty sore, but everything checked out okay. He was given some pain medication and told to take it easy for the next couple of days. He drove over to Jenna's apartment to check with Officer Brown before he headed back home. All was still quiet. He reported he hadn't seen any black sedan with a dent in it. On the drive home, he was putting the pieces together. Ralph more than likely hired someone to take care of Mike and Jenna, knowing he couldn't draw attention to himself or he would be a dead man. He's already slipped up twice. He would ask the Lieutenant to put an officer with Jenna and Mike until they could catch this guy.

Chapter 29

$\mathcal{M}$ ike woke up the next morning and felt like a freight train had hit him. He was sore all over, and his neck was killing him! He knew these hotel beds were uncomfortable, but man! He took a hot shower and felt better. He dressed and headed down to the first floor to get a bite to eat and check out before his appointment. As soon as this meeting was over, he was going straight to the airport to see if an early flight was available.

Mark was busy on the phone, trying to get a rental. He woke up with his body aching all over. The pain pills helped some, but he was still feeling it. The police arrived earlier and questioned him about the accident. He debated on whether to call Mike or not. He finally decided to wait. He would be home tonight. No sense worrying him. He wanted to make sure the meeting went well. It could be their chance to expand their restaurant business. With it being Friday night, he called in an extra hostess. With his face slightly bruised from the airbags, he didn't want to be out on the floor unless it was absolutely necessary. His rental arrived that afternoon. Mark went to shower and drove into work.

Jenna was busy at the apartment, preparing dinner for her and Mike. Mike had texted her and said he would be getting back around 7:30. It was 5:30. She set the oven at 275 degrees and placed the lasagna inside. She went about fixing the salads and the garlic bread and placed them in the fridge. With that done she went back to her bedroom to shower and change into something pretty for Mike. She chose a pale yellow, sleeveless v-neck dress with a flower design diagonally crossing the front of the dress. The dress fit her like a glove, falling just above the knee. She wore her dark hair down with soft curls flowing gently down her back. She applied her makeup and finished up with putting on the necklace Mike had bought for her. The diamond sparkled against her tanned skin. She took one last look in the mirror, and she was ready. It was almost 7:30, and Mike should be here any minute. She went into the kitchen to check on dinner.

She opened the oven and heard a voice coming from the living room.

"Hi pretty, bitch! Remember me?" She recognized that voice and chills went down her spine. She shut the oven and looked over the counter to see Ralph sitting on her couch. Shocked, her heart started to race, and she thought she was going to pass out.

"How did you get in here?" Jenna asked nervously. Ralph stood up and slowly walked up to the counter.

"I have my ways," he slurred. She could tell he'd been drinking. She could smell the liquor from here. "We have some unfinished business to take care of."

"What do you mean?"

"Well, before we were so rudely interrupted, we were just about to go and have some fun."

She took a deep breath. She only needed to keep him talking till Mike got here.

"Did my boyfriend not make it clear to you that night? He's going to be here any minute, so I suggest you leave!" she said, her voice shaking.

"Now do you think I would be here if he was a threat to me? I took care of your boyfriend last night. Even if he did come, he's in no shape to fight me."

He started walking around the corner. Jenna ran for the door. He caught her half way there pulling on her hair and slamming her against his chest. She screamed.

"Shut up, bitch!" He pulled harder on her hair and ran his mouth down her neck. He took his other hand and ripped the bodice of her dress exposing part of her breast. She struggled to get free.

"Let go of me!" she screamed.

"Stop fighting me!" He turned her around and slapped her across the face with the back of his hand.

Mike got out of his car in front of Jenna's apartment and hurried up the stairs. He heard Jenna scream. He went to open the door. It was locked.

"Jenna!" he yelled.

"Mike!" she screamed.

Mike's heart started pounding as fear for Jenna gripped him. He took his shoulder and slammed it against the door. It moved slightly. He did it again, and the door flew open. He saw Jenna with her dress ripped down the front and Ralph holding her with a knife to her throat!

"You look pretty healthy for a guy who was in a major car accident last night!" he growled. Mike had no idea what he was talking about. He took a step towards them. "Come any closer, and your girlfriend gets it!" he snarled.

Mike tried to reason with him. Seeing Jenna with tears streaming down her face and fear in her eyes, he needed to stay calm.

"Let her go Ralph, this is between you and me."

Out of the corner of his eye, Mike saw Cuddles down on her haunches in attack mode. In one slick move, Cuddles let out a howl, leaped up on Ralph's back, claws in his neck biting his ear. Ralph let go of Jenna screaming as Cuddles drew blood. Mike moved in, grabbed Ralph's hand with the knife and squeezed till he let go.

"Okay, Cuddles, I got this!"

Cuddles jumped off and ran out the door. Mike pulled his arm back and was ready to slam Ralph with his fist when a shot was fired. Jenna watched in horror as Ralph fell to the floor, blood coming out of his chest. Mike turned around but saw no one. Jenna came running into his arms. She clung to him crying uncontrollably.

"Jenna, sweetheart," he held her tightly in his arms. His emotions were running high, he almost lost her. He kissed the top of her head. "Sweetheart," he pulled away from her. "Come sit down on the couch. I need to check Ralph." Jenna stayed on the couch and wiped the tears from her face with her hands. Mike went over and checked his vitals. He was dead. Mike quickly called the police. He pulled up Zack's number.

"Detective Williams," he answered.

"Zack!" said Mike. "Can you come over to Jenna's? Ralph's been murdered. I've already called the police."

Zack was at the restaurant having dinner with Mark.

"I'll be right there!" He ended the call and took one look at Mark. "There's trouble over at Jenna's. I have to go."

"Are Mike and Jenna all right?"

Panic started setting in.

"I think so, but Ralph is dead."

"I'm coming with you. Just give me a minute." Mark hurried and talked to the head bartender and then his hostesses. Zack was waiting by the door. "Okay, let's go!" said Mark.

When they arrived, the police and ambulance was there. Mark and Zack came into the apartment to see Ralph being put on a stretcher with a sheet over him. Mark, with his heart pounding, went over to Jenna and Mike and gave them both a hug.

"Are you two okay?"

"We're fine," said Mike. He looked his brother over. "But what happened to you?"

"My car was hit from behind and slammed into a light pole last night." Now it was starting to make sense. How he woke up this morning and Ralph commenting on how he looked coming into the apartment. A police officer came up to Mike.

"I know this has been pretty traumatic for you both, but I need to ask you some questions."

Mike took Jenna over to the couch. The officer sat on the love seat. Mike and Jenna answered all his questions leading up to the shooting.

"Did you see the person who fired the shot?" Mike shook his head no.

"When I turned around to see, there was no one there," said Mike.

"Okay," said the officer, and he closed his tablet, "I may have more questions for you tomorrow, but for now, I think I've got what I need."

Another police officer came in the front door holding a black and white cat in his arms.

"Hey, I found this pretty cat under your bush out front. Could she be yours?" he asked.

"Cuddles!" both Mike and Jenna said in union. Mike took her from the officer. He held her up and looked into her pretty green eyes.

"You are one brave cat!" said Mike proudly. "This is one time I'm happy you attacked that man and saved your mistress!" He brought her down to his chest and petted her before he handed her to Jenna.

"Well, that explains the scratches on his neck and the bites on his ear!" said the officer.

Mike smiled, "Ralph never saw her coming."

The police were just leaving when Sasha ran into the apartment. She ran over to Jenna. She took one look at her friend and exclaimed, "What happened? Are you all right?"

Sasha hugged her friend.

"I'm fine," said Jenna and pulled away from her friend. "Could you help me out of this dress? I want to take a shower."

"Sure." Sasha led her back to the bedroom and helped her out of her dress. After her shower, Jenna put on some sweats and an oversized shirt. When she looked into the mirror, she saw a bruise coming out on her cheek from where Ralph hit her. She picked up the dress and threw it in the trash. She never wanted to see it again. When she came back into the living room, the men had cleaned up the floor and temporarily fixed the door. Mark and Zack were getting ready to leave. Jenna went up and gave them both a hug and thanked them for being here. They said good night, and Mike shut the door. Mike turned and took Jenna in his arms. He held her close. After a while she glanced up at him.

"I fixed you dinner but I am sure it's ruined."

"It still smells good." He smiled down at her.

"Are you hungry?" she asked.

"I could eat something." Jenna took him in the kitchen and checked the lasagna. It was all dried out. She took it out of the oven.

Sasha came in just as she put it on the counter.

"Looks like dinner went to the wayside." Jenna and Mike watched as Sasha took a knife and cut out a small square. She popped it in her mouth.

"Not bad. You know if we take the top layer off, add some more sauce, sprinkle parmesan on it, it would be great."

Mike and Jenna glanced at each other.

"It's worth a try," said Mike. He was starving. He hadn't eaten since lunch.

Jenna shrugged her shoulders, "Okay." She really wasn't hungry after what she had been through tonight.

"You two have a seat at the counter and let me handle this," said Sasha. Sasha went to work, and they were soon feasting on the dinner Jenna had made earlier. Jenna just nibbled on hers. She couldn't shake the picture out of her head of seeing Ralph shot and him falling to the floor in a pool of blood. Mike took Jenna's hand in his.

"I think I should put you to bed, little one. You've been through a lot tonight."

She slid off the stool and followed Mike into her bedroom. He pulled back the covers for her. When she climbed into bed, she caught his hand.

"Stay with me," she pleaded.

Mike searched her eyes. He saw the fear and anxiety and wasn't about to refuse her. He slipped his shoes off and crawled into bed with her. He reached up and turned the light out. He wrapped Jenna up in his arms beside him. He heard a gentle meow. Mike patted the bed, "Come on Cuddles." She jumped up on the bed and walked up on his chest. She took a turn around on him and promptly curled up and went to sleep. He gently put his hand on her back and wondered when he had got so attached to a cat.

Just before they fell asleep Jenna whispered, "I love you Mike."

"I love you sweetheart," he whispered back

Manchez was in bed with his wife when his phone rang. He sat up on the side of the bed. He looked back at his wife. She appeared to be sleeping. He answered the phone.

"Yes, Victor."

"Sorry to bother you, sir, I know it's late, but I thought you would like to know that the problem has been taken care of," he said with certainty.

"Where and when?" asked Manchez.

"Sir, he broke into an apartment and tried to rape a woman. When the boyfriend arrived, there was a fight. I was able to get a clear shot into the chest. I took him out just after 8:00."

"Did anyone see you?"

"No, I was long gone before the police arrived, and no one was outside the building, I made sure, sir," said Victor.

"Good! I will call you when I need your services again. A check will be put in the mail to you on Monday morning."

"Thank you, sir," said Victor.

Manchez ended the call and lay back down next to his wife. She turned around and pressed her big breasts next to his chest. He loved her breasts.

"Umm, who was that, honey?"

"No one to worry your pretty little head," he said seductively, "And since you're awake how about a good hard romp to relieve our stress from today?"

He started moving his hands over her body.

"Oh, yes, Marco, it's just what we need!"

The next morning, two officers of the Honolulu Police Department came to investigate what happened last night. Jenna and Mike answered all their questions again. When they left, Jenna went to put on another pot of coffee. Mike followed her into the kitchen.

"What can I make you for breakfast?"

Mike put his hands on her shoulders and turned her around.

"Jenna, love, you don't have to make me breakfast. I would be happy with some toast, and I can make it. I want to know how you are doing through all of this. Can you talk to me about what you're feeling?" asked Mike softly.

What was it about this man that could bring out all the emotions in her? She searched those deep blue eyes and only saw the love and concern he had for her. The tears came streaming down her cheeks. He pulled her into his chest and let her cry it out. When the tears slowed, she gazed back up into his eyes.

"Mike," she swallowed, "I really thought that Ralph was going to beat and rape me. In the back of my mind, I knew you were on your way but what if something held you up?" She shuddered. "I can't get the images of a knife at my throat and Ralph getting shot out of my mind."

"Oh, Jenna, I wish I could turn back the clock and had been here so this would never have happened. But whoever killed Ralph saved me from killing him." He bent his head and kissed her soft lips. He raised his head, "Jenna, love, I will always be here for you. Anytime you want to talk, I will listen. We'll get through this together." Jenna put her arms around his waist and hugged him close to her.

"Thank you," she whispered.

Back at the police department, the officers came back to Zack's office. Zack was sitting behind his desk. He had the officers sit down.

"Anything new to report?" asked Zack.

"No. Jenna and Mike's story is the same. We checked with some neighbors, and they didn't see anything. Whoever killed Ralph knew what he was doing. He shot him and disappeared," said one of the officers.

"Well, we know Ralph was connected to Manchez. I'm sure he had something to do with it. We just can't prove it, yet."

Zack sat back in his chair.

"Jason is our only link to nailing him. We are all going to have to be alert and watch each other's backs if we are to put Manchez away."

Chapter 30

A couple weeks later, Mike surprised her on Sunday morning, dressed in a suit with a bouquet of yellow roses in his hand. She invited him in.

"For you, my little one," his eyes shone as he handed her the flowers.

"They're beautiful, Mike, thank you!" she breathed. She went to get a vase to put them in. Jenna set them in the center of the table and stood for a moment to admire them. Mike came up behind her and put his arms around her.

"Do you mind if I go to church with you this morning?" he asked.

She turned around and gazed up at him in surprise.

"Are you sure?" she asked.

"Yes, I would love to come to church with you."

She smiled, "Then I would love for you to come!" She went to change into a dress, and they were soon sitting in a pew. Mike took her hand as they listened to Pastor Kingsley's sermon.

The Pastor talked about salvation. How Jesus died for our sins, so we could be free.

"In the Bible, Jesus talks about taking his yoke upon you and giving your burdens to him. Anyone of you who are ready to become a new person in Christ, I ask that you please come forward."

Mike surprised her as he stood up and walked up to the altar. Jenna watched with tears in her eyes as Mike gave his life to our Lord and Savior. Mike turned around and faced the congregation as Pastor Kingsley introduced him as a new brother in Christ. Mike walked back with tears in his eyes to take his seat. He put his arm around Jenna and held her close. Jenna gazed up at him with tears of her own. Her heart overflowing with love for this man, she whispered, "I love you."

He gently squeezed her to him.

"I love you," he whispered back.

After church, Mike took her to a nice restaurant on the other side of the island. It was a quaint little place set not too far from the beach. There specialty was fresh seafood and lobster. Jenna ordered the lobster while Mike ordered the steak and lobster combination. Jenna and Mike talked about him becoming a Christian, how it made him feel inside. He couldn't describe it. It was like something exploded inside him. He knew then deep inside his heart, it was the Lord. They enjoyed their dinner, and when they stepped outside the restaurant, Mike asked her if she would like to take a walk along the beach.

"I'd love to!"

They walked along the boardwalk to the beach. They took their shoes off and walked hand in hand along the beach till they came upon a bench. Mike sat down and pulled Jenna down with him. He put his arm around her. Jenna laid her head on his shoulder as they quietly watched the ocean waves rush to shore.

"Jenna, love."

Jenna raised her head.

"Yes?" she asked. Mike was nervous about something, she could feel it.

He took her hand in his.

"Jenna, I know we haven't known each other very long, but I want you to know that you complete me like no other woman has ever done." He stood up and took a small box out of his suit pocket. Jenna's heart started to pound. Mike went down on one knee. He opened the box. "Jenna Marie Hathaway, I love you with all my heart. I want to spend the rest of my life with you. Will you marry me?"

Mike held his breath.

Jenna, with tears in her eyes and the biggest smile ever, said, "Michael James TreVaine, I love you with all my heart. Yes, I will marry you!"

Mike let out his breath, took the ring out of the box and placed it on her third finger on her left hand. The one karat solitaire diamond with a sapphire on each side was set in a white gold band that sparkled in the sun.

"It's perfect," she sighed. He stood up bringing her with him.

"You're perfect. And together we are going to have the perfect life."

The magic of his kiss, two hearts beating together as one, she knew it couldn't get any better than this.

Epilogue

June 5, Graduation Day. Jenna sat with her fellow classmates, waiting for her name to be called. As she reminisced over the last couple of days, she was happy her parents were able to fly in a few days before the commencement. When they met Mike, they liked him immediately, and Jenna was surprised to find out that he had called her dad to ask for her hand in marriage before he proposed. Mike took Jenna and her parents around the island to see some of the tourist attractions. They especially wanted to see the Arizona Memorial from World War II, where over 1,100 of our Navy men lost their lives when the ship was struck and went down beneath the ocean. When you looked down into the water, you could actually see the ship. The names on the great wall gave Jenna chills as she envisioned what had taken place when the ship went down.

"Jenna Marie Hathaway," her name was called, and she nervously walked up to the podium. She looked out and saw Mike, Mark, and her parents cheering her on as she shook hands with the professor and placed her diploma in her hands. Pictures were taken, and she returned to her seat. After everyone received their diploma, hats were thrown in the air as students cheered that this day had finally come, and they were graduates of the Class of 2019.

Mike had set up a luncheon for her and Sasha, inviting all their friends and parents in the lanai at the restaurant. Palani put together, with the help of one of his cooks, a buffet with many of the traditional Hawaiian cuisines. Megan and Tammy went around serving drinks and making sure everything was ready for everyone to sit down and eat. Jenna was by Mike's side while he was talking to her parents.

Her heart was bursting with joy as she looked around the lanai, everybody laughing and having a good time. Her eyes stopped at the entrance into the lanai. There was a man with a camouflage uniform on. A matching camouflage cap was perched on top of his dark hair. His skin was weathered, and he looked tired and worn out. His blue eyes locked with hers, the same blue eyes as his brothers. Jenna was just about to nudge Mike when he placed his finger to lips. He started walking towards them. He put a hand on Mike's shoulder, "Is there a party going on here?"

Mike knew that voice. He turned to his older brother.

"Peyton! Oh Peyton, you're home!" Mike hugged him and called Mark over. "Mark, it's Peyton!" Mark looked and rushed over to embrace him. "My God, you're finally home! Is this going to be permanent?"

Peyton with a tired look in his eyes said, "Yes, this was my last deployment. I'm home for good."

Both the bothers cheered. Mike introduced him to Jenna as his fiancée and to her parents. Megan came over and asked if she could get him a drink. When she came back and placed it in his hand, he thanked her and took a drink. He stepped away from his brothers and walked over to the railing. He looked out over the ocean.

After 12 years in the armed services, he wondered what the hell he was going to do with the rest of his life. Mike glanced over at his brother with concern. He wondered if this was what he truly wanted. Mark and he would talk to him when they had more privacy. Mike turned back to his love. He gazed lovingly into her eyes happy to be celebrating her special day with her parents and all of her friends. He couldn't wait for another special day when they would be united in marriage and would spend the rest of their lives together.

THE RECIPES FOR KALUA PORK AND
HAUPIE PIE THAT ARE FEATURED IN THIS BOOK.

Kalua Pork

- 5-7 lbs. of pork butt roast (also referred to as pork shoulder roast)
- 1 ½ tbs. of Hawaiian sea salt (or regular sea salt if you cannot find the Hawaiian salt)
- 1 tbs. of liquid smoke sauce

DIRECTIONS:

1. Set oven at 275 degrees.

2. Place butt roast on large sheet of aluminum foil, dull side. Rub the roast with the Hawaiian salt. Rub the smoke sauce over the roast. Wrap the roast up loosely in the aluminum foil and place in a deep roasting pan. Place in preheated oven and bake 7-8 hours.

3. When done, take roast out of the foil and place on cutting board. Shred with a knife.

4. Serve with cooked green cabbage or rice with slices of fresh pineapple wedges. Also can be served on a bun with your favorite chips! Enjoy!

Gluten-Free Haupie Pie

- One 9-inch gluten-free pie crust
- Pie Crust Directions:
- ½ C. shorting or butter
- 3 ½ C. gluten free flour

DIRECTIONS:

1. Cut shorting into flour.

2. Mix together 1 egg, 1 tbs. apple cider vinegar, and ½ C cold water. Add to flour mixture, stirring with a fork and roll out. Makes 3 pie crusts.

3. Place pie crust in a 9-inch pie pan. Pierce crust with a fork before baking. Place in oven and bake at 375 degrees until golden brown. Remove from oven and let cool.

HAUPIE MIXTURE:
(I LIKE TO USE ORGANIC PRODUCTS, BUT NOT NECESSARY)

- 2/3 C. whole milk (organic)
- 5 tbs. of tapioca starch or flour (organic)
- 1-14 oz. can unsweetened coconut milk (not fat free or light; organic), or you can use organic coconut milk from the cooler and measure out 14 oz.
- 1 C. whole milk (organic)
- 1 C. granulated sugar (organic)
- 1 C. semi-sweet chocolate chips

DIRECTIONS:

1. In a small bowl, combine 2/3 C whole milk and 5 tbs. of tapioca starch and set aside.

2. In a medium sauce pan, over medium heat, whisk together coconut milk, 1 C whole milk, and sugar. Bring to a simmer, whisking often.

3. Stir tapioca and milk mixture before adding to coconut mixture. Add the tapioca mixture slowly while whisking constantly.

4. Remove from heat and continue whisking until the mixture becomes thick. (This is haupie.)

5. Place about half of the haupie mixture in a bowl and set aside.

6. Add chocolate chips to the remaining mixture in the sauce pan and stir until chocolate chips are melted and well combined.

7. Add chocolate haupie mixture to cooled pie crust and smooth with spatula until even.

8. Add the remaining haupie mixture and carefully smooth over top. Cover with upside down plate and place in refrigerator for 4-6 hours.

AND NOW FOR THE WHIPPED TOPPING!

- 1-1/2 C. heavy whipping cream
- ¼ C. sugar
- ½ tsp. coconut extract or vanilla (optional; I like to use vanilla.)

DIRECTIONS:

1. After pie has cooled, whip cream with ¼ C. sugar until peaks form. Place on top of or smooth over haupie pie. Cut and serve.

2. Enjoy!

Serves 8—unless someone can't resist a second piece!